I0783521

Spirit
Lake

A Novel

Ben Dolan

Darkly Bright Press

Spirit Lake
by Ben Dolan

Catalog Number 024

Library of Congress Control Number: 2025938242

ISBN: 979-8-9899449-9-6

Publisher's Cataloging-in-Publication Data

Names: Dolan, Ben, author.
Title: Spirit lake : a novel / Ben Dolan.
Description: Cochiti Lake, NM: Darkly Bright Press, 2025.
Identifiers: LCCN: 2025938242 | ISBN: 979-8-9899449-9-6
Subjects: LCSH Albuquerque (N.M.)--Fiction. | Future, The--Fiction.
| Psychological fiction. | BISAC FICTION / Literary | FICTION /
Christian / Futuristic | FICTION / Psychological
Classification: LCC PS3604 .O53 S75 2025 | DDC 813.6--dc23

darkly bright press

www.darklybrightpress.com

Spirit Lake

Ben Dolan

Prologue
(and Epilogue)

(You can read this now, if you want. Or you can wait until the end, which is where it belongs. There's no stopping me either way.)

Sky watch. Monday morning. My last carrot soda condensates a few centimeters beyond, on my left hand; beautiful, clear beads dwell in the sun for a moment before the matte-white synplastic dashboard absorbs the moisture in that magical way that still causes me to wonder, just like it did decades ago, with your mother, as we toddled our way northward to Santa Fe in a different SD, simpler than this one, more beautiful in a way, but similarly bedecked with the water of our sweating drinks.

Mounted above the vehicle's sprinkled dash is the impenetrable screen at which I stare. It pulses dismissively as my sentences lengthen. Even as I write these words, they populate a different screen, the one in front of you now, the one I've spent too much time gazing into. Behind the screen before you is the thick pane of glass that has always so effectively separated me from the city below, from the cracking streets and cooling fans and black-lit bars. Beyond the city, the desert is the horizon. Beyond the desert, the cosmos. Beyond the cosmos, the desert.

I cannot help but wonder if, indeed, you're reading even as this very sentence unfolds. You'll discover, below, that I intended to begin this whole thing with "The inscrutable Daniel Glidden." But instead, I begin with me. And you. Though I appreciate the heightened suspense of observing a disembodied narrator type the last lines of his story (a story you're just beginning), I did not intend it to work out this way, our near miss. When, a couple of days ago, I heard of your approach (in the most unfortunate way, I might add), I could not have foreseen this dramatic exit.

Know this: Deserving or not, I've left you everything. A man deleted needs nothing like all that. Don't read too much into it. You're all that's left. I go, afloat in dew.

1

The inscrutable Daniel Glidden sent a message not long after ten on this bleeding Friday morning. Normally such a moment was the butt end of my pleasure-reading time. Today, however, perhaps premonitorily, had been leaking out unstoppered since sunrise. The message said that you were in town, that you wanted to know about your mother, and that he had given you my address. The former two details surprised me in timing but not in content, as it's natural that one would want to know about one's mother, and in many ways, I've wondered how many years would lapse before you appeared. The last detail, however, the part about my address, I could not understand, since he knows how closely I guard my privacy and, also, how basically impossible it would be for you to access my apartment building without prior authorization. But, of course, we are talking about Daniel Glidden—I suppose you could say my Daniel Glidden, for if he is anyone's, he is mine—the professor, the self-provocateur, the emotional exhibitionist, the public weeper. Indeed, besides the fact that he was the first and last to publish your mother's poetry, these traits, I'm assuming, are precisely why you went—or, rather, like the moths of old, why you were unknowingly attracted—to him. For men such as him draw people to them. Men such as me do not.

Publishing suits billboards-of-men like Daniel. They find it comforting to perpetually reveal to the world their location down to ten square meters. They are gratified by anonymous attention; they gain followers and friends and gazes. Men like me, however, tend to silently evade (which was, at first, what I planned to do to you); we are visible only by leavings; we are nervous that even our tiny bumps and jostles might pinpoint us to a spot on a digital map within a thousand square meters of the chair in which we sit nightly to peruse old hard-copy books and to pick the dried crumbs of soy shake out of our graying beards.

But Daniel Glidden and his ilk will never pass away. How could they? All stories would cease, and we the overeducated curmudgeons would end the human race simply via disgusted neglect. Even now, after all these years, it seems he and I are in some sort of indissoluble union, a lived fiction in which two characters are never more than a chapter's breadth apart, regardless of the time and space and disdain between them. This is the first time I've thought in such terms, but such terms seem accurate.

He didn't say he had given you my cell but I couldn't imagine that he hadn't, so then I felt that I simply had to wait for that disconcerting "new contact" noise to fart in my living room like some uninvited family member. The cell, indeed, lies there, on the single table beside the drooping couch, debased and nude in the fuzzy circle of dust that the daily picking up and putting down has formed. I await the sound. The verbiage of today's communication is telling: Fifty years ago, one would have been notified in a grainy reproduction of last year's pop hit that a new *caller*, a supplicant, a suitor, was incoming, whereas now one is made aware via synth boop and digihorn that a new *contact* approacheth, a new opportunity, an unforeseen chance for netting someone. This, of course, produces a little anxiety, for I want no callers and I need no contacts. The ones I already have only cause me difficulty.

Let me be honest and say it again: I am not just being coy; I do not want contact. Repelling has been my primary social activity for the last decade or so. This has been natural for me. But I must admit that it wasn't simply the inconvenience of your arrival that had clamped my stomach. Something about your arrival, something entirely outside of its bad timing, had escalated the general unease I usually feel when presented with the possibility of contact.

The first diagnosis I made was not far off, but ultimately superficial. My discomfort, I thought, was simply that empty-intestine feeling I used to get when I was expecting the rare benevolent guest, back in a time when expecting a guest was within the scope of my withered reality. It had been so long that I'd forgotten the twist of it.

Then I remembered that soda helps. I found one deep in the cooler; I knew I would. Just two months ago, an impossibly young doctor told me to abandon such chemical nonsense. Returning home, I stashed a four-pack in the Defridge and then walled its memory off in my brain, leaving there (in my brain) only the tiny coded keypad whose multistage password would include *abnormally heightened anxiety* + *time pressure* + *your mother*, and would then permit access for precisely this sort of emergency. This is, perhaps, the only skill I can absolutely claim to have mastered, this compartmentalization of neural codes. Once, in an effort to test my talent, I hid from myself ten paper hundred-dollar bills for four months, and only when a preprogrammed notification (a message from a lawyer whose bill I knew would come due, but to whom I'd intentionally given the incorrect account information) reminded me to look behind the rear dust-jacket flap of a last-century Stanisław Lem volume did I, in an explosion of disordered images, remember my test.

Soda now unhidden and uncorked, I spent the better of the past few hours sitting on the sad couch next to the dusty cell table, wondering exactly how I will respond to you, the new caller, when you do indeed call, for I'm sure that Daniel has told you that I am the one you should talk to concerning your mother. He's probably said something grandiose like "If I was her publisher, JP was her coauthor." I wonder how I should respond to Daniel now that, for the first time in years, there are details he and I must discuss. I am annoyed, I realize, that Daniel is in any way involved in all this, just as I was annoyed forty years ago. It's true I was deeply involved with your mother, and that Daniel, well, was not, but I now see that, in more ways than one, he has the power in this situation precisely because you came to him first. He simply could have said *nothing* about me in order to monopolize your attention, which would have been fine with me. But I deduce that such monopolization was not the greatest danger. Even worse, he could sow false narratives in this virgin emotional soil you've presented him. He *could tell you things,* as we used to say. This would be a certain academic irony, for a cornerstone of my teaching career has been in hollering at my students the refreshing truism (though my spirit has dwindled so much lately that now it's just a rather bitter pronouncement) that there are no such things as false stories. Lies are as real as truth.

But I won't waste too much time talking about Daniel Glidden now, false or not. Perhaps there will be a moment in what seems to be this inevitable contact in which I can explain how, through no fault of his own, Daniel has become the server that hosts all my woes.

Yes, here's the point of all this: I was throat-deep in a perfectly ambiguous but cutting response to Daniel, and I had already begun drafting a curt rejection of your geographic advance, when I realized something quite refreshingly simple. You hadn't yet called. And you still haven't. This is radically important. That you have not yet called suggests to me that either Daniel is keeping you from me (or me from you) by not giving you my info *or* (or!) that you indeed have my "probie" (you'll perhaps discover in what follows that my students, if they've changed me at all, have drilled into my head their ridiculous slang . . . forgive me) and thus are not approaching this haphazardly. Though I can't completely rule out something childish in Daniel, I do prefer to trust his general innocence regarding these things, to gamble on the likelihood that he'll disregard the pain your mother's memory might inflict on both him and me and you and simply say, "You know, you'll really love talking to Joe about all this." This, Daniel's simple ignorance, normally as impenetrable and nuanced as a laser-wired prison wall, is for probably only the second time since I've known him a great relief rather than an infuriating obstacle. For I try to do nothing haphazardly, nothing vengeful. Even spontaneity I first prefer to parboil in planning. And perhaps you detect this (or, miraculously, perhaps Daniel has mustered all his powers of wisdom and suggested it!) and so are giving me some time to prepare. And this preparation is much appreciated.

It also has moved me. That you haven't yet called or texted, that you circle above like a wary seabird, has caused me to reconsider my plans concerning your advance. Had you showed up on my doorstep, you would have set loose a string of habits and ancillary coding that would have pushed me underground for years, probably forever. I would have made evading you an entertainment, in a way. I would have communicated to you via rejection.

But I see your carefulness, and I admire it and want to reward it. Also, I am old. I am not as fast as I once was.

Thus, rather than let the coming storm overwhelm the dam and wash away everything below it, I suppose it's prudent to begin slowly emptying the reservoir. So, in the time I have left, I will begin writing what you will want to know, for in telling the story I make it real, and in making it real I make it transferable, and in making it transferable I am finally rid of it. And of you. And (please God) of Daniel Glidden.

2

Before I tell the story of your mother, it seems appropriate, here at the beginning, to reveal what I know about you. In the last hour since my happy realization about Daniel's predictable ignorance and your good intentions, I've done a good bit of research on you, as I'm sure you did on me when Daniel gave you my name. Ah . . . I remember now that you would have known at least my first name already, for it was printed with her poems. But I'm guessing on the R & D front I have a slight advantage: For somewhat boring reasons that perhaps I'll explain in an effort to buy time during our awkward and imminent face-to-face interaction (see? I'm not without humor), I have editor/reader privilege in some of the highest tiers of the DC/Oxford Bio project, which, even as it publishes information on your pop singers and your Scottish princesses, is also collecting and culling and storing megatons of petty data on individuals who (at least yet) do not capture wider public attention. The scare-news stories about data monopolies and identity devaluations are true on that front, but the DCOB is less like a sinister, hoard-guarding dragon and more like an absent-minded quadrillionaire who bought a foreclosed mansion so labyrinthine and sprawling that it contains within it vast areas, secured by their impenetrable obscurity, where tiny little societies still live on, functioning as if their creator were still extant and watching and smiling. In other words, the data is still being farmed just like it was before, but the taxpayers own the land and the barns, and the DCOB, like I said, is about a third as interested in you as *you* are. And so there is a modicum of safety introduced simply by the sheer inefficiency of nationalized enterprises such as these. Consequently, an article several years ago about the nascent power in the DCOB's resources was dead on. The article died largely unread. Nothing is more boring than unexploited resources. I say all this because of the likelihood that, to you, the DCOB is unimportant, if not unknown. Understanding its importance, however, is paramount. I am one who toils in its vast fields, and I've been roaming through one particular section for years.

There, for example, I have discovered, among other things, that you are a professor in the Centex Consortium. This makes us peers, in a sense, but more importantly, such knowledge helps me understand why now, after forty-one years, you have decided to rise up from the Procrustean Texas limestone and begin what I'm sure you've long intended to begin:

weaving together the story of your mother, and, by proxy, you. I see that you've published three "books" (even after all these years, I still am not accustomed to using this word without quotes—I will henceforth suppress this urge), the first when you were twenty-six, the second at thirty, and the third at thirty-four. Such temporo-intellectual symmetry is admirable, but it has now been nearly seven years and . . . nothing. Not even a trailer has come out with your name in its end lines.

So, a little speculation. You need a book. If Centex is anything like our Southwest States Network, you recently had to go through another competitive hiring committee process, which perpetually has standing before it a DNA-fixed twenty-six-year-old who is prettier and less flash fried than you, and she has a good book (though not as good as your first, apparently—its awards are impressive even to this old academic) and she will work for much less money. The Centex execs on the screens and in the expensive chairs are, there in their glass-walled playroom, basically holding the two of you like dolls, one in each hand, comparing your busts and eyelids, and suspecting perhaps, though the busts and eyelids are clearly slackening in the older, there might be some cheap and potentially problematic gimmick in the newer version, that it might not be as well made or as trustworthy, and so even though their male loins tell them to choose the twenty-six-year-old, they're willing to pass up the newer model this time around—because you, the older, could be on the verge of something big, or, more frighteningly, she, the younger, could be on the verge of *getting* into something big, like, for example, motherhood, a sickness no exec would wish upon his bottom line.

But I do you some injustice. You're still relatively young and, based on the smattering of recent photos of a government-sponsored conference you attended, you're still quite beautiful, if that's something an old man like me can be permitted to say. The photo that caught me was a simple one. A boardwalk on the brown Sotex Coast, a sunset incorrectly aligned, a much younger person (your child, cousin, neighbor, lover?) in the crook of your armpit, an old-timey Ferris wheel arching across the left border of the frame. Your eyelids and eye corners are brown and spotted and wrinkled (like your mother, you have conscientiously avoided the procedures and products, I presume), but the eyes themselves are vivid still, something that most people don't realize is lost when the rest of the face is continually polished to a sheen. We (humans) are best looking when we age in the way we've always aged. I suppose there is some neural node in our brains that still finds age beautiful and its defiance abrasive. I imagine you look now what your mother might have looked like had she another fifteen years in this world.

Because of *Coordinates'* surprising success, I was inoculated early on against such ignominious academic proceedings as a Rehire, for *Coordinates* was and still is, to use another old phrase, a cash cow, and I have remained its reclusive, devoted keeper. I would not have survived a Rehiring Committee. But I have occasionally looked on in silent horror as my colleagues were examined thusly. I cannot deny that I feel the stirrings of some sort of duty, then, to help you confound those bottom-lining invertebrates while simultaneously squashing the next wave of twenty-six-year-olds with sub-mediocre books. Yes, now that I'm presented with materializing and transferring this story, I see how it could be immediately helpful in assisting another embattled colleague to stave off the interminable advances of the Brainless Monetizers. Even now, as old and apathetic as I have become, I still love the idea of pinching my enemies, of settling scores. But to tell myself that this is the reason I write would be false. It would leave you rewarded but unsatisfied.

I cannot deny that I feel rising in me a certain sense of greedy nostalgia, a growing desire to keep it all for myself, mostly because I can't, in good conscience, do it justice. If *Coordinates* is about our techno-choked and lonely country and the triumph of American apathy over American democracy and ultimately the tickings of my saturated mind, the story of your mother is about something else in us, in me, something more visceral and digestive, and because I am JP Stone and not Daniel Glidden, because I loved your mother and didn't just interview her one fine spring day as she folded silverware behind a moist, faux-mahogany bar top, I find the materialization difficult. The story resists solidification; it is still largely contained in gut and lung and adenoid. I much prefer to sell the solidified products of my mind and keep my organs and their secretions to myself.

Finally, I have discovered (really, been reminded of) one more thing about you, which, I think, is a good way to begin the story of your mother. That is, you're forty-one years old, and your mother entered my world almost exactly forty-two years ago (June 29, my sixty-eighth birthday, will be forty-two years). After growing absences and silences, she and I lost touch completely in late September or early October of that same year. She was long gone by the time the ice cracked in Spirit Lake the following spring.

Now we arrive at the two things the DCOB doesn't know. (And what the DCOB doesn't know, usually we do not either.) There are omissions in the lines for your birth date, and for your paternal source. How paltry, a casual observer (though there are no strictly casual observers at this level of the DCOB) might think. There must be some cross-wiring, for birth dates are as obtainable as fingerprints. They're everywhere! Clearly this person is of such little national importance that these tiny holes have remained unmended and unminded by the minders and menders (like me) constantly crawling these warehouse shelves.

But, of course, you and I both object to such dismissal. You're an author, a successful academic, a full professor. You're a thinker and a voice in culture.

Though they don't make them available to the proletariat, the DCOB generates algorithmic guesses as stopgaps. Birth month: March? The days it gives are based on the occurrence of world events that tend to spike birth rates day to day, and though such predictive science like birth surge dating perhaps has a statistical use, it is pointless for our purposes, for you weren't born in a range, but on a distinct day, and that day matters very much.

Then, the other omission. Paternal source: "mult. poss." (the DCOB is full of such meaningfully vague usages as these "multipossums," as we DCOBers say). There are four in the list, the first two preposterous: Daniel Glidden, Grey Aaman. Then David Geores. And then me.

3

There we are. Rather, here we are. It may sound a bit like a diabolical kids' book.

I am not your father.

Daniel Glidden is not your father.

It is funny to say, but it's worth putting it down: Grey Aaman is absolutely not your father. (Grey? Is that you? I can see your twitchy grin even from all these years away. Sorry you've got to be involved with all this.)

I never thought I'd write such a grouping of sentences as the above. But, of course, such hidden obviousnesses are now precisely why I write. A conversation between you and me without such predetermined exactitude could yield confusing and even ruinous results. Ruinous? you ask. How can a simple conversation, an old story recounted, cause such tumult? Less has toppled governments.

I write it again; I sing it from my glass crow's nest; it echoes in the desert and cosmos and cosmological desert: I am not your father and Daniel Glidden is not your father. Poor Grey, neither.

Though it has little to do with biological aptitude, it's worth saying that Daniel Glidden is what we used to call asexual. I don't mean this offensively, it's just that I don't know the more modern and acceptable term for it. More importantly, your mother, I think, disliked him, not because he was asexual (this was pre-Jameson, you'll remember), but because, for one, he wept publicly when he read his own poetry at his bot poetry events, though at first she found this pathetickry endearing. However, once, in her presence, in fact on the occasion of their first meeting, Daniel unknowingly read aloud to a group of us some of her anonymously published poems from the uni's undergrad journal. While reading, he mocked them by fake weeping. It was incredibly childish, but he couldn't have known who wrote the poems. We were at a long table made of uneven and tilted smaller tables. He held a greasy piece of pizza in one hand, the cover-bent mag in the other. Neon signs hung on the wall above him. A drooly U student sat much too close to his left shoulder. Daniel, alive with the rapt attention pouring over him, held pizza and mag shoulder high, poked out his lower lip, and read in a way that was so like how he normally and sincerely read poetry that his mockery was all the more hideous. She knew that the poems were not good (she had told me so herself, and I certainly didn't disagree), but there was something awful about *Daniel Glidden* mock weeping over her anonymously submitted poems. Except by some wild accident, Daniel Glidden and your mother's DNA are unlikely to have meiotically danced.

Grey Aaman is definitely not your father. Admittedly, Grey Aaman, unlike Daniel, was a mysterious man. As far as I know, however, he never actually saw your mother in person. For this reason, I had never before considered him a character worth naming, but I suppose the reasons for the DCOB's rather wanton paternal suggestions should be fleshed out, and they will be, in time. But Grey's odd appearance here at the end of all things, I realize now, is not unfortuitous; he can be put to work. Grey Aaman should not stand for a distinct and historical person, but should stand for a quantity. That is, Grey Aaman should stand for the portion of your mother, the exact percentage of her infinitude, that was never mapped, not by me, not by any human, and not even by her. Could Grey be your father? Well, yes. As far as I know, he had the physical plumbing and basic social aptitude for such a thing, and he lived in the same city and was about the same age as your mother and she did not despise him. But this describes thousands of men. Grey will, from now on (except when we meet him, finally, in the back of that stuffy, long-gone server room, whirring with fans, that used to stand so unobtrusively at the heart of the U), stand for a possibility, therefore, and not a person. The possibility of anything that's possible. The possibility that the well of a human soul was truly as deep and unfathomable as your mother used to believe.

This is all rather crass, I know, the checklist of anti-fathers, but we must begin by saying things aloud. Because I'm assuming that you want to know who your father is. While I am perhaps a valuable speculative source on the matter, the truth is that the farthest I can proceed in this weird biological algebra is solving for the variable of me. And me plus your mother does not equal you. All other conjectures beyond this simple math—I'll show my work soon enough—are at best logical and at worst wild guesses, for the immensity of your mother's existence, as typical as it will seem, could have certainly permitted a secret southwest quadrant lover, a late-night fling, even a trip to a fast-dealing fertility specialist (you'll be surprised to know that insemination of single women was, then, still a rather cloudy legal realm after the Louisiana "money moms" scandals).

So now I'll say it once more: It's true, I am not your father. In time, I will lay out the gory and embarrassing evidence in support of my defense. But take it on trust from the beginning that you are not my offspring. Such trust will help you begin to accept the genetic validity and totally regrettable introduction of the fourth suitor, an alcoholic, soot-faced pyromaniac. (I assure you that the serrated edge of this insult will be dulled by the photographic evidence of its objective truth.) He is, ruling out the Grey factor, almost definitely your father. This is a sad enough truth that I have felt in me a bubble of sympathy, a certain hiccup of remorse that bids me to wish that I was, indeed, your pappy, because having such as he among your ancestors is like being a carrier for a rare disease that makes for good news stories. His name was, and still perhaps is, David Geores.

But the bloat of remorse fades when I belch and remember that it's been a few miserable weeks since I carbonated my ulcerous stomach. I remember a great song from my childhood in which the singer said he'd never seen a hearse with a trailer hitch. I suppose if I have to go, there's no reason to take a good stomach with me.

4

After an hour break and no news from you or any other, I feel compelled to sit back down again. It is fun to see the chapters tick away. I thought that the above writing would be enough to set me at ease, to warm the water a bit before you and I step in, to make the order of necessary proclamations clearer, but two more cold carrot sodas have only mitigated and not eliminated the foreboding intestinal pressure that says you might call at any moment, and that urgency pushes me to continue the release. I mean, I said it: I'm not your daddy. I can bring out the receipts from the surgery. I can give you Angela's number. So why am I sitting here again, thinking definitely about writing more?

Sometime near the halfway point of carrot soda number two (three, if you count the one I drained before I first began writing), I determined why it is I still felt so anxious: my death. Again.

Really, it began by realizing that I don't *need* your mother's story. This is a shock, something like the dark surprise of my former colleague who scrapped and saved and fasted for decades in fear of retirement, only to realize that, having become used to scrapping and saving and fasting, he had in retirement nothing more hopeful than cash reserves enough to last two or three more emaciated lifetimes. I don't need your mother's story, because my career is ending; the patched-up, flimsy vessel that was *Coordinates*, not *Spirit Lake* or your mother, has borne it nobly to this port.

Your career, however, is just reaching its most productive childbearing years. If you can get this narrative monetized in the next year, they'll give you enough infantile post-U fellows to keep you busy into your decrepit centenary, like they did with Bloom.

Along comes a foul-faced little truth. I have not, up to this point, fully confronted the reality of the last part of my life, which is what some people call retirement. Even more alarming to me is that I didn't partition off this line of reflection with keypad and password. It is, instead, a neglected corner of self, a place I thought unnecessary to visit.

Now, having arrived there, I find it depressing. Your arrival and your academic need show me that all I have left is this singular reservoir of narrative art. *Spirit Lake* is all that is left. It is untouched and rarely visited, and then by no one but me. The ninth installment of *Coordinates* was long enough ago that I cannot remember its exact release date, and the rather sickening but absolutely magnetic doctor's models suggest I'll clear ninety-five even if there is "no change at all" in my soda intake and negligible exercise regime and spartan diet.

It is truly delightful to hear the hiss of nitrogen escaping these metal cans, is it not?

My academic life is nearly complete, just as yours will be at the legal limit, and, without what begins to seem like an impossible-to-attain waiver from the ASA, I will soon awake to the final day in the yellowing classroom and the final blathered 4:00 p.m. message from a panicking post-U. Supposedly I will toe the edge of the twenty-five years of the desert beyond the working life's cosmos, and this is the desert I am expected to cross, whether I like it or not.

I hate you a little for holding this mirror so close to my wrinkled neck and pale-veined hands. I take back what I said about age. The unstoppable crumbling of age is beautiful only in static image; living it is not so much horrifying as it is boring, and I can see why so many professional academics make it about five years before they're calling their doctors and beginning the paperwork. Women seem to survive better, but just last year (I had forgotten this fact until the second carrot soda, whose micro-carcinogens have always had wonderful effects on my psychological fortitude), my former colleague Brenda Link Patel waited, with immeasurable patience and poise, nine full months before they issued the approval. Nine months from irrevocable signature to irrevocable pill. She'd only been retired for three years. I had lunch with her one day early on and she told me that retirement felt no different than when, as a teenager, her home country, Kashmir, was ceded to and then not accepted by Pakistan, and for months everybody mulled around doing nothing, waiting only for war to rip the air and "either kill them and/or narrativize them" (that's from her video installation *Deadreal*, a work of generally unappreciated brilliance). Her memorial service was exquisite. She'd had a long time to plan it, after all, and the university-provided consultant we have here is very good.

I must be old. I'm beginning to enjoy memorial services and their emceeing propagandists. They are the only social events I've attended recently.

But if I am indeed old, I don't feel it. Your mother's face appears to my mind as if we were only recently walking in the piercing Albuquerque sun in the U district, talking about mountain streams and the future of literature. What's true is that I'm nearing seventy, that age deemed by the Supreme Court to be truly old, and I was in my twenties when I met your mother, and only a few months before that I had finished my post-U fellowship.

And your arrival has also revealed to me this other truth that I have not been willing to admit: I will be known, if I am known, for *Coordinates*. Though I dreamed of more, I awoke only to it. I will not be known for *Spirit Lake*.

Hopefully, you will.

Yet I feel this undeniable compulsion to suddenly spew it forth.

So take good notes. This is only an outline.

5

Back then, as your mother waited in the wings to come onstage, I thought it would be the triumphant summer of my first book of criticism, which I had titled, even before writing it, simply and elegantly, *Bot Poetics*. It would be my debut as a cultural voice, a critical force. I was a poet, then, when there were still pure poets, and for the two years of my fellowship, I had been particularly infatuated with bot poetry, which, after Gorr published her first "book performance" and then, almost simultaneously, Cortez Laughlin his critical exploration of Gorr (history, indeed, would vindicate those of us who later felt like Gorr and Cortez Laughlin were really just partners in an admittedly brilliant executed model that had been rather hesitantly endorsed by the Brainless Monetizers), had exploded into academia in a way that made us all a bit giddy. If this was the beginning, we thought, to what galaxy would this trajectory bring us?

I received a paper copy of Cortez Laughlin's work sometime in the last semester of my post-U. It was one of the first books to be edited, marketed, printed, packed, and distributed by the same megacompany, an organization for which "literary publishing" was a necessary column to advance forward, despite the losses, in a greater battle for "holistic incorporation," as the execs then called legal worldwide monopoly. It was a hedge division, a single production tentacle that was too culturally important to abandon simply because of financial loss.

Despite what the penniless and now-aging anarchists say about the fearful past and the almost-realized apocalypse of perfect technological singularity of that era, the megacompany's aggressive moves produced, for a few years, a nearly utopian publishing environment. Gone was the obsession with the "marketability" of a manuscript. Gone the hierarchy, gone the eternal and foppish editorial meetings in which a single book was excoriated, then palm fronded and praised, then murdered, then resurrected, all to test its weight in silver. Gone was the publishing elite. Gone, all of it! Instead, a flush of totally unqualified literati were hired to make recommendations for publication, and like monkeys with stamps they ferried innumerable books through the lax process. Profit was not the point. They called their friends. They wrote fantasy books about dog knights under pen names. They published things sight unseen. The megacompany's leadership made their market grab seem truly philanthropic: "Books for everyone!" was printed over and over again in obnoxious typefaces on their cardboard shipping boxes.

It was in one of these cardboard boxes that Cortez Laughlin's book arrived on my crumbly doorstep (to think—the demolition of that group of eight little yellow-painted, window-starved hovels was hailed in the newspaper just ten years ago as "mopping up" the last traces of asbestos in the city). Inside, it was oddly nested in shredded newspaper, a material becoming rare even then, and the shreds themselves, I swear, were pieces of cultural artifacts from the 1960s, either original or skillfully reproduced, and there was a vague sense, on rifling through the little fortune-cookie-esque slips, that one might come upon an article by Martin Luther King Jr. or John F. Kennedy, or some dustup of Led Zeppelin or disco. I know now that Led Zeppelin and disco belong to the next decade, but back then I heaped all the premillennial American ephemera together, and to see it surrounding this impossible matte-black book that said, simply, *SAY* and, below that, *How Lysandra Gorr's Art Works* and then, at the very bottom, in small caps, RAUL CORTEZ LAUGHLIN, was enough to sell me on emigrating to a new, greener academic country.

I decided even before I read the book that the most academically impressive book was the book about another book. And the book that made you a cultural voice was the book about a group of books. I knew then that I would write the seminal critical work on the genre I had tended for years. I would stop farming; instead, I would feast.

That June I'd had my head down. *Bot-Poetics* (I'll henceforth retain the hyphen for historical accuracy, but its permanent inclusion was an editorial mistake, perhaps indicative of the poor thing's fate) was itself born a day before my birthday, and, though I hate to imagine David Geores horizontal—except in handcuffs and squirming beneath a state-issued boot—I cannot help but mention the likelihood that you were conceived sometime as I finished *Bot-Poetics*, for it was right as I was completing the first draft that I met your mother.

I like this June moment, our first scene with you and I and your mother together: I couldn't have composed it better myself.

Backstory: Daniel lived in this old house downtown that had been bought, gutted, and re-roomed in a two-month frenzy. The house's white-painted chimney I can still see these forty years later from a certain angle in my kitchen, though of course the day must be not be smoky, nor the autotemper activated, which happens when the smoke clears enough to allow through the sun's sharp beams. Come to think of it, I only now realized that—for how long I don't know—I have made it a habit to stand at the kitchen sink and, before commencing washing my two dishes, I lean my body slightly to the left in order to achieve the right angle to see the white monument to my past. However, if the day is just unclear enough, I lean all the same but don't look for it; I let my eyes wander unfocused over the rooftops of old downtown, then lean back after a few seconds to scrub the soy shake-flecked glass. An odd habit, no doubt, but the oddest things become routine in old age.

He shared the resurrected house with four others. His lodgings had a bed and a desk and a small kitchen, and a window that didn't open (most windows still opened back then) that a few months later we would secretly rebuild so it opened and closed with a tiny Arduino that he controlled with his cell. Just outside the window was an enormous pine tree, and I can remember the way that pine tree's needles would swish on the glass while I watched in silence as Daniel swirled a new cone of code in front of my very eyes, like some twentieth-century ice cream parlorist. But these things were ahead and had not yet arrived. I was only just then standing on the wooden porch of his house for the first time, staring at my cell, waiting for him to respond to my "I'm here" message while the white chimney loomed somewhere above me. He had invited me over for "a little fun." I couldn't imagine what he wanted. But there I was.

He finally beeped me in to the house. I ascended a set of faux-concrete stairs, turned right, and was presented with his beige door, which said, simply, GLIDDEN. I knocked and almost simultaneously heard "Come in." When I entered, it looked as if he had been standing in that one spot—a strip of fading carpet between bed and desk wide enough for only one skinny person to stand—for the entirety of the hour in between my arrival and his initial message asking me to come over. He had his hands clenched at his side (now they are always out in front of him—a man balancing); he was bent over a bit in the middle (now a permanent stoop); his holey jeans stretched over his bony legs as if over vertical pipes (now those pipes hold up a little paunch); his tall, thin head (now bald) was leveled exactly at my face; his round-framed glasses shone (he still wears the same style); his blond hair was gelled straight backward in a terrible way, terrible because the hair was too short to really lie down correctly; his thick eyebrows (now brambles) seemed equidistant from both hairline and glasses frame. He smiled wildly.

"Joe!" Back then I went by Joe, before I realized that no one would publish something by Joe Stone. So for *Bot-Poetics* I invented a middle initial—my parents had thought such things frivolous—in order to abbreviate it into a much more academic acronym. I chose the middle initial *P* because once I had a dream in which, standing waist-deep in an interminable ocean, I heard the water itself speak a name that I knew was mine but had also never heard. I could not remember it upon waking, but I'm sure it began with *P*.

"Daniel?" Based on his manic stance. I was going to ask if everything was OK, but he interrupted. Pine needles swished on glass.

"Do you like pot?" His facial expression barely changed.

"Uh. Sure, I guess." I did not, but I hadn't yet learned to be ruthless. Ruthless or not, I felt self-congratulatory. I had, the day before, written the final word of a 63,705-word draft of *Bot-Poetics*, and though I was sure there'd be an important peer-review process in which renowned poeticists would recommend some very technical and thus ultimately flattering revisions, I felt that I had given myself the best birthday gift possible.

"Look!" And he pointed at the foot of the bed, to his left, where a clear bag full of gummy cubes sat. There were orange and yellow and red. I noticed that, beneath the plastic bag, the blue fleece hotel blanket on his bed was perfectly smoothed and tucked. I glanced up at a glossy photo hung low on the wall, a bit too close to the flat pillow. In the picture was a collection of eight or nine differently sized people in front of a fountain, all of them in a similar white shirt and triangle-smile expression. Any of them could have been Daniel.

When I looked back at Daniel, he had the exact same smile. He didn't move. The state had legalized marijuana only recently, and Daniel, though no longer a Mormon in faith, was still a Mormon in approach and wanted to rebel even now in an orderly manner.

"Nice," I said.

"Which color do you want?"

"What dose are they?"

For the first time, he moved his feet. He pivoted robotically (small tangent: I saw him make the same movement just a few days ago in the department lounge when I pointed out to him that there were free pastries in a box near his left elbow).

"Dose?" he asked.

I took a step toward him and pointed at the line that listed the THC content. He asked if that was a lot. I told him I wasn't sure, even though I was pretty sure it was. He immediately plucked a red one from the crunchy bag and put it in his mouth. He laughed like a child. He said something about it being his first time. He handed me a yellow one, and I put it in my mouth. It tasted like a lemon floor cleaner now banned in most states, and which I have, indeed, tasted, though not willingly. I tried to swallow it but could not. For a few strange minutes, we stood across from one another, silently chewing.

On his desk he had a paper copy of a book of poetry written by some obscure Beat subpoet named Kaufman. Daniel did a 180 pivot on the same foot and grabbed the book. He told me that he believed this guy was the original bot poet. I was, by this time, so tired of hearing what people called bot poetry or bot-like poetry that I felt a drop in my stomach and a burning desire to invent an excuse to leave. Instead, I tongued the cube into my cheek and said I hadn't heard of Kaufman. Daniel said nobody had. Then he read a poem to me, a forgettable one, the first one in the book. He saw that I was unimpressed, though I nodded. His eyebrows descended a fraction toward his eyes. I was still standing only a step away from Daniel's door. He held the book a bit too close to his face and flipped the pages.

"This one I love," he said, then turned the pages to show me. It was written in all caps. I remember almost nothing of it, and care not to rehash it all here. On and on it went. I just now found this poem (his name had worn and twisted into Kellogg over the years) simply by typing in the single fragment I remembered: MY LITTLE GIRL MOTHER.

How appropriate for our task! For it was only about an hour and a half later, that is, about an hour and fifteen minutes after Daniel said he wasn't feeling *anything* and so unrolled the crinkly bag again to pluck out two more; about twenty minutes after Daniel, Kaufman in hand and still standing before his desk, though he had moved on to talking while coding on his cell with the non-Kaufman hand (I was sitting on the bed by then, and had refused a second cube), interrupted a poem with a few moments of silent book staring, then looked up at me and said, "Joe, you're going to have to escort—no, bring! *bring's* the word!— bring me to the hospital"; and about three minutes after we parked my old trad car in the black-hot parking lot and, like a piece of bulky furniture, I carried Daniel, who was moving his long legs wildly and superfluously in simulation of walking without actually walking, into the waiting room and watched as a grim old nurse shook her head at Daniel's rubber body; it was then, just then, forty or so seconds after I sat down in the waiting room, that I saw your mother for the first time.

6

She was sitting in the row of chairs across from me, bent over in pain and looking intensely at her cell. (They were big, inflexible things then, sort of like tribal talisman—people walked around with their cells held out in front of them like existential flashlights.) She was crying. She wasn't weeping, like Daniel would in front of crowds, prodigiously, snottily, or like I'd seen my favorite cousin weep when her yearbook picture had been switched with that of her worst enemy. No, your mother wasn't gasping or blubbering. Tears leaked at regular intervals from her eyes, and every three or four seconds she used her noncell hand to wipe her chin off. She had small brown hands, and her dark brown hair was long and wavy and full and pulled back into a complicated and logicless bun. Her features were sharp, her eyes were large, and she was beautiful in the way that all women at some point in their twenties are fleetingly beautiful.

As you've probably noticed from the images you've inevitably found (which, try as I may, I can't seem to liquidate completely) I am not a handsome man, necessarily. I don't like haircuts and I prefer not to shave. As a rule, women are not interested in me. I have hated them for their disinterest, even when, most of the time, I recognized that a large part of most people's days require them to simply ignore the people around them. Nonetheless, I could feel my disdain building for your mother even as I watched her cry. She was absolutely not interested in me, I thought, and, even worse, probably unable to understand, much less appreciate, *Bot-Poetics.* To comfort myself, I tried to guess at the cause of her inconspicuous mourning. A car wreck in which her foolhardy boyfriend was maimed but from which she emerged unhurt? A dying but emotionally distant mother? A radically uncomfortable menstrual period? Then I hit it: an abortion. (Remember, this was forty years ago; abortions were still medical procedures.) She was here to dispose of precisely the thing that would be like a car wreck to her foolhardy boyfriend, the living death of her mother, the only uterine activity worse than a radically uncomfortable period. And, I calculated, she wasn't weeping in sobbish waves or tearing at her hair and moaning, because she understood that this was "for the best," that her life was a territory barely large enough for her own small appetite. To bring a hungry and desiring being into such a subsistence economy would kill the whole population of that two-person country. But still she cried, because regardless of all this good sense, her body ached for her imminently dead motherhood, and it pushed forth tears and weighed her smooth forehead down simply because logic and sadness do not speak the same language.

How strange it would be, indeed, and how more and more convinced I become of the idea that you were, in your own pre-cortical, amphibian way, observing this moment, or, if nothing more, at least present.

And her first words to me were "What are you *looking* at?" My eyes lifted from her bereft middle. Her face was turned up and her red eyes were clamped onto my face. "How about you don't look at me, and I don't look at you, and we'll call it good?" she said, lifting the damp back of her hand to her wet chin. I've remembered this line because I thought it so clever and also so direct. She sucked some snot in on the second "you." Your mother was like this; tragedy or deep disappointment exhausted her normally diplomatic bearing.

I said that I was sorry. I looked down, imitating shame. I felt none. She said something in return about people staring at her chest regularly but that a hospital waiting room was just too far. I nodded, then I recovered in precisely the way I'd seen my father recover so many times when rebuffed by a scandalized, tight-hipped PTA mother or stuttering college student in the produce aisle at the tiny store near my childhood home. "I was just trying to think of something to say that might make you feel better," I said. (The first lemon cleaner rinse had occurred, in fact, when I first used that line, though sarcastically, after telling him in a rage that I thought he was disgusting.) She glanced back at me. I sat up straight in my chair. The ploy had worked.

She sniffed again, but for the first time exorbitantly. She looked at me and I'm sure she was trying to weigh my sincerity.

"Well, you could tell me that *this* is no big deal." She twisted in her seat and pointed down at her left calf. The colors there were kaleidoscopic and glorious at first glance, especially when cast against the background of the gray knap of the carpet. Upon examination, the picture became hideous. Almost the entirety of the skin's surface from the Achilles to the back of the knee was riddled with black and deep red and white. The white, I realized, was pus. I looked at her other calf. It was supple and perfectly muscled and hairless. I preferred it. But these are the illogicalities of new romance—one must stare not at the calf one prefers but at the calf the beloved prefers you to prefer!

"That looks awful," I said.

"It is awful," she said.

"Does it hurt?"

"Yes, but it's more the principal of the thing . . ." She looked over her shoulder at the swinging ER door.

"What happened?"

She exhaled grandly. Just as she began to speak, I noticed that the old, short, pucker-faced nurse that had wheeled Daniel away had emerged from the doors, stopped, turned her head in a slow periscopic scan, found me, and taken four large strides to a distance not exactly private. Before your mother made any headway in her story, the nurse announced *mezza voce* that she'd seen a lot of Daniels—"if that was even his name"—in the last month, and that there were bigger problems for this hospital to deal with than "willful stupidity," and so, she wanted me to know, she had, in her words, "plopped him in a chair in the hallway, given him an IV and a pulse monitor, and told him not to move for an hour, which he is taking very, very seriously." I said nothing. I think she wanted me to be upset, to fight back for Daniel's dignity, but I agreed with her entirely. Daniel was then the epitome of innocently willful stupidity. I found it amusing and slightly charming, though I probably wouldn't have even given Daniel a chair in a hallway. Then, in a radically changed tone, she addressed your mother. "Honey, come on back and we'll take a look at your leg."

As they walked back toward the hallway where I assumed Daniel was sitting, his eyebrows soaring, knees jutting out of pant holes like table corners, hair matted in strange ways, repeating something like "I've overdosed on ganj" to the variously ill and injured passersby, I heard your mother say that she had gotten the tattoo the Friday before last, and it had been fine for a couple of days but then . . . The hallway doors closed behind her, an enormous, red *E*, then an *R* of the same typeset flapping alternatively into view. I realized for the first time that the black streak vertically bisecting her rotting calf wasn't a bruise or some black hole of the infection but was, instead, writing of some kind, and I knew that I really, really wanted to learn what it said.

Of course, being the old narrator I am, I see now how appropriate that infected tattoo is as an opening image in our story, for its content—not bacterial—would unknowingly become the central image of the denouement of our story (yes, it must be, trust me), and the unknown probability of you in her womb the conditions for the climax. I have never put these things together in just such a way, and in a way it solves some narrative problems that I've toyed with here and there over the years but always (for my own sanity) abandoned.

I often tell my students that narrative is the "equilibrium of meaning" in which all things, no matter how disparate, must align, stabilize, and intertwine into a central pathway or vector. Those elements that do not behave thusly simply cease to narratively exist. And so Daniel Glidden's potscapade and an infected tattoo on a beautiful and covertly pregnant stranger suddenly unite in a single narrative direction, and this doesn't surprise me at all. In fact, I'm a little excited about how crestfallen the eugenically controlled twenty-six-year-old tenure hunter will be when she has gotten this far in the narrative and realized that she will not win the professorship on looks alone.

I sat still in the angular waiting room chair for another fifteen minutes, then walked the room looking for a soda machine. I stopped when I realized there was none (the old soda—the caffeinated, dangerous stuff— was being slowly guilted out of all public facilities), and stood there, just outside the war-torn country of arm chairs, but a safe distance away from the check-in counter and, a few paces down, the swinging ER doors. Behind me people coughed and poked at the hospital's scuff-screened tablets. A TV blared the news above my head. The R door opened about a half meter, a young woman poked her head out and then retracted it, and just as the door closed, I thought I heard Daniel moan. I remembered my last trip to the hospital, for a spider bite on my lip. I had handed them a jar with the tiny brown spider in it and the woman said, "You're like the four percent of people who actually bring in the thing that bit them." She smiled, and when I didn't respond, she shrugged and said I was fine, that it wasn't a brown recluse or something even remotely as nefarious, not only because brown recluses looked leggier and angrier but also because by then—it had been an hour or so since the bite—there'd already be plenty of necrosis. "Necrosis?" I asked. "Dying skin," she said. "Your lip would be already showing signs of rapid death."

Your mother eventually reemerged. The doors swung happily behind her. She went to the gray, belly-high counter and spoke with the featureless young lady who pointed to different things on the tablet in response to each of your mother's questions. Your mother signed and dated there, initialed here, paid (yes, paid) a co-pay. The calf had been bandaged with what looked like plastic wrap and toilet paper. She punched a final thing on the tablet, turned, caught my eye, and then kept turning as if no eye had been caught, which is a distinct skill of women in their late twenties. She pulled her cell out—that was my cue, but I didn't see it then—and began walking slowly down the tiled wash that meandered through the carpeted plain where we'd met. I glanced at the tileway and saw how it ran past me, then ultimately dissolved into a wide delta near two sliding doors, beyond which was the cloudless

Albuquerque sky. She moved slowly downriver, too slowly, even for an injured person. Now I understood. I felt my heart beating rapidly.

Just as her shoulders were in line with mine (though I still looked upriver toward the foolish Daniel), I leaned toward her on one foot as if whispering her a secret. "All better?" I asked.

"Hardly," she said, looking up from her cell, then shaking it like a pill bottle. "But I got drugs." She smiled. I saw her teeth, and they were perfect but for some enamel thinning in the valleys.

"Is there any necrosis?"

"Necrosis?" She paused. "Nice word."

I laughed. "I'm a poet." Then I took the deep breath in exactly the manner I'd planned to take it. "Are you interested in getting coffee before you take the drugs?"

She saw my smile. "Not really. I can literally feel the pus dribbling like syrup down my ankle." I raised my eyebrows. She laughed. "I'm a poet too."

I see now that neither of us could have known if the other was serious about being a poet, or if it was just one of those asinine jokes that alleviate the awkward swelling of the ankles above love's tender new feet.

Again I channeled my father. I looked dejected but not pitiful, like I'd had a good idea but had been shown the legitimate obstacles to its execution. "Besides," she said, "your friend will probably need some help soon." Daniel. I hadn't forgotten about Daniel at all, but I'd miscalculated how leaving him behind might look to her. So I laughed and said that I'd almost forgotten about Daniel. I pushed my hands through my hair. I think she took all of this as I intended it to be taken. She smiled, for the second time, and I revised my opinion about the enamel thinning. Must have been the lighting.

"Give me your number," she said, "and maybe when my leg isn't oozing sap we could get coffee before drugs."

I remembered then the pot gummy I'd eaten and I wondered if I was, indeed, presenting myself in the way I thought I was presenting myself, for at the moment I felt an unprecedented mastery over the game. I spoke my number aloud (no slurs, from what I could tell) and she tapped it onto the screen, then lifted it to my face for confirmation. The rigid screen was shattered—it seems that all screens back then were shattered—but the number was correct. She sent a message; I felt my back pocket jiggle. (The message said, and I quote, "hey.") So, I thought, she was not just placating me, and I had no reason to hate her. She was truly and just barely interested.

"Hope your friend's OK," she said. "Shit can sneak up on you." She took a step. "What's your name?"

I told her and she typed it into her cell. Then she looked at me, didn't say her name, grimaced (though somehow pleasantly), said "See you," and limped through the sliding doors and out into the world where I lived.

7

What do you know about bot poetics? This is an important question. I've been going on and on like a grad school professor, assuming you know the basics not only of the genre but of the movement that birthed and then murdered it. You'll forgive me if I assume your ignorance of such an illustrious genre in which the likes of Daniel Glidden were once well known. A primer is necessary before we proceed. You must know the strange country you've sauntered into.

Bot poetry is produced, quite simply, using computer code as the primary or secondary generative "mind." Many bot poets in the latter years of the movement attempted to cast some mystery around the genre, I think in an effort to save it from the very obscurity they'd unknowingly willed it into. In truth, however, bot poetry is not radically different from traditional poetry. People loved the "technological component" of AI-produced verse, but it's a truism now to say that there has always been, since the beginning of poetry, a "technological component." All poetry is technological, in that it is communication forced into a machine that packages it in memorable and meaningful ways—ballads as mnemonic devices, sonnets as prepackaged seductions, slam as emotive political performance, etc. etc. The bot poet, then, depending on his facility as a programmer, was not "generating" poetry much differently than was Petrarch: both were using a prebuilt technology—in Petrarch's case, ABBAABBACDECDE; in a bot poet's case, Sindhu or Javaplus— to produce a packaged product that both fulfilled expectations and smacked of infinite possibility.

And please. I'm not trying to defend bot poetry or my orphaned *Bot-Poetics*. If I've learned a single thing from decades of department meetings, there is no good defense for profitless genres (the lost daughter genre, the dead mother genre, the mysterious religious practices genre—these are profitable, still, after all these years, and so your *Spirit Lake* will shine).

But why, indeed, am I going on about bot poetry? Your mother, alive in a sense, is just barely beyond the hospital doors! Let's follow her. Yes, I see her there. But you must believe me that your mother and Daniel Glidden and Grey Aaman and David Geores will be mere sprites, shadows of truth, unless I can paint in true colors the Jurassic culture in which we all then existed. And perhaps the most representative carnivory I can show you from that time is the culture gorging itself on the entrails of poetry (both literally poetry and all that was poetic). For this tragedy was at the core of my soul. Thus, it is necessary to distinguish the bot poetry genre (a grazing and beautiful herbivore) from the bot poetry *movement,* which, or, I should say, *whose members,* would have been more righteous in abandoning their love child, rather than eviscerating it.

The ill-fated *movement* was lifting its treacherous skirts then, preparing. It was novel enough that die-hard practitioners (S.e.e. Hofsed, Boony Storn [a bot-produced name], our Daniel Glidden himself) were being interviewed by national news outlets. There was much intellectual fomenting and fervor. A presidential candidate mentioned one of Storn's bot poems in a stump speech. A rap subgenre rose up like mold in all the hot air and became somehow connected with the abstract mural scene in Chicago. The bot poetry *genre,* or rather the *technological form* (to keep myself consistent with my own definitions established in *Bot-Poetics*), which had been long standing and well explored if sneered at by mainstream literary types, was becoming popular. Its stock was soaring, its peak invisible beyond the offing. And I, I was the all-seeing eye watching it happen.

I know for sure I was the first to see the ways the movement moved, and how the genre would flex and warp under the weight of popularity. *Bot-Poetics* would establish me as the intellectual shepherd of this vast artistic diaspora. Soon enough, I thought, I would be getting calls from news agencies and award boards.

Part of the frenzy had to do with the scarcity of capable creators. At that time, "programming" was not taught to every living child and their pets. I had learned a bit of HTML and HTML2 in a high school internship, but for the most part, "programmers," as we called them, were rare and highly sought after. But programming then was grueling, idiotic work devoid of unifying theories. Programming was a bunch of cavemen teaching one another how to start fire by the magic and complex bang-rock ceremony. It was only years later that any formality would take hold, primarily when that pseudonymous L8man wrote that long and winding philosophical framework into the notes alongside the code propping up teetering eBay. His notes set the stage for the Code of Code, which fifth graders now memorize.

Back then, many of the programmers had gotten into the coding game out of sheer adventure and a desire to ascend quickly. They craved the joyous power one feels in having mysterious control over cultural levers. They basked in the social equality previously inaccessible for a sharp-elbowed, sun-deprived programmer. Among others, Baby+ (an infant-supply warehouse) and Dairy Queen (a greasy burger joint) threw dripping gobs of money at twenty-two-year-old programmers. Small countries were offering government posts. The enormous tech companies were losing in the race to recruit them, especially after the great flops of the Hack Wars, which sent many of these men—and they were, not exclusively but mostly, men—careening into global politics and international espionage and gray-market wealth. Many became culture makers; the group of them became culture itself. Their language and humor and interests began to be mainstream. They were like rappers in the century's first decades; their touch was Midas's.

Most of the programmers were not computer heroes. They worked at big tech companies on tiny little U-turns in the tangled network of online plumbing. But they had not been trained for this dank work, which was, like all trade work, repetitive and unlit. They realized quickly that the tech companies were recruiting philosophers and royals but then were giving these Brahmans (L8man's terminology!) thankless, menial jobs in the black crawl space beneath the internet. They were glorified typists, custodians of code, digital plumbers. Heady intellectuals were handed a laptop and a map and sent out to clean the festering back alleys and drainages of the massive global network of fraying and circuitous code.

Despite the trudge, many persevered out of sheer necessity. Slowly a (rather dark) culture developed, which I know a bit about, and which bit you know I know, if you've seen *Coordinates 4*.

Strike that—I won't assume you've seen *Coordinates*. I know, however, that you've seen the signs around Centex for the "programmer's reunions," which are so akin to last-century VFAs that they have, in many cases, bought the latter's crumbling bingo-beer halls and turned them into part museums of obsolescence, part pot dens. You probably missed, however, last year's relatively unreported court case around the New Vermont Programming Reunion.

There's an image somewhere of the old men sitting around a collapsible table covered in computer parts, and they are fat and scraggle-bearded and wearing their ironic NASCAR for Dummies shirts and draped with wire-and-circuit-board necklaces. At that particular meeting of the NVPR, the old code grumps, half drunk, wrote an elaborate program to produce unbelievably eloquent speeches filled with hatred and vitriol, one of which was then accidentally "read" aloud in Maine at one of those "improvisational" political campaign events, where candidates, often medicated and usually too poor to hire decent consultants, regularly (and now legally, as of the Ball Sampson Bill) mouth the words that a speech bot is simultaneously producing and amplifying in the candidate's digitally reconstituted voice at that very moment. I'm sure you've noticed that some candidates have even stopped the lip-synching, and now they shake hands or squeeze shoulders. One even painted a pointillist utopian landscape during the artificial speech.

The NVPR court case was essentially about *who* spoke the hate—the speech bot, the candidate, the mustachioed womanizers of the NVPR? There were many doctors, brought in by the defense, who testified about the power of Pseudonol, which the candidate claimed he had, in blind deference to the handler from a hired management firm, ingested in copious amounts; half-life tests a week later could not confirm these mythical quantities. An ungendered expert on Ball Sampson testified, but they were almost incoherent in explaining the purpose of the law, which I think was a better defense of the bill than even its authors could have imagined. The speech-bot builder testified too, and said, at one point (this is why I'm telling you about all this, though I suspect you have by now already toyed with the idea that I am an aged and supercilious rambler), "The only people to blame are people."

(She was brilliant, that builder. I messaged her one night and eventually discovered that she had seen the first two *Coordinates* and had been inspired by them to write "art programs," as she called them. An attempt to meet failed after she suddenly descended into radio silence, wrongly making me feel lecherous.)

I won't withhold from you the ultimate significance for you and me of this woman's concise mantra in the teleological tangle. That is, my youngish friend, it will be easy to blame systems, to blame communications, to blame technology and religions and governments, but you must resist this popular pastime, and you and I must be willing to speak the names of the people to blame.

But code, at the time, was a phenomenon. It was lurching upward and dragging some of the most socially inept, morally immature, politically backward programmers up with it. Into such a cold code world enter: Daniel Glidden.

8

Before the poetry, Daniel worked in a Boston / Eastern metroplex megafirm where he wrote operational software for self-driving cars. He was sick of it. He always told me that the break had come the moment he realized that he worked in a converted closet with two other guys sweating mere centimeters from his back and who quickly clicked out of salacious videos when he'd turn around to ask them to scoot forward. They were three white men in a box,

> *one of whom*
> *was Daniel*
> *too.*

I've always loved those three simple lines. They're right here in his first book (yes, paper, so no quotation marks), which I've extracted from the rear of the book closet in my bedroom (for which referential purpose is practically the only reason I go in there anymore). The book was reviewed well by a number of our more learned contemporaries, but, according to the stats page for the modern version, pretty much no one has ever read Daniel's first work except those benevolent critics and the execs that gave him the first professor position. And me, of course. And the biannual student stalker type that plagued all of us before our hair started to gray.

The most important thing is this: Bot poets, unlike the rest of academia, whether they admitted it or not, knew in their creative gut that poetry as a viable contemporary literary form was dying, going the way of the jester and the TV variety show and the aphorism; the most conscious among us believed we were giving it a glorious wake. The murmur of that time was not terribly different from the conversation that is swirling around the novel now, though Cervantes's baby certainly still has much life left to live; bot-produced novels, excluding romances and children's books, are still rudimentary and awful.

In the weeks before I first met Daniel, I had cemented my belief once and for all that there was no future at all as a bot poet. I believed, instead, that there was only a future in studying bot poets and their genre. (This, of course, is the great survival intuition of the insular academic, for nearly all genres are studied for much longer than they are enjoyed.) In other words, the only chance for survival was becoming a bot poeticist. Gorr and Cortez Laughlin, in their twin books, basically ushered in this new era without intending to. A nearby but perhaps simpler comparison is the biologist who realizes that saving their particular endangered lizard is impossible, so they might as well save themselves and become a professor who specializes in a newly extinct lizard. Much was said in my younger years about academia consuming all human pursuits that were not easily monetized (see current religious history departments, the ballooning musicology trend, small business and entrepreneurics). In my lifetime, I have seen such prophetic fulfillment: the professorship has expanded to accommodate refugees from all unprofitable enterprises. More specifically, with its cousin politics, it is the last remaining island of "careerism," which perhaps seems antiquated to you, but monogamous and immobile brains of my generations have not been able to survive happily in the unstable and mutable "jobist" lifestyle that now is the norm. We needed, we still need, highways to drive on, channels dredged. You are right to think that perhaps a little jobism might redeem our benighted retirements. It is a good thought, though it is too late for me to learn to ride off-road.

I was not, on that Friday night, in the mood to even eulogize bot poetry. Instead, I'd begun to slink behind it hungrily, waiting for it to finally drop dead. We were at a new student gathering. I think it was at Joe's, whose beer-soaked intellectual locker room we'll encounter more fully later—for now, let's just poke our heads in. At these particular gatherings, which I'd been to twice before, recent grads of the program were asked to mingle and lie and glad-hand, and we were *encouraged* (usually in a threatening, terse message from Sharon Colby, the head fictionist) to *not* discuss the fake-prof scandal that was still boiling below the surface of the Narrative and New Poetics faculty. Instead, says one message I've yanked from the archives, "talk about your bright future as bot poets."

Daniel was the nearest to my elbow when I ordered my first soda from the bar. We began talking. He asked me what my experience was of the program. Here was the opening through which to shove my "bright future." I could tell he was zealous and optimistic, so I spoke honestly: I was glad to have two years to realize that poetry was a sinking ship and that I should swim to the nearest watertight vessel before I drowned too.

"Watertight vessel?" he asked, taking me surprisingly seriously.

"The professorship," I said, casually.

He was visibly shaken. His unbeered hand dropped to his side, his pale white face fell. I saw a red flush around a couple of acne bulbs irritated by an electric razor job almost indubitably executed in the parking lot ten minutes before his entrance. I exulted, thinking that such an effect—the feeling that I was a kind of doomsday prophet— if magnified, would make the yet-to-be-written *Bot-Poetics* infamous. Infamy, I believed, was absolutely the fastest way into academia.

But he did not walk away. Instead, he recovered. He took a sip of his orange beer and then asked what kind of poetry I wrote. I told him I *had been* making bot poems, but before I could go on, he brightened and raised his hand out to stop me. He said wetly that he was a bot poet too, and that he understood the feeling that poetry was dying, and he'd even written a couple of good drafts on the subject, and he could show me if I just gave him a second . . . The TVs churned behind the bar; eager new admits were nodding and smiling in response to the wisdom of their more experienced peers; Sharon Colby pulled her robe-dress tightly across her middle and looked over her shoulder, hoping someone walking in was anyone but a writer.

While I waited, I prepared the cutting sort of criticism that would make me seem both very smart and not unkind.

What he eventually revealed to me on his cell, however, and what hints I'd get from the following conversation told me that Daniel was gifted as an art programmer. My most revised poetry script was childish in comparison to the little bold knobs of code he could produce in a single ten-minute session at the bar, which he did, right then, while I wiped the soda can condensation from my hand onto my new shorts. And while he coded, he narrated his life, almost as if this were a Gorrian performance for which he'd prepared.

He had grown up a Mormon in a time when Mormons were concentrated and largely contained in Utah and the Utah-touching borderlands of the surrounding states. Later, deep in the black heart of the eastern cloud cities, he remembered Mike Smith's satirical work and discovered that Smith had studied at an Iowa MFA program (almost all MFAs are now largely dissolved into the Narrative and New Poetics departments, though those departments are slowly being consumed by others . . . I suppose you could call this period Cretaceous), and so Daniel began applying. He had almost no creative work to show, but because he had plenty of money saved up, he was willing to pay full price for any program mercenary enough to take his money. It does not surprise me that our bony, vape-clouded institution was the first to put their palm out.

All of this he poured forth grossly, shamelessly. Occasionally, he interrupted the autobiographical flow to speak to his cell's compiler as if it were a naughty toddler. This first impression was not good, but I'd learn over the next couple of years that Daniel did have a spark of genius. His love for order and exactitude had been exploited by the corporate wrangle and, now that he was around "creatives," he was willing to be a little sloppy. In the absence of obsessive tasking, what came through were the delicious (in poetry) paradoxical logic lapses that Mormons are (well, were) so excellent at cultivating, and this quality, paired with his alarming persistence made him, in my opinion, an excellent and perhaps the last true bot poet.

That's right. I said it. I was studying the nearly extinct lizard, and there before me was the most beautiful specimen I'd seen.

Take these lines from a quick "Daniel Glidden" search, which are not perhaps the best examples but will do:

> *Who are Alanis?*
> *Who is Alana Re?*
> *No one. They, no one*
> *In particular, AlanalA*
> *[. . .]*
> *in a coda, a code I did not write*
> *but that rights me.*

Reach back to undergrad literary history and note the similarities to Beat poetry (see Kaufman's poem way above), but rehashed in the wildness of code-produced phrases. I know for a fact that this poem was built with a code that produced pairs of distinct words that abut one another in alphabetical succession in some outdated dictionary. He loved writing the code but he also loved the transrational treasure hunt, the beauty of making meaning out of some phrase like "pracksis bells" or "soup but soup" that, at least at . . .

9

I have placed an ellipsis at the end of the above paragraph because the cell blurped from the table near the sofa. After the surge of adrenaline and the bitter relief in discovering it was not you, and then a brief and stunted conversation with the person who it was, and then the five or so minutes after hanging up that it took me to still my hands enough to return to this missive, no, this outline, I had forgotten completely where I intended to go in recounting such minuscule detail in Daniel Glidden's hagiography. So, in returning to a place as near as I can to my original departure, I find talking about myself finally unavoidable.

First, let's ask this. Who decides worthiness? The creator? (Never.) The audience? (Hardly.) The critic? (Mostly.) The critic decides worthiness. He sits at the head of the cultural table and says to the creator, "Serve," and to the audience, "Eat." He is the controller of aesthetic value in a world in which everyone is both creator and consumer. His harem is populated by artists. His servants are investors.

I tolerated Daniel all those years ago because I knew he was precisely the person who would assure I'd have a job for perpetuity. He believed in poetry and beauty, but he also worked like a nineteenth-century Nevadan farmer. There at the bar, it didn't take more than half a soda and half his beer-moistened biography before I figured I would be the Cortez Laughlin to his Gorr, and I would sell books of criticism about people like him to people like me. They would in turn assign them in the classes that they willingly taught for little more than basic health insurance and grocery money, and I would eventually be hired as a professor at a more prestigious branch because of a small but hungry readership of bottom-rung professors and their bored students. It was not an empire I was imagining. I have no delusions: we were all toiling in an obscure mine, taking out mid-grade ore. We forget that wealth and status are local phenomena.

Things went a different way with *Coordinates*, of course. *Coordinates* saved me from myself, because, as it turned out, I would never be permitted to ascend to the critic's throne.

So, here we are. All this talk about code and bot poetics can lead us only to my poor *Bot-Poetics*, whose shameful downfall I have up to now avoided describing.

Let's look directly at it, no sense in hiding. As of today, the listing for my one "book" of criticism, the aforementioned and incorrectly hyphenated *Bot-Poetics*, written that June in the hot fury of realization that the work I'd been trained to do in the New Poetics program was about as useful and meaningful as bracelet making, doesn't get a viewer per day, is "accessed" perhaps once every third month, and, as far as I can tell from rather complex searches, has not been quoted or perhaps even browsed by important cultural admins beyond the two or three myopic pseudo-literary doorknobs who called it "alarmist" and "cannibalistic." But let's not stop there, let's rip the bandage off: Once, the publisher offered it as a free download, just to get my name in circulation, and of the nineteen downloads in that week, I got four messages and one handwritten letter (anachronisms abound in the Mesozoic!) from New Poetics students in other states that attempted to prove me wrong but invariably finished with what I called the "say it ain't so" paragraph, as if, after exhausting all their preliminary arguments, they had actually convinced themselves that I was indeed right, that all was lost, that this message was their last breath above water.

I *was* right. The failure of *Bot-Poetics* was really the failure of people to read it, and such a failure proved the very argument it was making about the emptiness of the culture into which I published. How many books have drifted thus into self-affirming obscurity? My book claimed that poetry had so turned in on itself that it had become like Paris and Santa Fe, which is to say that it had become an amusement park in the theme of itself, making only one outcome possible, and that outcome is invoking saccharine nostalgia, thus making it impossible to teach to anyone below the age of thirty, and *bot* poetry, traditional poetry's unlikely savior, was the giant but not evil corporation that wanted to come in and tear half of Paris down (the chintzy, ridiculous part where no one actually lived but where cell-blind tourists roam like the bison that once ate the grass in their flat, interstate-laced home states) in order to create something new and radical and interesting. By then, however, too many professors' syllabi and pensions were vested in the Poetryland model, and their subsequent campaign against bot poetry succeeded in eliminating its influence and also succeeded in dooming the study of poetry to, at least in one famous case, the anthropology department.

All of this I explained to Daniel at length within the first weeks of our friendship. Daniel was absolutely unfazed by my pessimism. I think this is why I liked him initially, and it is undoubtedly why I have liked him less and less since. Back then he would listen to my lectures and, in later meetings at twinkle-lit coffee shop patios or in the orange light of barrooms, he'd even quote from my previous diatribes. I still have an odd sentimental weakness for the memory of an afternoon meeting at the river (then in its last year or two of flow), in which, having emerged from the forest of cottonwoods into an open place where we could see easily the brown ankle depth moving past us like an empty conveyor belt, Daniel and I stood quietly, contemplatively, until he looked at the water and quoted one of my more obscure (but secretly favored) verses:

> *Suns are no rivers.*
> *We disown rivers.*

It was a magical moment.

Soon, however, I'd realize that though Daniel heard what I said and retained it enough to flatter me, he believed little of it and, I think, actually slightly despised me for it. To this day, our parallel careers are half-playful, half-serious middle fingers directed at the other.

I think I have a chance of pulling ahead here at the end, though. I have noticed, lately, that Daniel seems tired. Like you, he hasn't published anything in years, not even a series credit. This last *Coordinates*, the ninth, was, for the first time, entirely without his collaboration, though he had certainly been less and less important in every series since the second. On top of that, one of his post-U fellows came to me recently (which is rare in itself) to say she felt like Daniel had checked out. *No,* I wanted to say, *the boat he was on has finally sunk, and he has stopped swimming.* But, of course, the dog-paddling post-U student was on that boat too, and regardless of bravery, no one but that actor in New Zealand and the cult in Alabama has chosen to see what we all know exists on that Antarctically cooled super server: the medically modeled and 89 percent accurate (those are their numbers) forecast, *down to the week* (believe it, just search in the *Times* from a month or two ago: the six-month range standard of government budget models is old news!), of each of our deaths. I just told the forlorn student to put her head down and keep narrating. I've told hundreds of students that exact thing in response to the broadest range of problems spoken aloud in my office in the last twenty years. Roommate troubles? Put your head down and narrate. Purposeless? Alcoholic? Broke? PYHDAN. Pyhdan pattah, like rain on parched earth. What I used to give them—carefully curated advice about their situation—never worked. They'd drop out or commit crimes. They'd stalk me for months, send me death threats, pen my name into suicide notes. Now I tell them to put their heads down and narrate. Usually all things are repaired or simply survived, even if not much that's narrated is worth consuming.

10

After writing that crash course in the history of bot poetics and also Daniel, I spent a minute or two in dejection. What time I had before your arrival was, perhaps, depleted unnecessarily by the above diversion. Nevertheless, it will remain; I will not reread or remove; I will barrel forward. And! You had not yet called. Therefore, I decided that I would finally message our man.

I will reproduce the subsequent conversation here verbatim, because I think it will be enlightening for you once you and I meet, for besides series narrative and the demise of bot poetics, I've probably studied Danielitics the most, and he is bound to be a unifying subject of our unfortunate but required interlocutions. Principle #1 in this narrow academic field: Daniel Glidden is not a complex being, nor is he apparently simple. Perhaps he sent the following from the bathroom.

> *Me:* Thanks for letting me know about her, Daniel. I'm surprised you gave her my address, though, as you know quite well she won't really be able to just "show up." What is it that she wanted?
>
> *Daniel:* She wants to know more about her mothrr [*sic*—years ago Daniel, consummate bot poet, turned off autocorrect in one of those characteristically superstitious moments of paradox. He does not, like most other reasonable people, use speechtext]. She said she read the poems in a back issue of Cold and found my contact info that way.
>
> *Daniel:* She asked for your adress..[*sic*] I told her about security. I rolf [*sic*] her to call you ahead of time.
>
> *Daniel:* Im [sic] having dinner with her in an hour Id [*sic, sic*] ask you to join us but she seems to want to meet alone.
>
> *Daniel:* And we're having ramen, yor favorite [*sic*; sort of *sic*: I despise ramen]
>
> *Daniel:* I'll let you know what she says ☺
>
> *Daniel:* I'm a little nervous, [ ][ ] [not *sic*; the symbol did not transfer correctly]. I haven't thought about her in decades.

I am, now, trying desperately not to do what I used to always do with

Daniel, which is expect him to follow through with a timeliness that could be expected of anyone else alive, except for one other person I know, a certain concierge who you'll have the pleasure of meeting soon enough, which proves, I think, the basic truth that I am surrounded by unreliables. He said he'd "let me know" (a phrase I detest with a hatred that, at least once, has caused an embarrassing tussle in a department meeting), but I know that he won't "let me know," or he will "let me know" and it will be at the least opportune time, like next year, or like tomorrow evening after you've already called, or, even more horrible, after you've showed up at security and I've seen your probing visage staring at me through the doorscreen.

Such security, by the way, is a great advantage of living in this half-empty high-rise downtown. This awful building can be seen from almost any point in the city, but it is a monstrosity, inspired by some state university architect who made $4 billion about twenty years ago on a government nuclear waste deal and so decided to "give back" with a cantilevered glass-and-stucco obelisk at the center of a city that grows in every sector *but* its center. They found pueblo remains in the pit they dug for the foundational beams, and those are on view in reception, which, after the unavoidable moment of confusion, you'll find on the fifteenth floor, so oddly placed because the builder guy believed wholly in the imminent explosion of drone travel. He wanted to be the first to welcome helicoptered people to his building via helicopter-level reception area—thus the enormous and vertiginous concrete pad hanging from the middle of the building like a toddler's play table. But twenty years later, there are no manned drones (and with that golfing and baby-making Independent's reelection, it seems that there will not even be many *unmanned* drones besides the SEC eyes, much less PCs) and the fifteenth-floor reception is just an annoyance, for I must take two elevators to get to my apartment, one from the garage to reception, and one from reception to the forty-first of forty-three floors. Those who live on floors below reception must ride the second elevator back *down*, some returning to a room so near the garage that, I imagine, the quiet squeak of tires on glossy pavement punctuates the frivolous gallivanting of their empty dreams.

This building is representative of the same foolish optimism that makes people seem successful in ventures that are outright failures. Bot poetry is no different from architecture or medicine or transportation: There are the visionaries, and there are the marketers. The marketers are trying to make money on the visionaries before the visionaries make money for themselves, and marketers try to make money long after the visionaries have departed, and visionaries become marketers when they've run out of ideas.

Daniel has become a marketer. But back then, despite Daniel's simplicity, he was a true visionary.

He mentioned, above, *Cold*—this publication is something I should pause to biographize a bit. This journal, which is still active, was the first "online" journal to truly do something different (in fact, I recently read one review that said *Cold* was the first of the Third Cult pubs, a genre so bloated now that it must be about to die), and undoubtedly the first to truly get people excited about an artistic landscape in which bot poetry was not a weed species. *Cold* was not enough to save the culture from themselves, but it was remarkable on its own, so much so that even in the first three or four years after I left the New Poetics program, I tried to provide Daniel with as many publishable bot poems as possible, though I'd long believed it was all in vain. Something about *Cold* was literal and narcotic—I felt like I was sending my work into cryo, where things would be preserved in immaculate stasis until the next world needed them. Daniel's vision, developed during that first year in the NNP program, was that poetry should be "declassified," as he rather vaguely put it in one of those early manifestos. What he meant was that bot poetry should look like poetry and poetry should look like bot poetry and all of it should look like country music or World War II propaganda posters or dog food bags.

But this avant-gardism didn't get him anywhere, really. It certainly wasn't what made it alive. His ascent to fame only came about a year after founding, when *Cold* became the first to use videditing (executed by a black-lipsticked woman named Emily, perched amid artificial pet parakeets in a dank apartment, for hours learning to use what was then a bootlegged and jury-rigged software from China [the docupic *Eleanor's Birds* from a couple of decades ago was based on her posthumously discovered vlog]) to any sort of artistic effect—one of the things that made *Cold* truly widespread was the now clunky but then quite wonderful video of a younger version of a (then) recently dead, wildly famous heartthrob actor reading the last few sections of "Song of Myself" while sitting on the edge of a precipice at the Grand Canyon, then falling off the precipice at that last line: "falling to fetch me at first keep encouraged." It was circulated in some places as "lost footage" of the heartthrob's career, in others as nonfictional proof that his life hadn't ended on an ill-fated philanthropic jaunt to a disease-ridden African island. *Cold* was being discussed in the national press.

Daniel quickly released a fascinating follow-up, though this one was more artistic and didn't involve any famous living or dead person, but simply demonstrated, by swapping faces of crowd members with others in the same giant blinking crowd, the power of videditing software in the depiction of moving images. It was a characterless but otherwise creepy insinuation that he was at the helm of a technological revolution. People had been tricked by the heartthrob thing, fascinated by the prank, but they were converted by the "Crowd." *Cold* exploded, a cultural tire fire. Emily and/or her parakeets built a software framework and wrote into the code a powerful ethical overlay that made boundary-breaking art almost automatically. We pumped in poetry; *Cold* put it in precisely the pill form that culture could swallow.

But the real breakthrough was this: A famous pseudo-intellectual rapper whose name you likely know saw the video and decided he wanted to collaborate with *Cold* on a rap / slam / bot poetry mix-up, which (here's where you probably can pick up the thread) became the horrid and inescapable "Semitrue," and that unfortunate insemination begat that still-thriving American genre that is half exploding speaker tube and half grinding key change.

Daniel was aflame in those years. I saw him weekly for coffee or a soda, and in those sessions he simply spouted to me his disbelief. He didn't believe it would all hold together. He didn't believe it would go anywhere. He didn't believe Pseudo-Intellectual Rapper would actually commit. He didn't believe that PR's PR folks would allow for full collaboration. He didn't believe that the collaboration would be popular. He didn't believe that its popularity would mean anything for him. He didn't, couldn't, wouldn't believe in the position the state uni was offering him. I listened and nodded. What's true was that he was publishing poems and literary-tinged videos and mash-ups that were getting mass attention and then celebrity attention and then, the last step in intellectual dynasty building, critical attention. (If there is a map for literary fame, I suppose that's it.) What's also true is that the ailing critic Bloom (who had up until that year seemed truly immortal) wrote a short piece that seemed to suggest he believed *Cold* was taking up the literary torch for which he'd long sought a worthy heir. What he actually said was "Hubs like *Cold* make me wish I had twenty more years," which seems to me akin to an inveterate but now dying hunter commenting wistfully on a flock of mangy pigeons he glimpsed through the hospital window.

What's also also true is that by the time Daniel finished the New Poetics program two years after we met, he was making twice as much on the royalties and ads connected to *Cold* as the U was offering for a professorship position, but so disbelieving was he of *Cold*'s staying power that he accepted the position and merged *Cold* and its profits with the Narrative and New Poetics Department, making *Cold* an institutional project and effectively memorializing it before it was dead.

Here lies *Cold*.

Though, even the dead usher in intrigue: you found me by finding her in *Cold*.

And you're perhaps sharing an appetizer with the keeper of the dead.

11a

I had been teaching at a high school in town and had only my bot poetry publications to show. But I had just finally finished editing the rough cut of the first *Coordinates*, and Daniel thought it was brilliant. It was my *Cold*, though it certainly did not garner such desirable attention. Last time I checked, they were still using it in a freshman comparative in one of the smaller branch campuses of the Centex Consortium, so perhaps you've had to sit through it.

The original idea was much simpler than what it became. In fact, the original idea was nigh stupid. I had just bought a discount SD vehicle, one of the first of the Chinese-made auto drivers that was legalized (then, hurriedly, made illegal after a couple of fiery crashes; then, even more quickly after the anger and black taping, relegalized after "testing") in the first true wave of affordable SDs. Albuquerque, forty years later, has a fifteenth-floor drone reception but, still, rather awful SD infrastructure, but I bought the car for a singular forked reason: I could avoid taking the cacophonous and fecal-smelling A bus, which I'd taken only once, to a new faculty meeting, and which I would never, ever step on again, and, gloriously, I could read while commuting. The car was a XiPi 2. (XiPi 1s had been selling in Poland and Hungary, etc., and were having big-time language problems.) It had two seats instead of the one that you see so commonly in XiPis now. I alternated which seat I sat in, even though it had a basic manual steering setup, as was then mandated, and the steering wheel turned and tilted in a creepy homage to trad-driving culture. When I sat in the "passenger seat" (this redundant phrase, naturally, one only hears uttered by old folks), I had a vague feeling that I could be risking my life, but, of course, nothing ever happened besides once arriving quite early in the empty parking lot of Desert High Cool, a reputable air-conditioning vendor, before I realized I would need to manually program my workplace into the navigation instead of relying on voice rec.

I was not excited about the car, necessarily; I only craved the independence. I was one of the first SD buyers in the city, and a couple of news outlets wanted to interview me. I turned them down. I simply wasn't interested in the silly moral debates about the life-or-death-decision-making algorithms in SD cars, and when the infamous "You or Them Update" came around, I promptly and without qualms checked the THEM box (euphemistically labeled as the "Maximize Passenger Safety" choice), as I'm sure THEM did as well.

Daniel, however, having worked as a peon for one of those Eastern Metropolis firms, seemed excited about the SD's implications. The day after I bought the thing, Daniel and I were in the garage of the apartment I used to rent in the Northeastern Heights. Daniel was fiddling with the screen and discovered an EXT setting that could accommodate, he thought, a cell or laptop. We all had laptops then, so he got his, and I watched from the right-hand seat as he accessed the Neanderthal brain of my new SD.

"Incredible," he said.

"What?" I said.

"I have access to everything. All the source code. Everything."

"Don't touch it," I said. I imagined my car getting stuck in some endless left-turn loop downtown.

"I won't."

But I could see that he was definitely touching it. Suddenly the automatic seat belts quivered.

"All of this should be prohibited. It really is a poorly guarded doorway into the car's brain." Daniel was, in this way, a prophet. Maybe six months later, a teenager would program a XiPi to drive without a passenger and park itself in his friend's garage, but in the process he somehow eliminated the car's ability to turn itself off (believing as it did that it still had a passenger) thus filling the garage (and eventually, the garage apartment above it) with toxic fumes that killed the very friend (and the very friend's dog) that the teenager had only intended to prank. The gas XiPis were forcibly recalled and made secure, but the low-level code monkeys who rewrote my car's code at the volcano-themed dealership in Rio Rancho didn't see (or didn't care, or didn't know to care) that, by that time, Daniel had already programmed the *Coordinates* function into my car, which was so called because the icon on the screen was just called COORDINATES. Considering also his other famous title outing—*Cold*—it's not too harsh to say that Daniel was not a gifted titler. I suppose he loved the sound of *co*.

I will admit a sort of paternity. *Coordinates*, you could say, is the love child of that once-friendship between Daniel and me. It was born in that XiPi, from two young academics toying with code, each with a different desire but one with an absolute and naive trust that ideas matter, while the other had in his crumbly apartment a rather short list of all possible contingencies if "no career materializes."

I can count on one hand the people that launched the life I have lived for almost half a century. I should be more grateful than I feel.

11b

It's 21:00 now. While I swallow my soy shake and contemplate what I've written, I imagine the scene. You and Daniel at dinner in an orange-lit, narrow ground-floor restaurant. His beer is warm, probably half full. Your glass of wine has only a tactful sip remaining. He is poking at his cell, attempting to pay, to order a car. And you are tired. Daniel exhausts even the most tolerant among us.

I feel happy about your exhaustion and the late hour, because it means that you will probably not call tonight, which buys me more time to prepare and also provides precisely the cushion my schedule needs to prevent chaos. Now that the anxiety has been weeded out, I find little sprouting bodies of depression growing here and there, mostly *for* you, because Daniel is not exactly the man he used to be. I imagine that what is presented to you is a bearded, balding, blubbering old man who has likely cried in your presence at least once already, who is having trouble detecting and collecting with his pale tongue the crumbs gathering like scared chicks in the crease of rust-and-white hair where his mustache and beard meet, who listens with immaculate attention to what you say but somehow, in an indescribable process of memory, stores what he's heard so far from his consciousness that you could tell him, flat out, that you were absolutely his biological daughter (which you are not, but which might be a fun line to toss in his direction) and he would simply say, in response, "My biological daughter, huh? Well, that doesn't make the sense that I would need it to make in order to feel comfortable." He is probably telling you about *Cold*, about your mother, whose poems appeared there but who, as far as I know, never saw *Cold* in any of its varied forms and probably wasn't even living when the younger version of the dead heartthrob didn't fall into the Grand Canyon.

This is likely the first thing that will genuinely surprise you in this whole trip, that your mother was almost definitely not living when the only substantially unique bold knobs of her making were welded onto the cultural transfer pipes that Daniel was forging. And you will be disappointed but also a bit thrilled by the fact that Daniel will really only be able to lead you so far down that particular trail, and he will say or has already said, "That's something you'll have to ask Joe about."

While we're talking about what your mother didn't see, it's worth saying that your mother also never saw *Coordinates*. I think she would have loved it. She was all about adventure, spontaneity, wild choices, which, perhaps, helps you swallow the darker side of such a life: She sometimes drank copiously, and she told me that she occasionally had many boyfriends at once. In fact, David Geores, the front-runner for paternity in my book, was my—what do they call similar politicians in different countries?—ah, yes, my "counterpart" in the global economy of your mother's attention. That is, excluding the Grey Aaman factor, David and I were in direct competition. A guy named Luke or Lance or Lane, who might also be your father but who can be dismissed from this trial simply because of the seeming impossibility of timing, competed with David before I arrived, and preceded me by as close as three weeks. It was, if I remember right, Luke/Lance/Lane's sudden departure to Alaska or Alabama or Albania that had inspired the occasion but not the immortal content of your mother's tattoo. But I do not feel at all grateful to him, despite the unintended impetus he provided. Instead, I have mostly to thank some unknown and immoral tattoo artist, a Vietnamese woman who your mother said served under-the-tattoo-table pho to those clients in the position to eat it, whose filthy needle caused the glorious infection in your mother's leg and brought us together in the downtown Pres waiting room.

12

That tattoo must have healed slowly, because it was more than two weeks later that your mother messaged me. I was, by then, in possession of a full draft of *Bot-Poetics*, but I realized that I had no idea what to do next.

I was on summer break. Summer break has always been a wasteland for me. My peers exulted while I walked away trembling from the imprisoned safety of school's interminable roil. *Bot-Poetics* had saved the first half of summer, but it was not enough to sustain me through the latter half. As July neared, I grew ever more shiftless, unsleeping, overly reflective. I revised sentences, moving clauses around like paint swatches. While rereading Cortez Laughlin, in pain, late one night, I admitted to myself that my first chapter, "Prebotics," was anemic, perhaps outright superfluous. It was undoubtedly intellectual pseudonalia. When I reached the end of that particular Cortez Laughlin chapter, I stopped reading and threw the book into a corner. I was deathly afraid—in fact, I was paralyzed with certainty—that the book's subsequent chapters would always unveil the frivolity of my own. So I paced, literarily, literally. In early July, I revised that first chapter nine times—I was wrangling with the earliest bot generators, the ones that produced infinite numbers of tiny poetic globs like this one:

> *I am a dark*
> *on*
> *the night after*
> *The*
> *past love*
> *goes stale*

This was supposedly a simple chapter, a preamble, really a sort of legend for understanding the genre I'd explore more thoroughly in the book. But I was floundering. I couldn't decide whether to be explanatory or clever or compelling. In one section, I tried to explain that the initial struggle for many bot poets was coding punctuation and line breaks, for there in the dots and tittles were whole cosmos of untouched thought. Now I say this so simply, what it was that I wanted to do. But then, ideas spiraled outward into space and the chapter grew and grew and creaked under the weight of itself.

All I was hoping to say was this: Such simple formatting conditions seem like baby code, but the struggle of those early years lay in developing an analytical language for a transrational skill. It was eminently difficult to code for good punctuation in prose (some British teenager accidentally solved this, though, with the Jcode library, and in exploring this annoying innovation, I spent the unbroken entirety of forty hours spanning a weekend that July), but it was, in our minds, nearly impossible to code for poetic punctuation and spacing. This is because poetry thrives on what could be called organic punctuation—punctuation based not entirely on rules but on breath and feeling. No, no! Here I am again, fiddling with my toes! It's not the punctuation, JP! You learned, like Croce, that poetry is just language, and that language cannot be meaningfully deconstructed any further; words and pauses exist, but they do not add up to language. Poetry is meaning, and a bot cannot mean. How utterly simple this all is, how totally undeserving of an entire book. Do you hear me, my young self?

But back to *feeling*. Just writing the word again in this context reminds me of the burn of that July's atmosphere. Simulating *feeling* (do not read *emotion*) in a bot poem was really the initial challenge for all bot poets. (On a structural, and not a sentence, level, bot novels are right now struggling with the same problem, that uncanny sense of artificiality, like when the protagonist of the last bot novel I read said to their unrequited love before plunging to their deaths, "Death is ending." Knowing that a bot had produced this phrase caused an uncomfortable sense that there was nothing more behind this vague pronouncement but basic syllogism, and this discomfort is what makes only the very first bot novel interesting.) Though all of us could admire the excellent lines and rhythms that were pouring out of our lean-to programs like nickels, none of the early bot poets could achieve the eloquence of a single poetic sentence, enjambed in the perfect way and punctuated as exquisitely as our forebears' had been. The above poem represents this struggle. Of the thirteen words, the first eight seem bot produced, while the last five seem organic, if unoriginal. Achieving the wonderful sonority of "on / the night" while avoiding its obvious red herring feeling, and achieving the basic metaphor of "The / past love / goes stale" while avoiding generating sickly sweet clichés . . . such basic goals were really the name of the bot poet's game. We believed with our whole beings that readers could understand, though perhaps not explain how they understood, the difference between "I, even still, love you" and "I even still love you," but a bot could not be "coded" to meaningfully (re?)produce these basic poetic gestures.

All this early movement in the bot poetry world was rather slow, and I was only a toddler when the earliest generators were built. I, of course, have expressed the struggle perfectly here, because I've spent years revising it in my head. Back then, however, hunched over in an apartment whose singular window was a broad, retro-frosted, thin-paned thing in the shower stall, staring at an outdated and unblanked screen, typing miserably and deleting everything in nearly the same stroke, I could barely get a sentence out without thinking of my downward-drifting career, which my father had predicted when I received my NNP acceptance letter just before his death and which downfall my mother chronicled in a handwritten timeline she photographed and sent me before her own death, many years later, as if she had promised my father to bring him a detailed report when they met up again.

I was on soda number four or five and deep in the jungle of that first chapter when my cell jiggled on the desk. I'll reproduce this conversation verbatim too. (The money I've poured into archival services is finally yielding results.)

> *Your mother:* Well, the pus has dried and the prescriptions run out. I'm back in the game.
>
> *Me:* Great. Let's get coffee?
>
> *Your mother:* I'd prefer beer.
>
> *Me:* I only drink soda.
>
> *Your mother:* Alcoholic? Mormon? Joes has soda. Meet you there 930?

This was before the switch to twenty-four-hour time, and I remember being desperately confused here. I couldn't determine whether she meant 9:30 at night, which was only an hour distant and seemed oddly late and (rather tactlessly) built for a casual hookup, or 9:30 the next morning, which seemed like a worrisome time to meet for beer, and perhaps changed the tone of her first question into one searching for a partner in addiction. Either way, notwithstanding the omitted apostrophes and colon, I was concerned that I'd misread your mother when I thought she was interested in brains and thoughts. But those weeks had hollowed me out. My pants no longer fit and even Daniel was sending me alarmed messages. I knew this 9:30 meeting, whenever it was, represented a line tossed toward me in the murky flood.

The strategic genius of the next message even I, forty years later, find surprising and quite wonderful.

> *Me:* 9:30? I've got a pretty full morning tomorrow.
>
> *Your mother:* We won't stay out too late. I got to work in the morning too.

13

Places like Joe's are why we Joes must acronymize our names to get even the most basic intellectual respect. Joe's, both particularly and as a genre, is gone now. In fact, ten years ago, the coffee shop that replaced the dog groomers that replaced the art gallery that replaced Joe's exploded in the middle of the night. There was only a gas leak, probably from the very same meter I locked my bike to. The gas sneaked in through an open window, accumulated in the men's bathroom; the building was decimated. No one was hurt, and only the little gyro place across the street had broken windows. I have been by since to see the rubble, which, for years, sat absolutely untouched, until recently someone cleared the tiny space and put up a COMING SOON sign for a set of drive-in lift lofts, built by the son of the same deranged architect who built my current residence.

I went to see it, the gap, a few years ago, before they cleared out the wreckage. It took me some doing to get the SD to navigate there correctly, because I didn't remember the street, and nearly every surrounding business had been demolished or retrofitted to accommodate the influx of wealthy Middle Eastern students to the university. (Carey Bowen has a foolish song about this: "These new cars can't drive you / down Memory Lane.") By then the neighborhood had become an SD-only sector, so the police dispatched a guy to investigate my erratic activity. I saw him pull up behind me in his black bubble. I jabbed at the SD's screen.

Some neighborhoods have supposedly installed off lines that trip the distributors or something in non-SD cars and force them (and their undoubtedly criminal cargo/passengers) to stop, but I doubt such hard barriers exist. I think the specter of off lines is an off line in itself, and no one has actually installed such expensive deterrents, because no trad car really has any reason to venture into the SD neighborhoods except to steal stuff, and people who steal stuff from SD neighborhoods already drive stolen SDs, and the snackle that proceeds into an SD-only neighborhood in a trad car is reported by seven or eight neighbors before the car consumes even a few ounces of fuel on such fuel-less and forbidden turf.

A few neighborhoods, however, genuinely have electrostet detectors, which can pick up the human inconsistencies in managing the acceleration of an electric motor. The truth is, I suppose, that an SD car does not falter, does not retrace its steps five times, does not swerve or cut turns or leave its blinker on for too long. I kept programming and reprogramming new addresses, so my car would stop at one place, then U-turn and stop at another place, then circle the block and stop again. Eventually, it began to protest, robotically. *Are you in need of navigation assistance?*

The police behind me I'm sure saw it. A thin man in black and blue, who I'm almost sure took my Narrative One class maybe five years before, tapped on the glass and, when I succeeded in lowering it, asked for my ID number. I provided it, he scanned it, and on his little device he thus perused my profile for what seemed like many long minutes, his insolent finger swiping aggressively across the too-big screen. He asked, then, if my car was malfunctioning. I said it was not, but my memory was. I couldn't remember where a place named Joe's had been. It had exploded, I told him. "Oh yeah," he said, and though I could see nothing through the standard-issue opaque screen-specs, his eyes must have glimmered.

"I was at the U when that happened!" he said. "Let's see, put your car on follow and I'll get you there."

I waved at him when we arrived at the fenced-off rubble. He burbled onward.

Standing at the plastic boundary, I tried to reconstruct the old dive bar in my mind. Such reconstruction I'll repeat here, for your benefit.

It had been long and narrow, and the shape of the bar itself seemed to suggest that it was surrounding some other hidden place, for the establishment opened into a foyer populated with too few tables surrounded always by far too many chairs; the bar, beyond them, formed a natural barrier on the opposite side of the room. To the right, the wooden bar made a left turn and entered another narrow hallway perpendicular to the foyer. On the right hand, across a narrow walkway from the long, unbroken bar, were high-backed booths, squeaky and wide enough to fit only two narrow asses on each seat. Then, twenty paces or so down that hallway, the bar turned left again into another room perpendicular to the hallway and parallel to the foyer. Joe's, therefore, was a giant angular (and backward) C. And, as far as I can tell from my conversations with your mother and my infrequent visits, the three narrow spaces were absolutely distinct in culture.

The front space had a herd of wobbly tables standing about, waiting to be screeched across the floor, and at these tables often sat soccer teams and church groups and cheap bachelor parties. No one ever sat at the bar itself there in the front. The waitresses gathered near a cash register there when things were slow. The owner did paperwork there. It was too light, too familiar up there for drinkers and thinkers. Lights from turning cars beamed in and you could just generally see the less attractive features of your compatriot's face.

The side hallway, however, was always occupied by beautiful, sad-looking people. It had a long string of red rope lights where wall met ceiling, and beneath that rope light were the various framed newspaper articles and printouts that mentioned the seedy establishment's mediocre accomplishments over the three decades of its life, and beneath those were the booths. Usually, I sat in the booths. The patrons of "the side," as Joe's employees and regulars called it, wore dark colors and had deep and furious opinions about the playlist, which they tried to monopolize. They were often staring into the bright portals of their cells. They wore hats with narrow brims, pants with narrow hips. They were vegans, some of them; others had traveled to India, Slovenia. Many of them had lived at some point in one of America's many Brooklyns; at Joe's, they lamented their exile in Albuquerque, which had nothing even close to a Brooklyn.

The back room was the most artificially illumined, and it was crowded with nonhuman objects. Besides the barstools, there were a few booths and a few tables. Hanging from the ceiling and walls were a troop of neon signs advertising beer companies that had mostly died in the big beer slump. In a declivity near the entrance to the bathroom were three ancient pinball machines. I imagine only a few people in the city were interested in these petty anachronisms, but these few were always and forever in the back of Joe's slapping the machines' particleboard sides, and they were loud (the people), and they occasionally wore costumes, sometimes of cartoon characters I recognized, and sometimes of creatures I did not recognize. Sitting at the bar in the back was an interesting anthropological choice, even if it was excruciating. Indeed, "the back" will be the setting for a rather crucial and brutal moment in your story.

Once, after losing a bet with your mother about what David Geores would say next (odds were basically fifty-fifty), I played one of Joe's pinball machines. I found it totally inane; it was Scary-Burning-Trailer-Park themed and required only that I slap the two buttons at the side, which I did for what seemed like nearly a half hour. After a few minutes of button mashing, a man in a broken-tusked walrus suit (a yellow one— that detail is important) and two women in sexy semi-dragon costumes came up and watched me play. The neon lights held us in their glow.

The bar clinked with glass. They seemed impressed. I just kept saying, over and over, "Where's the skill? I mean, when do you make a *decision?*" I was actually getting angry, for there was some connection my mind was making to the (by then) grim future of *Bot-Poetics* and the flashy hollowness of this big electronic box I was beating. The costumed others around me, dolts all, began hollering and wowing every time the ball plunked into one of the illuminated holes and thus fished out from the machine depths impossible millions of points (the broken-tusked walrus, seeing the gush of points I milked from the machine, literally bit his flipper so hard with his apparently whole-toothed human mouth that I think it bled through the polyester), and by the end, two uncostumed automatons had joined broken-tusked walrus and the semi-dragons (who were now embracing, their sweaty, overflowing cleavage cleaving to their partner's). When they saw my final score, they swore at me and said they just *couldn't understand* and they bought me a beer that I didn't drink. Over the next year, even long after your mother was gone, I reentered Joe's six times, and each time, somebody'd say, "You still got it." People cared deeply about success in obsolete activities and not at all for things a machine couldn't be programmed to do itself, like, for example, poetic punctuation or writing *Bot-Poetics*.

What I love about my high-rise apartment now is that it is laid out much like Joe's. The living room at the front leads, on the right, to the long, narrow hallway big enough for my screens and desk (where I sit writing this), back to the lightless kitchen with the fancy equipment that, besides the cooler, I almost never use, and eventually into the center of the Ɔ, my bedroom, where I also spend very little time. I usually sleep in the front room, with the church groups.

14

The hour at which I locked my bike to the gas meter outside Joe's normally found me pants-less and betomed, orange lamplight falling on browned pages. But not that night. That night was hers. In a haze, I strode to the poorly hung front door, pulled on the cold handle, and stepped across the threshold.

I couldn't find your mother in the front (there was a group of little kids and two weary adults passing pizza boxes over the kids' heads) or in any of the dark booths or at the scratched-up bar or in the back at the flashing machines, so I just chose a booth and slid in. I was probably yawning wildly.

I rarely went out at night, and when I did, it was usually to some official NNP event in hopes that I would endear myself to a future super poet in my program so completely that they would feel compelled to help when I contacted them a few years later looking for leads on good academic jobs. Thus, I treated everyone equally, daily walked one of four different routes between shared offices to say hello to the disgruntled occupants, and regularly kept dates with all but two suspicious (of me) women (who, ironically, would publish a cowritten collection a few years later and would get hired as a married couple, though they were not in fact married or even in love, at the new "Stanvard" in Colorado, and whose Scandinavian names you probably could recite in your sleep, knowing now their brief biography).

Eventually, I saw someone come out from behind the bar. It was your mother. She had an apron on and she was not limping, though the leg was still wrapped. I realized then that I'd seen her before here at Joe's, that she'd never served me in particular but had been in the front, perhaps, while Carl or Brian or whoever disdainfully sprayed my carrot soda into a cup. There was no way I could have recognized her under the white hospital lights, crying, when the only time I'd glimpsed her previously had been in the half redness of Joe's shadows. She looked exactly the same as I'd remembered her, except, without the puffy eyes, her beauty gained some maturity that I hadn't noticed before. She wore a Joe's T-shirt, but I made a point not to look at her chest. She had her hair pulled back in a different way than it had been at the hospital. Half of it hung down in a brown, lush curtain, the other half she pulled away from her face and into a bun held in place by a remnant lock wrapped and tucked.

Apparently (here's where things start to fuzz out), she had had a busy night and was behind in her side work, so she'd be another fifteen minutes behind the bar, but if I sat up at the bar, I could talk to her while she folded silverware. I agreed and she asked me what type of soda I liked and I, apparently, said, "Yes," and then "Soda would be great," when she again asked me what *kind*. This exchange clued her into my dishevelment, and she was worried that I was some earthborn doser. I sat at the bar and drank my soda and watched as her slender hands folded the napkins over the forks, over and over again, so methodically that she could do it without looking, like an old-fashioned baker kneading bread, and I'm sure my fixation made her more worried. I was so tired I nearly closed my eyes for a moment.

I'm sure we talked about our jobs, where we lived, mutual acquaintances. In fact, the two suspicious (of me) women of Scandinavian heritage spent a lot of time at Joe's eating the cheap vegan pizza, and I had at least once come here intending to accidentally run into them, though that attempt had soured quickly. Your mother told me later that they were great customers, those two, friendly and interesting and encouraging (your mother had mentioned to them that she, too, wrote poetry), which did not at all jive with what I knew of them.

(I cannot help this indulgent side note: I am still mystified by the overwhelming praise in the reviews of their teaching. I saw, in fact, that they were featured in one of those busidemic magazines for the Stanvard hydra, but I was gratified to know that they had published nothing of note since the squalor that was *Coils and Ropes and Things I Have Stored*, or whatever the hell they titled that phlegmy book of pseudo-prosody. The revelation that they were indeed legal sisters and not lovers caused less of a ripple in academia than I had expected, and I have rarely been so furious as when I saw that one of my students had submitted to me a short summary of a critical biography called *And When They Grew Up They Conquered U*, which had been written by one of their fawning post-U's at the very U that they were supposed to have conquered, a post-U who had probably been nearly struck dead by the fact that the sisters would be willing to give to their totally unaccomplished neophyte biographer unpublished poems of theirs to include, a post-U who would have probably never considered why such superstars even had unpublished poems they were willing to hand over to a drooling groupie.)

Your mother said later that I stared like a cat at her hands folding the silverware, but what's true is that my eyes wandered between her hands and her face (via the soft ridge of her breasts, but never lingering there), and I remember this because I felt something surge in me, something that had more to do with the silverware-folding hands than the off-limits breasts, something that, as far as I could remember, had never before surged, though maybe it had bubbled. I'm guessing this is why, when I reached the end of my brief and tragic narrative about the pre-failure of *Bot-Poetics*, which I had shamelessly and uncharacteristically lay before her in all its sprawling horror, I began drinking the beer she slid to me.

That is, she commiserated. And people commiserate with beer. She was people; I was people. We drank beer and lamented the state of poetry. She told me later that this was the moment where she first thought we'd get along, when she realized I (1) cared about poetry enough to be distraught about it and (2) would drink a beer if handed one.

That was probably the third beer I ever drank. I have always liked beer's soda similarity, but I have never liked feeling buzzed or drunk or aloof or sneeled or in any way impaired, and the beer of that time, as Daniel often said, "would have killed more than a few Mormons." In fact, he still says this, even though very few people still drink beer or know anything about Mormon teetotaling; he probably has already said it to you tonight. I've seen him, now twice at our annual department dinner party, order a beer, walk immediately to the circle of people that contains the newest faculty members, sip the beer, say the thing about killing Mormons, survey the laughs, and then carry the beer around unsipped for the remainder of the night.

I was drinking beer, and I had not eaten much that day or the day before. We kept talking. What I learned about your mother that night I actually regathered three nights later (again at Joe's), when she graciously rehashed the biographical paragraphs from the tale of that first night as closely as she could, for I could not recall many details with any fidelity. The biography that she supposedly described over silverware folding that night ran thusly: She had finished her degree a year before, she had applied to Narrative and New Poetics programs across the country but had been rejected outright from all of them, she despised bot poetry and loved Sappho and also the poets of the middle and late twentieth century, and she believed that poetry was not dying but sleeping, hibernating, and was relatively useless in this cultural winter but would emerge again someway, somehow, and that all she wanted to do was (and she didn't even pause here, but put her two hands up in the air and made quotations) *solder bold knobs on old pipes.* She had prepared this particular move ahead of time, I realized, when, after our first meeting in the hospital, I had mentioned that I'd published some poetry, much of it, especially that poem, easily available to any amateur stalker. I, after being paralyzed with genuine surprise apparently, lifted my glass and drained the remainder, partly just to buy time.

I remember setting down the glass. I remember hearing your mother's name roared from the front of the bar. I remember clearly the slight cringe when she heard the roar, the delay as she finished folding a napkin over a fork-spoon-knife stack, then the slow turn of her head to the right, to meet the oncoming apparition, the lardy zombie of a man who, to this day, I regret meeting in such a state as I was then, for he, seeing me, 1) silly with booze and 2) talking sloppily to the nymph he tortured regularly with his presence, thought that I was like him.

15

It is difficult to begin talking about David Geores.

It is late now, just past 23:00. I can't help but think of Daniel and you. Unless he has unveiled some unique part of the story I didn't know he possessed, Daniel has long exhausted the information useful to you. He's probably talking about the "secret spots" of Albuquerque—all of them contain pinto beans and old napkin dispensers—or maybe he's making plans to take you up the mountain. I imagine your dinner was at that one trendy place downtown with the fake cigars everywhere, the place he believes knowing about proves that he hasn't lost touch. If somehow your meeting has survived until now, I imagine he's toying with his cell, trying to get its operating system to run those old things he made four decades ago. You, I'm sure, are courteous, but I hope by now you've found a way to wiggle out.

I, too, watch Daniel fiddle with his cell. There's more at stake for me. That is, I hope Daniel will (those four words in that order represent a large part of the conflict between Daniel and me) indeed "let me know," as he said he would, though I am almost certain he won't before sleep. Perhaps you've already parted ways. If, in fact, he was embarrassed by the conspicuously unchanging beer level in the glass he so enthusiastically ordered and so drank the whole beer quickly and lustily in your waning presence, he is probably barely able to get his stout finger to hit the right button on the SD's screen to get him home. If he didn't have the beer, he's probably sitting alone in the idle SD now, which waits patiently for him to enter a destination command, even while he is *still* trying to run the shell OS on his impossibly complicated cell, which has functions he barely even understands. I am tempted to call the fool myself and interrupt his Sisyphean thumbing. An unwell part of me wants to look out through the thick plate glass to the pool of soft light where the restaurant's SD landing is (on Oprah Street, formerly Eighth). I want to see the glow of Daniel's illuminated cell blink as he answers my call.

But Daniel is not my current adversary; he is only a distraction to the story at hand. David Geores had just put his bulk onto the stool next to me at Joe's, and I had descended into a stupor. Now that I'm thinking about it, he is more than very probably your biological father, which will prove as problematic for you as he was for me.

I should begin with a disclaimer: I wasn't so much jealous of him as I was constantly interrupted by him. In the coming weeks, I'd spend two or three days planning something spectacular for your mother: I'd research obscure museums in the city, I'd plan a meal for us to cook together, I'd rip some pages out of a book of inferior bot poetry for a cut-up exercise, and then, prepared and fortified with carrot soda, I'd message your mother. But there'd always be "something with David." Something like drinking beer at Joe's or eating pizza at Joe's or just chilling at Joe's or come meet us at Joe's or I gotta get him out of Joe's or, a few weeks later, she'd "let me know" (God help me) when she and David left Joe's. That is, I went for pizza and chilling at Joe's for three or four weeks, and too many times I sat there glumly, undrunk, nodding politely at his babble, and then helped her carry him out at night. But, in the aftermath of the fire, I'm guessing I made it quite clear that I did not ever want to sit again with David at Joe's.

Because it's likely that David Geores is your father, I hate to speak too negatively of him here, but I must call a circuit a circuit: David was, is probably still, a raging alcoholic and poorly recovering addict. He was slightly older than your mother and slightly younger than me, but he'd been almost five years in recovery from an addiction that had left him basically penniless and hospitalized in Kansas City after he'd spent a few days riding hard and going nowhere on a thousand dollars' worth of meth. Meth, at that time, was not the innocuous medicalized super high that it is now, because then there was no Zamprom or instant detox. The stuff burned tubes like lava in one's brain crust. David's brain was not so holey that he couldn't function, but he certainly liked to believe it was. This was David's schtick. He was raucous and rude and black mouthed but at the end of the drunken night he'd apologize softly in your ear—he had moistened mine with his hot breath more times than I care to count. He'd say sorry, for example, for calling academics "skinny little shit rakers" or for saying "Mama Stone was probably celibate." If Daniel Glidden's line was about Mormon-killing beer, David's was that he'd "lost his filter to methamphetamines."

David was a mammoth: very tall and broad and meaty, already potbellied from copious beer. He had a sort of a beard—a patchy mane of wiry hair poking out from his round chin and neck. He had small eyes, a flat nose, a big mouth. His eyelashes were disturbingly long. And, at least before the accident, his ears departed from his head at slightly different angles. (You have, fortunately, dodged most of these traits, though you do seem tall.) He, too, supposedly wanted to be a poet (this story, you'll see, is soggy with them); he had met your mother in a writer's group. David, however, as far as he'd let on, hadn't written more than a single poem, which he worked and reworked (or forgot and rediscovered) constantly. It was always called "Gneiss" and its first lines I remember well because he recited it at almost every Joe's session. Your mother had a game, of sorts, in which she'd egg him on until the whole thing poured out. I don't know if I've gotten the enjambment right.

> If I was a man and my sister
> Was a woman and
> She got married and had my child
> Would that child be my gneiss?

Though the rest of the poem changed and morphed, and though the poem would, in one version, be about incest and in the next a simple contemplation of unclehood and in the next about generational trauma, this first stanza never changed.

The moral of the story is that David Geores was unhinged, his brain pocked with divots and goiters. Rather, David Geores was hingeless; there was no resetting him in the frame. Which episode in this short run should I cast before you as an example? The time he diabolically forced the little Fiat to wreck itself? The public nudity? The enraged tree trimmer whose equipment David straddled and watered? These were, of course, dramatic but somehow meaningless in our—your and my—story. So I'll tell you about the fire.

Before they developed the Rivergone area, the Rio had water all year and was lined by forest on either side, which we called the bosque. A fast bus right outside Joe's could drop you at the river in ten minutes. Somehow, one night, David, already drunk, decided that he wanted to go build a bonfire in the bosque. This was illegal and taboo in so many ways, for the trees in the bosque were already beginning to dry out and die, and the burgeoning camps of homeless people were constantly being flushed out of the reeds to prevent the inevitable fire that burned up sections of the bosque each year. These days wildfires are normal and have long ceased being spectator events. Back then they were frightening and also inescapably symbolic of the end times that the Evangelicals of those years were smugly preaching.

David, however, was unstoppable. He was standing up in the booth, and your mother was telling him to sit down, and David said he'd sit down when they left for the bosque, and I told your mother that, first of all, he didn't make any sense and, second of all, we'd get arrested. I told David he looked like an idiot standing there for all the depressed playlist kids of the side hall to gawk at. He had to bend his neck to keep his head from hitting the ceiling. He bounced and raised his arms like an action figure and called me some name. Your mother told David to shut up and that she'd go to the bosque with him. "What about JP?" David asked. Your mother looked at me, and I could tell she was scared in a way that normally she would not have been, so I said I'd go. David climbed down and stumbled past the teenage soccer team stretching pizza cheese with their grass-stained fingers and, as we followed him out, I told your mother that we should just jump off the bus at the last moment and let David ride around until he was sober—I was sure he wouldn't be able to get the right stop, and perhaps would just fall asleep there in the back. Your mother agreed. Just before she rose up from the barstool, I thought I saw her cross herself, like the Catholics of my youth, only backward, moving right to left then to heart.

I didn't care to what God she prayed, for I was close to an unprecedented victory. I finally felt like my gravity was pulling her away from the drunken planet that was David Geores.

When the bus pulled up, we helped David on. The orange light from the ceiling made Halloweenish the few ghosts sitting there in different stages of recline. An old woman clutched her purse and clearly lost hope that she'd have an uneventful ride home. David said hello to no one and everyone. He was, however, smoking a cigarette that he refused to put out, and his idiotic greetings had drawn the bus driver's eye, which loomed large in the concave mirror above the windshield. The bus driver said if he didn't put that cigarette out he was going to call the cops. Your mother said to David that the only way they'd get to have a bonfire is if he threw his cigarette out. David, feigning total defeat, attempted to flick it away, but the cigarette bounced off the door frame and landed on the bus floor. The old woman said, "Oh my God." The bus driver, however, thought he'd expelled it. I heard the air breaks lift. I jumped off. "Let's go," I told your mother, but she was simultaneously reaching for the glowing cig and helping David sit in one of the seats reserved for the elderly. The doors shut and I watched the bus move west down Central toward the river.

She sent me a message (which I found in my archive just now): "Just meet us there. I'll order a ride home. I'll tell him there's a big bonfire his roommates made at his house." I unlocked my bike and steered it into Central and rode faster than I ever had before. I'm not sure what I was afraid of, for nights like these were David's Tuesdays and Wednesdays. The slight dilation of your mother's eyes and the mysterious reverse-Catholic gestures haunted me as I rode.

It was a twenty-minute ride if I pedaled hard. I thought I was going to save your mother from this buffoon. I would not insult him, I decided. I would attempt none of my intellectual feints intended to confuse him into silence. As I roared through downtown, I practiced what I would say to David. "David," I'd say, "I know you're a recovering addict," I'd say, "and I know you're drunk," I'd say, "but none of that is an excuse to hurt others, especially her," and I'd point to your mother and say, "I'm taking her home. You do what you want to do." But I couldn't seem to figure out how I'd "take" your mother home, considering I had only my bike, and ordering a ride and standing around for ten minutes wouldn't exactly be the romantic exit I was hoping might finally cause your mother to fully yield to me.

The city blazed by. The SD scourge has ruined Central, because back then you could push hard on the pedals just after University and begin coasting at Sycamore or Spruce and, if you hit the green lights, you wouldn't have to pedal again until Second Street, about three kilometers farther. That night, I hit the green lights. Lowriders and minivans struggled to keep up with me. One woman in a passenger seat even laughed and told the driver, I think, to speed up, which he did, but then he was slowed by an old man in a Ford who planned, sometime, to turn right; I nearly took his mirror off as I streaked by. I soared, and I imagined, too, that if I had some light plastic wings, I could glide above downtown and land right on David's wonky right ear as he stumbled out of the bus.

As I neared the river, I started smelling smoke. *Impossible,* I thought. The guy could barely walk; there's no way he's already started a fire. But once the silhouettes of the big cottonwoods came into view, I finally saw it, a red glow, maybe a hundred paces north of Central in the bosque. I heard sirens roaring already. How could he have already ... ? I turned onto the river trail and pedaled hard.

The scene was confusing when I finally got through the parked cars and hose lines a couple of minutes later. There were fire trucks everywhere, their lights pulsing onto the tree trunks like flashlights over columns in a catacomb. A wall of flame was roaring maybe fifty meters away, and I could see the outlines of people standing nearby and watching the fire. Three streams of water doused the forest in between the people and the fire; steam hissed and rose in clouds, obscuring the fire for an instant, when a hose shot too far. I looked for your mother and David, assuming that they'd been arrested, but I didn't see them in either of the police cars. I felt a bittersweet (but mostly sweet) sense of finality. This would be the last straw with David. Your mother would not forgive him this.

Then I saw David's silhouette. He was the only one with his arms raised. His massive figure looked twice the size of your mother's, and he was holding something in his hand. I pushed my bike closer and called out to them. "JP!" David yelled. As he stumbled toward me, I saw that his shirt was in his hand; he'd taken it off, no doubt, to feel the effect of the flames on his enormous front. Your mother walked behind him, laughing and covering her mouth with her hand.

"David was screwing with us. This fire had been going for hours." He had, apparently, been sober enough to decode the message on his blotter app and then invent this story about the bonfire.

"How'd you find that out?"

"He showed me the app just before we got off the bus." Your mother laughed a little then. She shrugged. I felt my victory crumbling.

David had, by this time, returned to face the fire and lifted his arms again. And I'll never forget him in that moment: the dark silhouette of a shirtless man exulting in the presence of a forest fire. I have no idea what he was happy about. A searchlight floated angrily in the limbs, then found David. The light on his back revealed two long scars that paralleled his spine: I'd find out later that they were the tick marks made by two pieces of rebar that hadn't been sufficiently covered by the cement culvert he'd slid down while high (in "Methland," he told your mother, he'd slid down a snake's tongue and been gored by its fangs). A voice blared over the fire truck megaphone: "Sir, please take twenty steps back. You are in danger." David didn't move, but kept his arms up and screamed, like a child, "DAAAANGERRRRR!"

I told your mother that David was broken, lost. She said yes, but that somehow he made it through. She was bathed in moonlight, kind of a soft white blue. I could see that she did not love this man but that she felt deeply for him, even cried for him. The she said, "He reminds me of my brother." Your uncle. I never heard anything more about the man. I assumed he was no longer among the living.

Perhaps it was this moment of sympathy warmed over by the firelight, but right then she was more beautiful than I'd ever seen her. Her face was, here and there, lit orange by the firelight, and her brown eyes shone as she watched David pump his fists idiotically and hoot. Some firemen were making bowlegged strides toward him. She laughed again.

Your mother often dragged David home at the end of the night. I don't know how long she'd been doing this before we met, but I know for sure that she continued to do it even after the fire, until something happened that August or September that she would never talk about, even when I asked. All I know is that at Joe's sometime in late September, he passed our booth with almost no acknowledgment. I feigned concern then, but I felt elation. She cried a bit, then recovered.

I think you could guess what I assumed David had done, and why your mother finally ended their interaction, though I certainly didn't feel much pity for her, because she had cultivated this give-and-take expectation over who knows how many weeks. But we must be discerning, here, because the focus of our investigation is your more-than-probably-father, and it's right here when he, for the most part, leaves the scene. David, I must say, seemed too much of a drunk to be a predator. By the time I'd met your mother, David was drinking wildly and always. During the short time I knew him, I honestly don't know (please read this not as leftover bitterness but as empirical reflection) if David would have been physically capable of executing the particular mechanical steps of child making anytime after noon. However. An important detail exists in an offhand comment your mother made as (spoiler) we walked down Central, hand in hand, toward our first night together: your mother said (1) she didn't know what had happened to David and (2) he "hadn't been this way at first."

That night of the fire, six weeks or so after we first met in the waiting room, she called a ride and stuffed David in (he was soaking wet from the hose spray) and said, "Goodnight, David. I'm going with JP." And David, wasted and shivering, just said, "K," and shut the door himself, and your mother and I, finally alone, walked back into town. I see that night as really the beginning of many things: m and your mother's romance, her separation from David and all that he symbolized, and my own sense that there was, after all, unpredictably *good* things that happened.

My bike was gone when I returned for it the next day. I was unmoved.

Once, a few months after your mother disappeared, I was drinking soda in a side booth at Joe's (a mistake, I'll admit now) and I somehow was in the thick of a discussion with the bartender about your mother and her "eclectic friendships." The bartender—a chubby, pasty guy who wore a pristine baseball cap with a tiny flexible screen embedded in it that displayed in succession the logos of his favorite teams, though the change of image was so sporadic and imperceptible that he seemed to have always just and only that one team's hat, no, that one—was newish and so didn't yet completely dislike me, nor did he know who David Geores was. I told him he was this loud, insane guy who used to hang with your mother, you know, the guy that started that big kerfuffle with the normally-tusked walrus (color: blue!), the guy who always hollered, "If I was a man and my sister . . ." Surely he'd heard of him. No, he said, but he'd heard that your mother liked "characters," and there had been this one strange guy, he said, who perhaps had done something to her . . .

Right then and there, in a practically unprecedented public spectacle, I stood up, cleared my throat, and recited the whole of David's "Gneiss" with the most contemptuous and cartoonish voice I could muster. Because of the whole blue walrus thing and David's subsequent cowardly hiding, I'd never actually had my chance to confront him and tell him what I thought, and I suppose that's why I chose to bellow out his stupid poem in Joe's that night. It felt like I was defending your mother, somehow. (This is when I was still convinced that David had in some way contributed to your mother's disappearance.) After one false start, I performed excellently.

Once, in seventh grade, at an end-of-the-year pool party, a similar moment transpired. I wasn't exactly a mute, but I rarely spoke to anyone but my closest friend, and we two often huddled in corners and shady spots whispering conspiratorially. There were few people in our class who'd heard me speak, except when Mr. Patton insisted I answer one of his inane questions about meiosis or frog intestination. It was my younger brother, John, a delinquent sixth grader with a lisp, that I parodied that day, as a group of oddly retrospective peers sat on the pool steps, their lower halves submerged, their sunlit chests showing the budding signs of adulthood. I was near this group, waiting for exactly this chance, for it was the first party I'd been invited to (a teacher had handled the list), and I was bitter. John's name surged into the conversation when Tia Brasheres lamented his unending and stalker-like pursuit of her twin sister, Taya. I pounced. I did the scene of John stumbling through his lines in the school play. Most of my peers laughed and slapped their knees in total shock; they'd seen the video over and over. A couple of girls stared at me, clearly disgusted. But I was good. Really good. Several young men of the soccer player type would remember that performance for many years. John would hear of it eventually.

My impression of David Geores, admittedly, was intended to be rancorous. I bellowed. I flailed. I spat profusely (David slobbered like a tranquilized elephant). I did not need the applause from the crowd, which I got, in smatterings. I needed only this moment of release.

When I sat back down, the bartender still had no idea who I was talking about. He laughed and nodded from behind his cell. He had been hired, unbeknownst to me, as a part-time beer pourer, part-time marketer (the hat was his own invention), and he had begun videoing me when I paused to clear my throat and practice my monster voice. He posted the video on the Joe's feed that night (the idiot didn't even look up the news coverage about the blue hale-tusked walrus)—*Come get poetic at Joe's!* I didn't know about the video until Daniel messaged me and said he wished he could have been there for the fun. I never went back to Joe's. I think it's likely that David didn't either, though for years I thought my filmed affront would bring him out of hiding. But it's true that I never saw David Geores in person again.

Before I left that night, however, the bartender said, in a tone that was half joke, half accusation, "Yeah, you seem like her type."

16

Writing that last chapter exhausted me deeply.

So, after drinking another soy shake and showering, I lay down on the couch in hopes of getting some sleep. The semidarkness of this apartment has always been comforting to me. Sleeping at such monolithic elevation (the forty-second floor) produces a sensation that few experience in their lifetimes: The night is lit from below. When the reflective blanket of pollution is rolled up in the windy spring, and when the wildfire smoke finally dissipates in the late fall, and when, during those two short seasons, the moon is new or unrisen, the effect of being in the apartment is part dream, part magic. The ghostly old city glows itself upward, and in my apartment my shadow looms large on the night-gray walls, the bottom-right corner of all the framed prints glinting white. These nights are rare, but I find myself waiting for them year-round, hoping that some strange gust of wind or a rare storm returns to our burned world and tamps the evidence down enough so that we can see again.

Tonight was not one of those nights. But as I lay there on the couch looking up through the plate of ultraclear glass at the head of the couch, I longed for one. The haze outside was thin enough that I could see seven or eight stars. After a few sleepless minutes, I could not withstand the urge to go out into the black night.

I have no balcony—the shameless architect wanted to save money where he could. However, on the thirty-fifth floor, exactly twenty floors above the "drone" reception but on the opposite side of the building, there is a similar concrete pad jutting out from the massive structure. This was to be the drone approach for the fine dining restaurant that was planned to serve the building's posh clientele. If I am any indicator, however, there was a grave miscalculation in the demographic research. Albuquerque has never been and will likely never be an "urban" place, in the same way that New York and Dallas will never de-urbanize. "Urban" is not a physical descriptor; it is a mindset, a self-perception that requires a certain organ that Albuquerque doesn't have. If I were an urban geographer or social engineer, I'd write this thesis: There are cities in which the forces of urbanity have been socialized away, sort of cleansed from the residents' genes, and so, untouched by some sudden population inrush, forever the place will be an underwhelming, uncrowded, uninteresting though slowly densifying environment. The futuristic novels of late, the ones that imagine that Waco or Lincoln have become these whirring space ports like London or Dubai—they deny not only present reality but the thread of reality that has made Waco and Lincoln what they are, the same thread that the novel is supposedly continuing. These novels are the wet dreams of the cities where there is no penthouse wealth and no invisible tier of fame.

Though I don't know the man, the dernal who erected this building surely read the fabled *Root 66*, because, in it, the unnamed city of the future that is supposed to be Albuquerque is a garden of towering steel and hovercraft-type vehicles and climbing vines. So this building, my home, was propped up in the sand, the first and last step toward that sci-fi future. Much of the clientele that prepurchased apartments never moved in. To this day, the wealthier residents in Albuquerque, unaccustomed and even suspicious of downtown living, choose the low, split-level homes of the U district, or the four-story townhomes in the new SD-only neighborhoods. They bought apartments in the big building downtown as novelties, investments, mostly because they heard that Nigerian speculators were salivating for anything American with windows and elevators. But there is no reason to live downtown, and so no one does, and because no one does, there's no reason to make downtown livable, and so there's no reason to live in downtown.

Thus, we more marginal species make our fleeting homes here. I, for one, enjoy a downtown where no one really wants to live. I may mock the fool who built this impossible metal phallus here in the center of it all, but, in truth, I love him for his architectural quixotism, and I especially love his superfluous, cable-hung drone approaches jutting out from the side of the building on the fifteenth and thirty-fifth floors.

It was late by the time I shut my door behind me, long after midnight, and the little outing began badly. It'll help you to know that, to save operational costs, the fast lift, the one nearest my apartment, is usually shut down between midnight and six, and the few residents above the thirtieth floor are forced to use the lumbering freight lift, for which I once waited seventeen minutes. It is windowless and almost always reeks of vapor. Once I found there, on the blotchy blue carpet, a single, foot-stained flip-flop and, stuck to it, a half-sucked after-dinner candy. I don't know who actually lives on the floors below me, but I can't imagine they were target residents.

The freight elevator climbed slowly but steadily toward my floor. Finally came that last bump and the hiss of the hydraulic doors beginning their tired routine. As the doors slid open, I found myself computing exterior input when I'd been expecting to sift only interior: a human form, a woman, a woman younger than me, a very beautiful woman not much younger than you stepping out onto my floor, a very beautiful woman not as young as your mother had been but certainly younger than I am now exiting the freight elevator on the floor where, last I checked, I alone occupied an apartment (there are seven) year-round. The freight elevator's yellow light seemed more harsh than usual, and when the woman stepped out from underneath it and her face finally came into contrast, I thought it was you, you the daughter of your mother, the neglected offspring of the woman I once loved; terror and rage struck at once. I hadn't considered this possibility, hadn't foreseen this particular forescene. I was struggling to make sense of what it meant. I thought your first appearance in the story would be via a buzz from Juan Miguel downstairs and then your face on my doorscreen. The blocking for your part on stage would then move in a sort of slow curve between the abandoned couch (my ersatz bed), then the cleared table in front of the big window looking out on the city, then deeper into the side hallway, where my desk sits (and this writing atop it), but there is nothing more me than this, my narrative voice echoing from a distance.

The woman, who could have been you, stepped off and looked at me for a moment and even began a smile, but when I returned only an expression of confusion, she realized that I was not whoever it was she was expecting, or expecting not to expect.

"Hello," she said (note: with absolutely no accent).

"Hello."

"Is this forty-two?" (Note: the "i" sound in "this" was a bit brighter than that in normal Standard American English.)

"Yes, it is."

"Thank you," she said, and moved down the hallway, a rolling plastic case trailing behind her. She turned the corner. My heart raged. Thoughts screamed past. I kept listening, trying to judge which door she was headed for. The freight elevator dinged—someone was summoning it from below—and if I didn't get on now, it might be another twenty minutes before I'd see it again. I heard the doors lurch. I thought I heard a voice bump down the hallway. I stepped quickly on.

In the slow descent (the infernal machine pointlessly stopped at floors forty and thirty-eight and thirty-six, opening its doors to no one or nothing but hallway light), I tried to understand who that woman was, but could make no headway. I had not formally authorized any visits, and she was not, as far as I could tell, the aged evolution of some short-lived post-U tryst long ago (of which there were two, decades old and poorly concluded). Slowly, the most important truth of the matter settled into my consciousness. She was not you; you were not here. I felt a fullness of relief then.

I asked myself, however, that if, indeed, I knew you were coming, how could I feel any "fullness" of relief, knowing that you *would*, at some point, arrive (not to mention that someone *else* had arrived, quite oddly, on my floor)? As if from another room in my head, a voice immediately answered: Because now you have time to finish.

The dread reality struck me then. This thing that I was preparing, this document, this sketch, was my last work, my last offering to the world. I would be giving it to you. And it was not yet finished. I did not want you to arrive until it was finished.

Of course, as any artist knows, the moment in which you're no longer tinkering, in which the vision becomes solid and undeniable, is, as I said, dreadful. Dread: fear and awe. You are attracted to it, even while you're wildly afraid. You want to bury your head. What's ahead is pain and exhaustion, a sort of death. Getting immediately to work is impossible. So you continue on with what you're doing. You avoid eye contact. You descend to the thirty-fifth floor.

At the thirty-fifth floor the lift bumped to a stop, the doors reluctantly parted, and I walked out. I considered hitting the UP button and returning to investigate the forty-second-floor intruder, but decided against it. Must be the Hungarians.

17

About the Hungarians. I had met the owners of both units that weren't still for sale—42-1 and 42-2. They were couples slightly older than me, best friends, and they lived next to each other in either Buda or Pest, and when the political situation in America cleared up for Eastern European immigrants, they planned to retire here, here in urban-less Albuquerque, where the daughter of one couple and the son of the other had emigrated (they'd been in the US since college) after they had married and their sudden storybook romance had been consummated. Duplicate pictures of the same Hungarian wedding were displayed in similar places in both apartments (the foyer, the kitchen, one of the bedrooms). I'd seen the bride and thought her clownish in her thick makeup and mechanical facial features, but of course I had no taste for the Eastern European aesthetic, as proven by my nearly visceral reaction to a painting of a tree I'd seen in one of their foyers.

In the three or four years that they'd owned the apartments, they had only visited once besides their original purchasing visit. I'd avoided them entirely during that short visit, though they knocked on my door at least twice. I watched them on the security camera as they spoke to each other using primarily their voluminous eyebrows and large uplifted hands.

When they had come to my floor to view their new investments, and caught me in the hallway and cajoled me to come with them into their empty caverns, I had not known how to react but had not been as undone by their imposition as I'd expected to be. Though their accents were infuriating, they were otherwise pleasant people. The two nearly indistinguishable men, especially, seemed to like me, seemed to believe I would look after their apartments in their absence. They both were a little overweight, narrow hipped, and mustached. One of them had a tattoo of an old-timey beer bottle on his left hand; the other was perhaps ten centimeters taller. (One, the tall one, some months later, called me to say that he'd read *Bot-Poetics* and thought it would be a wonderful book for their daughter-in-law [the tattooed man's daughter] to translate into Hungarian. In Hungary, apparently, because of the world-renowned university Ethics and Fabrication Department, there was "a much interest in automation of the human processes," as he put it, "and the poetry of humans is very the human of humans, if you understand what it is I say to you," which, despite all odds, I did, and I wished that I'd written something to that effect in the intro to the book. He said he'd talk to his daughter-in-law. I await her solicitation.)

A day after they secured the places, they gave me their hardkeys and their codes (which, for the sake of simplicity, I have walled off completely in my brain) and asked that I, please, look in on things and be sure the bimonthly maid and maintenance crew weren't stealing the bedsheets. I did nothing of the sort. Look in, that is. I've only gone in the apartments twice. Once was a carrot soda emergency. I don't remember which couple's was which, but I discovered quickly that they had no soda. Instead, I helped myself to a mineral drink, Romanian in origin. It was not good, but it staved off desperation. I considered filching some bedsheets, but I thought that that would just implicate the poor maid. I otherwise remember little about their apartments.

The freight lift woman, I decided, was likely the storied translator daughter-in-law. My first impression was that she looked older, or perhaps younger, than their children must have been, but to be honest, I have no clue how old those syrupy Hungarians are. All in all, I have noticed, in the last couple of years, a blossoming blindness to age, a somewhat annoying inability to identify youthfulness, especially from the many pictures available digitally. I think it's because the women in my classes are always the same age and are, more and more, the same people entirely, right down to their leathered waists and hennaed clavicles. Nevertheless, I had pegged the Hungarians as fifty-two. It seemed impossible that this woman was their daughter. As I walked down the hallway lit with those old LEDs, I felt the fire of obsessive fixation near me, and I sprayed weakly a stream of logic back at it: No one has access to my floor without authorization; the Hungarians have been, historically, loose with authorization, but they have also never permitted someone unrelated to ascend to our floor. A burglar would not be hefting an obviously heavy suitcase and wouldn't ask such an obvious question as which floor she was on . . .

I had for many years pursued my suspicions about the people who moved about unchecked and low browed in this building, only to find my investigations unfounded or even crazy making. Only eight or nine months ago, I had begun waiting in the freight lift during normal hours (when the other lift was sliding up and down happily) to see if I could catch the enemy that had several times attempted entry into my apartment during hours he thought I was out. Three days after he tried many incorrect codes and even attempted to manually unlock the door by shorting the mechanism with an old-fashioned screwdriver (he had no idea that I was vomity and feverish, but very, very lucid, only two meters from that door), I finally caught him gaining access to one of the Hungarian's pads. When I accosted him and was dialing reception, he repeated several times, "Elnézést, elnézést," which I eventually discovered means, in this context, "Pardon me." He claimed—in a thick accent somewhat like my neighbors'—that he was the couple's "um, uh, friend," and though he had been in America for several years, still confused American 7s, which, especially in the pretentious script of the apartment numbers on our doors, looked like European 1s, and so he had, each of the three days before, mindlessly tried to get into my apartment, Apartment 42-7, instead of the correct one, 42-1. Here he produced his cell and scrolled to the message (in Hungarian) from his "friends," whose names I could not read, then he good-naturedly held the cell up to the numbers on the door and I could see his point. He laughed and said, haltingly, that he was "from behind the back of God" in Hungary, but now he lives here in Albuquerque with his wife but, well, um, uh, they had made a little bit of argument, you know about this, do you not? And it seemed that one different man is maybebespeakingortouching my my my wife. This last bit drained his humor. He became still. He looked at me furiously and I saw for the first time that he was intoxicated in some minimal way and that somehow for an instant he believed that perhaps I was the man who'd been maybespeakingortouching. I smiled and nodded and went to retrieve my empty soda cans and folding chair from the freight lift. He was, as I'm sure you've guessed, the tall guy's son. I confirmed this in a painful exchange of international messages. I couldn't understand why he did not simply say so.

For the next few days, I kept repeating in my mind that wonderfully musical and nonsensical phrase: "from behind the back of God." There are hundreds of ways it can be enjambed, and often, when I'm walking very intentionally between point A and point B—for example, when I'm walking across the clacky floor of the fifteenth-floor reception to reach the garage elevator on my way to teach a class—I find myself fiddling with this phrase, enjambing it and reuniting it over and over again, "from / behind the back / of God . . . from behind the / back / of God." I once met a professor who liked to say that poetry was just prose with more white space, and he was right on some level, but really what he meant was that poetry is prose in which white space *means*, and this, therefore, means that poetry is mathematically infinite and prose is not, because poetic white space is a variable and not a value. Poetry is algebra; prose, arithmetic. In poetry one solves for the white space, while in prose one just adds everything up.

I am now concerned that this woman's presence might, somehow, make even more complicated my already difficult reality. If either the man who is maybespeakingortouching her or her angered pseudo-Hungarian husband appeared here, I'd have to call Juan Miguel, who is yet another actor I'd prefer to give no more than a bit part to read (and who would rejoice in such sudden revelation of scandal). But let's leave that woman to her mysterious methods for a moment, for the whole point of that sally, other than procrastination in the face of a job of work, had been to see the city from the thirty-fifth-floor drone approach and (now, back in my room), the whole point of recounting this sally was to tell you about an epiphany I had there.

Having conquered the LED haunt of the empty hallway, I walked through the recently repurposed restaurant (now only a couple of old women do rehdana in here each morning and illegally burn incense) and out onto the drone approach. Whatever it is you're feeling as you read this, I implore you to descend to the thirty-fifth floor to see this spectacular view. On even a middling night like this one, one can see fifty or so kilometers to the south. Eventually, when the smoke moves off this fall, you'll be able to see even farther.

Just below me was the south part of downtown, the old riverbed still visible mostly by negation, outlined the way the grid of roads bends just slightly, everything jogging to the left until, about six kilometers farther south, you could see a huddle of big white lights on in the river's path. They were likely filming the umpteenth enviro-educational movie, probably the "bats" segment, whose creatures they would animate onto the nighttime dry river background with basically the same software that Daniel used so long ago to pitch a famous dead heartthrob over a famous precipice. Visible another few miles downriver were the flashing lights and hovering glow balloons from the reservation's casino park; beyond that, the southern suburbs, beyond that, blackness, though a mountain shape was visible in the glow from the little SD stops behind it. Ladron Peak. It remains untouched after all these years. No reason to live on it, no reason to walk on it, no reason to dig in it. Even at three thousand meters it is now entirely treeless, snow being as rare there as birds, and the few trees Ladron did have had been valuable enough to justify ascent with crawlers. Now Ladron is brown, useless, and thus has no recent story. Robbers of two centuries ago hid there, in the remote copses now cut down, knowing no one would come looking for them in such desolation.

Between my building and Ladron stretched a complicated system of lights and blacks, a motherboard of city. I stared at it, followed its paths, noticed its nodes. The security drones hovered in swarms over the southwest quadrant, destinations in which zone some family-oriented SDs won't even accept, though of course such robotic anxiety is probably unfounded. If you listen closely, you can hear in the southwest quadrant the human-controlled roar of gas engines, loud music, the occasional explosion of a gun. I, of course, do not go there, but I have always loved watching the southwest quadrant at night from this vantage. The little glow orbs that flash almost imperceptibly behind drone rotors make that quadrant, from this far above, seem like it's decorated with incandescent light bulbs, the kind we had as kids. I watched the drones move in and out, side to side. The flashing police lights throbbed obediently on the streets beneath them. My experience tells me that all existing things—cities, literature, academia, families—have a southwest quadrant, a forbidden, supposedly sinister, portion, a place that must be vigilantly patrolled and contained and embordered, a place that thrives on broken pieces and gasoline and potato chips and northern Mexican sack weed and government intervention from incubator to incinerator.

You can probably see where I'm going with this. I realized out there on the drone approach that there is no better place to "start" (rather, continue) this thing I'm writing. I must reveal my southwest quadrant; otherwise, your patience might stall and die. For how many years have I included the single nominalized adjective "vulnerability" among the bulleted lists I hand my narrative-drunk students, those wannabe creators? I hadn't really fully considered how I would tell you about the next part of your mother's story, the mountain peak and Spirit Lake part, for that chapter was the most unbelievable and—I dug up an old and long-buried worry as I lay down on the couch tonight—implicated me in your mother's disappearance in a way that I wasn't sure I'd be able to explain. In fact, I have, to this day, never attempted to explain it, nor, for that matter, have I been compelled to do so, and so it has simply remained somewhat unexplained. And all of this in me is more like a southwest quadrant than a Ladron: There is much to tell and much to see; it is not a boring obscurity or value harvested long ago, because the truth is that your mother is not living, and only I and two others knew it and still know it for sure and not simply circumstantially, as, for example, the DCOB and Daniel Glidden and surely even the sledge David Geores and you, you motherless daughter, knew it, know it.

I toed the edge of the drone landing, and leaned against the steel fence. It wobbled a bit, and I felt the stomach drop of vertigo. I stepped back, turned around.

When I reentered my apartment, it became clear to me that many things would need to be prepared before your arrival. For some reason, the height and distance of the drone approach had caused a wave of energy in this admittedly aging college professor. It would be appropriate, I decided, that, when you enter, you'd see my life's work in front of you, greeting you. And so I began to search around for the physical copies I possessed of the work I've done. I found the first four *Coordinates* rather easily—the glossy, totally symbolic packages had been sitting, unmoved, on my desk for all the years since I'd made them. The remaining *Coordinates*, produced by a much larger corporation, have not been memorialized in physical copies, and that's just as well, for the data of this world is now eternal in ways of which the old tapemen only dreamed.

Finding a copy of *Bot-Poetics* was not easy. I could have sworn that it was in my book closet, and for some reason I remember it standing shamelessly between a volume of Plutarch's Lives and Spiers's essays. But I could not find my failed little bastard child there. Nor could I find it in the boxes beneath the bed, though in one of the four boxes I could convince myself to search, I did find a couple of things—mere secondary relics, but relics all the same—that might be useful for you in the narrative you'll write about all of this. Those I left there, in the bedroom, on the other side of the bed, in a red plastic box with black writing.

As I searched, I could feel a rage building in me, which was inexplicable, for you might have *more* respect for me if, after all, there is no paper book to display and thus you remain unaware of my maiden literary voyage. I searched my desk drawers too, but there was little there—I felt a pang of fear that my empty drawers indicated something about my life, but then I remembered that, though his desk was chock-full, Canetti's genius madman didn't have cloud storage nor the automatic retention of the ever-present archivist bots watching his every keystroke.

What I found in my desk, however, was enough to distract me from what I did not find. I found two hardkeys. I've placed them in my lap, and now, well, I should say, in thirty minutes, at precisely six, I will venture out and fulfill my neighborly duty in my absent friends' stead, for I have not been able to rule out a single absurdity: One couple, I don't remember which, once mentioned renting their apartments freely on an open vacation rental market; I made it clear that this would be unacceptable. I never heard anything more. I likely wouldn't. What better way to sneak up on me than to rent the doorway across from mine?

18

I have returned.

After a soda and a scone I found in the bottom of a grocery delivery bag, I went out into the hallway with two keys. There were a number of things I took as givens: The freight lift's doors had revealed her to me sometime around a quarter past one; I returned to my apartment at five to three and by then she had either (1) entered and remained in an apartment on the forty-second floor or (2) had fled the forty-second floor via freight lift alone (before I went into my apartment, I checked the fire escape slides and found them stored as they should be).

My goal for this particular mission was two pronged. I intended to gratify my curiosity/suspicion about the woman from last night's inexplicably late encounter, but I also intended to see if the Hungarians had retained a paper copy of *Bot-Poetics* somewhere in their apartments. The latter would be a weird excuse if I was caught in the former. It was a few minutes after six. I calculated generously: it took, likely, twenty minutes from our encounter to enter the apartment, get her bearings, glance at the screen near the door, find a place for her rolling case, remove her clothes—she had a skirt suit on that would need to be unwound like a swaddling cloth, being sure that the hidden tie that held it all together did not suddenly pull tight and require five minutes of half-undressed fiddling with the knot—and shoes, toilet, tend to her teeth, and tuck herself into the untouched bed and think whatever thoughts she had before she finally fell asleep.

A typical person, I figured, that falls asleep at 1:35 does not wake up at 6:00 unless there is some pressing business or prescribed chemical assistance, either of which very well might be possible—she had looked relatively accomplished and a bit harried.

I did not know which door she had entered. So I chose the apartment that the young man who tried to forcibly enter mine was *actually* looking for. I knocked on Hungarian door #1. No answer. Perhaps she was still in bed. I put the key near the manual port, but withdrew. I knocked again. The door moved a bit, just barely, and I discovered that it had been propped open, thwarting the automatic return mechanism. I did not look at what propped it open, because I understood that the security camera, on detecting movement near the door, would have begun filming, and the fact that the "ajar alarm" wasn't sounding suggested to me that this was partly Juan Miguel's doing, and that he might well be watching me right now. I thought, first, that I should knock on Hungarian door #2, because if my knock on Hungarian door #1 had woken her, she would then hear me enter Hungarian door #1, and then, if I exited Hungarian door #1 and then knocked on Hungarian door #2, she might wait to see if I would walk in just to catch me in the act of intrusion, thus making it embarrassing for me, though of course I had been given a mandate ("Please view our apartments from time to time, to be sure no items become amiss"). So I stepped over and knocked (loudly enough to wake someone in natural sleep) on Hungarian door #2. Again, nothing. I returned to #1. I entered the key into the slot carefully and waited for the hollow click. I pushed open the now unlocked and ajar door, and stepped over the paltry object that had interrupted its arc.

Nothing, really, was different here since my last incursion for the carrot soda, maybe two years ago. Nothing, that is, except for the big window covering the entire back wall, which, from a distance, looked impossibly dirty, as if some of the few remaining miscreant Albuquerque birds had survived mass starvation and learned to graffiti their anger onto the window with the only paint available to them. I walked up closer and saw that it was not dirt but scratches, and then, after stepping back again, I saw that a gigantic mushroom, complete with its characteristic spots and asymmetrical hat, had been etched, via tiny crisscross scratches, into the glass. It even had a smiling mouth and tired-looking eyes; it was as tall as me. Nearby, posing as a cousin of the white-faux-leather, semi-modern furniture that both Hungarian families must have bought in bulk, I saw one of those foldable two-step ladders, and, in the grooves of its foot treads, tiny dusticles of glass. And nothing else. If the Hungarian maybe-son had burned holes in the carpet or scrawled Hungarian expletives on the wall, maintenance had already taken care of it. I thought I could smell the cooped-up odor of new paint, but I couldn't be sure.

I went to Hungarian bedroom #1A and saw nothing but the same untouched bed I had seen during the carrot soda campaign. In Hungarian bedroom #1B, there was a slight alteration: The mattress had been removed from the bed frame. A bookshelf revealed nothing useful, though three paper Stanisław Lem books stood in between two ceramic lambs, and I thought about Lem's most famous protagonist, who was, of course, in the same situation I was, faced with the same choices, though of course he floated in the pseudo-atmosphere above Solaris, and I'm floating in smoke above burning Earth.

The door alarm hypocritically sounded its soft warning about being ajar. Still there was no sign of the woman, no plastic case. I couldn't understand this. Juan Miguel's sly movement had so clearly prepared the way for her to enter here, yet here she was not. So I decided to retreat and try Hungarian door #2.

I knocked again, loudly. Nothing. This door was not propped open. I deployed the second key and went in.

The plastic case I knew intuitively would be there was indeed lying there, flayed open like an animal shot down right before its escape. I had to push it aside with the door in order to enter. Its intestines spilled out and they were undoubtedly a middle-aged woman's: different colors of folded cloth, a modest bra, a gaping zipper bag with tubes and cheap screenpapers, a velveteen pouch, a cheap screenreader, unencrypted and displaying (I pressed the button) the 143rd out of 233 pages of something titled *supermodernism* (no capitals), and from which a random sampling produced hypersyllabic phrases like "demonstrably erroneous" and "weakening of historicity" and impossible retoolings of words, such as "salvational" and "syntagmatic." To be better than halfway through such intellectual goulash suggests that she was a committed academic, which made me both more horrified and more curious.

This apartment was laid out like mine, and like mine it contained only one bedroom, and here with this woman's suitcase at the door I felt, for a moment, like I had reached a museum exhibit that was two of my own memories combined into one, like this was a suitcase that had just been schlepped to an academic conference in Canadian Chicago or Miami, like this was an apartment that at its bedroom center had a different woman, a woman of Taiwanese heritage in black professional garb, a woman who had barely made it across the threshold, so exhausted was she from networking and re-recording the same talk three times for stream, and thus I forgot how angry I got when there were bra straps grabbing at my feet the moment I walk into my apartment, not this building's apartment, but an apartment near the U, the next apartment after your mother.

Though I said we'd begin with satellites, I suppose this as good a time as any to begin our little tour of one avenue in my southwest quadrant, though it wasn't until this suitcase at the door (a satellite, if you will) that I thought the remaining three boxes under my bed would be worth what seems like a rather odd detour. Those boxes, of course, are marked with an A, and while seeing them earlier only fed the fire of confused anger that had begun with the furious and profitless search for *Bot-Poetics*, I see now that they must be dragged out, for a very specific reason.

19

Meet Angela. Angela was my wife, my only wife. In America, at least, she technically still is my wife, but Taiwan is outside of the Social Rights Consortium, I think because of the eugenics thing, and so allows for the strange situation we've gotten ourselves in. I didn't think she had anything to do with this narrative at all and, in fact, I worried that in your searchings you might have somehow discovered our marriage and dragged her into your own version of my narrative, when in actuality she belongs there about as much as the medically retired Brenda Link Patel. I now see that she (Angela, not Brenda) has one vital role that I had overlooked, and that is to testify on my biological behalf. She will not be coming back to America, except perhaps for a visit to San Francisco or the White House with her new family, so she can bear witness in absentia. Whether or not you contact her (how you would, I do not know) is not for me to control.

So she could tell her parents and brother and kindergarten teacher and across-the-street neighbor and vegetable stand guy in Taiwan that she was "officially" paired off, Angela was the one to push for marriage. I eventually agreed because I realized that for Angela a marriage certificate was something akin to a degree for Americans: We've done it, it says, we're finally independent, we are OK. She was a post-U student in another department—which department doesn't matter at all—on campus. I was six years older than her and a new professor in the NNP program. I married her at the surprising end of the haze of years after your mother's disappearance. In fact, it wasn't really until we were actively talking about marriage that I realized Angela had fallen in love with me (or, at least, had "attached" to me), and when I considered how much time we spent together, the hours at the little gyro shop that would eventually be shaken by exploding former Joe's, the long walks between her place and campus, the meals she'd make me in her tiny little apartment, how carefully she'd attended to the elaborate late-night complaints I'd strung out about my new job or my distributor. (I'd published *Bot-Poetics*, finally, with a tiny little imprint operated from what seemed like an alternate universe in Guam. At its head was a flabby demiurge: The guy would say to my face that the book was selling well when the stats page said it had sold only a handful of copies.) She would listen to me deride my peers (the first and second *Coordinates* were getting great reviews but had somehow turned a few colleagues against me). She would comfort me when my mother called and talked only about John. I began to get scared, not of being married to Angela—she was nice and pretty and seemed like she was OK with being the wife to a reclusive and anthropessimistic academic who perhaps did not have the capacity to love someone—but because I realized then that I had lived for several years in almost perfect automation.

It seemed to me, in fact, that the career strides I'd made, the completion and publishing and failure of what I thought would be my glorious critical debut, and the surprising success of *Coordinates*, were all achieved by a person who was me but who also wasn't, like I'd programmed myself living my own life in the way that I had planned but without the concern for its ultimate outcome that I had had previously. Those years were lived incredulously, because fundamentally I could not "fit" your mother's disappearance/demise into the program. Half of me had burned badly; I walled it off and lived in the other half. Of course, I knew your mother's absence was irrevocable and final and so on and so on, but I could not somehow find a place for it in the code. I suppose you could say that the original problem of bot poets (the answer, good pupil, is C: simulating *feel*) was precisely my problem in those first years after your mother. Indeed, I could achieve the look of living, but not the feel. Once during those months, I even sprinted outright from one of Daniel's "smaller" parties, where I'd gone in a state of unthinking and premature social recrudescence. On my way out, I leapt the fence bordering his pretentious new-professor house, and it wasn't until three blocks later that I was convinced that the three women eyeing me in the corner of the party had not looked upon me with criminal intent, indeed, had not even been dangerous. It was true, though, that they had been staring. They told Daniel later that they were concerned about my vacant look and my clothing, which was dirty and dark with sweat.

Angela's first words to me, in fact, were something like "Are you OK?" when I was backed into a corner at a later faculty/post-U mingling event that I had to attend in order to fulfill my contract. She was beautiful—immaculate, really—and her slightly swallowed r's and sustained eye contact was as attractive as her face and body. But what became clear by our second date, which I had agreed to only to avoid a difficult cell conversation, was that Angela believed in me in a way that far outstripped most people's concern for socially inept men. It was a blind belief, a naive confidence in a goodness that I hadn't ever really displayed or developed. She believed that all humans were, ultimately, savable, no matter how burned.

Such blindness resulted in much pain.

She thought I was the authority on pretty much everything besides cooking and children, and she thought *Bot-Poetics* was genius and she planned to translate it into Taiwanese and the trendy Canto-Mandarin when she had time.

Though the pendulum has, as far as I can tell from the snatches I get of my students' personal lives, swung back in the direction of women as shining domestic beings, such a female desire was totally out of the ordinary thirty or thirty-five years ago. In fact, it was brave for a woman to even make known her desire to be at home. Angela was and did. It was the second-greatest conflict of our relationship that I insisted she "work outside the home" (as that one ditch-sitting Missourian, in the second or third *Coordinates,* had said his own plump wife never did do, as she sat silently smiling from the adjacent chair), which she did faithfully but almost always with incurable fatigue. Angela could spend a weekend making pickles and scrubbing grout and resewing my pant legs to fit more exactly my inversely proportionate legs, and then she'd wake up exuberant on Monday. Or she could spend a Friday night at a social event and then a Saturday morning womanning a boring panel at a regional conference in Kentucky and subsequently need a week to recover. These things I did not accept when we were married, for they were the opposite qualities of your mother (though your mother was young enough that her bent for domesticity was perhaps never tested, and I suppose, too, that it was never clear what career she might have achieved beyond bar mistress), and both Angela and I were often unhappy because of this.

But the greatest conflict came a few years in, when I began to feel that, finally, we had reached some agreement on her need to network and submit papers. Though they drained her, she was extremely capable. I felt she had finally accepted the utter absence on my part of any expectation to eat anything more elaborate than cold-cut sandwiches or to sleep in a room that felt "homey." She had, I thought, relaxed into our intellectual machine shop of a life. Things had stabilized and even seemed to be improving between us. She was waking up on Mondays after conferences or research binges much less forlorn. One Monday morning, I did hear her gagging in the bathroom, and after a week or so of her retching (I dared not ask), I came up with the explanation that her Taiwanese domesticity was literally being exorcised by modern America.

You, though, have probably already guessed the truth. She was pregnant. But before you lift your investigative, theme-tracing finger and demand an hour-by-hour recounting of the nighttime (and sometimes noontime) romances between your mother and me, which (except for a single night, the last night, in which there was absolutely no copulation) I will never give you, I must interrupt your zealous father searching and provide this little darkness: Angela miscarried. What this has to do with you will become clear presently.

The baby wasn't bigger than a berry. I heard her weeping in the bathroom, and when I finally went in, I saw her sitting on the floor in the narrow niche that housed the toilet, holding the tiny thing in her hand, like she'd found a sea creature and unknowingly killed it. When I asked what it was, she said it was "our baby."

I was overcome. I had not known that she'd had her IUD removed; we had not spoken a word about children, and had we, I would have used every evasive technique that I knew, including tyrannical prohibition. So, on the one hand, I was furious. Truly enraged. I nearly hit her. But I could not, of course, both because I'd never before hit anyone (not even David Geores) and also because she held in her hands our tiny little never-child, the only one I nearly made. I was deeply affected by this reality. I wanted to go put my hands under it and weep too, because what I realized for the first time was that I never had considered any legitimate future outside one with your mother. This life with Angela was just a sort of holding pattern, a marriage made on a deserted island while waiting to be rescued, or not.

Inexplicably (and this I share with you out of sheer generosity, for it is, in your story, superfluous sentimentality), as I stood there in the doorway of our shared bathroom, the vac fan humming above us, Angela sobbing into her own bloodied hands, I remembered a moment with your mother, a first night, a late night, a bathroom night. It was the night of David's bosque bonfire. I woke up from a deep, contented sleep and heard, just barely, the childlike hiccups of suppressed weeping from your mother's bathroom. Her room was small, filled with cloth and blankets and pillows, much of it unwashed for months, all of it smelling of her. The bathroom door, I had realized earlier that night, did not close all the way, and it speaks volumes about your mother that I, in the black of that lovely night, for the first time in my long memory, facilitized in a bathroom whose door did not close and lock. I didn't even realize I'd done it until I'd done it, and flushed, and climbed back into the warmth of your mother's bed, and felt the firm grip of her long fingers around my wrist.

When, however, I awoke sometime later, I found her in the bathroom, crying, and despite feeling immense fear, I asked her what was wrong.

In the darkness of the bathroom, lit only by a tiny sliver of window above the shower, I felt the weight of my body. I watched her silhouette, which was bent in a sitting position on the toilet. She held her hands out in front of her as she tried to calm her crying. Nothing was in her hands, of course, but she looked at them as if she were reading over a contract. And she said, simply, "Please, JP Don't . . ." Then she paused, and I didn't breathe. And she never said anything after that. She just cried a little more, and I sat at her feet and rubbed the tops of her bare thighs.

I loved her. I knew it then, and I think she knew she loved me then, and we were very, very afraid of what that meant, so we said nothing, and she cried out of fear, because two people who love each other can do nothing but draw pain toward themselves them like magnets. To fall in love with another person is a sort of suicide.

I thought I was immune to such things with Angela, having already hurled myself years before into the gaping chasm of your mother. I supposed Angela and I had worked out an arrangement that allowed for us to live like single people as a couple, to pass the time while waiting for at least a partially natural death. But the tiny, blood-borne shell of a human in her hands was not just something people do to pass the time. This was real pain and real death, and we'd made it for ourselves.

20

Daniel, you . . . you!

Daniel of the morning!

Just now he has messaged me with a regular trove of information. He says, among innumerable pointless cul-de-sacs of thought, that last night's dinner was rather depressing (naturally!), that he cried in front of you twice (of course he did, and of course he told me he did!), that you seemed rather annoyed to know that he, Daniel Glidden, knew almost nothing about the woman who bore you (he was at best a fly buzzing wildly in the *next room* during those months!), and that you look an awful lot like your mother (I'll forego detailing how unqualified he is for pronouncing such judgments). He told me that you said that you'd call me *after* a 9:00 a.m. appointment you had made, which was both glorious and mysterious, for it means that I had at least until 10:00 to get my thoughts in order (it's only 8:22 now), but it also meant that I wasn't the only thing remaining for you to accomplish in Albuquerque. I wondered for a few minutes if you had gotten in touch, somehow, with our old pal David Geores, but the logistics of your meeting him confused me. So I decided to dispose of prideful posing and instead just ask Daniel directly if you had mentioned someone named David. It took him eight more minutes to respond than I would have liked, but he finally said no, you hadn't mentioned any David. Another message came four minutes later that said the 9 a.m. appointment was with, as far as he understood, some aging business owner in Albuquerque. Aria Dang? I searched her name and found her listed on the winner board of some highfalutin culinary contest for Vietnamese fusion cuisine. Then I found that she has a restaurant in the foothills. Her name was mentioned in an outdated thread on body art and in a couple of old trad-car listings. Ten years ago, she was featured in a business blog article: "Aria Dang = Reinvention."

I found this particular clue enigmatic. After some research, the closest I could come to making sense of it was that one of your books had dealt with the grandchildren of veterans from the first Vietnamese war, so naturally Aria Dang was a professional stop for you. I had never heard of Aria Dang and was glad of it, for I was perfectly satisfied with the idea that your mother's story should be suspended in the plasma of daily life until you and I meet. As one of my professors said in the NNP program, "Suspense equals expectation plus delay."

Daniel Glidden (unknowingly) personifies this formula.
Where was I?

21

The miscarriage. The miscarriage set off another phase in my life not dissimilar to the blurred years after your mother. It was a time of moral diffusion. I did not want to repeat the fertilization or the impromptu and unwilled abortion, so I insisted that Angela return to the doctor and have the IUD reinserted. She refused. I told her that I wouldn't be coupling with her until I had proof of the reintroduction of effective contraception. She said she wanted a child and that contraception was not an effective tool for having a child. I said it was an effective tool for keeping our marriage intact. She said nothing and went to bake onion muffins.

Her strategy following that misconception, I must admit now, was perfectly conceived, if you'll allow the pun. She would just wait me out. And she knew that she *could*. For six weeks, I fumed and fidgeted, and that was when I began getting used to sleeping on the couch. But by the tail end of week seven, my thoughts, fueled by sopping, violent dreams and admittedly steeping, during the day, in a buildup of hormone waste, plummeted off some unforeseen precipice: I *liked* that she was holding out on me. I mean, with our insurance, the possibilities for asexual fertilization were practically endless, but suffice it to say that for the cost of a couple of extra conference appearances a year, she could have easily been impregnated without my participation or awareness. But forget medicine! She had plenty of post-U groupies, idiotic, moist-crotched boys who thought she was the most beautiful and brilliant woman they'd ever met. And it was true (they hadn't met your mother). And they knew I was a reclusive semi-tyrant, and that any child of mine would be malformed and huge headed. They could have done Angela a service in the nine minutes it would have taken from the moment she made the proposition. And, hell, forget even the post-U's! She could have just fooled me, as she'd done before, forged a doctor's receipt, lied about the IUD. But that she held out and pursued no alternatives meant she wanted *my* child, my genes, and my cooperation. One day, while my students were working quietly on some nefarious time waster the U had developed as a way for them to give me feedback on my teaching, I realized that Angela's tiny cold war was, perhaps, one of the kindest things that ever had been done to me.

I still slept on the couch, but I began to soften. Over a (wonderful) rice dish one night, I asked her when the "waiting period" was over after her miscarriage. "Waiting period?" she asked. She didn't even look up from the textbook she was reviewing for a friend, thinking that I intended to resurrect the old fight. "Isn't there a mandatory time period before the next attempt at conception?" Finally she understood me. I did not look at her, but I could feel her looking at me. Yes. And she said a date three weeks from then.

Those three weeks were perhaps the best of our relationship, and they mark almost perfectly the midpoint of our marriage. During those silver days, I felt like I had something of hers, and she knew she had something of mine, so we were kind to one another, forgiving, careful. We were two formerly hostile countries thriving in anticipation of a mutual exchange of resources. I made her tea one night and her eyes grew so large in gratitude that I felt, for a moment, something like a reciprocal love fondness gripping my metamorphic heart.

But, long, miserable, gory story short, the following three years would not see the political agreement fulfilled. We had another miscarriage six months later, this time at a half-empty downtown restaurant, this time with more blood and less sentiment. And nine months after that, a false alarm, a miscarriage's blood but not its pain avoided. And then nothing. For a year and a half.

I eventually went to the doctor. I hadn't had my pants down for thirty seconds before he said, "Varicose veins. On both of them." I asked what that meant. I learned that these two deep purple veins I'd always had, one that wrapped around the left testicle almost entirely, and another that wandered around the top of the right, caused excess blood flow and therefore excess heat in precisely the place you don't want heat, because sperm died when hot. He said the chances of conception were dismally low and, in the case of successful conception, chances for fetal survival even lower, and in the case of fetal survival, chances for a normal, healthy child are something like one out of ten thousand (percentages might speak more clearly: that's .01 percent, which is, statistically, more rare than dying in an SD that drives itself into the ocean [there is, nationwide, a .023 percent chance of that happening]). But, he said (here the saggy-cheeked old doctor stood up straight and quite compassionately put his hand on my shoulder), with my insurance, outside of a simple, inpatient surgery to correct the varicocele, the possibilities for assisted fertilization were many. I grabbed the waist of my pants and said thank you and I'd be in touch.

I submit to you this rather embarrassing medical history as proof. I can supply subsequent imaging results too. The chances that you are my daughter are not just metaphorically low. Unless, of course, you are very good at masking your deficient IQ (which skill would, I think, be precisely the definition of high IQ), there is no way you are my child, even though even I can see that the timing matches up somewhat.

But to return to Angela in order to return to Hungarian door #2 in order to return to your mother. The thought of having my dough cut open was a bit much for me to bear. I at first refused to consider surgery. Also I felt strangely proud, as if there was nothing wrong with my anatomy, and it was, instead, the world that conspired against me. So I also refused artificial seeding under grow lights or whatever they do to grow babies in the lab.

Angela didn't take this as the bluff that I perhaps expected her to. We descended into a silence that seemed to compact itself like soil; each new day added a new layer. Within a couple of months, she sent me a very loving email wishing me the best of luck but saying that she wanted to have children, and so she was returning to Taiwan and to her parents, who would find her a match easily, and in that match she would become a mother. She wished that her kids could have been the offspring of such an "intelligent, eloquent, powerful" man like me, she said, but it seemed like the price was too high for the both of us. I quote her not entirely out of flattery but out of a hope that you will believe that your mother was not totally insane in loving me.

I remember thinking after receiving that email that I couldn't agree more. And so for roughly thirty years, there was no suitcase blocking my entryway, until that moment behind Hungarian door #2, to which door (which isn't my door, I know) we return now.

Besides the furniture (same as next door) and wall hangings, the apartment was the duplicate of mine, down to the real marble countertop and coffee maker (both upgrades included as a move-in special). I spiraled my way down the sparse side hall and through the duplicate kitchen. The bedroom door was closed.

I hadn't considered the possibility of another Hungarian door, which had neither code nor key and which was, if it was like my bedroom had been before I had the lock changed, unlockable. So I considered my dilemma. Was it more rude to just walk in? Or to knock? Just walking in would have the advantage of innocence ("Sorry, just doing my routine check on the place . . ."). Knocking would be a tacit admission that I knew someone was in there, and that I thought that they should know that *I* was in *here*.

The decision was too much, and I started to think about how scared the woman might be if indeed I just walked in or if I knocked. So I backed up and walked out, being careful now to make as little noise as possible.

Thankfully, I retreated without discovery. I'd gotten what the narrative gods had sent me there for. I returned to the desk to write about Angela and my varicose veins, which now, upon rereading, I worry might make you feel a bit sorry for me or her. You shouldn't. I've had as good a life alone as I would have had with Angela. For, not long after that, I realized that other people are often unintentionally the source of my deepest unhappiness, and that such a person like me should probably be careful to keep others at a safe distance for the sake of both parties. As for Angela, maybe ten years ago she sent me a nice note and a picture of her oldest son's high school graduation.

As for me. I have no children.

22

I am annoyed at myself for the unnecessary mess I've made.

Our conversation over cell, just concluded, was not a good beginning, and I'm sorry for that, though such a downer was perhaps unavoidable. I was both surprised at your timing (clearly the meeting with Ms. Dang did not last long) and lurched from a kind of reverie. I didn't, in the moment, have the wherewithal to explain to you the nearly three hours that preceded the call, which were impudent, stupid hours that I would delete from the archive of my life in an instant, if I could. Perhaps one day we will have such technology. I'd pay plenty.

But I shouldn't fool myself. I am a narrativist; I live and die by the archive. It was precisely the archive that boiled my bottom and caused me to bubble forth the disgruntlement I simply couldn't contain during our call. Indeed, shortly after I retreated from Hungarian door #2 (I glanced under a couple of articles of clothing on the way out—only more clothing was revealed) and then wrote the above about Angela, I relapsed into that old addiction, and within minutes was deep, deep in the archive, watching old security camera footage and browsing the messages Angela had sent me.

Some of those old messages were inane and funny ("I have logged onto your shoe" and "Rice and boiling, please"), little relational crumbs whose source only she and I would understand. But others were more painful to read, and though the ache I still feel in my groin means I certainly haven't forgotten the misery of those years after the miscarriage, I did forget the many and various ways I had been pierced through.

I found, for example, a long message from the time near the end, when we were fighting constantly about doctor's visits. Before I went to the doctor, tests seemed to suggest that if there was anything wrong with her, the deficiencies they had found were normal in modern women, easily rectified by store-bought supplements, and rarely the cause of infertility. This pointed the spotlight at me. She sent me an unwarranted message while I was in office hours one day, explaining in semi-grammatical bulleted paragraphs that if I loved her (it said that: "if you love me"), I would "bring [the] testicles to a medical examination." What I think we both knew by then was that I did not "love" her in the way she was talking about, and that her "if you love me" line was not a way to plead but a way to outline the boundaries of our different countries in preparation for the final war for independence. The boundary we shared, apparently, was "if you love me." I ceded all territory beyond that. This message from her was a formal political declaration in a way. It hurt to read it. I may be stone, but I still feel pain.

Also there was some entryway footage from my last apartment of *precisely* the situation I was describing: the open suitcase and the strewn bras, though sometime during those three bad years she had a cosmetic operation that essentially made bras obsolete, so the suitcases of the latter years (after a brief disappearance in our calm middle year, the suitcases had made a vengeful reappearance at the end) were thus less strappy. The last suitcase, though, I remember distinctly. It wasn't open, and had on top of it a little disposable pamphlet (even then, such things were long outdated—had she made this one, knowing I'd be more likely to read something printed in vegetable ink?) with SOCIAL CONSORTIUM DIVORCE LAW emblazoned in purple across the top. I acted like I didn't see it and asked, in a perfectly measured tone, if she would please move the suitcase out of the entryway. She came into the room crying.

But my memory is racing ahead of my archival compulsions. I decided, in those hours before you called, to try to find that very moment from the security camera footage in order to determine how many days beforehand the unheeded warning about her departure had come. I guessed six days, because she sent the message on a Saturday, and Sunday was the day she usually returned home from conferences. Why this is important—finding this day on the footage—is a reasonable question, and one I'm only asking myself now. Three hours ago, it was not a question. It was a necessity.

The video files had been compressed with a code that minimized their storage requirements but could restore their quality almost exactly on decompression. The decompression process is not particularly fast, and so I began by decompressing short spurts of time: the Sundays and Saturdays in the range of a few weeks (I thought it was likely that my memory had done its own storage-saving decompression). The camera at the other apartment was motion activated (the ones here use a complex algorithm for vibration and sound, and the camera flicks on about a moment *before* the door opens), and so anytime the door opened or closed the camera began recording, and always a millisecond after the initial motion, which makes every video seem sudden, a sort of boring explosion in the chain reaction of life.

I watched each entrance and exit from those weekend days: Mine were less frequent than hers. Though I did see a purse and a set of large boots that I can no longer identify (she brought them into the foyer from elsewhere in the apartment and I later carried them out only to return without them in four minutes), I found no suitcase, much less a suitcase with a pamphlet on top. Strange.

I expanded my search. Maybe it was a weekday conference in a nearby city. The decompression of the weekdays took much longer. In the meantime, I checked my cell and drank a carrot soda.

But I found no suitcase in the weekdays. So I decompressed whole months. Four of them, the four proceeding the final message from her.

While the program chugged along, I went out into the hallway and paced, vaguely hoping that the woman might come out of Hungarian door #2. The doors for the fast lift opened and no one disembarked, so I stepped on and rode down to the thirty-fifth and strode out to the drone approach, now transformed in the daylight. The sun was blinding—an odd occurrence during fire season—and I only lasted a few minutes before I retreated back to the forty-second floor, where nothing had changed besides the completion of the decompression.

I watched every single entry and exit from those months on 10x speed. The boots reappeared and disappeared. A guy from the SD battery dealer stood for what seemed like hours in the entryway, staring at his cell. Then there was a flash of luggage—stop the film!—but no: It was the odd-shaped bag of a friend from Taiwan who came to visit her about a month before she left. We came and went, came and went, but there was no luggage. I decompressed two more months and drank another carrot soda, but by this time I knew what I'd find. No luggage. She had stopped going to conferences in those months, I'm sure, because she had stopped believing in my vision for our life.

How could I have remembered something that never occurred?

I considered the possibility of a malfunction in the camera, but unless there is a benevolent god of footage that goes around removing pain from people's archives, I thought such a malfunction extremely unlikely, as there was (based on a count of a sample month) exactly as many entrances and exits as there should have been; none were missing. I also considered the possibility that I had been my own benevolent god, and had deleted such problematic footage out of consideration for my future mental health, and also knowing well by then (after the Big Co. raid of the years before) that perhaps my most self-destructive tendency was to flagellate with archival material. But this theory didn't stand up to the previous sample count I'd made, which, again, suggested nothing had been removed. If I'd deleted the footage, then, the only answer I could come up with was that I'd known that, later, I'd count the entrances and exits and find one missing and thus affirm a trauma I had attempted to erase, so back then, holding the proverbial scissors, I'd copied a section of mundane entrance footage from some previous week and inserted it into the hole where the suitcase and the note should have been. And if this was the case, I somehow deleted this deceptive editing from my memory, while, mysteriously, retaining the memory I'd intended to delete. So the project before me was comparing (I opened three windows simultaneously on the screen for this) the days of the weeks preceding her message with the days of the weeks preceding those weeks to see if any of the footage had been reused. This was a difficult task, because our entrances and exits were so similar to begin with, and because humans, for as new as all things seem, are for the most part automatons. In fact, I noticed quickly that I always stepped in with my left foot first, brought my right foot in as I shut the door behind me, and began removing my shoes almost before the door had shut. *All* the footage looked copied, but I could see some differences when I examined it more closely: my clothes, the items on the table at the end of the couch, the state of the pillows on the same.

Why detail this for you? Because you called just as I ruled out a third day.

I was startled out of my idiotic searching. The sound of a "new caller" shot me through with dread. I glanced at the clock and saw that it was almost midday. When I answered, you began exactly as I thought you would.

"Yes, hello," you said. I practically mouthed the words as you said them.

To think, these are the first two words you've ever spoken to me. If, in a parallel universe (a beautiful one, with David Geores), you were, indeed, my daughter, this would be an important moment.

"Is this JP Stone?" I said it was. You introduced yourself as your mother's daughter and said that via your mother's poems in *Cold* you had tracked down Daniel Glidden and had gotten lots of wonderful information about your mother from him, but he suggested that you meet with me.

I said something like "Aha, yes."

Then you asked if I had known your mother very well. My reply was bumbling and halting and circuitous, for the question surprised me. "Briefly, if you count knowing people well as a function of time," and even as I was saying it, I knew that this was not the right tone or character to portray, that it sounded more like a demented, aging academic of the sort that reads uncapitalized publications like *supermodernism* just to "keep up with the field." I recovered, though, and said I did indeed have some information to share with you that I thought you would like to have. I told you about the dam and the reservoir and how it was good not to let the storm overwhelm the dike. You said, "I'm sorry, I don't really understand. Are you talking about a dam here in Albuquerque?" And I realized that I had been talking metaphorically in response to your question about where we might meet. Finally, I invited you to my apartment without confusion. You asked when might be good.

As I spoke to you on my cell, the footage of me and beautiful, sad Angela entering and exiting our apartment ticked away on the screen in front of me. Perhaps I was not perfectly coherent on the phone because I was simultaneously considering how long it would take me to go through all the Angela footage. This is why I said, "I unfortunately can't meet today. Would tomorrow work for you?" You said it would, but that you'd be leaving Albuquerque in the evening. I suggested lunch. You said "Thank you, that would be nice," and asked if you could bring anything, which is as old-fashioned a courtesy as anything I've encountered recently. I thought, first, of what I had in the apartment. Carrot soda and soy shakes. Then I thought briefly about having you pick up gyros, but I ruled that out simply because nothing sounded worse to me than you arriving with plastic containers of steaming meat wraps that I'd have to choke down in order to not seem totally perverse. So I rashly decided that I'd pick something up, which meant, I knew, that two hours would be lost in the moments preceding our meeting. Nonetheless, I told you so: I'd pick something up. You said fine, and that you'd see me then.

Then you said, "Uh, JP?" I felt my rock heart twist; no one had said my first name as a question in decades. My students call me Professor Stone and, excepting Daniel, my colleagues just call me Stone if they say anything to me at all. "Yes?" I said. "Do you have . . . any . . . images of her, like archived? Pictures that I don't have access to?" I thought for a moment. The answer to the question was a resounding and painful yes. I had hundreds. However, the tone of my answer—the suppressed anger and piercing accusation, which I won't write down here—I'm sure surprised you, because you didn't say anything. Of course, you couldn't have known at all what you were asking for.

When I heard your stunned silence, I corrected course, and so said in a gentler tone: "I might have some photos, but my archives are so disordered and data that old tends to degrade on low-cost servers, which I regretfully had to use during the lean years. But I'll check."

"Thank you," you said, with real emotion. "I'll take anything."

We said goodbye and the cell beeped you away.

23

I immediately regretted the two concessions I hadn't planned on making: acquiring acceptable food and "looking into" pictures of your mother. I don't mind careful invention when it's necessary, but for some reason, I knew that these photos were precisely the things you deserved but also precisely the things I did not want to yield, the photos and all the other bits of information I have in my possession but cannot open. And I was worried that Daniel hadn't forgotten at all and might have mentioned the "double lockbox" to you, and perhaps had even gone so far as offering you access, at least, to his part of the lockbox after, he assumed, I would inevitably evade your probe.

I'm glad, however, that I bought time. Having said no straight out would have incentivized you to return to Daniel. And I'd like to remove Daniel from this story as quickly as possible. He is one of those characters that tend to weigh the plot down excessively. So now I must determine if and how I'll ask Daniel to dig up the old hoard and unlock his box without getting him any more deeply involved in this than he already is.

But, God, I do not want to. Have the whole of it, the story and the characters and the brutal conclusion, but do not take those things, those little crumbs of time that only she and I shared. Perhaps I'll make you new ones! I'll find Daniel's old videditing Emily and ask her if she could re-create some Joe's scenes, maybe a couple of pictures with your drunken probably-father mashing at the pinball machines amid laughing at the walruses! Ah. Emily's probably dead (she looked nearly dead back then), and even falsifying the photos in a convincing way would require parent photos, the real ones, and all of this could never be accomplished before you arrive, and, anyway, what's the point of evasion anymore?

How can I explain this? How will you ever understand why I am loathe to return to that little hoard?

Daniel. I must contact Daniel.

24

But let's begin with something even worse: Big Co. Years after your mother's disappearance, Big Co. (whose actual name has been so thoroughly litigated and entwined with surveillance software that I hesitate to use it here, for fear of engaging some long buried data-laced trip wire and thus bringing upon my anonymous head some sort of auto-generated lawsuit and its subsequent phone calls) was finally busted up. This was a political and social upheaval that affected the oxygenated, ambulatory world very little, but in the chronology of intellectual history, as I'm sure you learned ad nauseam in grade school, it has been compared to the burning of the library in Alexandria. This is ridiculous, because little is actually gone. Instead, much was dispersed. In fact (you were too young for this to matter), there was a sudden outflow of data that, combined with the USGS glut, made the few years after your birth an era of incredibly fair and to this day unmatched distribution of electronic wealth among the very citizens on whose digital land this company was so successfully farming for free.

This may sound ridiculous, but on the day they had appointed for the government-mandated breakup of Big Co., there was a small gathering on campus, in the old faculty lounge that had become a sort of server farm but had maintained in one corner an empty space where people could meet. A few of us, sitting on long benches previously associated with some on-campus religious facility, were witnesses to, attendees of, the massive outpouring of data that, if I remember correctly without searching, occurred precisely at 10:15, as if Nia Yazzie and her gang of data communists had destroyed Big Co. early that morning, paused for coffee, then opened a first come, first serve bazaar that totally and absolutely defied all court orders regarding the dissolution of the trust. The government shut it down a day later, but they were about fifteen hours too late.

In the preceding hours, however, I remember mainly the silence that hung over the seven or eight of us who sat with our laptops open, our ancillary drives attached, backup drives balanced on our pale knees, waiting, reining in our hope and anxiety even as minutes later things ballooned out of control. I remember the buzzing of the fans and the rapid on-off of the server coolers. A technician came in sometime around 9:30 and asked us if we had the authority to be there, and I showed him my newly minted faculty badge. The mustached technician wiped his sweaty hands on his thick pants and said, "NNP? I don't know that department." I told him it stood for Networking and Nanocomputing Program, or something idiotic like that, and he believed me and shrugged, preferring not to power up his scanner. Just before he turned to leave, he looked at the strange group of pajamaed misfits and asked if we wouldn't mind being sure the main door locked when we left.

We'd already been there for more than ten hours and I had emptied something like seven carrot sodas. Then it happened. At 10:15, there was a surge from all global directions as thousands of people—some with very, very sophisticated pre-built programs—pounced on this data flow in order to immediately try to sell it to more naive parties. Grey Aaman, who had been appointed to the watch just ten minutes before, said, "Guys, I think it's happening." And there, on an obscure clearinghouse server used for the photographic offal of government-sponsored galas, there was suddenly an ocean to wade through. All of us roared. There was a wild shuffling of limbs as we clambered to our computers, which were already doing the work we'd asked them to do. Folders upon folders.

Nationally, probably globally, this was a gold rush in fast-forward. Because much of the most valuable data was elaborate and high-resolution satellite imagery, huge mapping and surveillance outfits rose up and crested and crashed in a matter of days. There were also large-scale demographies—packaged data about white people in North Carolina, Black people in municipalities without police departments, old people in college courses . . . Pasty high school students throughout the world grabbed all they could and spent the next month or so trying to hock the waste in the vast infopawn network that grew up almost at the exact moment it was needed but then died when even their attempts to "pay by the kilo" didn't dissuade massive data dumps into their machines. Only Pawnline survived, and we know its scent well. A strange genre of business—sellers of contact information for the owners of user names and emails—rose up in as a sort of loose mafia and persists to this day, after surviving two court battles. This was all basically before you were old enough to own a cell license.

We in the lounge / server farm had come for similar reasons, as a sort of raiding party, and we had waited outside the gates with a singular plan: to storm into the flow and find our treasures and sprint out with every last data pebble we could hold. In the week preceding the event, we built digital war wagons and made elaborate plans. From our computers hung, like unripe fruit, detachable hard drives, backup batteries, good luck talismans. A quiet young man who didn't want to tell us his name had four computers. One woman—there because no one (yet) knew she was the biological daughter of a famous and not-at-all-cool criminal mother—had even written a triage plan for the group, based on a system in which we drew straws for precedence. We had to draw straws because everyone in that room had a pressing reason to join this campaign. The information we were seeking was not useful to us at all, necessarily. The problem was that it could be useful to the world: criminal records, surveillance photos, incriminating emails and profiles, appearances in maps and lists and databases that one didn't want to appear on. A few among us were covering tracks. A few were angling for control. A couple were vengeful.

We were, in many ways, a group of semi-repentant lowlifes. In a meeting a week or so before, we had all gathered and, first, promised to speak nothing about one another outside of the group, and, second, told each other our basic needs. In other words, we confessed our sins. We weren't wildly specific, but even the specificity we did achieve was unprecedented. I spoke about your mother for the first time since the last time I'd spoken *to* her. No one nodded, but nor did they smirk. We were backed into corners, all of us. There was no ego left.

In fact, my acquaintance Grey Aaman (sorry to bring you back into the story at this low point, my friend), a stocky, balding guy from the North, strangely, many years ago, had somehow found his name and picture on a map of sex offenders—it was a user-generated map built totally anonymously, and it persisted despite numerous judicial injunctions because it was a tool of the self-styled "Call-It" culture, whose famous formula was that twenty off-target defamations was worth one ousted sex maniac. And they had a point: The particular map in question, the one of suburban Detroit on which Grey appeared, had actually led to the conviction of a serial rapist.

The backstory was that Grey had had a bad breakup. The guy, furious and often drunk, had vengefully reported Grey to the Call-It map. Grey hadn't been the most upstanding ex either. That was years before. By Big Co.-llapse, the map was old and long abandoned and had been taken down from the outer crust, but Grey was there to ensure that no one (and we knew for a fact that there were Sudanese blackmail bots already clicking their pincers at the cracking dam) could touch the information. Call-It had been replaced by innumerable clones, each as poisonously idiotic as the last. But his new job was too precious to him to risk the resurfacing of such misinformation. This is why Grey screamed like a toddler when, at 10:19 or so, he saw that he had secured the entire Call-It directory, beating the dozens of others, spread out all over the world, who surely wanted it.

(After Grey's shriek, the woman there to take hold of her twisted mother's DNA profile and genealogical data screamed back at Grey, "Triage!" Grey, in a moment of remarkable grace, swung his gaze across the landscape of cans and cords and computers and seemed suddenly to be born: He immediately jumped up, ran to his backpack, traded the now-full external drive for another, returned to his screen, and began clicking his way toward the DNA alleyways in this global bazaar.)

Another woman, a grade-school teacher with long, wavy hair and a flat face, was there to remove the images from her amateur pornography career. Despite our best attempts to explain that her images were not hosted or owned by Big Co., and therefore the photos' roots would not be up for grabs, she persisted in her blind hope. A couple of other people, their faces lost to me now, were there to execute similar life revisions. Two nervous young men—undergrads—sat near the outlet fan in a corner and never told us what they were raiding beyond "some stuff that happened when we were kids," but they maintained a place on the triage sheet that said, "Aspen and Vasily will indicate" (I remember their names only because they later built a nearby private prison and named it after themselves), which meant that, if their triage number came up and they still needed help, they'd guide us to their treasure.

I was there for your mother. Grey had actually been the one to bring me in. One day he came into my office, shut the door behind him, and asked, "Are you ever concerned that people might find out something about you that you prefer for them to not find out?" I thought he was *beginning* a blackmail conversation—he and I had shared an unbalanced and dangerous post-U student (Grey taught the intro New Poetics courses) for a single semester before changing departments—and while I nodded and scrunched my eyebrows, I initiated a rapid scan of potentially blackmailable memories and found there an embarrassing moment in an Uber outside a party a few years before, which Grey may have witnessed from the sidewalk. I said that, indeed, such a possibility concerned me. Grey said it concerned him too. Then there was a heavy pause, and I prepared myself to pay Grey whatever he asked. But then he told me about Nia Yazzie and her group and the semisecret website she had built and the court case against her that would not resolve itself in time. I acted worried, but really I was incredibly excited. I asked him to tell me more.

I think Grey was looking for confirmation that I had skeletons in my closet too. I knew how he felt—there is nothing more lonely than owning a secret—but I did not plan on letting him into my closet.

Grey needed help. For a couple of weeks, he and I worked together on a program, only looking politely away when the other coded in the particular target of their raid. Grey, however, got drunk one night and told me all about his target in long, unreadable messages (which I now cannot find). In some bizarre way, he seemed to still love the guy who had begun this awful anti-journey and who was now in prison on some drug charge. I did not reciprocate with any revelation of my own. In the meeting, I said that I'd had a "tumultuous romance that ended in a disappearance."

I had done extensive research and discovered that really there would be only limited releases of personal information that hadn't already been made public, and all of this would come primarily from "inactive" or "suspended" accounts. Most of the gold rush was for rather inconsequential tailings, the waste rock of Big Co.'s many decades of monopolized ore hauling. The most likely yields from this release would be information about and from people long gone and accounts long inactive. Like the wavy-haired teacher, many people developed a semi-apocalyptic belief that this was the way they'd be able to erase anything and everything. In this way, Nia Yazzie had been touted as a hero, but really she was a scrapper; the government had feigned fury but in actuality they were turning their heads as thousands of scavengers emerged to carry away an immense pile of information waste that really just cost taxpayer money to maintain.

I had a target that was certainly inactive. When 10:15 hit, I figured I'd be the only one in the world interested in such information. But I couldn't risk it. I wanted everything. If there was someone else out there interested in your mother, I wanted to be sure their nominal curiosity did not somehow impede my love.

10:18. My program purred and purred. I figured the slowness of the program's gathering was a result of the targets' disparate locations.

10:20. I opened the collection folder. Nothing.

10:21. I refreshed the folder: A series of low-weight text files appeared. My heart fluttered. I opened them.

10:23. The silly end-of-year survey forms for a group of Ohio plumbers took me some moments to fully comprehend, but by 10:24 I understood that my program had failed. My inferior coding skills revealed themselves. For the first time in my life, I screamed in public.

Grey, having helped the woman ahead of me in triage, circumnavigated the sobbing grade-school teacher and came to my rescue. He hollered questions at me as if bullets were singeing our arm hairs. I told him my program failed: "I've got Ohio plumbers, it's all over, a survey of plumbers, God, no, I couldn't . . ." Grey said he could help. He flipped open his computer and deleted a swatch of his code, pasted a new piece in, then said, "Give me your target."

I hesitated. I had long made a habit of withholding anything about your mother and me. But I was unsure who might be out there looking for the same dry bones. So I told him. By 10:34, he had retrieved more data than his already-laden wagon could hold, so he leapt to my computer and extracted my hard drive, and I remember the great relief I felt when I saw my drive come up on his screen and begin to accept the data he had shunted toward us. I held on to his arm without thinking. The program eventually said NO RESULTS and I immediately ripped the transfer cords from Grey's machine. The irony was that Grey had asked for my help in building his code.

We retreated. I grabbed my laptop and Grey and I stood between two humming server banks and off-loaded from his drive the relevant files onto my machine. That done, I gripped Grey's arm in perhaps the deepest thanks I've ever felt. I left quickly and, I regret now, without having checked Grey's machine for copies or remnants. I believe Grey, in his glorious retirement, has given much of his digital archive to the university, and, there, those little organizer bots must have found rather personal information regarding your mother, which, I think, explains the DCOB's incongruous suspicion that Grey might be your father.

I hope this was sufficient narrative evidence to help you rule out the real Grey Aaman.

He would have made a good father.

25

It's been years since I thought about that day. For many, many years, however, I thought about it very much. I'll admit that I've never felt more connected to a human being who wasn't your mother than I did to Grey in those moments.

I spent the following year and a half combing through the data that I gleaned with Grey's cunning. I culled it, scrapbooked it, enshrined it. I separated it into chapters. In this chapter goes all the data concerning your mother's emails to family members; in this one, emails to close friends; in this one, emails unsent, perhaps several revisions of the same one. Several chapters had to do with her poetry, which, as luck would have it, was all saved somehow in Big Co.'s labyrinthine cloud drives. A very special folder with several subchapters was dedicated to the images, messages, and inadvertent recordings (for a period of months, her phone had mysteriously recorded phone conversations that occurred between 21:00 and 23:30 each night) culled from her cell.

I am distant enough from this strange time that I can readily admit the occult nature of my interests and activities then. For example, a month or two was dedicated to developing and revising the above classification system. I'd think I have it finished and then in some obscure directory I'd find a hidden patch of documents grown during her mainschool years, little short answers likely copied and pasted into some quizzing software and then forgotten. Such a discovery would break open a formerly simplistic class of data (MAINSCHOOL COMPOSITION) because I'd discover upon further inspection that this quizzing software had been employed sporadically in her mainschool years and, apparently, by a few professors at the U (there are many who belong in mainschool, both in mind and spirit), thus creating a body of data that was homogeneous in tone and purpose but heterogeneous in life stage. In order to accommodate this new subclass (PROMPTED SHORT ANSWERS), I'd have to reform entire classes, unpacking MAINSCHOOL and U entirely and repacking things into different boxes. One night, a week or so before I finally collapsed the classification system into its ultimate (genius) simplicity, I remember realizing that in one series in the PROMPTED SHORT ANSWERS directory, a systems psychology professor had, it seemed, asked in a quiz for both personal reflection and creative writing that responded to and expanded on more cut-and-dried short answers from earlier in the quiz. Thus the short answers (1) ranged in kind from pat to personal to poetic and (2) were referential in ways that would require the pat to understand the poetic. This caused me great distress. I did not sleep well.

The night I finally broke and decided to make the classification the very thing, the very story itself, and not the precursor to it, was when I found in an email communication to a much-hated professor at the U (a man I know, a man so bitter he was intolerable even to me) that she had composed partially via algorithm. I was alerted to the message simply because of the old grump's name, but I saw very quickly that there was something different about her prose, something stilted and, in some instances, absolutely preposterous. One rhetorical question that still rings wildly in my memory went, "Do you really think in such fluffernutter as gerontology?" (I once jokingly said this under my breath to an old nurse checking my ever-waning pulse). But what I realized was that she never sent the email, nor was she in any way versed in code, and so I started to guess that she likely had not composed the algorithm herself but had borrowed it and used it to produce a message that blew off the necessary steam before composing a subsequent and totally tame message to the same old man asking simply why her test had been so severely different in content from her classmates' (which question [she didn't and wouldn't know] would be answered years later in a racist rant before the U committee that would fire him—as is their habit, years too late—and on which I sat).

This email sent me into skyward spiral. How do you classify someone's life? How do you make sense of these things? Is this *hers*, this unsent email produced with an algorithm she didn't write? Is it as much hers as the poem she wrote the summer before she began at the U, which contemplates the philosophical bent of mountain grasses? Is her application to Joe's (completed on Big Co.'s Applications Application) half Joe's, half hers? And if she lied on that application about the fact that she worked at a chain restaurant for nine months and then admitted that day to a Centex friend in a cell message that she changed the "nine days of hell to nine months of experience" on the app, where should I classify such things, when, indeed, the nine-to-nine simple algorithm of her cell message is its own sort of poetry? Is the poem I wrote about her back, her long, naked spine, somehow *hers* if, indeed, I am, was, *hers*, and should my poem fall in next to her own about me, which is really just a vague cloud of emotion that has only sentimental value? Is the picture of her grandmother's dog that died when your mother was three poetic if it appears in a folder that says IDEAS FOR POEMS?

All these questions are rushing back, and it's taken me these hundred-odd pages to realize that the questions rush now not toward me but toward you. A hundred pages ago, I was cringing, but now, eyes just barely opened, I see them pass like a herd of some immense animal. I am unscathed.

How will you not be flattened by it all? You come looking for her and what you will get are the bones left after she gnawed them, the wrappers of things that pleased her, the thoughts she inscribed into computerized bits. You can re-create a female character from these things, no doubt, but you are a fool and the worst kind of fool to believe you can build anything more than an automaton that puts out a stylized version of what you put in it. No doubt you are looking for a woman who explains who you are, your idiosyncrasies, your sadnesses, your perceptions. Perhaps you will find yourself here. How can it be otherwise? How can you hear her, and not just Big Co.'s algorithmic sampling of her? Because you are more her than any other, that's how.

Back then, what I understood was that all things are permissible, but not all are beneficial. I decided from there on to make my own gospel of your mother, to spend my time not wondering about where things belonged but, instead, rebuilding her. For though the poem may never achieve the *feel*, we still try. Thus, I had three folders: TO BE CULLED and HER and NOT HER. In HER I would place "nine days of hell to nine months of experience"; in NOT HER I would place what she wrote for "desired pay" and "mode of transportation," though of course the process of breaking down the information gathered just by the Big Co.'s Applications Application might take a whole night. Thenceforward the process became emotional, visceral, rather than archival. Sometimes I would spend time in the HER folder, relishing in her presence, rejoicing in her tenuous resurrection. Other times, usually Mondays, I'd cull items in the TO BE folder, and nothing was more comforting than realizing the sheer volume I had there, and basic calculations suggested that, at the rate I was culling, I'd have enough material to last decades.

But two human truths conspired against me. First, I realized that while I culled slowly and deliciously, I was losing the biospiritual glue that could connect disparate Big Co. data into HER. That is, as time passed, I lost her more, lost the feel of her, and so the borders of HER grew fuzzy. I'd have a hard time remembering, for example, if Octavio Paz was her favorite poet or her favorite poet to hate, and so a pithy little poem about Paz written in extreme draft form could seem forced (if she hated him) or enigmatic (if she liked him), and I could not pinpoint where such data might belong. It hurt me to see that I was losing her even as I was preserving her.

Then, the second truth. Sometime in May of the second year after your mother, Daniel, already the interim chair of the department after Sharon Colby finally lost her suit against a colleague in the department who'd programmed a bot to run his online courses, sent me a message and said that a couple of students had told him that I'd left early from three classes, and, when he checked, he saw that I had failed entirely to enter any comments or end points into the system for an entire school year. What was going on?

For the first time in months, I seemed to wake up. I looked around. I was in my foothills apartment, surrounded by empty cans and soybrick wrappers and wearing a button-down office shirt and no pants. It wasn't wounded vanity that caused me to reel then, it was a realization that if this was what my life looked like now, how might it look in fifteen years, when I'd lost all memory of being with your mother, having replaced it with the scads of memories related to culling your mother's digital leavings?

I looked at my computer and saw files there that concerned your mother, her communications with others, her poetry, some of her unsent messages, folders that she had named and accessed, and as my memory began attempting to "call up," as we used to say, the various landscapes in your mother's world I'd walked through for the past fifteen months, I stopped it. I saw how this new way of relating to your mother was encroaching on the way I had remembered your mother. And I knew for sure that your mother was most HER when, indeed, she was living, her head rested in glorious discomfort in the crook of my arm. After she was gone, I became mesmerized by a simulacrum of her.

So I told my memory to stop. I deleted the process. I realized that neither she nor I was going to survive if I continued on in this way. So I begged Daniel to do two things: first, to publish two poems in the fledgling *Cold* written by that woman I'd known a couple of years before ("Remember her?" I said. "She *died?*" Daniel said.), and second, to encrypt with his own code an already encrypted set of data I would send him, which he would then return to me. Here's the particular exchange, which explains the double-lockbox phenomenon.

Daniel: Basically, you want me to lock in my own programmed lockbox a lockbox that you'll send me, then you want me to send it back?

Me: Yes, a double lockbox.

Daniel: Can I ask why?

Me: You can, but I will not answer.

Daniel: Is it illegal or incriminating?

Me: Neither. I promise you it will never cause you any trouble.

Daniel: The government has much more powerful decryption technology than I think we could guess.

Daniel (again, after a pause): Even I can break most run-of-the-mill encryptions.

I took this as a threat at first. But then I called his bluff.

Me: The government doesn't give a sweez about the secrets of two mediocre writers in a mid-major city in a region fast becoming a fiery desert. Encrypt the files and send them back.

Daniel: OK, OK. You owe me one.

I have owed him many, many more than just one. *Coordinates* really had nothing to do with him beyond the programs he wrote for the XiPi, but at first, I included him as a cocreator. When, on the third series, I said that perhaps, instead of cocreator, I'd make him a "contributor," he said it was bad timing, for in Phoenix next month he would be performing/presenting that strange and short-lived *Cold Coordinates* variety show he had developed. For the first time, then, I wondered at what power Daniel actually had.

Daniel Glidden is not a stupid man. That he continued to exert this influence of indebtedness over me suggested that he had more in his possession than just an encryption key. I had trusted Daniel too much, or perhaps proceeded too rashly in those unbalanced days. I began to suspect he had forced open my lockbox.

Since then, Daniel and I have developed a strained dance, in which I am the leader but he's doing the leading. A few years later, he has asked me to teach classes that a man in my position would normally not be asked to teach. Through seven *Coordinates* series he remained a cocreator, though he didn't even know I'd begun the third through seventh until I showed the rough cuts to him and asked for his input, which was always negligible and trifling. He postponed my evaluative review for years; he said this was merciful, but I think he was bent on keeping my salary low.

But his naive messages this morning suggest to me that something else might have been happening all this time. Perhaps I have been acting out of fear instead of resignation. Perhaps Daniel knows nothing, has nothing but the encryption key. Perhaps his willingness to include in *Cold* what work of mine he can was not some way to bolster his own profile—I have long thought I was doing him a favor by sending him critical works and *Coordinates* excerpts to publish—but was, instead, his clumsy, impersonal, but nonetheless genuine attempt at professional exchange. Perhaps Daniel has simply taken at face value what I've offered all these years.

I thus decided to message him to ask for a meeting so we might, finally, face the truth and exorcise these wrinkly old demons. I asked him if he was able to come to my apartment building today. He said he was free now, and so, as far as I know, he's on his way, though, for Daniel, this is a rather vague description of the elaborate and painstakingly slow action of "going somewhere."

26

Outside of the encrypted treasure now guarded by the (weeping? or cackling? we'll soon find out) troll named Daniel, I retained my only guilty pleasure, one benign enough that eventually I found it ineffective as an analgesic.

There is a satellite image of your mother. It is not hidden. I will bring you there now.

It is restricted by obscurity, not by intention; finding it is a matter of knowing the route, not the code. Even if I gave the coordinates to you, you would not be able to find her without my guiding your hands. So, let's begin.

35.817171, -105.740528. These are the coordinates I want you to begin with. They are a part of the most beautiful international language that humans have ever composed. The decimal place down to the millionth is particularly helpful, because we can both (I'm already there, and you're close behind) arrive at a common place roughly ten centimeters square. We won't have trouble finding each other there. It doesn't matter which map you choose for the first part of this search, your birth year or the current year, because we're just going to begin by getting our bearings. Oddly, environmental overhaul seems to have left this small area untouched for the last fifty years.

Ah! Nice to see you here.

We are now hovering above the southwestern edge of an alpine pond called Spirit Lake, as the crow flies about twenty-three kilometers from the gates of the theme park in Santa Fe. Now, depending on what year you're looking at, you'll likely see in your field of vision the blur of forest and the black space of water, and, in between, a thin white line parallel to the lakeshore. That's a long, perfectly straight, surprisingly resilient spruce log, though in the more recent images it has lost its structure and is only a ghost line, but even in the most recent images you can still see it.

Next step. Go to the USGS archive and enter the week (they took photos weekly) that corresponds with exactly seven months before your birthday. Use the same coordinates minus the last three decimals in each. It will spit back at you the file for a slightly zoomed-out picture of our pond, a high-resolution photo of a spot a thousand meters square: Spirit Lake (which is almost perfectly four hundred square meters) is in the middle.

Find, again, your thin white spruce line.

Good.

If you zoom in and look closely, you'll notice that the line is interrupted about a third of the way from the right. Now zoom in on that interruption.

Yes.

You found her.

That interruption is your mother. She's sitting on the spruce log, contemplating the lake. You'll see her brown hair and her white arms. I believe her legs are crossed, but the resolution makes this particular feature difficult to confirm. Where am I in this image? At this particular moment I was back in Albuquerque, teaching a class, I believe. How do I know it's your mother, then? A great question. Hold on to it.

Where to next? Move southward on your map slowly, to the tree line that immediately flanks your pondering mother. This is the beginning of a rather large and totally featureless forest of spruce and ponderosa pine. If, at the tree line, you slowly move to the east, you'll soon encounter an odd angle that looks like a tree has grown a square crown instead of a round one. But this be no tree! This is the roof of the "cabin" where your mother lived for the months of your gestation. It is also the structure where you were supposed to be born. But let's not look in there yet. This is merely a survey expedition.

We'll need to move southward a bit, though not far, to begin this story correctly. Subtract three-thousandths from the decimals in the coordinates for the same week. Now you'll move a kilometer south to 35.814. No, there's nothing wrong, or at least there's nothing wrong on your end, though what you see is an almost perfect horizontal bisection of the image, suggesting some sort of digital corruption. What you're looking at is the northern portion of an immense burn scar that, maybe a year and a half before this photo, was left after a fire roared through these mountains. It is still mostly black in the image you're looking at, though in the most recent images it looks more like a row in a garden.

Humor me while I tell you about burn hermits.

This scar was the legacy left by the first big burn of the modern fire era, and it also was the first burn in New Mexico that the governor labeled "uncontainable," and so called off fire suppression, which saved lives but, even better for the governor, saved tons of money in the short term. The fire burned for weeks, and it totally destroyed the ski area that for decades had justified keeping this particular area of the mountain accessible. Then the mudslides a year later decimated the upper portion of the road to the late ski area. They cleared the one nearest to Santa Fe in order to get people back to their hiking trails, but they encountered another slide about a quarter mile in. They brought in a drone and discovered that something like three-quarters of the upper half of the road had been destroyed, and would, at least for the next few years, continue to suffer from destructive mudslides. Thus, the decision was made by our all-knowing leaders that they would not rebuild in its entirety the road until mudslide danger had been mitigated. Such construction required its own funding and, in a poor state, roads for hikers are simply difficult to justify when a majority of your schools are still using paper books, and the ski area, which had been getting less and less usable snow each year, was only making money before the fire because they had no debt (and they had no debt because they'd built the thing in the 1960s on taxpayer dollars and then charged taxpayers to use it). Not until about eight years ago was the road finally reestablished to within a few kilometers of the old ski basin. Fires burned through the mountains regularly in the years between your mother's death and the rebuilding of the ski road, and they have totally decimated not only the forests but also the tourist culture. Forests grow back fast; tourists, however, remember. A video was circulated in those years of a hiking family literally burning to death while their phone streamed to a satellite their final moments. The mountains emptied out and Santa Fe became largely the park in the old city and its employees.

Burns, however, encourage some long-hidden spores to germinate and grow. Mushrooms and moths and trees that hadn't been seen in decades suddenly sprang up. More importantly for your story, however, was the human springing. Into the mountains all over the West went what came to be known as burn hermits: people who used kilometers-wide burn swaths as buffers for the world. They were not homogeneous in their views besides one—escape. Escape the proliferating internet. Escape pollution. Escape taxes that bought nuke upgrades. Escape Armageddon. Escape unemployment (which rocketed in the Southwest). Escape surveillance. Escape cultural immorality. Escape economic disappointment. Escape their mothers. The movement began near Shasta in California and then moved eastward. A good thick burn scar would greatly reduce and in many cases totally stop the stream of mountain visitors (search for, say, Yosemite's numbers from the last century, and compare them to now), mostly because no one wants to walk for an hour in a charred forest, especially where there are no trails, especially when the uncharred forests before and behind seem ready to ignite. These burn scars made relatively accessible areas "remote." Thus a well-placed burn hermit could be a couple of kilometers from a road but see maybe ten people a year. If he or she avoided being iconized on social media, they could last years out there. Even when the burn healed, what grew up most precociously was a hedge of aspen, not exactly impassable but certainly not pleasant to push through.

Your mother did not intend to be a burn hermit, and I daresay were it not for a singular and totally inane literary event organized by none other than Daniel Glidden, she might still be among us.

So we must go back there. Before Daniel birthed *Cold* into the world, he attempted to organize something akin to a literary think tank. He called it the Albuquerque Semi-Bots, and at first he just needed bodies. He begged me to join, and, because I was living in the foothills and doing nothing but trying to understand how to teach high school by attending stultifying pedagogy meetings at my new job, I agreed, if only just to satisfy my need for intellectual stimulation via deep criticism of other's vain attempts at satisfying their need for intellectual stimulation. I brought a notepad simply to take notes for an essay I planned to write on the demise of the Semi-Bots. I asked Daniel if I could invite your mother too. He asked if she was a writer. I said she was, though I had at that point not read anything she'd written (this was before Daniel's tasteless rendition of her undergrad poems), but for some reason I believed in her ability primarily based on her tattoo—

27

—her tattoo!

Forgive me for withholding it. I'm losing my balance. I must steady the story not with burn hermits nor the Semi-Bots. I will return briefly to the story of your mother and me. It's long healed, by now, the pus-leaking calf. She showed it to me on our first Joe's meeting, just before she tucked the first corner over the hundredth set of silverware, and just before I took my first sip of my third beer ever. I remember it as perhaps one of the most suave moments in an otherwise romantically clumsy life. I said, "You know, I'd love to see that tattoo when it's not hidden under a pus bubble," and she laughed and said, "OK," and came around the bar to where I sat. She had to roll her skinny pants up above her broad thigh, and she grunted audibly in the process. Her brown hair fell forward, the muscles in her arm tensed. Then she turned her back toward me and lifted her leg. I'd never had a woman turn her back to me like that—it was positively crushing. I forced myself, again, to look at her calf.

The writing in the tattoo was stacked, letter by letter, and composed of a wildly complex calligraphy in which the letters seemed to swirl out of nests of curving lines. In the red light of Joe's, it took me a while and a few guesses to make out the vertical and more prominent words: *Orange Under? Orange . . . ? Or range . . . thunder? Vunder?* She laughed and continued folding silverware. I asked her to let me see it again, and I got off the barstool and got very, very close to your mother's beautiful calf, and suddenly I saw it arise from her leg in perfect clarity:

O Strange Wonder!

The exclamation point may or may not have been just a decorative filigree. *O Strange Wonder?* I asked her what that meant. She said it was her favorite line of poetry. When I asked from what poem, she said, "I knew you'd ask me that," and she said she didn't know, exactly. It was a poem that her Romanian (only now does it occur to me that the Eastern Europeans are claiming their own significant territory in this narrative!) grandmother used to recite in accented English on Sunday mornings before she'd make a polenta and sour cream dish that your mother loved but could not remember the name of either. As she walked back around the bar, she said that maybe one other person had asked her which poem it had come from, but for the most part, she said, as soon as people heard it was poetry, they just said, "Nice," and told her about their tattoos. Then she stopped folding silverware and said in a surprisingly serious tone, "If you like me, don't ever tell me where that line is from. I know I could look it up in five minutes. I never have and I never will. I don't want to know." Because I'd already felt the itch to pull out my cell and identify its source, I asked her why.

She said that when she was twelve her grandmother died. But there were so many pictures of her and her grandmother, so many saved messages and files in her grandmother's name, that, by the time she was deep into her teens, she realized she'd forgotten almost everything about her grandmother and now remembered only the pictures and files referring to her grandmother. But that Sunday-morning poem, which she remembered much of, had never been recorded, not in sound or image or writing, and so it was the one remaining memory your mother knew was hers and not a memory of a digitization. Rather than remember the poet who wrote it, or the poem itself, she wanted to remember only her grandmother reciting it, only the words she used (which were probably wrong), only the way she inflected certain parts.

I thought her romanticism quaint and admirable, and I, too, found myself trying to locate important memories that were truly unrepresented in machine code. I found quite a few, but they . . .

. . . ah, I hear now the tinkling of the reception notification.

Daniel Glidden has come.

28

I have returned. Rattled, but ready. For the sake of clarity, I will not yet tell you about the conversation I just had with Mr. Glidden. So, where was I?

"I found quite a few, but they . . ." . . . seeking in my mind undigitized memories.

I found quite a few, but they were all miserable. My father in various public places doing variously embarrassing things. My mother, one winter evening, burying a puppy beneath the dirty snow in the backyard. One memory, of sunlight on snow, was indeed calming, but nothing that I could call up gleamed like the grandmother in the kitchen. I asked if she'd recite the poem for me. She said maybe one day.

O strange wonder, your mother. If there is a singular moment in my life in which I envied anyone with pure and rather wrathless envy, it was then, when your mother held before me not the memory itself but the case she kept it in. It was not a cliché necklace cask; instead, the memory was implanted in her skin, buried in her being, undivorceable, totally unified in one person. And I understood then, though more in gut than in mind, the reason for poetry's demise, and though my *Bot-Poetics* attempted to say the nearly ineffable truth and, in a way, *Coordinates* circled around it for years, I fear that such divorce, such separation, is perhaps the one thing that cannot be narrativized, because it is precisely the empty spot, the absence where narrative demands presence, the thing that makes life "feel" like life, and the thing that can only be approximated in our thousands-of-years-old code.

29

The global burns and the sea rises and the destroyed coastal cities and the quiet but widely destructive politics of that time revealed to us regular Joes the incalculable emptiness of the universe, the space just beyond the edge of the line (like the black screen at the end of even the cheesiest of old movies) in which we humans drop off but time and matter remains steady. Many of us had invested fully in the end, in the idea that beyond us was perhaps nothing. The fertility rate had dropped "suddenly" (but not that suddenly) in every Western country; the "liberal arts" had seen an unprecedented spike in interest; concerts and festivals and church services proliferated. There was a real desire to see the present more clearly, because we feared that tomorrow we'd wake up to nothing. On the literary level, there was widespread local organization even while the big publishers died out. Everyone was publishing; screenreaders totally leveled the playing field; "books" were everywhere and nowhere. Around the more serious writers sprouted clubs, meetings, societies, tiny fragmented gatherings that communicated via cell and forums, reading groups. The Semi-Bots, and then the subsequent cloud of people hovering around *Cold*, were the flowering bud and fruit, respectively, of this last cultural harvest. When I told your mother about the Semi-Bots meeting, she was excited.

The first meeting was uneventful. Your mother brought the undergrad literary magazine she published in and read one of her peers' poems, not her own. The poem was about floating trash islands in the Pacific. It was fine, and would have done well for max end points in a lower-level NNP class. Beyond its topic I don't remember a single bit of it, though, and prefer not to go searching for it, for fear of coming up against your mother's anonymous work and feeling again a fury at Daniel that might make it even harder to ask for his decryption.

But, since we are allowing things through the dam, I see that it is impossible to not recount the moment later that night, after the meeting, when, in the front room of Joe's, Daniel asked to see the lit mag your mother carried with her. She provided a disclaimer: It contained a lot of real stinkers. Daniel said he'd seen a lot of stinkers in his time and that they didn't bother him. But Daniel had already drained an entire beer (oh, if only it had been the Mormon-killing kind!) and had asked for another, so he began reading some of the more egregious mistakes in the journal. He read aloud three haikus about a dog in a Chinese family. People laughed at the first and second, so, encouraged, he attempted to read the third in an ambiguous Asian accent. Then, in his normal voice, Daniel began to read aloud the next poem, written by an anonymous author about a dead bird outside an urban window. Halfway through, he executed a giant, lip-flapping, deep-snorting sniffle, tilting his head and shoulders back as if emerging from the blackest waters of sadness. He couldn't finish the sniffle, though, because he began laughing, and others laughed too, not really at the poem but mostly because they glad to be free of the racial disaster he had previously seemed headed toward. He took a sip of his beer and said the thing about killing Mormons, and finally, normal, non-Daniel conversation resumed. Your mother stood at the bar for eight minutes without turning around. I did not go to her because it was only at minute seven that I realized that seven minutes was three minutes too many and the seven minutes meant that the dead bird must have been outside her window.

I sent Daniel an evil message that night, slashing giant holes in the tires of his new group and his ridiculous idea for a journal. Even though I wasn't sure then, I told him that the poem he'd read and mocked was your mother's. He wrote back "omg no way." But Daniel had no God anymore, he was now behind the back of God. I just told him he'd perhaps trampled on the last of an endangered species, which was a bit overblown. The poem wasn't that good. He apologized exorbitantly, said he'd contact your mother, begged me to come to his next group meeting.

Your mother messaged me a day later saying she'd talked to Daniel and agreed to attend the meeting the next month. Daniel told her some author would be there. He had written a book she was interested in. She did not say anything about her poem.

In between the first and second Semi-Bot meetings was a universe of violent and vivacious life: four David Geores evenings, the fourth being the bosque fire. After that were a number of beautiful moments with your mother, including a night on the West Mesa. That night, tucked into the mesa's black cloak, we talked about many things, mostly about religion and God, which we seemed to agree on in theory but not in practice. Neither of us thought religion was good or God particularly real, but for some reason she said (and this she spoke as we stood facing each other with our bare feet buried in the mesa sand in the moon dark) that she felt a kinship with religious people because they believed in something that everyone else thought was stupid. I asked what it was that she believed in that others thought stupid, and she said there wasn't anything in particular, there was only the experience: She *felt* like someone who believed something that everyone else thought stupid. I laughed and said that was like saying you could feel like a poet having never written a poem. And she said, "Yes, actually. That's a good way of putting it." At that moment, I yanked my feet from the sand (there was a tiny cactus spine in my middle toe) and stepped toward her, and she, at the same moment, stepped toward me.

I must stop there, reroute, not for the sake of the story but, instead, for my own. These moments with your mother will remain undigitized or narrativized; I will retain them in the same way that she retained her grandmother's Sunday-morning kitchen.iel.

30

Instead, I present to you a plot point.

You undoubtedly are waiting patiently to hear about the meeting I had with Daniel an hour or so ago. For we have followed him, at this point, for years. He has become a character, a hologram, and, I suppose, so too have I. And as Daniel and I grow into characters in a story you're reading for the first time, a story in which you're an important but unrecognized sub-subplot, I feel building in me the natural resentment of a storyteller. Now that you're practically standing on my doorstep, I feel even more than before the gravity of the demand you're making on my story. Your mother flooded into my life and has never fully drained out. I sense that you—tacitly, sure, but quite sincerely—would like for me to open the gates a bit wider, to release more into you. You came to Albuquerque for this reason. This is natural, and it's a tension that I've long exploited in my life.

Resentment is at the center of a good narrative. It's the tension that both drives the narrative but also keeps the impossible pair (the narrator and the reader) going together along the same path. The narrator resents the reader for demanding, always, *more*, as flattering as it may be, for they know that they cannot, ultimately, sate insatiability. The reader, likewise, resents the narrator for concluding, for finishing, for pulling the well dry and shrugging. I think you know that this moment is approaching, that there is no story that can satisfy the empty truth about your search, which is, to put it crudely: Your mother is dead and can only return to you in memories that are not your own. You and I will part ways and, if I release everything to you, I will feel emptied and you will feel only a little less empty, and we will continue living our lives in these only slightly altered states: attempting to dam up stories about existence that make us feel full, managing these reservoirs so those who come to drink from them aren't allowed to suck up every last drop.

But here stands (well, stood) Daniel. We cannot continue to bar him from appearing. As attentive as you are to my words, your head will turn to see him stride into fifteenth-floor reception, where I told him I'd meet him, while I am descending on the fast lift, watching the digital floor numbers fade into one another. I had decided to conduct our meeting on the thirty-fifth-floor drone approach. Neutral territory.

When I arrived, Juan Miguel, the young man at the front desk, was talking to Daniel about a "glitch" in the apartment network that had in the past allowed people to use the freight lift after hours without the requisite key code and had just then, apparently, allowed Daniel free access from the street. I heard the last bit as I walked up. I said to Juan Miguel that someone had come onto the forty-second floor from the freight elevator just the night before. They had? Who was it? Juan Miguel asked. I told him I had no idea. They were staying in 42-2. He typed something and stared at the screen. Yes, he said, there was a preauthorized occupant for these days. (I ignored the solicitation in his meaningful vagueness.) But he couldn't understand how she had basically skipped reception and used the freight elevator without the code. I said it seemed like something he'd better figure out.

"Yes," Juan Miguel said with a solemnity I'd never seen, "I suppose it is." He then turned around and walked into the reception area's unseen bowels. I considered hollering in his wake that such a reaction was probably *exactly* how an unknown woman skipped reception, but Daniel was standing there watching in silence and I thought it better not to give him any more fodder for the cruelty case he had long been building against me.

"Let's go up to some place a bit more private," I said to Daniel. He had on the same style of clothes he'd been wearing for forty years: jeans (though without holes) and a clean, unwrinkled, but ultimately too-small cotton shirt that really only served to show how much he (and by proxy, we) had aged. I noticed, especially and for the first time, the divots in the crook of both of his elbows. The holes there were pronounced, three or four centimeters deep, bordered on each side by felty skin that folded over the two tendons of his inner forearm. God, how old we are, I thought. How ironic it is that these two old men are meeting to talk about their undead twenties, how strange it is that they walk so much nearer the precipice of death and still can think of nothing but the mountain passes of their youth.

Daniel looked at me, still leaning on the reception counter. "Well, what is this about, Joe? I'd like to think . . ." he said. I remembered then, in his sarcastic ramble about pleasantries and beer, that it had probably been a decade since we had had a face-to-face conversation, just us, outside his office (he never came to mine).

I told him I'd "let him know" shortly. He didn't catch the joke. Or he did, but he couldn't see the humor.

We didn't speak in the elevator, and by the time we got the thirty-fifth floor, I imagine he had worked up a number of scenarios to fear, or perhaps was preparing to suppress his joy in hearing about my early retirement. He followed behind me through the incense-smelling meditation room and, when we arrived at the doors to the drone approach, he said, "Joe, that's enough, tell me what this is about." I asked if we could just step out onto the landing, and then I would tell him.

"Hell no," he said. "I'm even more afraid of heights now than I was as a younger person." I'd forgotten about this too. Or maybe I hadn't. "And there are barely even railings out there."

"We'll stay near the doors," I said. "The fence is quite strong."

"Why? Why can't we just talk right here, inside, where I won't get sick to my stomach? What's the matter? Are you spooked by that woman? Did she call you?"

I saw that he was, on some level, relishing this, though he was forcing his face to seem almost caring. I noted the hint—mostly in the risen eyebrows—of pleasure. I hated this. I hated that, yet again, Daniel Glidden was getting his way. Out on the drone approach I felt unfettered, triumphant. All options were open; there, time ended its protestations. But in that incense-and-sweat-reeking room I felt hateful and trapped.

He had something I needed. I saw that he had no innocence left, at least none concerning me, and that this situation was unprecedented in our lives, and probably would be the last thing we ever had to do with one another.

"Daniel. Thirty-odd years ago, I asked you to encrypt a mass of data for me."

Daniel feigned searching his memory, then feigned remembering. "Yes," he said, "I remember that. The 'double lockbox.'"

"Indeed. I need you to open your portion. It's for her. My lockbox contains tons of information and files having to do with her mother, and she deserves to have them."

"What happened between you and . . . her mother . . . back then?" Instead of looking at me, however, he looked out the window.

"That's not something I want to go into now."

Then he laughed. His eyes shone. "Is, is . . . that woman, the one I had dinner with, your *daughter?*"

"No."

"Joe!" He ran his hand through his remaining hair. I would have almost preferred laughter over his seriousness. "Can you be sure?"

I hesitated because I heard the elevator doors open across the room. I looked toward the hallway, and I saw someone slowly materialize. It was the woman from Hungarian door #2.

"Can I help you?" I yelled toward her, hoping to end this little interruption quickly. She stopped and shifted her weight and turned her head as if to go another direction, but then realized that the only direction to go was ours.

"Oh, I'm sorry," she said. "Is this reception?"

"It is not."

"Forgive me," she said. She stood there for a moment longer, as if she had another question. Then: "Are you the man from the forty-second floor?"

I now could tell that there was a hint, a wisp, of an accent—it was in the phrase "Are you," which sounded more like the trisyllabic "ahr-duh-yoo."

"Yes," I said.

"Did you come into the apartment this morning, where I am staying?"

"Did I what?"

"Did you come into the apartment this morning, where I am staying?"

"No."

"Someone came into the apartment this morning when I was in the bedroom. The apartment . . ."

I felt Daniel looking at me.

"Ma'am, I don't know who came into the apartment this morning where you are staying. But it probably has something to do with the fact that you are not the owner of that apartment, you arrived at an extremely odd hour, and you totally bypassed the normal check-in policies. My guess is that someone concerned about the security here checked the apartments, probably based on my signaling to them late last night that you had mysteriously emerged from the freight elevator and entered into the apartment of my Hungarian neighbors."

"All right, Joe," Daniel said quietly, only to me, turning now toward the window. "That's fine. Just let her go."

"Anyway," I said, and tried to moderate my tone into softness, "I am trying to finish up a discussion with my colleague here. But there are security cameras in the entryways of all the rooms, of course, and I'm sure Juan Miguel at reception would gladly check to see who it was that entered the apartment this morning."

She looked at me in a way that I couldn't understand. She seemed like she wanted to say something more but then looked at Daniel, pursed her lips, turned, and walked out.

Daniel was staring out into the sun.

"Listen, Daniel. The woman is not my child."

Daniel shrugged, toed the metal frame at the bottom of the window.

"Don't you remember what happened with Angela?"

This seemed to confuse him, maybe even anger him.

"What does Angela have to do with it?"

". . . don't you remember why she left?"

"You never told me why she left."

"We couldn't have children."

"Sure, but that's not really a valid excu—thing to say . . . anymore . . . I mean, with all the technology . . ."

"My testicles, Daniel." I was becoming very, very impatient. "I have varicose veins and rotten balls and they prevented successful conception. I refused to get the corrective surgery."

Daniel froze and stared at me. This was genuine. Finally, he said, almost in a whisper, "Refused?"

Daniel's poetic life had all but stopped after *Cold* had begun steaming along. But twenty years or so after the magazine started, a series of anonymous poems—bot produced, it seemed—ran over a couple of issues that basically lamented isolation and childlessness and missed opportunities with some long-ago tryst. I knew the poems were Daniel's. I had forgotten about them, until I saw how he looked at me when he repeated my refusal.

"Daniel. It doesn't matter *what* I did, because this was years after I met that woman's mother."

"I see," he said. Then he looked down, and I could no longer read his pain. We stood there in silence. After a minute or so, Daniel looked up at me. He seemed to want to say something and, for the first time in our long history, it seemed to me that he decided against saying it.

"Do you have your cell?" he asked, instead.

"What do you mean?"

"Your cell? Do you have it with you?"

"Of course."

"Give it to me."

He took out his cell and then took mine from my hand, then just as quickly handed it back and said, "Turn off the hand rec," then took it back once I had. I stood there for a minute or two as he tapped the twin screens with both thumbs.

"There," he said. "The encryption program I wrote back then is yours. I'm deleting it from my cell—see?" He held it up to my face, and it was, in fact, being removed. "I have never, ever, in all those years, used it to decrypt anything, Joe." I could see that he was (of course) leaking tears. "I know you don't trust me, but I never would have done that."

I stared at him.

"Are we done?" he asked.

We were.

Finally.

31

I doubted very seriously that the pseudo-Hungarian would pursue the surveillance camera path, and had she, I doubted even more that Juan Miguel would relent to her request, unless she somehow knew the particular ways to play the Juan Game. And it is to this little logistical sadness that we now must attend.

Juan Miguel, and his father before him, perform extra-regulatory favors for people if they participate fully in the Juan Game. In fact, he (Juan Miguel) seems to believe that rule bending and regulation slicing is part of his job. He was, after all, trained by his father, the infamous Juan (just Juan) who now is, thankfully, dead. Juan was an absolutely maddening man, hired among the original staff before the building's grand opening. Juan had been educated as an old-fashioned PhD in some South American country that no longer exists (I forget which), but his refugee status here and his, at first, rather limited command of English resulted in his taking a job for which he was certainly overqualified except in his ability to communicate his overqualification. This made him feel inferior in complicated ways and, I think, caused him to develop the massively complex Juan Game.

He was married, but his wife I never saw. He had more than one child—Juan Miguel has referred before to his brothers and sisters—but Juan Miguel is the only one I've encountered, and even he showed up suddenly eight or nine years ago, draped in a slightly-too-large teenager's suit, and was put to work perpetually shining the preposterous marble patchwork of the reception floor.

Juan Miguel learned from his father what I called the "fatherboard" trait. In the beginning, however, there was the motherboard. The big building ran entirely on an enormous computer housed on the forty-third floor. That motherboard controlled all things: lights, fire suppression, generators, trash removal, sewage and water, security cameras, SD parking and maintenance, solar gain repression, sound cancellation, even the regulation of the damn automatic toilet cleaners. The list goes juan. Juan soon installed himself originally as the "fatherboard," the social switchboard that gives life and meaning and narrative to the motherboard. This informal advisor to the queen can, at first, seem benign. He might, for example, mention to you as you stride toward the garage elevator that he had noticed last night that your entryway lights had been on override and were still aglow at 2 a.m., and so he had overridden the override, to save energy.

The first thing you need to know (and you *will* need to know this) about the Juan Game is that Juan acts with impunity, even though he claims, even complains, to be hamstrung by regulation and social norm. Overriding a light override is easy for him, without even using the front door security cameras (which, of course, he can gain access to "in extreme necessity," as the residential contract nebulously stipulates). As mildly invasive as this might seem, he is doing nothing more than a computer might do and does, which is observe your patterns and attempt to mitigate anomalies.

But then! Juan woud likely say, when he next sees you, that he noticed that you almost immediately overrode his override of your original override. (You balk at this linguistic tangle; he has planned for this.) So, defeated, he suspended the CPS and allowed you full control until the lights are unnecessary after sunrise. He then would smile as if asking a question that he ought not ask. The accurate response to this, which I learned from years with Juan, is a nod, silence, and a quick shot back, which, for me, was often inquiring as to whether my car was on its way toplevel. Calling up my car after seeing me in the lift cam was one of Juan's actual duties. If my car was late, it suggested he hadn't seen me on the lift cam, which suggested he had not been watching, which suggested, simply, he hadn't been doing the simplest part of his job.

Others, however, have not learned how to exit the Juan Game, and Juan Miguel has raised his father's invention to something like poetry. Once, while I was waiting on an important delivery, I watched a fascinating, if somewhat alarming, discussion between Juan Miguel and another resident. A young man from the underfloors (cheaper and many-bedroomed and heavily marketed to wealthier U students), probably a spoiled underachiever from a state with better education, walked by with that vague, shortsighted indirection that indicates someone using those idiotic celltacts or whatever they call them (they are the bane of the U teacher's existence). Juan Miguel spoke up and the young man startled a bit, blinked his eyes, and turned.

"Sir, your door was left slightly ajar last night, and when the computer alerted me to the issue, I discovered that someone had left a small shoe in between the door and the jamb."

"Oh. Yeah?" The young man seemed to finally succeed in focusing his eyes. I was near the door to the drone approach and I couldn't see whether or not he appeared incredulous. To leave apartment doors ajar was prohibited in our building, and was also just stupid. Something strange had happened once with a snake on the underfloors.

"Yessir. I was a bit perplexed. I, of course, considered the fact that perhaps you had intended to leave that door ajar." This was the portion of the Juan Game in which the master slowly lulled the player to sleep by exerting evidence of his superior intelligence.

"Aha," the young man said. Stumped.

I marveled, then, at Juan Miguel's likeness to his father, and saw how fully involved the younger was in this intragenerational game. Though I didn't get the syntax right, I did predict the gist of what Juan Miguel said next.

"Leaving doors ajar is prohibited, sir, so I removed the shoe." He bent down and brought out the shoe, which could have and certainly should have been left there in the apartment. It was, unsurprisingly, a woman's shoe. It had many hanging cords.

The cheap silvery color and the hanging cords. Those were the thing. Juan Miguel would have left any other shoe.

"Oh, sorry," the young man said, and took the shoe that Juan Miguel held out. There was a moment of pause. I understood, then, what was probably happening. The stats for one's apartment are constantly being aggregated and updated by the CPS. When someone moves in, they have the option of choosing "users" for the stats app, which is basically deciding who gets access to this information. At my previous apartment—the one I shared with Angela—I used the information only a couple of times, once to determine whether or not Angela was lying to me while I was on a *Coordinates* run, and another time to see if one of her friends had indeed left the apartment, meaning it was safe for me to return. It was much easier and simpler to use than the video archive, because, for example, in an instant one could see precisely the numbers of entrances and exits, and their exact time stamps. The young man's parents or overseers, I'm guessing, had access to these stats, and perhaps even used them against him. The clever shoe-in-the-door trick would cast enough legitimate smoke into the stats, even if it caused an error.

Any typical and professional receptionist / building manager would have ended it there. Visitors shod in any way were certainly permitted. But I think the young man picked up on what Juan Miguel was trying to communicate by handing him the dainty shoe.

"My friend . . . I have a friend that . . ." the young man began, still not sure how to play, "feels somewhat intimidated . . . by . . . uh, the reception area, and sometimes she has to leave in the middle of the night . . . and she doesn't want to bother you up here, so I just give her the freight-lift code to get her to the street." This did not explain why she'd left her shoe. The young man was lost.

Juan Miguel smiled. "It all compiles perfectly, sir. Rather than give her the freight-lift code—which now I must change—just tell her that it is better if she checks in with me, whether she is coming or going. I can override your door lock, for example, if this is what you would like. Or I can override the CPS."

"The CPS?" This poor fool had probably barely passed his mainschool exams.

"The computer tracks entrances and exits, and that information is available to the owners of the apartment. Are you the owner, sir? "

"My . . ." God, Juan was good. "Yes. We are."

"Then, for the sake of simplicity, it is better to suspend its tracking when there's an erratic but temporarily regular activity, otherwise it learns bad behaviors." Juan Miguel smiled.

"Oh." Long pause. "O—K," the young man said. He nodded. "I'll tell her just to check—which nights do you work again?"

"Six Monday through twenty-one Friday, sir."

"Monday through Friday."

"Yes, but Hillary, who's here Friday, Saturday, and Sunday, follows the same basic procedures. I'll make a note here and let her know. Which room are you in?"

The young man told him and began to walk away slowly, back in the direction he'd come.

"Sir!" Juan Miguel hollered after him. The young man turned. He had wrapped the shoe in its own cords and held it like dead thing. "Of course, overrides are part of the stats, and the management company in Denver sets a quota for overrides. So, if this is something that . . . if your friend will be visiting often, it might be best if we considered an alternative . . ."

This is where it all had been headed. I actually smiled, deeply impressed. Even his father would have been baffled by this long game. The young man stared. Juan Miguel glanced at me.

"We'll talk about it some other time, sir. I'm glad we worked it out."

I never could understand precisely why Juan Miguel wanted to become so involved in the residents' seedy lives. As far as I know, he's never asked for money, though I'm sure he receives it here and there. Somehow, I don't think it's about money. I suppose it's only natural that certain inexplicable tendencies are passed on and even concentrated between generations. His troglodytic father, spy bot though he was, never even hinted at an expected bribe or a favor beyond a positive performance review, which everyone but me gave him. (This infuriated him. Once, when I picked up a package from him, I discovered that it had been torn on three sides. I asked him about it, and he said that he'd accidentally ripped it and was sorry. Then he said, "Sir, on the performance review you'll get today, there is a line that says 'Cares utmost for residents' packages and possessions,' and I think it would be only right for you to put 'not at all.'" Of course, the performance review appeared on our doorscreens only twenty minutes later, and I saw his strategy immediately. He had never before so much as bent a package corner, and so I'm sure got only perfect marks on that front. He knew that I would, out of pity, not score him "not at all" on the package question, but, perhaps, "needs improvement," which would inevitably single my anonymous survey out, thus proving that I was the one person who even considered giving him anything below immaculate marks.) Each of the Juans were, as my mother sometimes called my father, a caged hawk.

32

I followed Daniel in silence down to reception, and he walked away without saying any sort of farewell. This was fine by me.

Juan Miguel watched Daniel walk out and then asked if he could do anything for me. I asked him why he was here on a Saturday. Wasn't it Hillary's shift?

He said she'd had some business to attend to, and he was happy to substitute for her.

"Ah," I said. Then I dove in. "Did the woman from 42-2 come down here yet?"

"She did, sir. We got everything squared away. I'm not sure how she bypassed us last night."

I hesitated and watched Juan Miguel's eyes. I had practiced for this.

"Juan Miguel, isn't it against the rules to allow guests to arrive unaccompanied after midnight?"

"Yes, it is." His surety was buying him time.

"I understand that she was preauthorized, Juan. But if she didn't stop by reception, how did she get the lift code?"

"I am still unsure about that. But I think she probably got it from the residents—"

"The residents who aren't residents, but who are owners, and which class of people—as it stipulates in the contract—do not have 'admission privileges,' so as basically to avoid this precise unfortunate situation?"

"I am going to change the lift code this afternoon. Your key will be updated."

"To be honest, Juan, I'm a bit worried. Just last week in that place in Uptown, some nonresident walked in with a boning knife and destroyed the knees of an old retired person on the upper floor, which apparently was a code-access-only floor. No stairs. Just like our building."

"Yes, I think I heard about that." Fool. You can't have already heard news I only now invented. But he was a skilled player, so he made a powerful move: "I did notice, sir, that this morning you unlocked 42-2 and—"

But I had prepared for this: "Because you simply seem unable to manage the night shift, Juan, I went in to 42-2 this morning—the owners, you'll recall, gave me their hardkey, obviously for good reason.

After seeing the suitcase at the door, I realized that it probably wasn't a criminal. Though, I must say, I was prepared for the worst. I didn't have the heart to walk into the bedroom where the person was staying, though."

"Yes, that sounds like a tough position." Juan's hands were sliding back and forth along the edge of the faux marble counter, and he looked up and out through the massive glass wall onto the drone approach, from whence no help would ever come. He had realized the gravity of being caught.

"Here we are, then, sir," he said. He was very serious. He looked directly into my eyes. His black irises communicated his defeat.

"Here we are." I had to stay in control. Gloating would not get me what I wanted.

Juan Miguel was silent. He saw that I was like him. Then he sighed.

The fact that you're reading this means that I have, finally, cashed out of the Juan Game. It only took a few minutes of conversation after that.

To you, I can say only good luck.

33

Some useful information: Your mother did not like SD cars. They were, admittedly, not as safe as they would become, but they were just slightly more safe than a nation of wheel-wielding, cell-addicted, holler-singing, pedal-mashing maniacs. I had a trad car in undergrad, but I had hated all of it: the laborious, endless managing of the wheel, the obsessive attention to speed and lane. Mine was a "midway," so it was not like some old-fashioned movie in which a person could pull on the gearshift and rocket forward into a stomach-sloshing turn. My midway managed everything but the helm: It reined in speed surges, it braked automatically if you weren't paying attention. An SD car was about as natural an evolution as a computer was an evolution of the typewriter. People bellyached about the collapse of society, but then they realized they could message their friends happily while commuting to work, or they could leave their Wyoming sheep farm, go to sleep in their "SleepD," and wake up to the sunrise at their backs and the Pacific Ocean throwing itself at the beach just a hundred paces in front of them. Your mother, though, ever the romantic, missed what she called the "tactile" feel of trad cars and often talked about getting hers back up and running and taking a long trad trip, just like in the movies.

Hers was not at all up and running. The gas tax of those years had beached tons of vehicles whose owners couldn't get waivers for EBT gas or couldn't afford to use EBT credits on gas. Much to-do was made about the first full city block that was "carless," which meant no parking, and only SD pickups and city bus access. It was officially named Garden Block, but it is known to residents and outsiders alike as the GNB, which I think is an evolution of the long-standing Albuquerque tendency to change names into homophonic nonsensicalities, best exemplified by the opening lines of one of my favorite bad student's personal narratives: "I'm not rich . . . I grew up in Albuquerque's Guard and Block." The GNB, people say, has a dedicated Police Drone unit, individual, rotored members of which are consistently downed by its innovative and organized residents. Once, they tossed thousands of yards of fishing filament back and forth between seven stories of opposing balconies looking in on a central courtyard where complicated sublegal deals were often struck. They wrecked four drones (surveillance drones, then, were about as effective as nosy eight-year-olds) before a unit of officers walked in with long-plume torches and melted all the filament, though not without two officers (as a locally popular video from the fourth floor shows) getting badly pocked on their cheeks with melted globs of filament falling down like last-century confetti.

Your mother moved in to the GNB when it was still relatively upstanding. It was a city block of apartment buildings, all of them eight stories, and each apartment block was a different primary color. I don't remember much about them besides these little alcoves that, at the time, people thought so wonderful: They were bathtub-sized indentations in the exterior walls, maybe four of them in a single block's facade, in which they inserted, preposterously, various desert plants. Eventually, they replanted all these alcoves with cholla cactus, which is nothing more than a hip-tall, branching stem covered in thick spines. I've heard at least one rap song refer to a childhood in the Cholla Projects. For the same reasons that I pay almost nothing for my penthouse, your mother paid very little for her room in the overbuilt and overly innovative Albuquerque development.

What matters, though, is that there was no parking. At the time, the GNB had an off-site parking lot in a part of the old fairgrounds where residents could park their cars. Your mother had a nonworking Chevrolet truck, a hand-me-down from your great-grandfather, who had driven it in the latter years of the last century. She had driven it from Texas to New Mexico a few years before, but some pump or valve had ruptured and was beyond her repair skill or budget. So it sat in the off-site GNB parking lot, rotting in the dry Albuquerque sun. She occasionally rode the bus over to see it and talk to it, or something equally as preposterous. On the Saturday after I returned from my first *Coordinates* trip, she sent me a message that said, "Meet me at the off-site GNB lot, sector G8. Blue Chevrolet truck about fifteen stalls south of the ice cream truck." This was by far the most mysterious thing I'd ever received from your mother. I hadn't seen her in over a week.

I didn't want to park the new XiPi near such a cesspool of dying combustion engines, so I reluctantly took the bus, where I was forced to stand next to a potbellied man who scrolled through pornography on his cell and showed the occasional specimen to his bandannaed compatriot, who giggled raspily.

When I arrived at the lot, I walked through a portal in the cement block wall. What lay before me was a sort of man-made monstrosity. I was in sector S, from what I could determine from the faded signs, and stretched out before me was a sea of vehicles, broken windowed, bird spattered, wheelless. I walked through the rows and tried to spot another sign. I saw a couple of tow trucks moving in some far-off rows. I walked farther, zigzagging through models and makes long forgotten: squashed Mitsubishi trucks, Chryslers and Toyotas with headlights dangling like put-out eyes, three or four Saturns. I bumped into dry-rotting mirrors as I stared in desperation up at the light poles. The signs that marked the sectors made no sense. Though I thought I had walked in a relatively straight vector, I encountered sector T on the other side of sector H.

I stopped near a new XiPi (red, and, in such a vast wasteland, a sitting duck) and spun slowly around, scanning the horizon. A few portable shade canopies were gathered ten or fifteen rows to the southwest, so I moved in that direction, thinking it was some administrative station.

It was not. It was a group of four guys, two of whom stuck out from underneath a pair of Volvos parked next to one another. This was before the incessant wildfires; the sun blazed white above us. They all wore very clean clothes and had their shirts tucked in. They almost looked like they were on their way to a country ball or something. They spoke Spanish primarily, but, while one guy tinkered with a complicated car part that looked like a steel heart, another guy told me in singsongy English that he hadn't even known those signs were meant to organize the lot. He just thought they were left over from the old state fair.

"So," I said, "there's no way you can help me find G8?"

"Ay, no," he said. "No. It's impossible."

"How do people find their way around here?"

"We know the cars. Like . . ." he kicked the shoe of one of the men under the truck and asked something in Spanish. The other guy said, "Bucket." Then the original guy said, "Bucket. Like bucket truck. There. See that truck?" He pointed to a spot over the tops of cars, and I saw the bucket truck of some defunct private networking company. "We use the cars," he said.

I asked him about the ice cream truck.

"Ice?" he asked. "ICE truck . . ." He looked down, got a little fidgety. "No sé. No ICE truck, man."

Then the guy under the Volvo said something and my conversant perked up.

"Ah! Helados! Yes, yes." He turned on his heel and pointed in a different direction. "There are three. Three helados. Red one over there. See it? A blue-and-green one very far away, on the other side, güey."

I think I saw a tall box of an old ice cream truck in the distance.

"See the red one?"

I nodded. I thanked them and began walking.

It was the red one. I finally found your mother, about nine cars over, sitting in her blue truck. Nothing was broken or missing from its exterior. She had the door ajar. She was drinking bottled beer. I did not mention the fact that she was nine stalls, not fifteen as she'd said, from the ice cream truck because—and I am reluctant to fork over an image so sanguine, but out of sheer duty I feel it necessary to release it to you—your mother was perhaps never as beautiful as I saw her then. Only her bare brown shoulders (she wore a white tank top) and her slightly narrow head were visible above the old truck's dash. She had on big black sunglasses and her teeth were impossibly white. She smiled at me. She had her hair pulled back, as usual, but the ponytail had been forced up a bit by the seat. On the steering wheel, I could just barely see one of her feet with the short, stubby toes.

"Hey, amigo!" she said in an exaggerated Hispanic, now extinct accent that we sometimes called Burqueño.

I smiled and leaned on the hood. It was not as hot as I'd thought it be. I told her I'd seen her uncles over there with the Volvos (jokes about her father's Mexican heritage and double-digit sibling count had already become a language of love between us). She joked back and said this was where they had their family reunions. I climbed in the passenger seat. Her brown legs, not long or thin, were impossibly attractive all tangled up in the steering wheel. She had the six-pack next to her. She offered me a beer and I said no thanks. Then she begged, so I took one and twisted the cap off. The beer was warm. I pretended to sip it.

I said I'd never done anything like this before, and she said she liked to come check on the truck every once in a while. Across the aisle from her (the truck had been backed in for the view, I suppose), was an even older Volkswagen, flanked on one side by a Kia and on the other by a Pontiac SUV that looked like a june bug. She said she liked to look at the three cars in front of her and smell the off-gassing of the probably toxic dashboard materials of decades past and imagine that she was back in a time when there were no cells or computers, besides the enormous ones in warehouses. She said something then that young people all over the country were saying at the time: "I feel like I don't belong in these times, you know?" I didn't know, but I nodded. She scratched the back of her knee and then let her hand rest on the zipper of her jean shorts, which bisected perfectly the forbidden and magnetic space that on Barbie dolls was needed to accommodate the pins that held the legs on.

She asked me then if we could go on a trip together.

I said definitely. I was beginning work the following week, but I would have considered the impossible—calling in "sick"—to get a trip with your mother in.

She mentioned the Grand Canyon.

I wouldn't have cared if we went in circles around Albuquerque for days, so I said that the Grand Canyon sounded wonderful.

"I work all week, though," she said. "And it's too far to do on a weekend."

I thought about it. We could take the XiPi over on Friday night. We could sleep while the XiPi piloted us to the rim, then we could spend Saturday hiking its rim and maybe take the new tram across. We'd ride back the next night, and that Monday I'd start my job as a high school teacher.

She said she didn't think she'd be able to sleep in a car that was being driven by Big Co. I said of course she could, she was sleeping in a society that was. And the XiPi's seats reclined fully into a sort of narrow bed the width of the car. She said she didn't know. I said it was the Chinese version of Big Co., anyway. She laughed. Lemme think about it, she said.

We talked more about trad cars (then they were just "cars") and SDs (in Albuquerque: "esdies"). We talked a bit more than I would have liked about Daniel and the Semi-Bots, whose second meeting was approaching on the Tuesday of my first week of school. She was excited to go, because the author that Daniel had secured was a post-U student from the Environmental Department who, on a research trip in the charred mountains outside Santa Fe, had discovered an older man living in a hut just beyond a burn scar. The post-U fellow wrote a book about the burn hermit.

"You want to be a burn hermit?" I asked her.

"No," she said, and finished the second bottle. Then she turned to me, put one elbow on the steering wheel, stuffed one foot underneath her. "I just like that they exist. They're pretty fascinating, don't you think? Just living out there alone, no technology. Sounds great."

I made some quibbling point about log cabins and freeze-dried food being rather technologically advanced, if considered in the whole scope of human existence. She smiled and shrugged and said something in words that I've not retained perfectly but whose punchline I'll always remember: The only scope she was interested in was hers, she said. Then she said, "And yours. Sort of." I took her hand.

You can imagine what followed. At some point, somebody yelled a greeting in a distant row and we sat up and looked through the windshield and saw that the mountains were aflame with the unburning pink fire of the sunset.

We walked to her place from there, and I told her about my family (depressing), my brother (less depressing than my father), my life after moving (much less depressing), and why I'd chosen the NNP program after I worked three years in the administrative department of a vegetable processing plant where my dad worked (*Joe* was the desk guy at an asparagus cannery, but bot poetry meant I could be *JP Stone*). Finally, I told her that I thought I was falling in love with her.

The suitcase/sec-cam debacle has cast into serious doubt my memory of this moment, as it seems to me that I actually said something like "I am, I believe, I am . . . falling in love with you." I'm willing to allow, however, that I may have said nothing.

I know for sure that she did not say she loved me on that walk, because the next week was filled with a mix of triumph and dread about her saying it. But this strange mixture of emotion could have the result of a situation in which I said it (triumph) and she didn't reciprocate (dread), or, alternatively, I didn't say it and should have (dread) and planned to on the trip (triumph) that, just then, on that streetlamp-lit walk to her parking-lot-less apartment in the future ghetto, solidified.

"Let's go to the Grand Canyon. In the XiPi. We don't need no stinking sleep," she said. She squeezed my hand.

Are words necessary? Must we say everything, really? A good story, I tell my students, can be judged by what's left unsaid.

34

I was ecstatic, miserable. I couldn't wait for Friday, but I imagined it with holy trembling. I occupied the week with work on the first draft of the first season of *Coordinates*. As I lay in bed those nights, waiting for a joke or pointless banter to tinkle in from your mother's cell, I allowed myself to plan some things for the ride to the Grand Canyon: We would have a couple of important conversations (which made me nauseous to even think about executing) about the future; I brought along two (paper) books of poetry I'd inherited when my father died; finally (this was before the law changed to allow alcohol in SDs), I brought only carrot soda and some good bread I'd . . .

35

I've added the ellipses to the end of the above paragraph because I was interrupted, strangely, by a call from, of all people, one of the Hungarian neighbors. I normally wouldn't have answered, of course, but I received, just a half minute before the call, a message that said, "It is I I am Emil I have apartment nearby your," and another that said, "I call you now." How this man got my cell information was explicable only by an after-the-buzzer play by Juan Miguel, that snot sleeve. The game was not over. I answered because I thought perhaps he would thank me for being so diligent in fulfilling my appointment as resident eye, though I had a feeling that the Hungarian woman was not unwelcome.

I answered. There was a storm of crackling, then a rushed silence.

"Stone?"

"Yes. This is JP Stone. How did you get this contact? I am . . ."

"Stone JP I am glad you are talking with me. There is information needed to give."

What I made out through the humidity of his accent was spotty. The mysterious woman is either his daughter or daughter-in-law; she is in "married conflicts" with either his son or son-in-law, who, he said "once went to your apartment, it was mistake"; the son/son-in-law was not healthy; the daughter/daughter-in-law is a translator at the U and he had told me before (his past perfect tense was far from perfect: "I have telled you once in past times") about her, and suggested that she translate *Bot-Poetics* into Hungarian.

"Stone," he said, after I had said "aha" seven or eight times. "Will you please go to her and speak? She is very sad, she is very, very sad. She does not translate anything for two months, and perhaps she has no more job. She translates your book and then job is OK."

I told him that I did not have the time to . . .

"Stone, I saw on the camera that you enter our apartment . . . this is not good because she is afraid . . ."

What a bother. I told him I would talk to her.

36a

All that I'll avoid for now in order to return to the more interesting story. On the Friday morning before your mother and I would head toward the most romantic of American abysses, I rode the happy little XiPi to the car wash, where I remember an older woman asking if this was one of those cars that "go by themselves." I said it was, and she asked if she could sit in it and have me take a photo with her cell, which I did. I took one photo with hers and one with mine. I still have that photo in the archive. The woman's skin is absolutely leathered from exposure to the sun, and she had a shirt on that said SAVE THE WILD HORSES and I wonder how she'd feel now, if she were still around, about the proliferation of cars that "go by themselves" and the eventual and controversial "saving" of the wild horses.

On the way back to my apartment, the XiPi pinged a message onto its screen. It was your mother, apostrophe-less and thus derailed.

"David in hospital. Its bad."

36b

I think I may have screamed. I know for sure I scooted into the left-side seat in order to bash the impotent steering wheel with the heels of my palms (this is one downfall of today's SD—there is nothing good to bash).

I collected myself and responded badly: "OK."

Your mother: "He was shot in the head."

This might, these days, sound implausible, like an explosion scene in a 3D movie that was beginning to drag. But what we often forget was that the laws in New Mexico really didn't change much until about twenty-five years ago. But, like David's face, the past has been blown out of proportion. It wasn't like the series suggest. People weren't walking around with guns or pointing them in fights. But it was legal to walk around with them, and there were Davidy sort of people that enjoyed what they called "exercising their rights" in this way. They were generally like the walrus folks, really—socially awkward and slightly afraid—and so this is probably what began this particular conflagration. People shot one another with their guns, which is, of course, why they had them in the first place.

The story that the Joe's cameras and the witnesses would eventually tell was this. David was drinking at Joe's, back in the back with the "walruspervs," as I'd heard him call them. (After whatever happened between him and your mother caused David to be excommunicated or ostracized from the side spot, he had moved deeper into Joe's.) He was there with another guy, a bearded Davidite who is best punished with obscurity and insults behind his back, because he was eventually convicted of absolutely nothing. This guy, a recently graduated and jobless post-U student in the math department, had joined David back there in a move of solidarity with his fellow socially self-destructive blowhards. This guy already hated the side spot clientele; this guy (we'd discover later, mostly from strange insult barrages he'd execute like carefully planned figure-skating routines in the comment sections of liberal-leaning articles on romance) already hated everyone; this guy made hate a hobby. David was a good partner in such a venture— the rift between your mother and him had sent him spiraling into the online hate economy of the day. From what the bartender told me later, together the two men "drank and hated." David, primarily, made fun of the people in the back of Joe's, while the other guy silently laughed, hunched over the bar. Your mother said she'd seen them do it before, sit back there cackling, David slowly increasing the volume of his mockery, the other guy fixating his eyes on her breasts or on the wooden bar or on nowhere in particular. She thought that this whole program was a weak attempt to get her to come back there and tell him to shut up. Instead, she'd send Cory or Preston or whatever unthinking brot was there to kick David out. Most of what David said was just the standard drivel that primitive minds like his level at anyone who didn't drink themselves into oblivion and grow out their ridiculous facial hair and wear hats advertising companies that wouldn't hire them even sober.

But on this particular night, the night before your mother and I were supposed to depart, somebody in yet another walrus costume (this walrus had both teeth, and was blue) finally said something back. For many years I hated the person inside the blue walrus costume for this. Why not just stay quiet and remain unseen behind those foam tusks? Was David even worth speaking to? Could he even understand semi-intelligent speech? Wasn't speaking to him something like talking to a mangy, mentally disabled panda? (Forgive me: I forget that we are speaking here of your biological source code.)

But the blue walrus did speak. Something snarky and perhaps slightly vulnerable.

David smelled blood. He was too drunk to even get off his stool, but he just kept hollering snatches of racial slurs (inside the blue whole-tusked walrus, actually, was a white guy named Aaron) and obesity-centered insults. He didn't even turn to the walrus. David's compatriot, however, did turn. The videos show that the guy spun around on his bar seat and faced the improbably creature of the arctic beaches. For a full three minutes, this moose just stared at the walrus' two trembling tusks as David bantered on and man inside the walrus tried to interrupt. David's friend didn't even laugh. The man in the walrus wasn't yelling, just standing there with his cell out in front of him, saying something that sounded like "Just go home, you big drunk ass," while he pretended to be reading messages, or something.

Then the guy next to David put his hand in his pants and produced a pistol, a tiny, seemingly fake .22 caliber, and told the walrus that he should stop talking. Just like that. "You should stop talking," the guy said. He didn't point the gun *at* Mr. Blue Walrus (this was absolutely the single pivot point in the subsequent, overly publicized but idiotically argued trial for assault with a deadly weapon charges), nor did he *wave it about,* as some other Walruses said (and which botched testimony [they spent an inordinate amount of breath describing the social distinction between more aggressive, yellow broken-tusked walruses and their *pacifist* blue counterparts] likely gave credibility to the guy's false repentance and diverted attention from his history as a wife-beater). He just held it up slightly, his elbow on the bar, pointing the gun toward the ceiling. David, from the videos, seemed to have no clue that his friend had produced a gun, because David was still yelling, facing forward, employing the finer muscles of his face in a way that he would never be able to again.

Then there was a blur of motion. In the video, it looks like David was trying to flex his biceps: he lifted his arms up in the classic bodybuilder pose. But he did it suddenly, and his right arm hit his friend's gun hand. The gun popped; all walruses (two yellow, a dirty red one, and the aforementioned blue) scattered; David's body jolted and fell. The entire video was on the news within days, primarily because the other guy had disappeared.

The next morning the manager texted your mother and said they were closing for a day because of "your asshole boyfriend." It took a few messages for your mother to understand what happened, but eventually she understood. When your mother went to the hospital, they wouldn't let her see him. It would be days, in fact, before we'd get any word about him. It wasn't because of the severity of his injuries, though, that she couldn't get to him; it was because he'd prohibited all visitors. Your mother took a few shifts at work to cover for the guy who'd had been tending bar and now was too shaky to even enter the building.

A few days later, when your mother finally messaged David and demanded to be let in, he relented. She was only there for thirty minutes or so, but he screamed at her and said that it had all been her fault. He then made her swear she wouldn't talk about what had happened to him. I didn't find the bit out about the screaming and the blame until later, when I read through some raided emails she sent her mother back in Texas. But I knew about the promise. When I picked her up from the hospital that Tuesday, and when I asked what unnecessary organ had been blown off of David's beer-saturated body, she looked straight ahead and said, "I swore I wouldn't tell, and so I won't." She teared up, then composed herself. "Mentally, however, there was no damage. The bullet missed anything vital."

David all but disappeared after that. A year or so later I tried to find him—this was after your mother was gone—but I couldn't get him to meet me. I sent him message after message, some, at first, accusatory, others pleading. He eventually responded, oddly sanguine, "I'm not interesting [*sic*] in talking to you JP"

Years later, after much cajoling and form completing, I was finally accepted as a contributor and editor for the immense DCOB. At the time, one would navigate to your mother's biographical profile and see what has largely remained unchanged for the twenty-five years of the project. They list her birth and death date (the latter I supplied). They list the places that are associated with these dates. They list her degrees. Her publications (though only the *Cold* ones). They list the interesting details of her childhood that would, if ever her profile was lifted from "semi-obscure" (the *Cold* publications and a rather prestigious Texas award for her lead role in a mainschool rendition of *Richard III* had prompted the "interest finder" algorithm to elevate her status) to "visible," become the pertinent elements of the story of her visibility: She won this or that award, she began acting lessons as a little girl, she wrote poetry with her semi-poetic mother (with a link to her mother's profile here, whose simple linking from a "visible" person would perhaps be enough to prompt the algorithm to raise her mother's profile to "semi-obscure"). Family includes you, your grandmother. In "Partnerships," my name is listed, and so is Grey's, and so is David's. Of the three, only mine is "visible," which is both a sort of social status (actually, I'm "known," the level just above "semi-known" and just below "well known," which is in turn just below "widely known," which is the only thing below the top tier, "famous") and a literal indication of how "visible" the DCOB profile is. The levels below "visible" are not accessible by anyone but DCOB editors. David's profile was initially rated at "semi-obscure" because of the Blackichu incident, but it was quickly downgraded by the algorithm, which assigns "expiration dates" to the notoriety of certain sorts of information.

When I first gained access to the underfloors of the DCOB, I naturally went first to my profile, then to your mother's. Finally, after hours of minute editorial suggestions, I went to David's. I had not heard anything about him for years, and so expected to see some suicide date on his profile. There was none. There was no information beyond the accidental shooting. Surprisingly, DCOB didn't seem to know precisely what happened to his head, which is odd, because medical records are siphoned through their system.

I tell you all this because of a change that appeared in the DCOB six years ago. I got on to make my quarterly check of the profiles I care about, and I saw that a single sentence had been inscribed under the current year in the "basic chronology" section: "According to taxation data, David Geores is known to be residing in the Mexico City Independent Economic District." I have not pursued this any further. That he had been out of the country since the accident would explain the dearth of medical records, and, even more important for your search (though, after recounting all this I don't see why it would be necessary), the absence of DNA information, which is not visible to the public or even lower-level DCOB administrators, but which I can certainly see. My DNA data I've kept away from the insatiable DCOB gullet only through persistent and intense informational warfare.

However, I can see yours.

37

We arrived at the second meeting of the Semi-Bots just an hour after your mother had seen what I assumed was an unluckily mangled version of the same horrid David, and so the sense of foreboding that settled in my stomach I attributed to your mother's bad visions and the tenuous nature of our attending the second meeting of a group led by a man who'd deeply hurt her. Foreboding is different than foreshadowing; I felt foreboding. In the coming months, I would turn this evening around in my hands like some intricately designed puzzle (*this* is foreshadowing), but I would also be puzzled by the deep and troubling feeling that proved a certain prescience. During the later Haze years, I invested heavily in the belief that, had I acted on the foreboding, I could have prevented us from walking the particular path whose trailhead was that second Semi-Bots meeting and whose terminus was your mother's early death. But the eventual dissolution of the Haze (accomplished unintentionally by Daniel's concern over my ability to do my job) brought with it a relieving, if perhaps even scarier proposition: I could never have foreseen accurately the outcome of our attendance. Feeling something is radically different than seeing, as I'm sure you know.

Indeed, if I've learned anything in my years of narrative study, it's the line I used as a tag on many a syllabi: "The only stories we are able to control have already happened." Those who continue to insist on the twentieth-century notion that narratives help us "live our lives" are dunces. Narratives help us in only one activity, visceral and vital. We narrate our pasts. Our material is none other than the information now stored, predetermined, already produced by the cryptic program of existence. Narrative is how we store memory. Narrative is how we see our pasts. It at times stands in direct opposition to how we feel about our pasts. Narrative takes from feeling's sweaty hands the job of determining what we retain and how, and what it all means. We can live without narratives, yes. I detest the soccer-dad, narrative-or-else professors who, like the shortsighted Bot-Poets of thirty years ago, thought that one must sell someone a survival tool at every turn, and so packaged literature in glossy indispensability. We can live without narratives, but that's pretty much all we can do without them.

You must know this about me. I believe wholeheartedly, and always have, in Aristotle's original definition of a poet's work: "It is not the poet's function to relate what has happened, but what may happen." It is only in recent years, however, that I've come to understand that the latter "what may happen" is still speaking about the past. When I was working as a bot poet, I had not yet fully embraced this truth. I thought that as a bot poet I could speak about the world *as it was at that moment* using the very thing—coding—that was shaping that world into precisely what it was at that moment. When I switched the object of my career to criticism, I was not only trying to find the best path by which to summit the pointy spire of academia but also slowly coming to recognize that I could not tolerate, and in fact hated, the idea of what may happen. Criticism thus presented itself as the purest form of discussing and evaluating what has already happened. I had elderly mascots there too. For example, there's the seventeenth-century poet John Dryden, who said, "They wholly mistake the nature of criticism who think its business is principally to find fault." But, as I've mentioned, I failed not in my attempt to narrate the literary past but in my attempt to paint in critical strokes pleasing to *the world as it was at that moment*. I retain to this day a belief that the reasons for my failure were, on some level, proof of my eminent ability as a critic, but I was so disheartened that I simply couldn't continue. *Coordinates*, then, introduced a third path, something that mixed both: narratology, or the study of story in personal history. This has become a wildly popular field. I'd even venture to claim, indeed, that it is one of the oldest human tendencies, like romance and religion, but this I do not advertise too much, else I'd be out of a job. It still amazes me that freshmen and even first year post-U's have no real narrative for their experiences. Many of my students viewed their pasts—even the sex-crazed argument of last night, or last week's traumatic dog park episode—as hodgepodges of impossibilities and disconnected complexities that are ultimately beyond their intellectual facility to piece together, or they are granite edifices unmovable because they're sunk already in an unreachable time. Au contraire, mon ami. They are not yet anything, as paints are not yet a painting. What *may happen* in your past (I've hollered for years) is yours to shape!

However, my teaching has admittedly become somewhat rote. The opening line for my class that used to fetch rapt attention was "Your life contains a best-selling story." I used the ridiculous word "best-selling" (I mean, the *Adventure of DarDar Dolls* books were "best-selling") because I knew they'd be enticed by the riches, but I also believe it, as cliché as it might at first sound. I always knew, however, that talking like this to an intro-level NNP class was like talking about Atlantis with an intro archaeology class. As you probably know well by now, teaching is (again, like romance and religion) mostly a showy smoke-and-mirror act, a garish performance intended to waste the time that the higher-ups believe most students—if left to their own devices—would employ at best semi-criminally. That they learn nothing is now becoming an open secret; consider our last president's widely applauded remarks about community college: "The point is not that people are learning the subjects . . . the point is that they're . . . [I don't remember what the pol bot said that students were doing, but you could insert here any vague, universally applauded human endeavor]". The problem is that few people anymore know anything about *story* and instead know only *plot*. The problem is that they refuse to paint and want only to sketch. The problem is our pasts disappear faster than our presents unfold. The problem is we can't even keep pace with our own careening lives.

But back to the Semi-Bots, a time when all of the above ideas were just zygotes in my intellectual womb. For here the plot gets complex, even if the story thins.

Daniel had been busy. The second meeting was more fully attended than the first. In fact, it was positively packed. I recognized a couple of regulars from Joe's, where I'm sure Daniel had made a few rounds. The Scandinavian sisters were there too, and were slated to read a poem for two voices before the featured author, Muhammad Wright, would be giving a presentation of *Behind the Burn: My Week with the Burn Hermit Cordell Jones*. The title seemed to be ironic ("My Week?"), but I got the sense from some promotional posterage that it was not, at all, ironic. I squeezed out a little witticism and made your mother smile and made myself feel a bit better. I saw that your mother was holding in her hands her cell, mashing its side button periodically, glancing quickly at the lit screen, looking for something incoming.

David Geores was incoming. He was, for his part, acting in his normal interfering ways. He had been cut off and then *hospitalized* and I still couldn't shake the weight he had draped over your mother.

Daniel was up at the front, babbling about the next meeting's agenda, which was totally forgettable. We were in a shabby old NNP classroom, the only venue Daniel could secure. I couldn't understand who all these people were. I thought then that I'd never attend another one unless forced at gunpoint, but I had no idea then that Daniel would, just three years later, be working to save me from the high school squalor and shoehorn me into the fracturing NNP department. I'd earn totally farcical but very, very usable Glidden Merit Points (at the core of my career, I was the top dealer in this currency) by attending the strange brainstorm/therapy group that the Semi-Bots became and that would become the first staff of *Cold*.

Daniel introduced the two women and they came on stage and read a bot-produced poem for two voices. I don't remember any of the poem's words (you can look it up in *Coils and Ropes . . .*; I certainly will not), but I do remember the eerie way they stood: totally still, arms loosely hanging at their sides, straight blond hair reaching to almost the exact same place on their fair-skinned biceps, blue eyes looking into some upper-back corner as they recited their ridiculous poem from shared memory. At the end of the poem, they smiled to indicate they'd finished but did not alter their odd gazes a bit, and the forty or so people who had come clapped incredulously. There was a brief question-and-answer session, which Daniel nervously cut short when there was powerful silence after the short woman said only "No" when someone asked if they read poetry daily. Then Muhammad Wright stood up.

He had the dark hair and complexion of the Middle East, but other than his referential name I could guess nothing more about him. He was unreadable, at first. He introduced himself as a former political activist and bioprotester, information that perhaps was intended to make edgier the semiformal attire he'd donned for his reading. His gray suit and blue shirt were cheap but trendy. His shoes were matte. He put his résumé up on the screen that Daniel had unfurled, and I remember now that there was a line for "Political Prisoner in the PRC." As if someone had expressed vocal surprise (no one had), he chuckled and explained that he had gone to China to use explosives on the enormous exhaust lines that expelled megatons of polluted mine water into enormous toxic lakes in the northwest of the country. He flashed an obscure NPR article on the screen that talked about the arrest of a "small group of protestors" in China's Gobi Desert. He had circled his blurry head in the photograph. Someone wondered half jokingly if such an explosion just meant the megatons of polluted water would then seep into somewhere that was not yet as far gone as a toxic lake. He said, "Indeed," and smiled as if the person would see the subversive logic.

Then he smiled again and said that he hadn't come here to talk about environmental issues but to talk about Cordell Jones, the first Black burn hermit and perhaps the most important burn hermit alive, the man all of us had come to hear about. Except me. I hadn't come to hear about anything.

"And yes," Muhammad said, "he is still living just outside Santa

Fe here in our great state." There was an audible shuffle of excited audience buttocks.

He flashed another picture onto the screen. Spruce and ponderosa formed the verticals, blue sky and a carpet of pine needles the horizontals. There in the center, just behind the first row of trees, was a little structure, a sort of hovel made from logs and sod. "Cordell Jones lives here," he said. "He has one room, which is perhaps, oh . . ." He paced the room out on the floor. It was not big. "He has almost nothing. He uses an antique typewriter and a tiny gas backpacking stove. In the winter, he packs in a whole bunch of meat and stores it in a trusty snowbank nearby. He has succeeded in growing root crops before, though when I was there last summer, they had failed because the snowmelt-collecting reservoir he built had collapsed." Wright paused and waited. Everyone was silent. Then he said, "The question is, Is Cordell Jones insane, or is he the only sane one?" Such niggling pick-a-hand-any-hand rhetorical questions from overdressed speakers were what had made me want to get out of school as soon as I had gotten from it what I needed. I gripped your mother's arm in mock suspense and said, in a whispered urgency, " *Which is he?* " Your mother smiled and shushed me. I thought, perhaps, that I was bit by witty bit pulling her out of David Geores's destructive orbit.

Muhammad Wright went on to explain the whole ordeal. He'd been researching the super-micro climate of "burn scar margins" and had one afternoon found Cordell Jones sitting on an unburned stump (left by some long-gone tree cutter), typing on a typewriter.. Both men were surprised, but Muhammad was the only one, apparently, who wanted to talk. Cordell immediately said, "If you take a picture of me, I will take the cell from you," and Muhammad knew that he had probably already done so to some other disaster tourist of the forest.

Muhammad didn't tell us how, but over the course of a few sporadic visits, he had somehow ingratiated himself with the hermit. He learned that Cordell was a former football player (this was long before pads and helmets were banned, and thus predates the rugby craze) turned musician (stage name: Core L) turned burn hermit. He had the build of a warrior, and the soft voice of someone who used it as an instrument, and the round, flat glasses of a man who reads constantly. His long dreadlocks he held back, Muhammad described for us, with the lace of his old football cleat, "the only tie / to the war / I have" (an excerpt from one of Cordell's typewritten [and then Muhammad-photographed] poem/songs clicked onto the screen). Muhammad explained that Cordell had gained some notoriety a few years before when he released a song that had criticized the old NFL, which had "drafted" him (really [Core L rapped], "enlisted our brains / as a flesh purse for they gains").

The song made him famous, on some level. He was asked to collaborate and to speak and to attend, but Cordell Jones was not a collaborator and speaker and attender. He was now the voice protesting exploitation, and he believed that all the people finally calling his cell and wanting his input were just trying to exploit him in their own way. He was living in East LA and, on a reflective hike, met a drugged-dry burn hermit who lived a miserable life just below the summit of Mount San Antonio, the biggest peak in the area. Cordell knew "burn-hermitude," as Muhammad so annoyingly put it, was the way to escape exploitation and just be a "true human."

I leaned over to your mother as he droned on. She was paying careful attention, and when I whispered something snarky, she at first pretended not to hear me. But then she turned to me and said, simply, "I remember that song. I used to love that song. I didn't know it was about football. I can't believe the man out there is Core."

All in all, Muhammad had only stayed with Cordell for the six or seven days it took to interview Cordell and get a few snapshots of his writing. The at first inexplicable irony was that Muhammad had succeeded in getting all this material from someone who seemed so hell-bent on remaining outside the demands of the insatiable listeners he had attracted. I began to suspect that, in fact, Muhammad had not told Cordell he was going to write a book about him. When Muhammad said that he (Muhammad) had "left in the middle of the night," it seemed to suggest that he had somehow tricked Cordell into autobiographicizing.

"I have a bit of audio," he said. He played a muffled clip of Cordell reading what I would come to appreciate as a subtly beautiful poem, though at first I didn't think much of it. It's published in Muhammad's book only, and were it not for Cordell's voice (recognizable only because it most certainly isn't Muhammad's), I might suspect that Muhammad had just fabricated it. It was not a bot poem, of course, so I didn't really have much to say about its technique. There are a couple of sics in there, but I copy it here for you as it is published in *Behind the Burn,* which I later bought but only so that I could access Cordell's work.

> in the snow at the rock edge of the mountain
> i found a tiny bird flop-flopping . . .
> it was like a hawk or a heron idk . . .
> it screeched at me,
> sank down into the white . . .

and hopped out again
you need help? i asked it
i couldnt get it's answer
so i left it to burn in the snow
claw of pain ripping the skin of My chest
fearing it might become
a symbol of hope
it didnt understand

When I first heard Muhammad's rather gristly recording, I snorted perhaps a bit too loudly. The premise of the poem wasn't awful, but I was lost at "it was like a hawk or a heron idk." It was, of course, nearly unthinkable that it was a heron, and the "like" in that sentence was enough to make me want to leave. The poem was obviously about his own trepidation regarding exploitation, as the speaker seemed to prefer almost certain death above risking objectification. I could not understand why, in the transcription (had Cordell written it thus, or was Muhammad simply writing down Cordell's spoken word?), the personal pronoun had not been capitalized while the personal possessive had.

I looked at your mother. She was still nodding, even in the empty silence at the end of Cordell's final words. I remembered, then, a couple of lines from the poem about the dead bird that Daniel had mocked so brutally: "There is nothing beyond it and me / it rests, though not in peace." I did not know for sure at the time if that was your mother's poem, but I saw that the two poems, in a painfully unavoidable way, had somehow united in Daniel Glidden's Semi-Bot meeting.

The question-and-answer period began with a series of questions about Cordell's musical career, which really hadn't come up at all in the presentation. One woman in the front asked if Cordell was, "like, recording anything?" The person in front of me sat up straight, and on the bony back I saw a T-shirt with the logo of the college FM station, which, since the decline and then deregulation of FM, had become something like record stores had been for undergraduates in my day, nostalgia centers where misfits could buy some social real estate on the cheap. I understood that a majority of the crowd was here because of Cordell's music. When Wright shook his head and said he had no idea if Cordell was recording anything but hadn't seen a cell or computer anywhere in the hut, there was a collective sigh. Nothing would have been cooler for these people than to know that Core L was rebooting himself in their very own mountains. A few people got up and left.

Finally someone asked quite matter-of-factly precisely the question that was on the rest of our minds: How did Wright manage to acquire all of this?

"Great question," he said. "I planned to stay there with him—" He looked at the floor, searching for the words.

"You mean, live out there?" Daniel asked.

"Yes. I planned to build my own little hut near the foot of a cliff sort of nearby where there was more snow."

"Why didn't you?" someone else asked.

"It was . . . too hard. After my cell and backup battery died, I lasted maybe two days." He laughed, and so did most of the small crowd.

Next question: "What does Cordell think of the book?"

"I don't know," Wright said. "I have not seen him or talked to him since I left last June."

"What did he think about the idea?"

"For the book?" Wright asked. He pulled at the hem of his suit coat. The other person nodded. "Cordell doesn't know I've published a book."

Now it was my turn: "So"—I cleared my throat pretentiously and then raised my voice—"you wrote this book about him without his permission." I did not lift my voice at the end to signify a question.

"Cordell did not want anyone to know anything about him," Muhammad said, staring at me.

"And the poems of Cordell's were . . . stolen from him?" Your mother put her hand on my arm and squeezed violently. I saw Daniel turn his head halfway in my direction, knowing that I was the perpetrator but not knowing what look to use if he faced me.

"They weren't stolen . . . I felt it was . . . an important story. I wrote it for my dissertation, and one professor from the department encouraged me . . ."

"Ah!" I said.

Daniel stood up and thanked Muhammad Wright for his time and for this fascinating story.

38

In order to transcribe the above poem, I had to extract the paper copy from the book closet. The cabin is on the front in a photo filtered as black and white, no doubt taken by Wright. In the photo, the cabin is almost indistinguishable from its surroundings, beside the fact that the line of its rough-hewn awning is about the only horizontal in a picture full of verticals. The book, however, is unremarkable, and part of me regrets keeping it for this long. I had not remembered that the book was so thin, the type so large, the lines so widely spaced. I guessed that the whole thing was maybe a two-hour ordeal, which, of course, was the trend of the time: oddball biography, mainschool-vocabulary level, reading time approximating a long film.

The non-FM people in attendance did not really care about Muhammad Wright's product, for most of them were at least knee-deep in the same sell-it-before-anyone-has-a-chance-to-think game. They rose from their seats and began chatting with one another and with Wright. This was not a reading as much as it was a show of support for the very vacuous society they hoped would survive long enough to carry their careers until mandatory retirement.

Your mother sat still for a moment looking at the top knee of her crossed legs. I could feel the weight of hot thought emanating from her, and I figured she was annoyed with me (this hypersensitivity I learned from my tea-guzzling mother's perfectly straight brow line), and that I would have to work my way back into a state of grace, and I became a bit annoyed too, at this prospect. Then she looked up at Muhammad, who was nodding elaborately in response to something Daniel was saying.

"Wait here just a second," she said. "I want to ask him a quick question."

She walked up to the front and I, struggling not to look at the supple place below her back, stared at the illegible tattoo on her calf. At the front, Daniel and Wright were standing shoulder to shoulder, nodding and speaking without facing one another. She interrupted Daniel by putting her hand on his shoulder, then she asked Muhammad something. Daniel stepped away and smiled an intrusion between the Scandinavians. Wright nodded a bit as your mother spoke, but then smiled as if hearing a bad joke, then shook his head. He looked straight at her and shook his head and, I saw, clearly said, "Sorry." But your mother persisted. She shook her head too, and Muhammad kept listening but looked around the room as if planning his exit. I saw her move her hand to his upper arm, and with the other hand he made a slanted chopping gesture, emphasizing every third word or so. Muhammad pursed his lips and tilted his head back a bit. She was still talking. Finally, Muhammad pulled out his cell. She pulled hers out too, and they compared them for a moment. Then Muhammad put his away and nodded. They shook hands. He said nothing.

"What was that?" I asked her when she came back to where I was seated. She avoided all eye contact.

"I'll tell you in the car."

Then, back in the XiPi, she asked if I remained interested in taking a little trip, though she still seemed irritated with my antagonistic questioning.

"Sure," I said. I felt my stomach lurch. I clicked her saved address into the screen.

"Next weekend, then," she said, still looking straight ahead, "let's go find Cordell Jones."

She'd cajoled Muhammad into giving her the trail name and general area in which Cordell lived, though he said it'd be very difficult to find him. The prospect of a long hike to a misanthropic and now deceived burn hermit armed with a typewriter was not exactly enticing, but I figured this was a good enough offer, as we'd have a couple of hours in the XiPi both ways, a few hours of hiking, and maybe a night under smoke-screened stars. She planned to work on Friday, so we decided to leave first thing Saturday morning.

I decided not to point out that we would be attempting precisely the thing that Cordell Jones had run into the mountains to avoid.

Holding the book in my hands now suggests a different truth, and that is the banality of it all. Some guy who was living in the mountains, some book peddler who shared a secret location that no one besides your mother was interested in to begin with, some mysterious and ephemeral shimmer of "something bigger" (than Albuquerque, than Joe's and its David Georeses, than the slow and imperceptible and often regrettable survival of mankind) that, of course, is sold in bulk to twentysomethings to this day, a load of cloud-spray that attempts to fog over the fundamental truth of our American existence, which is that we are not even so important as to call ourselves cogs in a machine anymore. If we are cogs, the machine has long shed us; we lie like discarded bones on the floor.

39a

The XiPi I'm in right now (now being later, a couple of hours after the very exhausting session of the Juan Game and perhaps the final Daniel Glidden episode) is much more advanced than the XiPi we took to the Sangre de Cristo Mountains forty years ago. And the road there is different too. Now there's a dedicated SD highway with a 175-kph lane, which I'm not in, not because this XiPi can't do it but because I prefer the 125-kph view of things. The SD route, in many places, is walled off for reasons I've never fully been able to understand, but my favorite section, the 30 or 40 kilometers in the reservation between Albuquerque and Old Santa Fe, is still open. From there you can see the trad-car route and its dozens of stoplights and tollbooths and bootleg kiosks. Beyond that is the desert, broken only by untamed arroyos and a cluster of container homes here and there. Beyond these is the backdrop of the dry and uninhabited Cerrillos Mountains. Beyond those, nothing.

I've still got ten minutes to go before I reach the reservation, though. As of now, I'm still in the mandatory slowdown of north Albuquerque, and I'm surrounded by thousands of SDs purring in the evening commute. Most of them have their windows blacked, and inside, I imagine, their insensate passengers are watching one of those asinine commute shows, or they're sending last-minute messages before their businesses' servers go offline at the legislated and normalized Standard Offline Time. or they're browsing 3Ds of women who look like their partners did twelve years ago. A few are listening to narratives; fewer still are reading them on screen; one in ten thousand are reading printed paper that they've carried around all day in anticipation of this very moment.

I am living anachronistically too. I'm typing in the old way. Not in the Cordell Jones way—though I did see a hipster student doing a "t-writer demo" in the quad the other day—but in the Bill Gates way, on a keyboard with my fingers, a keyboard that I thankfully left in the car after my most recent trip to the office.

A bit of explanation is in order. After my meeting with Daniel, I returned to my apartment. Only one thing (my decryption program) stood between me and the archive that I'd sealed up decades before. I immediately began pacing. I felt the return of that old combination, the sickly mix of urge and fear.

The decryption program worked splendidly, and, much more quickly than I expected (these cells are fifty times more powerful than the computer I used to encrypt the stuff back then), there were the old folders there before me. I avoided HER and opened TO BE CULLED. Her original folder names appeared. One was titled BREATHE, another OLD DOCS, another TAXXDOCS, another MOM STUFF. These I remembered, and their exact contents populated in my head even before I opened them. I scrolled through the thirty or forty folders, trying to seem casual, but what I was actually looking for was the folder where I'd spent the most time, the folder that had been a favorite late-night haunt. Inexplicably nestled between DOGGGGGGGG and SOC350, I found it: ABQ PrOOst. (Your mother often used a potty-themed mangling of the word when she referred to the *Albuquerque News*, which hadn't abandoned the *Post* in their title until after her death—an event they reported—and whose shoddy reporting you've undoubtedly read. But the forced lower-case r was a pleasant surprise: she had been required to read *Swann's Way* for a class she already disliked, and she found the book infuriating for its—what were her words—"annoying French obsession with non-events.") In that folder were forty-three documents, seventeen images, three videos, and one audio file. (I know these numbers by heart.) The forty-three documents ranged in length from roughly a thousand words to fifteen thousand. This, the longest document, was an "unsent" letter to me, though I have reason to believe that it was, indeed, sent, though not in the traditional way. The images were varied and, to the untrained eye, rather mundane: pictures with friends in Centex, a couple of me at Joe's, a picture of her and me in her room. The videos were two to five minutes. One was filmed in the enormous trad-car parking lot, another was filmed in the tiny kitchen of her apartment, and the third was in my XiPi while we were on our way to find Cordell Jones's hiding place.

At the top of the contents list, however, was the audio file that I knew I'd see but also dreaded seeing. It was filed first because it was simply titled "0326 Recording." It will be, of course, from your perspective, the only thing that really matters in those files. At first, I was surprised by my ability to look at it without catastrophe. But then I felt a creeping wave of nausea. I tossed the cell onto my couch-bed and strode out of the apartment. But then, gripped with fear, I jumped back in, grabbed the cell, and went out again.

I was not in my right mind, of course. Those years after the data raid had been lost in a gas cloud of addiction, compulsion, insanity, a circling and circling and never an arrival. The Haze: I was culling but I was also reculling. I was pouring digital sand from one cup into another. When grains fell out, I acted unconcerned, but then, launching from my bed as if in an air raid, I'd go empty out the NOT HER folder, return the contents to the TO BE CULLED folder, and in this way manage a few hours of dreamless sleep. "0326 Recording" is, as far as I know, the only file or folder I have not examined in all your mother's digital crumblings, though I have, strictly speaking, opened it. Perhaps it will be worth discussing more later, but for now, suffice it to say that "0326 Recording" was the center of the bleeding wound that was my romance with your mother, and to look directly at it was to look directly at the cancer eating the flesh.

I thought a few decades would steel my soul against this weakness. But seeing "0326 Recording" there, somehow still throbbing even after being locked away, unfed and unattended for years, I discovered that though I had fully recovered my control, I had not disposed of, so it seemed, the capacity for the intense and insatiable desire, the resolution of which had pushed me into the Haze and had also kept me stuck inside it.

In the hallway I stood for only a second, still nauseous, still feeling the irresistible pull back to the cell and the simultaneous feeling of intense self-disgust, the hollow pain of unfillable need that can only be vitiated with the futile attempt to fill it.

It must be stated here that there is no "recovery" or "renewal." It doesn't matter what the substance of one's addiction is. There is only forgetting, narrative revision. The reintroduction of the need threatens to bring back the old narrative, which is just as true and real as the one made to kill it. There is no rebirth. There is only the first one, the one that made you, then the subsequent pain of being you, and the stories you tell about all of it.

In the wilds of narrative combat, I thought only of the most expedient relief that was not surrender: another human. I took fifteen steps down the hallway and banged on the door of 42-2.

The clicks of shoe heels on the faux marble ("Same from lobby," the old Hungarian had told me, proudly) indicated her approach, and those sounds also signaled to me precisely what I was doing and how little I wanted to do it. I turned and took three steps back toward my apartment. Too late: She had opened the door. Too late: She said, "Stone?"

It was me, but I did not turn around. I walked to the fast lift around the corner. It was mercifully only three floors away. "Stone, wait!" she said. Its doors opened like arms and I entered and said, "Lobby."

The program had begun, and now it had to continue until output. I could not go back to my apartment; she would follow me there. I could not go hide on the comforting drone approaches. But I also could not admit to myself then (twenty minutes ago, now) that I really had nowhere to go. The apartment was not the answer—even if I was able to ignore her knocking, I'd first have to pass her in the hallway, where I'm sure she stood, hip angled out, eyebrows declined.

What do you say to a woman like her? Her marriage burns and crackles. Her career is charred. Her parents are a hemisphere away but even more distant generationally. No one could translate *Bot-Poetics*, because, like the very poetry it discusses, it doesn't even say what it should in its native tongue, for God's sake. But how, more importantly, do I translate the infinitude of my world and, in reverse, the infinitude of hers? How do two people, totally unconnected in narrative, begin to write a common one? Forget acquaintance, DNA, biology, attraction! All of it is inconsequential if there is no story. And, my friend, there is no shared story here. This is mine, *Bot-Poetics* is mine, and to yield it to someone else is to release it from my care, and to release it from my care is to relinquish my purpose as caretaker, and to relinquish my purpose is to admit the beginning of the denouement of the story I've been composing all this time. Everyone knows—and this I hope you'll remember and agree with—that the best denouements are the shortest ones. I intend it to be so in my case.

As the lift descended, I considered places to hide out for the hour or so it would take her to return to focusing on her own private disasters. But my world has become little more than the U building that houses my classrooms and office, my apartment, and the narrow lane between them. All necessities are delivered. So, too, are prepared meals, but these are getting fewer and fewer as my departing youth takes with it its already fickle appetite. If I were any other living person, I would go to a bar or café. The former I have long avoided. The latter I always despised.

You must understand that my imminent retirement will eliminate half of that world. All that will be left is my apartment, my XiPi, my cell. And my narrative. The apartment and the XiPi are really just containers for me and my glowing little pet, little friend, little handheld comfort and purpose. On my cell now is the archive, which I know I will never again encrypt, for I would never again ask Daniel for anything, and Daniel's the only one I know well enough to whom I'd even consider entrusting such a self-revealing task.

When the elevator disgorged me into the lobby and I asked Juan

Miguel to bring up my car, I feared that the pseudo-Hungarian might catch up with me, so I descended via the fire stairs to the garage and stood behind a concrete pillar near the platform where cars arrive. I immediately climbed into the XiPi when it pulled up. The XiPi asked its normal ask. I hesitated. I needed a place to go that would require nothing from me, a place to consider and conclude. This is a cultural problem with SDs that has not been satisfactorily reconciled, though very few people complain about it anymore. Sometimes people need to just "drive" after a big argument or when you were feeling existentially morose. People in just such a situation feel and need to be destination-less. They need to pull out into the night and make unpremeditated turns until two hours have passed. They need quiet without stillness. Years ago, there were, of course, plenty of SDs that included just such a setting— you hit the button and the car just drives until you tell it to stop—though I'm guessing for you such things were on their way out probably long before you could get your owner's code permit. The program was called, in most SDs, the JD button (the Just Drive mode; in modern Burqueño: "hitting chaydee"). I needed to hit the chaydee, but because of Fanessa Allen and her husband and their damned tearjerker of a viral video about their community that had been discriminated against in the old Ford-Honda JD algorithm, JD programs had since become all but useless because they were truly and perfectly random, and also, strangely, had become an illicit way for teenagers to avoid destination restrictions on their SDs (they just kept hitting chaydee until they ended up near the warehouse that sold the vaporizable or snortable or teethable punch-out du jour). Because they legally can't eliminate possible destinations, they could send me straight to the Southwest Quadrant, which as of now is about a third of the unregulated traffic corridors in the city, and is not at all somewhere I'd want to go in my very unfast SD, which doesn't even have a chaydee, anyway.

I remembered then, while I sat there pondering the rapid narrowing of my story, that Core L had a song about JD mode, though back then the JD mode was more often called Just Go, and some people believed that certain SD manufacturers had sold "stock" in the "jugo" algorithm, thus pushing their particular brand of SDs "randomly" through corridors where there'd be a higher chance of passing a business that had, perhaps, bought a fleet of SDs or underwritten some R & D, and that, perhaps, the rider would be interested in patronizing. Core L's song was about riding jugo and noticing the places that the car company thought he'd like—dispensary, liquor store, dimer, dimer, dimer, liquor store—and the places he didn't pass—the U, the public natatorium, the wine bar. Mysteriously: the hospital. "Never, never that place." Then I thought of your mother, who forced me to listen to Core L on the entire trip out to see him.

I saw the shadow blink of a door opening in my peripheral vision, so, in order to evacuate the garage more quickly, I said, "Office," and the car said, "Going to your office?" and I said, "Yes," and then it pulled away, past the rows and rows of SDs parked on the upper level, past the massive thermal turbines, past the empty guard kiosk, which has remained unattended since the building's opening (though the entrance it guards is carefully managed by both the mother- and fatherboard).

I was not going to my office, though. Not yet, at least. That was for later. But remembering Core L's jugo song and your mother's enthusiasm as we had purred toward Santa Fe in that first XiPi, I had a new idea. I scanned through a map on the screen and found the new road to the old ski basin outside Santa Fe. It looked to me that the hike that, back then, took us three hours would now take maybe half that, as the road went much nearer the pass that one must gain before descending into the shallow alpine valley that holds Spirit Lake in its palm.

The idea evolved rapidly, more quickly than anything I've done in years. Now, as the XiPi finally finds its way out of the globs of commuters and into the empty space beyond the northern city limits, a more long-term outing seems better than it even did originally. Originally, I thought maybe I'd just take a drive up the ski basin road again and, as I did so, write about the same drive of forty years ago. Perhaps my memory would be defragmented simply by passing familiar settings. I could then avoid the pseudo-Hungarian and finish the story of your mother and perhaps use the old exposure-therapy technique of forcing myself to encounter a minuscule piece of the terror: the road into the mountains that your mother only traveled (as far as I know) once alive. Perhaps then I could acclimate myself to her digital resurrection, and could sit with the archival version of her without risking losing a year or two, and could even, perhaps, finally listen to "0326 Recording" . . . but even just writing such things makes my throat close.

I found the road on the map. I knew that it had been (re)extended in the four decades since I'd last traveled it, and I clicked on its terminus. "Going to the Old Santa Fe Ski Area and Recreation Facility?" the XiPi said, and I almost said "No" simply out of the habit of disagreeing with its insane suggestions, but then I said "Yes," and the car took the next left, and steered me away from my office, which, oddly, felt like I was detouring around the foyer of hell.

39b

(feel free to skip)

Our central motherboards are working constantly to provide us with a Self. I am now subject to your program; I am being forced into its code. And what's true is that you, too, are in mine, have been for forty years, though you are really just a negative feedback loop, one that must be circumvented to allow for normal function.

How can you write a program for *feel?* It is expressed so simply as that. When we read a story that is billed to us as "true" (there is even a legal standard for such narratives now), it doesn't matter at all whether that story is "verifiable"; it matters only that it *feels* true. But, as I've begun to understand over these many years teaching narrative, it is not only the narrativist's job to develop "true feeling" stories. It is also the job of the audience. Take, for example, the Shulin-Ekso experiment with "companion bots," which are now sold widely and are still at the center of a cultural debate about "humanity" (a quick glance at a search shows a long-form narrative from a week ago titled "Parent Bot: Companion Bot Receives Guardianship of Adopted Child During Spouse's House Arrest"). Why aren't people all over the world leaving their Georesian partners and taking up with amenable, satisfying companion bots? Why are we still asking whether or not it's "OK"? Because to leave one's human companions for a bot would make one the "sort of person who" left their partner for a companion bot. Or the sort of person who was not loyal. Or the sort of person who preferred control of a bot over the unpredictability of a human. And so on.

It's this—the "sort of person who" thing—that we can't escape, because it is simply the metaphysical air we breathe. Its origin in us, its rather bleak control over our daily actions, its ability to starve us or intoxicate us or rape us or, on the contrary, cause us to keep living when there simply is not much reason for it, cause us to believe, cause us to write, is precisely what we forget is our motivating factor. We are desperately trying to figure out who we are, sure, but just as often and sometimes even exclusively, we are also desperately trying *not* to be "the sort of person who." Again I say: There is no rebirth.

Take your mother. She was beautiful, she was capable, she was alive with friends and intellectual potential. She could have done anything—

learned code, gotten into poetry school had she reapplied, started a shoe company, run for office—but what she did was descend the staircase of my apartment early one Saturday morning (we had hardly slept!) and step into my self-driving vehicle in a harebrained attempt to find Cordell Jones, because she believed (she did not *know*, like, for example, how we *know* that eating a soyshake will contribute to relieving our hunger) that Cordell Jones would help her along the path not to survival or to pleasure but to wholeness.

Or, alternatively, perhaps she wholeheartedly did *not* want to be the person who passed up an opportunity to find Cordell Jones, she did not want to be the sort of Muhammad Wright–like person who without the umbilical cord of popular culture and its cooling technological breeze would die, the sort of person who just gave in, got the chip (the chip was years away, then, but you get the point) and the membership (then recently legalized) and faded into old age over six or seven featureless decades. Was the quest to *not* be this or that person the driving force for your mother? Is it part of your quest, to not be something? I can say without question that such quests are not only futile—they are counterproductive. One always becomes the sort of person who. I am he. I am not proud.

I became more fully aware of this quest sitting in her apartment's guest parking in the white-sun morning of exurb Albuquerque, while your mother was calmly trying to give me the coordinates that Muhammad Wright had shared with her. These were the coordinates of the trailhead where we would begin our hike; they are essentially the same as the ones I'm driving toward now. She read them aloud for the third time. I entered them into the XiPi's screen. When the XiPi said to your mother that there was no address near those coordinates (meaning no building or point of interest) and asked if your mother still wanted to proceed, she sighed and said, "I know it sounds crazy, but yeah." The XiPis of that era, however, did not understand such complicated responses (they've gotten better at parsing out our many shades of yeses and noes, but they still don't understand that "third factor"), so the XiPi asked again, and your mother and I laughed. I realized that even she was not sure what this day would hold. She said, "Yes." When the XiPi bumped into gear and pulled away from the curb, your mother put her feet on the dash and said, "Play Core L's album *Side of Side*," and the first slow spoken-word lines (which I'd listen to so often in the Haze that even now I can reproduce easily their exact tone and lilt) poured out: "Saving mankind is a waste of time / because mankind is a timewaste kind / a bad winetaste, a bitter brew / long in making; now long past prime." As I watched the road pass underneath us, I descended from the lover's pink cloud and returned, for a lulled moment, to the world I normally inhabited. I realized that I was riding along with your mother toward a destination that had little to do with "us." I felt a tinge of jealous misery float into the car; I felt silence pull at me; I listened carefully to Core L and began building my angry case against his insipid pseudo-poetry. But then your mother brushed the top of my hand with her finger and I was reminded of the night before. The song ended and the next began. This one I almost liked.

So, just now, to heighten the effect, just as I pulled onto the SD route, in what I'm sure will become a chain of tiny catharses, very like the mini-strokes that presaged my father's death, I said, "Play Core L's album *Side of Side*." Cordell's voice immediately filled the XiPi, and I felt the sudden and nearly unstoppable desire to thumb through the archive on my cell and hover over "0326," even open it and play it, like I used to do, on 0 percent volume, feeling that titillating approach of culmination, but never allowing the fullness of it . . .

But I did not. Mostly for fear that the new XiPi would say, "I noticed '0326' was playing but muted, so I adjusted its volume to 20 percent. Do you want me to . . ." I shudder.

Though the evening summer sun is brutal, I've left my windows on full clear, mostly because I want to feel, if I can, transportive feelings, feelings that push me back beyond "0326" and to the moment when your mother and I were together. Like I am now, we were headed north, but the sun back then was beating into the SD on the opposite side than it is today, and there was no window blacking then. Your mother, in the right-hand seat, held her long, thin hand up beside her head to block the sun. Her face, then, was cast in shadow, though her coffee shins and knees shone gloriously. We talked about Core L, and I criticized his primitive rhyming and meter and concluded that whatever he was trying to do had failed. But I smiled. Your mother laughed and said she agreed with the criticism but not the conclusion, which was a favorite conversational line of mine that she used against me.

Then, for the second and final time, she quoted something I'd written. It was from a poem, probably one of the first I ever published, in which I alternated between stanzas of "my" poetry and bot poetry. The poem was about a destroyed and supposedly "impassible" road on the outskirts of the master-planned neighborhood I grew up in, one that jutted out, like a tail or distended colon, from the rear end of the development, opposite its gated and guarded mouth. It just led *away*, the road did, through forest and hillocks of coal slag, and you could supposedly take it for kilometers and kilometers (God, that will never sound as melodic as "miles and miles") until it deposited you in a depressing mine-dead town next to a Superfund river.

The primitive bot-produced stanzas were created using a modified version of the code that produced weather driving alerts in Pennsylvania. Your mother quoted lines from one of "my" stanzas, though. "An impassible road / is no road," she said. She looked at me and smiled, as one does when they quote something meaningful to another person. I think what she meant was that Cordell's lyrics may have been bad but they weren't so bad that they didn't communicate his meaning, and so thus they were successful. Or perhaps she saw a ROAD CLOSED sign. Or there was something in one of Core L's repetitive songs about bad roads.

What she didn't know and what I'd never have the chance to tell her was that, while as a teenager dawdling near the beginning of that road in order to prolong the depressing return to the stale and rotting house, I was struck for the first time by the fact that the road was symbolic of some desire in me, something deep and unspoken. Long before that, I had coded into the road some meaning that a pocked and disintegrating road doesn't inherently have. The road was just some rot-black, tree-choked byway. But for me it communicated something. It was that road that made me a poet. I wrote an unthinkably awful poem on my mouth-breathing laptop that night, and that was nearly the last one I ever wrote without a bot. However, almost without my full conscious awareness, I, at the last minute, copied and pasted a piece of the poem into a story I was writing for class about an old man in New York. I inset it, even, as a block quote. I think the old man main character read it aloud with a spartan breakfast.

One of my teachers, a benevolent and exhausted woman whose true talent had been sapped from her before she was forty, gave the story a middling grade but left a comment on the excerpted poem that said, "I love this! Where's it from? I couldn't find it in a search . . ." I have never forgotten this moment. If the road made me a poet (pleasure), that woman made me an academic (survival). I suppose that leaves your mother as the third factor.

Your mother had no idea what the road meant to me, and, now, looking back on it, I had no idea what the road (the road I'm on now, the one populated with silent SDs but that, back then, still roared with combustion and acceleration) meant for her. I'd only met her a month or so before, and the wild mystery of our relationship—did we "love" one another then?—was unlike anything I'd ever encountered. Where it would conclude, if or when it did, I could not understand, its arc I could not predict. Arriving at Cordell Jones's cabin was, I knew, not the end of anything at all, and so our errand to a rather concrete destination had, at best, only vague outcomes, obscure meanings, uncircumscribable purposes. We were not surviving or seeking pleasure. We were doing some third thing, and this tiny epiphany humbled me then. We suddenly seemed like children riding off into a vast and dangerous world. We were reading the symbol of ourselves.

How many of us are there? I ask you this in all credulity. Are you, too, an anonymous, impoverished poet pushing around the paltry trinkets of beauty you've managed to scratch up from your home desert? Have you found another, like we did, with whom to trade your rotten odes? If not, I am not the one—I've found mine, already. Perhaps your search should bend in that direction.

40

Only twice have I returned to Santa Fe in the forty years since your mother, and both times were with Angela and not long after the historical park opened. Now, as I approach it from the south, I see that the old city has morphed more than it has grown. The southern portion of town has retreated, and the large development flanking the highway that your mother and I mocked for its spurious attempt to make accessible the motto "Make Santa Fe your first second home" is now completely gone; in its place: a cluster of the same unpainted container homes that I passed in the reservation, scrub and weed, an abandoned trailer for carrying heavy equipment, a tarp tangled in one of the gnarled junipers. As I continued, I felt that I was approaching a city abandoned.

It took me several minutes of staring to understand what was different. Then I saw that entire neighborhoods had been removed from their places near the highways. Now there are a few big tents visible amid the brown tentacles of juniper and piñon. A plume of smoke.

The West burned; the West burns. People moved away. Rather, it burns less and less, but people are long gone, never even came. And those who came we despised. Santa Fe residents have hardened, have long moved back east, where wildfire is about as rare as resurrection. Albuquerque residents, those who never thought to leave, have weathered the cycle simply by retreating indoors and behind air filters. It is hard to say it now, because I've spent so many decades trying to accept it: These decades have been smoke and soot and rainlessness. Those of us who've stayed probably deserved it.

Recently, I have sensed a slackening in the air, a suspicious purity. It didn't take me long to find a recent article whose headline is enough to affirm my sense: "After Decades of Burn Cycles, Clear Skies." Other than a subtitle, no more writing has populated yet, and this suggests that it is not an article that could justify journalistic investigation. There is little that matters more than this news—that our summers and falls will not be blanketed in smoke, that our mountains will regrow, that our cities will expand and thicken—but the journalist, probably reading through the NOAA news push, just stated the fact, as they only do with articles that have no trend potential. Why no one cares, and why news organizations have been dying across the country, is that people are not interested in facts. Never really have been. They're interested in stories. But facts still blow like sand in our faces. What we are in need of and what we rarely get is a connecting narrative. We have the ingredients; we need a recipe.

Of course, the facts have clicked on. That is, you have arrived in a New Mexico that has been on fire, sometimes even in the dead of winter (the subtitle says that over half the total acreage of New Mexico's publicly managed forests have burned in that fifty years), for half a century, but you've also arrived in a New Mexico that has been cleansed, scoured, a New Mexico poised for rebirth, a new New Mexico. Without that story, the fact of less fire is uninteresting and even, perhaps, saddening, for we have become the Fire State, the constant glow, and before it dried completely, the Rio Grande carried our ash down to Texas and out into the Unified Gulf, and people knew us as burning people, as the land of burn hermits and the headquarters of the last exciting job in the country, helitack. We have forgotten entirely what it was like to be alive before the burns. We cling to them as ourselves. I, of course, cannot see life any differently than choked with smoke haze. I was not raised to believe in renewal or regeneration. How can fire survive in green resurrection? How can there be life after all this?

You must be different. I get the feeling that you're different. I sense in your arrival a hint of vernal union, and perhaps this is why I bristle and evade. Why did the Israelites never believe their prophets of old? Because a prophet might foretell that curses would persist, even after his hearers were dead. Ignoring is easier than resignation. What I'm telling you, of course, is a belief, a fantastic story, and not a verifiable fact (no promise about the world after I'm gone can ever be empirically verified), and it plagues logicians like me, for I love the idea that something of a particular human might outlast a human span, but when I look up from the story, my disbelief returns.

41

In order to avoid the congestion of the central Historic Park district, the SD is taking a flyover that connects to an elevated highway meant to bypass the city on the east side, and which serves primarily to get people into the mountains and the reestablished road to the ski basin. This time of year the Historical Family Park (code for Fully Plasticized History) is soggy with people, and Santa Fe is teeming with the yellow rental SDs and those annoying uniwheelers on which middle-aged moms careen, eyes wide, laughing loudly to cover their abject fear.

You probably don't know much about the park outside of the propaganda it spreads across the country. But the park doesn't matter. Here's what matters. During the park's establishment, many "residents"—most of them born and raised elsewhere—demanded clear access to the mountains. The city promised it but didn't deliver until a decade later. Now no one uses it, because those old wealthy naturalists have died and their children have inherited their homes, and their children aren't interested in the mountains, because in the mountains there are no electrified transportation options or historical musicals or funnel cake machines. The people who so desperately wanted access to the mountains back then couldn't stick around long enough. And back then, it looked like the mountains would never stop burning. The flyover is already in relative disrepair. I feels its bumps beneath me. The SD must reduce speed to safely avoid the holes.

Santa Fe was retooled in those years. Many of the older homes just beyond the park boundaries have been bought and razed and rebuilt into large resort-style manors, mostly catering to international tourists who *still* seem to represent the molecules of the long-rising tide of the Asian cowpoke tourist, who, ever since Texas began the sub-visa process, have found it much easier to come to New Mexico to fulfill their strange cowboyish dreams. Two high-rises—about half as tall as mine, but glassy and embarrassing nonetheless—stand near the flyover to the mountain bypass. One of these twins seems now to be an administrative center for the park. The other has the seal of New Mexico on it, and I assume it houses government operations. Half of that building is server, I'm sure. The other half—the elected officials—just serve the servers. (I read recently that our governor has published the forecast of her own reelection, built with an algorithm made by this young savant in Nortex who claims it can model human choice with something like 90 percent accuracy. In fact, the guy who made it says the algorithm *takes into account* the effect on voters the publication of such a prediction algorithm would have. Thus, an old-timer like me, who goes to vote for someone's pet duck or tomato plant for governor just to screw the gloating incumbent and their silly algorithmic smugness, has already been weighed and noted and discarded as inevitable rather than surprising. That is, there is a 99 percent likelihood that she will win reelection by 62 percent. The algorithm will take into account the amount of people who will simply not vote after realizing how futile voting is in the face of such an accurate algorithm. This is the algorithm's power: It even understands how widely it must advertise its prediction to assure the accuracy of its results. The algorithm makes itself more accurate simply by existing. I like this. Finally, the programs are telling us what to do. We have long been unsure, and have elected more idiots than not.)

As the SD steers its way along the eastern edge of Old Santa Fe, I alternate my gaze between the mountains, which are striated with dark burn scars and greenbelts, and the city below, which is brown and boxy and clean. From this vantage point on the raised thoroughfare, I can barely see the blanched heads of tourists moving about in the open-air SDs that are the sole occupants of Old Santa Fe's venerable streets. This is not the high season, but the relative absence of burns in the mountains over the last few years has, I've heard, encouraged summer visitors. In fact, when I look again at the striped massif ahead, I see only two plumes, one very far away whose upper portion seems to be blowing east toward insular Texas, and a smaller one farther west that rises up to become one with a sun-blocking cloud.

When your mother and I drove through Santa Fe that Saturday, no bypass had been built yet, and the city was choking with smoke. A fire in the Jemez Mountains on the other side of town (the second of the governor's eventually trademarked "uncontainables") was burning through a narrow swath of forest that ended at the government lab. A couple thousand folks in Los Alamos had evacuated a night or two before and were clogging the streets in Santa Fe, trying to find a room. Your mother and I had noticed the flood of traffic going the opposite way, headed to Albuquerque, and then we encountered the smoke a few miles south of the city, registering it only as a slight dimming of the sun, at first. By the time we exited the highway, we saw that Santa Fe was adrift in dull gray fog. Your mother said, "Look," and I leaned forward in imitation of her own arched position and for the first time both of us looked straight at the sun, which was like a slightly luminescent grocery-store orange hanging above us. This activity is commonplace for schoolchildren now, but then, such tremendous movements of fire and smoke were anomalies, signs of the end times that we didn't want to believe in but had been raised to wholly embrace.

A fire had just finished burning in the mountains where we were headed, too, and it only occurred to us in the smoke veil of Santa Fe's eerie streets that we ought to find out if we'd even be able to make it to the coordinates Muhammad Wright had given her. I remember your mother scrolling through her cell, looking for information. She shrugged when I asked if we would make it.

Then I looked on my cell. Farther up the mountain, things seemed clear enough, though, and a weather station in the state park suggested that air quality at elevation wasn't nearly as poor as it was in the city. The smoke in the city was thick. I'm glad we were in an SD—the traffic lights materialized only a few seconds before we reached them. Hanging clumps of chile still adorned porches. People still lived in these homes hidden behind the scrub and pine columns. They were probably at that very moment thinking where they might go to escape. The stunned little XiPi just wandered onward through the haze like a bat, blind by our standards but seeing invisibly. Neither your mother nor I spoke for many minutes as we moved through the war zone of smoke. Your mother eventually looked at me and asked if this was normal. I said I thought it would be from then on. I was not wrong.

My SD at the time had only a short electric range before it initiated its combustion engine to limp its way to a final destination. The SD noticed that our destination was beyond normal electric infrastructure, so it suggested that I fill the gas tank, in which I kept only minimal fuel to save weight. I assented and the car pulled into a gas station. The scene that resulted was a regular image of long-gone ephemera: Your mother hopped out (at a *gas station!*) and returned in a few minutes with a plastic water bottle (!) and a plastic bag (!) full of some salty chip. I pumped twenty-five dollars (!) of gas (!) myself (!), paid with a credit card (!), and then got back in the car. I forgot to say: While I was still pumping the gas, she kissed me—a light peck—in the gas-smelling smoke, and I thought perhaps that this woman and I would be together for many years. Unlike the plastic and the twenty-dollar's-worth of gas, a quick kiss in a sea of smoke is, I suppose, still a fathomable activity these days, though it's rare now that lovers are standing and waiting for something in such a privately public place as a gas station. We got back in the car and waited for the SD's rather slow processor to register our desire to return to the original route.

Just as we bumped forward, we heard a crunching sound in front of us and looked up. The trad SUV at the next pump up had pulled away with the pump's nozzle still in the car's fill spout, and the hose and metal finger of the nozzle ripped from its housing and fell like a severed limb on the concrete. The car lurched to a stop. The driver-side door shot open, and a woman got out and picked up the severed rubber arm. A younger girl, her teenage daughter, came around from the passenger side. The skinny teenager had her cell out and was taking a photo while trying to seem like she wasn't. Her mother looked at her and yelled something about how the daughter hadn't been paying attention and had let her (the mother) drive away with the nozzle still in the damn car. The daughter said, "Are you blaming *me* for this?" and the mother said, "Yes!" before coiling the hose near the pump's feet. The two marched back to their respective doors, entered and shut them, and then the brake lights flashed off. Just before they pulled away, I pointed to the rear glass of their car and said to your mother, "Look." She squinted and said, "What?" but then saw in the bottom-right corner the tiny orange sun with the A in the center that was the logo of the private high school where, just the week before, I'd taught my first miserable classes.

The SUV pulled away. Your mother mentioned something about working with brats and their children. Then she got out, jogged to the gas station building (in the SD's rather superfluous rearview mirror [!], I watched the two perfect and denimed U's of her rear end bump with each step—I include such graphic details as a way of complicating your mother, who, perhaps to you, might seem too old or too smart to be sexy, but she absolutely was, undoubtedly and wonderfully so), and returned with the short-statured station manager.

She climbed back in. "The little guy says that the hoses were made to break off," she said. The impatient SD clicked forward as soon as she buckled her seat belt.

"That's smart," she said, after a few minutes.

"What's smart?" I asked.

"The hoses on those pumps." I agreed, and I remember thinking how odd but entirely appropriate it was to think of something like a breakaway gas pump hose as "smart." A world of technology had already become our givens, it seemed, as if God Himself, and not Bobby R. Dyer (according to the US patents office), had given us breakaway fuel hoses.

42

And now, past the flyover, as the SD waits in the slow line of cars backed up at the mountain checkpoint, I must break away from that incongruous pit stop to say that I cannot escape imagining our lunch together tomorrow. I'll admit. I fear your beauty. I have tried aging your DCOB photo a bit in my mind to prepare myself for the visual shock. I've tried lengthening your cheeks, wrinkling your neck, moving the horizontal line of your breasts a bit farther down your torso, deepening and widening your pelvis. I have tried imagining the moment you materialize at my door, the moment you are standing in the entryway and being recorded by the sec camera for me to replay a hundred thousand times in the desert of post-retirement. I have tried to imagine our meal—me picking at some morsel of dim sum, you eating heartily and expectantly—and I have tried imagining how I will begin. It seems impossible to begin by simply reading "The inscrutable Daniel Glidden . . ." Such an action seems so parental, you the wide-eyed child, me the all-knowing narrator. Yes. This way is unthinkable to me. I have poured hours into this narrative and I see now that it will not much help me when you are sitting there at my unused table, when you are asking the very questions this narrative is meant to parry. I feel, even now, an unshakable dread, a feeling that by sitting at table with you, I am entering again into the very mystery that resulted in the disaster of your mother, your mother's disaster, the disaster that yielded you and me.

OK. Let me try something out. I'm thinking of lifting the faux bamboo of the dim sum packaging and then starting with this: "I hope you'll agree that your mother's story is so much more mine than it is yours, though she, of course, is your mother." I imagine that you'll ask what I mean by that. "What I mean is"—and here I'll remove the first dim sum from the little ring—"your mother and I were fully aware of one another and had a history together, whereas the history of *you*" (I'll raise the dim sum and gesture toward you) "and your mother is simply one of absence."

No. Having written that, I see that it's a ridiculous thing to say, because you have eight or so months in utero that I simply don't have— you existed *inside* your mother. So, a revision: "What I mean is"—and here I'll remove the first dim sum from the little ring, but then will pause, my hand suspended—"I know your mother's story because I was part of it; you were part of your *mother*, but you were not part of her story until the very, very end."

I'm getting closer, but this is too practiced . . .

This will be a difficult lunch.

43

The park ranger didn't even smile when she asked what I'd be doing on my visit to the mountains. Just to see what would happen, I said, "I want to see the place where my long-lost love died." The ranger looked at me, dead silent.

"Will you be harvesting mushrooms or tree products?"

"No."

"Enjoy your visit, and I'm sorry to hear about your loss."

I have seen photos from the last century of the entrance into the Sangre de Cristo Mountains just outside Santa Fe. They depict forest and rock. And the drive into the mountains, back then, was a sort of in-between version of those old photos and what I'm seeing now. Nun's Corner, a rock outcropping a couple of stories high, was the entrance into the first real fold of high mountain and was shrouded by trees in the last century (according to photos). When your mother and I passed it, it marked the beginning of a black section of burn maybe fifteen seconds long, then we were again in trees. Other than a few brief fingers of burns, a larger burn section didn't appear until fifteen minutes later and did not relent for a few minutes. The SD buzzed its combustion engine to life and the car surged upward. (The XiPi I'm in now needs no combustion, and the torque of its electric motor is so powerful it causes a rather nauseating feeling that I can only explain as biological surprise when the car doesn't slow at all on intense uphill grades.) At the end of that second, longer burn swath, the road had been gouged and melted, and the SD slowed abruptly (I remember your mother—already doubled over to look at the burned tree tops—hitting the dashboard sharply with her chin when the car balked; she yelped and we laughed) as it bumped over the concrete ripples. A person in spandex on a thin-tired bike ripped by, soaring downhill, avoided the ripples and fissures. When he passed our vehicle, I saw that he was wearing a mask. Your mother rubbed her chin and said something about the biker.

Today's entrance into the mountains revealed years upon years of burns. Everything, it seemed, had burned at some point, and like a still-living geology, there were layers of different ecology: here a black-painted hundred meters, beyond that a kilometer or two of new unidentifiable leaf, beyond that a longer section of black but with knee-high aspens. All variations of forest—scorched, infant, toddler, teenager—fly by as the SD climbs. I am passing now the old state park facilities, which had been permanently closed by the time your mother and I arrived here. It, at least, hasn't changed at all. It's as if someone has coated it in unbreathing plastex. The old lodge squats near the road and seems exactly as aged as it did forty years ago. Even the SKI RENTAL sign looks as if it were painted ten and not fifty years ago. A few of the bigger trees surrounding it look licked by fire, but not badly burned. Across the road is pure, untouched forest of huge pillars of pine and spruce. A bit farther on, torso-thick, white-kneed aspens hold up their scant leaves; I am surrounded by the neon green and snow white of adult aspen. Then I remember: This spot had been a blackened slope of wooden stalagmites when your mother and I passed this same place. There were still puffs of smoke lifting from the ashes. The smell of burning wood was intense back then. Your mother said, "It smells like fireplace," and I said, "You need to go on a camping trip."

In a few minutes is the Aspen Vista parking lot, which was, back then, the new end of the road. I feel my stomach twist with anticipation of arriving there. An old fire road, which had long been closed to vehicles, had reopened temporarily in those days to allow the ski area breakdown crew to get in and salvage what remained. We planned to walk up it to a higher peak, then descend into a valley where, your mother claimed, Cordell was supposed to be.

We had a couple of bottles of water. We had a couple of soy bars and a banana or two. We were not hikers. Hikers lived in Montana, we thought. Hikers were German tourists. We were searchers, writers. We were poets.

44a

That's it! I'll say, "What I mean is"—and here I'll remove the first dim sum from the little ring, but then will pause, my hand suspended, and allow you to see my arm tremble—"my story of your mother doesn't yet have much to do at all with *your* story of your mother . . . and I'm not really . . ." (I'll bring the dim sum to the small plate before me and act as if I'm searching for words) ". . . I'm just . . . I feel unprepared. There, I said it." A feigned tremble and "There, I said it," I tell my students, is one of the great keys to asking difficult questions in tense interviews; it comes up more than a few times in *Coordinates*.

44b

We started walking. There didn't seem to be any smoke at this elevation, and a few birds streaked over our heads, and it felt pretty good to be out there with your mother, even though this was not my idea of romance.

By now, you should have guessed at what happened next. Interruption, of course, as always. I could have taken your mother to the moon and, once there, just as we took our first looping hops, a twentysomething, poorly shaven guy would show up and ask if we didn't mind if he joined us.

This interruption was the heaving engine of a large truck driven by a twentysomething, poorly shaven guy. I swung around and watched as it slowly crawled toward us. The truck was old—boxy front and chipping green paint. It stared straight at us even as it jumped over rocks in the road. As it approached, it slowed. A young man leaned over and rolled down the passenger-side window with a crank. I couldn't really see him in the shade of the cab.

"Y'all want a ride?" he asked. "Or are you just hiking?"

This is how we came to ride a couple of kilometers up the mountain on a suspension-less flatbed truck, the driver of which, I think, wanted to flirt with your mother. When I walked up to the window to talk more to the guy, I could see that he was a minor lech (I was raised by one, so I knew the signs: the deep-set, shifting eyes accustomed to the low light of midnight; the dry lips; the smoking; the grumble of sleeplessness; the beard untouched for two weeks). Your mother acted oblivious in the face of his near drooling, knowing that, if she downplayed my jealousy so that we could ride on a truck part of the way, I'd be much less likely to call off the hunt early. She was smart on that front. I lied and said I'd prefer to ride out in the open air. I pulled myself up into the surprisingly cold steel at the end of the flatbed. Your mother thankfully insisted on sitting on the flatbed with me. The truck roared back into gear.

But now, years later, I'll pass Aspen Vista, because, with only a few hours of daylight left, I wouldn't make it far, and wouldn't see anything. The road beyond the Aspen Vista lot has been reestablished, and so I plan to make it to the old ski area parking lot, where, now, a tiny, cable-driven tourist lift—as far as I can tell from my research—will take me up to the top of something called Raven's Ridge. From there I could walk east for a kilometer or so and around a low peak, and, according to the topo maps, I'll be able to see Spirit Lake in the distance. The information about the lift claims that you gain nearly a kilometer in elevation in twenty minutes. If I can get to Raven's Ridge in forty-five minutes, then make the lookout in twenty, I'll be able to see the little lake below for the first time in more than forty years. I can, perhaps, see the sun set on its glass-calm water.

I honestly don't know why I'm doing it. There's not much curiosity to be satisfied, because I know I won't find much here. Until eight years ago, it seemed as if someone had been maintaining the small cabin next to the lake. I saw in a few photos over the years (which, since the loss of Big Co.'s monopoly and the dissolution of the USGS, were hardly updated as frequently as bimonthly, and at least twice weren't updated for an entire calendar year) obvious evidence of residence: in one photo, what seemed to be a large bucket or basin, in another, a black robe stretched out in the sun, and in another, a person, probably Macrina, bent over the edge of Spirit Lake performing some menial task of the everyday. But as soon as the road to the ski basin was rebuilt, I saw nothing more. Macrina, of course, would be in her eighties by now, and the road would have brought more visitors and more problems. For some reason, I have always believed that Macrina would die out there. And for some reason, I have always known that I could not return until she was gone. There have been no updates for her DCOB profile. But there wouldn't be.

Again, I'm outrunning myself. You haven't even met Macrina yet. You will, very soon. The SD is slowing now, and the signs say PARKING THIS WAY FOR LIFT. A couple of SD guide poles flash their brief morse at my little XiPi. It understands and pulls forward and into the appropriate parking space, right next to one of those rectangular sleepers that Europeans rent on American vacations. I see someone lean forward to peek through the glass, then lean back again, uninterested in an old man and his tiny Chinese transport. If all goes well, I'll see Spirit Lake in an hour.

45

I'm writing this in the last bit of natural light I have.

I have decided to stay here tonight.

I know you'll ask why. Perhaps you'll suspect that I do not want to encounter again the Hungarian woman, or perhaps you think I'm sabotaging the inevitable meeting between you and me. But I assure you that I am not so much afraid of the pseudo-Hungarian's meddling in my tight little world or your probing gaze as I am excited about the prospect of tomorrow. You and I planned to meet during lunch tomorrow, and I'm sure a quick message could delay that meeting until 13:00 or 13:30, which means that, by the time the sun rises at 6:15 and the first lift runs at 6:30, I will have approximately six hours. In my old age, an hour and a half walk down from the lift terminal to Spirit Lake (says the badly printed brochure I'm now holding) is probably more like two hours down and three hours up. This is five hours of walking and about six hundred meters of elevation gain. This will be challenging for a man like me, but sixty-eight is the new forty-five, and I carry no excess body fat, and the soyshake supplements from my doctor have kept me uncannily fit (how strange it would have been, had these shakes been perfected fifty years ago, to be deprived of the morbid satisfaction of watching my father wither away and finally puff out at sixty-three). I also have another thing, something not biological or instinctual: I have narrative force. It will, I'm sure, contribute in some way to the upward trend of my movement tomorrow. Of course, I'm afraid that my biology, in a vain effort to maintain the survival I've perfected over the last thirty-five years, will defy me, perhaps neglect to provide me with the adrenalin needed to accomplish feats that are somewhat outside of a desk-bound academic's normal range of activity. I will bring with me the emergency oxygen supplement from the case I keep in the XiPi. I will get to Spirit Lake. I will have approximately an hour, but probably less, to look around and do whatever it is I hope to do there. Even five minutes will be enough.

All of this came about because when I arrived at the lower lift terminal just a few minutes ago, the young man operating the lift, riding one of those half-medicated highs, rather rudely asked me where I was headed and if I had prepared for high-elevation hiking.

I said he could mind his own business, and that he could charge one ticket, and I held my cell out in consent. He was tall and badly dressed. He had an awful beard like mountain dwellers had always had, but whatever heritage he had received prevented the beard from growing any more fully than in tight little copses on his jaw. His eyes were glazed and he smiled with pot-brown teeth.

"Sorry, brot," he said, obviously used to such gruffness, "I just have to ask everybody. Some fool died up there last month." He reminded me of Juan Miguel in the way that he seemed to totally dismiss the emotion behind one's comments, and instead derived only the information of your emotion.

But I felt a sort of kinship with his belief in the foolishness of others. I asked about the distance from the lift terminal to the lookout.

"Lookout?" he said. He laughed, but then suddenly stopped. "What do you mean by that, brot?" He was sitting on a black stool near the lift's big wheel. The wheel was not turning, so I assumed business had been slow that day. The plastic chairs hung from the cable, which disappeared over a forested ridge hundreds of meters beyond us. When he asked me what I meant, he squinted his eyes and grinned, as if he was trying to determine some secret motive. Then he asked, "Are you one of those Old Thinkers or whatever they call themselves?"

"No, I'm a professor."

"It doesn't!" (I have always been baffled by this slang.) "What and where do you profess?" He emphasized the last word with an academic mockery.

"At State. Can I have a pass, please?" I stuck out my cell farther.

"It doesn't, brot! I spent a year there . . . failing in the business program." He laughed loudly. "You seem like you probably teach . . . calculus or something clack complex."

"I teach Narrative. Freshman intro all the way to post-U." I decided to answer more fully because I realized that this guy's hollow cheekbones and thin eyebrows seemed a lot like the sort of cheekbones and eyebrows that would get a failing grade in my class, and that, perhaps, already had.

He smiled at me and then looked down. I could tell that his memory access had been slowed considerably by the self-medicating (this is, after all, the entire point, is it not?) and then I saw him find the proper file, search it for an image of my face or a remnant of name (*Stern?* he thought while the processor sizzled. *Storm?*), and, finding little of use (which didn't surprise him), he decided to trust my implied memory, which was absolutely not memory at all (I intentionally purge the cache of all but a few student faces and names the moment they walk out of my classroom with their final disappointing grade) but instead just a statistical possibility.

He became very formal. "Unfortunately, you have to let me know" (I felt my stomach seize a bit) "what your plans are and I have to literally measure your heart rate with this thing and also record your water amounts before I can let you on. And that's policy, sir."

"Are you serious?"

"As a fire, br—sir. I'll lose my job if I don't."

I told him my plans. He then informed me that I'd never make it to the "lookout" I sought before sundown . He said the lift deposited you very near it but the ascent to the saddle between the peaks was something like three hundred meters, and by the time I'd made the saddle, the sun would be too far down to see anything but shadow. The guy who'd died the month before was an Old Thinker or Whatever but was younger than me, the lift operator said, and that guy had wanted so desperately to make that "lookout" ("That's why I ask about that word, sir, because the only person I've heard use that dick-old—sorry, I mean old—word was that guy who died") that he ran out of water while trudging up the saddle (the same one I planned to walk), then passed out and probably died sometime that night when his heart failed because of the dehydration.

"I had to go find the guy so the helicopter wouldn't waste all that money in the search, and when I got back, I couldn't do much but medicate for the next few days."

"You're saying I won't be able to see Spirit Lake if I go up now."

"No, sir. Even I would cruddle to get to the saddle before dark, and I'm . . ."

I suddenly felt ridiculous. I didn't know what to do. Nothing, really, was nostalgic or revealing about this parking lot, because this parking lot had not been in the story.

"Listen, sir, you're certainly welcome to sleep here. Those people in that big SD over there are from like Finland, and they're pretty cool, and theyr'e gonna ride up tomorrow morning and then make Lake Katherine, and Spirit Lake is on the way to Lake Katherine, sort of, and you could just like take a little detour . . . it's actually not much more time down to Spirit Lake than it is up to that"—he chuckled— "lookout. Whenever Whoever Those People Are come up here, they usually want to get to Spirit Lake too, and most of them take the first chair up and I've seen some of them come back down by lunchtime. If they don't die. That fool brot thought he could just walk around at a few thousand meters with a single can of water. They're like religious . . . so maybe he thought God or Shiva would rescue him. I don't know, brot, sir, maybe you're like in all that. For that old dude it didn't work out. I figured people need to have something . . ."

I walked away midsentence. Now I'm back here in my car, and the XiPi's cabin lights have come on as I feel it gently roll back downhill. A few minutes ago, Rodri, the young man who probably never was my student and who handed me this brochure as an unnecessary peace offering, climbed into the Fins' rented van and then there was the low thump of electroid drone song pulsing out of the van like it was a nightclub. The windows were opaqued, and the tune of their revelry was muted by the XiPi's noise cancellation, but I still felt the deep vibration of the bass, so I decided to sleep at the pull-off for Aspen Vista, which was, at least, a part of the story. I'll return to the lift parking in the morning.

The teenage aspens are tall here, and their silhouettes in the setting sun are a sort of beauty I've seen only once before, but, of course, not here, exactly.

I am finding it difficult to believe that tomorrow I will return to Spirit Lake.

46

The flatbed ride was jarring in a way I'd never before experienced. Your mother produced little scream laughs every time the big double-wheeled back end of the truck sunk into a boulder pocket or bounced over a rock ridge. My back compressed, and I tried to seem as casual as your mother. A couple of the bumps sent bolts of electricity searing through my back, and I believe that a minor spinal issue that has dogged me for much of my middle age was caused on that drive. The driver kept yelling back at us things like "Here comes a big one!" and "Watch out!" and, after a few disorienting jolts, I would press my hands into the truck's steel and lift my body off the truck bed and let my wrists take the shot.

The driver stopped after a few minutes and said, "You guys sure you don't want to ride up here?" We walked around to the side and opened the door but there was only the passenger seat, and at its feet was a big toolbox that couldn't go elsewhere. Your mother said she would sit on my lap. I asked the nearly burned-tan driver how much farther. He said twenty minutes. I said all right and climbed into the truck cab. Your mother got on top of me. But after a few minutes of more jaw-crunching bumps, I told the driver to stop. The cab was blistering hot, and the deep grass stench of his vape pen, which he puffed on like it was necessary for survival, was making me sick. I said I'd just stand on the flatbed and hold on to bars over the back window. "Suit yourself," the guy said. I assumed my position. Two advantages immediately presented themselves to me: I could now watch your mother interact with this guy through the back window, while also taking the hits with the built-in suspension in my extraordinarily sturdy legs, whose two stumps are indubitably my finest physical feature. The truck lurched forward; I gripped the bars tightly and bent my knees with each boulder. Your mother didn't even speak to the driver, so I let my attention wander outward.

At one point, the "vista" opened up and you could see a few kilometers of black forest: Only a small patch of green remained in the fold we'd driven up, a kind of verdant slash in the black, and near the top of one of the anonymous peaks was a deep-green teardrop that, I assumed, had only briefly burned. Down below, Santa Fe was shrouded underneath a thick layer of gray. The smoke's barely visible fingers stretched into the mountains too. Though we couldn't look directly at the sun up here, we had not escaped the smoke.

The vista closed as the tall black columns returned in a thick blur. We kept bumping upward.

The road eventually topped out and became smoother. One could see for kilometers in all directions; we were, for the most part, above the smoke, which seemed to loom even a hundred meters on the mountain below us. The sun was intense this high up. The flatbed sped up as the road smoothed out. We passed a metal box about the size of an old-fashioned dumpster. It looked like it used to have a window.

"That's the old Millennium lift!" the driver yelled.

I saw the big horizontal wheel on the pole next to the box. It occurred to me that the box had been where the lift operator sat. Every tree in sight had been burned. There was no wire on the lift anymore, no chairs anywhere, just that glassless cell for a medicated ski monk.

The truck stopped a minute later. I leaped awkwardly down from the steel bed; she unfolded gracefully from the passenger seat.

The guy leaned over toward the passenger window, vapor leaking from his mouth. "Deception Peak!" he said. "I'm going back the other way." He was headed up to the radio towers to meet up with a cell tower guy who had a crane truck up there. He'd be back there at exactly 16:00 (back then he would have said "four o'clock") and would give us a ride back down if we wanted one. We said thanks and that we'd plan on meeting him back here at four. I imagined the coming night alone with your mother in the XiPi, which had lay-flat seats for which I had paid extra in an uncharacteristic splurge. I only had to endure eight hours, then, of tromping through the forest in search of the first Black burn hermit. This did not seem insurmountable.

What's funny is that I didn't doubt we'd find him. I, like you, am a child of modernity, and whether I would have admitted it or not, I believed then that nothing was hidden that could not be found, and that what could not be found was never hidden in the first place.

The descent from Deception Peak to the roughly one-kilometer square area that Muhammad Wright had indicated was, to put it bluntly, quaint but depressing. I remember thinking with a certain alarm that we would have to *come back up* this particular path, which was an interminable series of switchbacks that had been hurriedly etched into the eastern slope of the mountain. The visible goal of our descent, as far as I could tell, was arriving in a flat valley that served as a shallow bowl for the surrounding gray peaks. I was sunburned within what seemed like minutes.

"I think I'm getting burned," I said to your mother, who was about six paces ahead of me. She stopped, turned, and let me approach. The valley unrolled behind her, and I swallowed a fleeting feeling of vertigo.

"Oh God," she said. "You really are."

"Aren't you?"

"No. I'm brown!" She stretched her arms out as if to prove it.

"Brown people don't get sunburned?"

"Not like French Canadians from Pennsylvania," she said.

I said I had never told her I was French Canadian.

"Aren't you?"

"Well . . . yes. On my dad's side."

"That's what I thought." And she handed me her jacket to wear over my head, and though I mumbled, the shade it provided was magnificent. She said I looked like some old monk.

Finally, down in the forest, we began our search. Though Wright hadn't mentioned it directly, it seemed clear to both of us that Cordell would be near water, and, according to our pixelated cell map, there were several small ponds in the area, so we worked our way toward the first, which was slightly to the south and east. There was a faint trail to follow, a game trail or an infrequently used hiking trail or both, and I thought for the first time how the forest really wasn't any large mammal's home. Of course, it was home territory for many mammals, but it wasn't a "home," a shelter, because no roof of any use sat atop its columns, and no walls blocked the wind or kept out predators, and no food was easily available for grass eaters or carnivores. It's almost as if the rocks called us back, yelled at us that there was nothing in that shag carpet of pines.

We hiked on. I listened to your mother's footsteps on the needle-covered path, and I wondered at the trees, who made no eye contact or gesture to indicate they recognized our presence. Birds flitted and cawed. A few white butterflies tumbled through the smoke-dusted air. The sun sent fingers to the forest floor. I was tired. I'd finished nearly my entire water bottle; your mother had finished half of hers. We stopped and looked around and I pointed the water levels out. Your mother just said she hoped we'd find Cordell, who undoubtedly had water. She looked at her cell, and with two fingers zoomed in on the place where we stood. "Just a few more minutes," she said.

She had, by the point, picked up a dead, stripped spruce branch and was using it as a walking stick. She lifted it into the air, like a priest in procession. "Come, Father Stone," she said. And I said, "Amen?" and kept walking. I preferred to watch my feet bump along the trail.

If I looked up, I had the strange sense that though I was walking at a normal pace, it took one and a half times as long as normal to reach little landmarks: a stump, a fat pine, a rock. I looked at my feet and wondered what the cause of this was. I was no hiker. The natural world had systems and ways outside of my experience. I was used to the distances of the world humans built.

After a while, I noticed that all along the trail little mounds of needle-dense sod were lifting up, as if something had emerged partly but given up when it saw light. I stopped and kicked one. A white knob was revealed.

I called to your mother. She came flopping back.

"Look." I repeated the kick.

"Mushrooms!" she said, and squatted to look more closely. "Can we eat them?"

"Not if you want to leave here."

There was a pause, which ruined the joke. "I don't," she said. "I don't want to leave. I love it out here." She looked up at me from her squat, then pulled the base of the mushroom and stood up, holding it in her fingers. It was cartoonish. It had a thick, bulbous stalk and a curved, too-small cap, like it was wearing a headdress that it had long outgrown.

I asked her if she really did like it out here, as it seemed desolate to me.

She nodded. "It's so peaceful."

I said if she ate the mushroom, things might eventually become very, very peaceful. She punched my shoulder, then held the little fungus up to my face. "It's cute." A black plume of hair hung over her sharp cheekbone. She brushed it back with the non-fungus hand. Then she pulled the mushroom to her face, smelled it. "Oh man. Smell it."

She held it up to my nose. It smelled like forest concentrate in the same way that a seashell sounds like ocean concentrate. She said she was going to look on her cell to see if it was edible. I suggested that we save that for later, and save cell battery and time by keeping on to the first lake. I could feel the subtle approach of the two-headed monster—disappointment and intense discomfort—and I sensed that we would be wandering for some time yet.

After a few more minutes of heads-down walking, I noticed that the forest went from slightly blackened on the base of the trees, but otherwise green and alive, to truly burned. Trees were still growing in this transitional area, but there were more black snags and generally less brown.

"This makes sense," your mother said, "because Muhammad Wright was studying transition areas." I said nothing, because logic is a pointless instrument in a logicless search.

We finally made it to the pond marked on your mother's map, which was surrounded by a forest that looked like something from a revolution. The pond was small, and it was drying up—all that was left in the bottom was the scummy dozen centimeters or so of water the animals had made so foul that even they wouldn't drink it. The satellite photo on your mother's phone was two months old and the lake was, at least we figured, filled with snowmelt then. We walked the perimeter, then made fifty-pace forays directly outward from the pond. But we gave up quickly. There was no way Cordell was near here. It would be like living next to a sewage-retention pond. There were no signs of human use but for an old glass bottle and a faux-leather strap of a woman's purse. All of this was too burned.

We agreed to head north, to another small pond on the map. Your mother stopped and stared at her phone. Earlier that week Muhammad Wright had, with his finger, drawn a rectangle on the screen over the map of this area. Your mother was clearly having a hard time remembering the exact corners and sides that he'd drawn. She said she was just trying to remember what Wright had done.

"So, what you're saying is that you're not exactly sure if we're only searching the lower half of Muhammad's rectangle, while Cordell might be in the upper half?"

"Well, yes," and she laughed. She was standing about ten paces up an even fainter trail, her hands over her eyes in an effort to see me. I stood in the shade outside the circle of sun where she had stopped. I did not laugh.

"It seems like we could look for this guy for hours in a theoretical rectangle that he's not even in."

"I suppose so," she said, trailing off and looking again at her phone.

"What do you mean 'suppose'? Maybe that Muhammad guy didn't even give you the right *mountain range*, for God's sake . . ."

"Why would he lie to me?"

And from here unfolded what I think amounted to the first (and, really, last) true fight that your mother and I ever had. Now, forty years later, it's easy to be honest: I was frightened and annoyed. She was alive with freedom and possibility. I hadn't thought to bring a soda with me, and I was desperate for one, thirsty but also headachy. The arithmetical quandary of our water worried me more than the absence of the soda, though. I just couldn't see how we'd go up that mountainside with only half (and dwindling) of our water remaining.

At one point during our argument, she came back into the shade and sat down on a short stump, her elbows on her knees. We argued about Muhammad Wright—who she claimed I disliked for no reason, and who I claimed she trusted for no reason—and about my tendency toward sunburn. Eventually, I said something about David Geores the Interrupter and she said it was pretty twisted to blame a guy who'd been *shot* for my own arboreal discomfort. "Arboreal discomfort?" I asked, and she said, "Yeah, arboreal discomfort, sir," and stared straight at me. I could tell she was still half joking, that this argument wasn't really what I'd thought, and that if we just sat in this forest and tossed a mushroom back and forth for the remainder of the day, she'd be happy. The mushroom stalk poked out of her left hand, and she looked utterly stunning. But I held back a laugh and grin and maintained my anger. I asked her how long we would be wandering in the woods before she felt satisfied that we wouldn't find Cordell Jones. She said, "I'll let you know." I went dead silent.

We kept walking. The truth was that I did not doubt we'd find Cordell Jones. I also had no reason to believe that Muhammad had given her anything besides his best guess. Instead, I figured that even *he*, city dweller that he is, would have struggled to find Cordell again. I thought we'd find Cordell at the worst time, maybe ten minutes before we'd agreed to turn around and head back. I was, especially, afraid of getting "stuck" with him, afraid of your mother saying, "It's too late to hike back out," and that we, instead, would be sleeping three wide in a burn hermit's chilly hut.

I walked ahead of her. She occasionally would yell "Hey!" or "This way!" when the GPS suggested we deviate from the little game trails we followed.

We arrived at the next pond. This one was full of water, and slightly bigger in diameter. The forest around it had recovered. Green boughs stretched toward the shine. I told her I'd check the other side. We walked in opposite directions.

On the other side of the pond, I found a campfire ring. I couldn't tell how old the burned wood was. Near it was a beer can with an expiration circle that listed a date in the future. I also found a cache of strips of torn paper that had been partially buried. I kicked them free of the dirt and saw they had writing on them in blue pen, a jaunting semicursive. I remember a few of the words well: "2.5 mm star bit" and "dripline" and "angle grinde." Almost as an impulse, I began making a poem with these bot-produced words. I stopped when your mother yelled from across the pond.

I said I hadn't found anything. I buried the paper again.

We began walking toward what the GPS suggested was a creek. We thought we'd follow that creek up to its source; perhaps Cordell was living in that corridor. As we walked, the forest changed almost imperceptibly from mostly unburned to mostly burned to somewhat recovered to untouched and shaded, then back to burned and canopyless. The places where fingers of fire had torn through the woods were varied based on the age of the fire, and, even in my mood, walking through the strata of former flame was a fascinating stroll through a living museum. I could see why someone like Muhammad Wright would have come out here. (I considered saying so to your mother, but I stayed silent.) In one section, there'd be luminous green growth of baby aspen, in others silt-black char, even, I could have sworn, tiny hairs of smoke still lifting up from ashy logs. In another section, clouds of white butterflies lifted up from the brown duff. One stratum had thousands of emerging white mushrooms; another section had fewer, already rotting flat ones; yet another had a third kind, brainish, almost indistinguishable from the dirt and somehow nefarious looking.

The forest was not recovering, I thought, as much as it was just being a forest. I tried to imagine what it would be like to *not* prefer or define the forest just in its old-growth phase, but instead to appreciate the forest simply as a living being of sorts, a cycle, a slow change. I have since always tried to think of forests in this way. I have, now that I think about it, tried to think of the earth in this way. It burns and floods, we adapt and recoil. There are very few, of course, who don't think that way anymore. The Old Thinkers or whoever Rodri was referring to might still be clinging to the idea that humans can overwhelm the earth, but the newest generations know for sure that the earth can overwhelm them, and they watch with a certain amount of humble wonder—the exact kind we lacked back then—when the volcanoes spread their inky fire and the seas rip apart another section of some massive, mobile city and a germ can sail in on the wind and within months murder unsuspecting scores.

Your mother was not one of these new thinkers. She really did believe in a downward plunge. The David Geores incident, I see now, had also been a symbolic bullet that she had barely dodged. I believed she looked around and saw that her life and its equipment were rusting in place. Her poetry was being mocked and scoffed at and rejected as not good enough for post-U programs. Her mother, your grandmother, was less and less responsive, and sent only enigmatic messages hinting at suicide (these I will not quote [though of course I have them], simply because it seems obvious that your still-alive grandmother has left behind the idea of self-deleting and embraced some other type of existence, medicated or otherwise). Her truck was incapacitated. Her apartment was poorly furnished. Her job was thankless and ultimately pointless. It was as if your mother had been born a farmer in an expansive and impossible desert. Her idealism could not survive in Albuquerque or Centex or any place, really, that you or I might think of as a place to survive in.

As we walked through the forest, these thoughts first occurred to me. I knew that I, on the other hand, had adapted well enough to the desert. I found the greenery of this forest, sparse as it was, oppressive.

47

It's strange to be slightly cramped in my SD, perched atop a mountain, narrating a story that I have never before narrated—though I have remembered it again and again. And in telling it, I see, now, that my character is not exactly the most sympathetic. Of course, my character is the surviving one, and after I wrote, above, that your mother seemed unequipped for living in the world, in this world, I allowed myself to ponder what, exactly, made me so equipped.

What's amazing to me is that in forty years, I have never before considered my character (narratively, I mean) up against your mother's. Here's an example: That man, the JP Stone of this story, back then, was certainly smart, even perhaps a kind of semi-rare brilliance. He was no national treasure of a genius. But he had an intellect that would pay the bills and make his name known. However, in comparison to your mother, that man was somehow deficient. I do not say so nostalgically. He was like a telescope and she was like a fish eye; what he saw with absolute clarity he saw narrowly and from a distance, and what he saw she could not see well. But she could see so much. She saw much. She saw kaleidoscopically.

Or another point: that JP Stone was a poet, attuned to the tremors of language's sound. While the anapestic beats of "mm star bit" and "dripline" seemed to him poetic, the raw material of this poetry was the trash and leavings of a thoughtless population. He was more a reader of tea leaves than a poet. Your mother, however, found something as simple as a mushroom's scent to be, somehow, *more* than just a mushroom scent.

Though I can't exactly empathize with her way of seeing, I do crave it. For now, what I see through my telescope is death, and what I hear in my ears is the dull thud of empties dropped by a society that produces and consumes beauty like cheap beer. (This image was less original than it seems; the car that pulled up next to me an hour ago has just ejected three empties from a window rolled down just enough.)

I wonder if all the pain that would ensue—for your mother briefly, and for me continuously—was a result of a type of seeing, or rather not seeing. That is, I didn't see anything out there but trees and burned snags and fungus. So it was easy to want to go home.

But I was not so lost as I might seem. For there was something I *did* see. I saw your mother. I *saw* something in her that *was* squarely not me. Some light or flame or wholeness. I couldn't grasp it intellectually, and I knew I couldn't. I don't know what it was . . . she not only saw, she was, and she was in a way that I wasn't. If she had just been beautiful, or funny, or athletic, or seductive, I wouldn't have mourned her loss these forty years. But she was some other thing. She was more like flame itself than she was like the forest. She was the opposite of my shriveled manhood. She was possibility.

You have traveled only miles to know this, but I have traveled decades to arrive here, to finally put into words the understanding I've been weaving all that time. And it's this: I was flammable material standing in the presence of flame.

Lest you think, however, that your mother was some deified super mortal, it should be known that she was still young and that these moments really were the beginning of her own selfhood. Her effort to find Cordell was the first dramatic step toward finding her path. I see now that had she not decided to live at Spirit Lake with Macrina, she would have made an equally dramatic step elsewhere or elsetime. She would have moved to Africa, to Mexico, to a cult's compound in Wisconsin; she would have quit her job and apprenticed with a plumber or pastor or pulque brewer. Something big would have happened, and I must remind myself of this when I begin to see Spirit Lake as a dead-end, single-track path branching from what could have been a long trek together. I have little idealism; I had much ambition. Now, after exhausting my ambition, I have only dread. Your mother could not have survived on my path. I could not have survived on hers. You could not have survived in between.

Mostly because of what it means about how to survive in this firescape, I regret that of the three possible, you and I are the remaining pair.

48

I have mentioned Macrina again, but this time we are near enough to hear the frivolous thud of her dull hatchet on a soft log.

After several hours and a quiet lunch of soy-bars and bananas in a burned-out clearing that had erupted with grasses and big hairy flowers, and after searching around a total of three actual ponds (and searching *for* one that the satellite photo swore existed but was nothing more than a strange crop circle of fallen gray tree corpses), and after following probably three kilometers of dry creek (where our drinkable water finally was depleted), we reached Spirit Lake.

We did not know it was called this, of course, and would have probably scoffed at such a cliché. (I would have, at least. I do, still.) It was bigger than the ponds we'd encountered so far, and it was clear and free of scum, and big rocks lay just beneath the water near the shore, as if they were seeing for how many eons they could hold their breath. We sat down on a log that rested atop a big hump at the lake's outlet—where the creek we'd been following began—and from this moraine we observed the pristine lake.

This was, indeed, a lake. The big mountain we'd descended seemed unbelievably far away, but perhaps this was because of the air's smoky deception. The trees around this lake were not burned in any way—they had escaped the cycle of fire.

Both of us had reached a clearing beyond anger and were now just silently worried. We would never make it back by 16:00 for a ride down—it was nearing that time already.

As we sat there, we heard rising up from the whisper of the trees the thunk-thunk of . . . of what? It sounded like someone was hammering wooden nails into rotten holes with a wooden hammer. It was barely audible, and it faded with the swish of pine boughs, but then, unlike the lake's boulders, resurfaced.

"That's *someone*," your mother said. And, of course, she was right. It was. Had to be. I was thinking of two things: how long until sundown (three hours or so, I guessed) and whether or not the diarrhea induced by swigging lake water would wait until halfway up the mountain to explode from our young bowels. The discovery of a person—a person thunk-thunking, nonetheless—was a sort of relief. But if it was not Cordell, I figured that replenished water and more exact directions would only lead us into another Muhammadan rectangle. I wondered what it would be like to sleep out there, with only the other's body for warmth . . .

We followed the sound and traced the lakeshore. When we had walked for a few minutes, though, it seemed that the sound was coming from across the lake, not ahead of us, so we circled back. We argued a little about echoes and sound speed, but your mother grabbed my hand and kept walking counterclockwise around the pristine water. After a minute or two, it became clear that the thunking was indeed ahead of us.

What materialized first was a tiny structure, a cabin, you might say, the same one you saw when you looked down from your future satellite seat. From above, it looks square, as you probably noticed, but this is only because the roof was made with pieces of rectangular plywood, maybe a meter by a half meter, that had been patched together over logs, then wrapped with tar paper and sealed with some long-banned impermeable, then covered with layer upon layer of charred spruce bark. (I remember this because within an hour or so, I would find plenty of time to examine it closely and note its construction.) The cabin itself is basically octagonal. It is built rather primitively, a stacked-log construction, but this is only visible once inside. On the outside, the cabin had been roughly stuccoed (which is why I didn't recognize it from Wright's photo; Macrina had had a few guys lug in a couple of sacks of weatherproof stucco, which she mixed with the water from Spirit Lake). As we got closer, we could see bits of grass and sticks poking out from the red-gray wall.

The thunk-thunk grew louder. "Hello?" your mother called from a few paces away. The thunk-thunk stopped, but nothing more happened. We came nearer. From the doorway of the cabin, which had no door, we looked in. It was no bigger than my apartment's bathroom (a convenience I'm missing right about now—I was sure, when I exited the car to empty my bladder, that the rustling thing in the nearby bushes would any moment come roaring out, ending this story a tad sooner than I'd planned). In the back of the cabin was a waist-high bench with a big sleeping bag on it. At the foot was a table, made from a bent piece of roof plywood. Above the table was a window—a simple half-meter square plate glass that was set into the stucco on the outside, and another pane stucco-sealed on the inside; its foggy translucence was likely a result of this odd double-pane construction. Along the opposite wall was a woodstove, a stainless steel, rather sci-fi-looking woodstove ("from a living room in a space cartoon," Cordell wrote), whose sleek exhaust exited at a wall hole similar in craftsmanship and height to the opposing window's. There were books underneath half of the bench bed, and there were black plastic trash bags underneath the other half. There was a strange-looking Christian cross flanked by two old religious paintings (though I could never find exact matches, I'd look them up later: they were Christ and Mary, his mother, in the Byzantine style). The place smelled of burned pine, slightly floral. The floor—a few square meters, at most—was covered in what I at first thought was a blanket woven from grass but what I realized was just long dry grass stems spread all over like in a children's book's barn.

"Hello," someone said behind us.

"God!" Your mother jumped and half turned. I spun around and hid my surprise. My heart raced. Probably from dehydration.

We have come now to Macrina. And so the end is nigh.

49

The woman who stood before us seemed incredibly young at first glance. Her long, black-gray robe minimized her curves (small breasts, I assumed, and wide hips) but could not hide the fact that she was not thin. She wore glasses, and they perched slightly off-kilter on her prominent, meaty nose. Her eyes were round and brown. She had very thick eyebrows that met in the middle with a barely visible bridge of hair. Her brown hair was pulled back into a ponytail (later I'd see that there were gray strands amid the brown). Her face was narrow and her features defined, and all of that looked wrong on top of such a round, shapeless body. Naturally, she was sweating.

We stood there in silence for a few moments and it dawned on me that she expected us to speak first. So I spoke up.

"Do . . . you live here?" I asked.

"Yes," she said. "I've been trying to, at least." She smiled and looked away, back toward the hidden spot on the other side of the cabin where she'd been thunking.

"We're out of water," your mother said, "and we hoped you had some."

"Water? Yes!" the woman said, and she sprung into action as if she'd realized we were old friends. "We have an entire lake!" She moved between us and into the cabin, pulled a small black case out from underneath the plywood desk, and unzipped it as she emerged.

"Follow me." She began walking toward the lake. "I'd give you some that I already filtered, but I'm mixing mine now with unfiltered." She shrugged and smiled as she walked. "It sounds like good wine or something when you say it that way." She laughed happily and, kneeling with effort and groans at the water's edge, began unpacking the case. Standing next to her so that the shade of my body covered her back, I could see sharp-lined crow's feet appear next to her eyes. She pulled a plastic cylinder out of the case, set it down, then opened a door on its side that swung outward and revealed two solar panels (one in the door and one in the cylinder).

"Sir, if you don't mind, these little panels of mine cannot be hidden under a bushel."

I moved slightly to the left. I wasn't precisely sure what a bushel even was (a collection of stemmed things? the basket which held them?), or what it had to do with a shadow.

"Oh my gosh, thank you so much," your mother said, when, seeing the woman pull out a long plastic straw and place it in the lake, she realized the contraption was a water filtration system. We both unscrewed the lids of our plastic (!) water bottles. The little machine whirred to life. I expected a gush of water—what came out was a trickle.

"This might take a while," the woman said after we all watched in silence for a moment. "I have it on its highest setting, and such low voltage . . . apparently . . . can only produce a drip-drop." She sat down and put her legs out in front of her. I looked at her leather-sandaled toes, which were dirty and much, much browner than the dough white of her arms that had been momentarily exposed when she pushed her sleeve up to better place the straw in the water.

"Where have you come from?" she said.

"Deception Peak," I said. Your mother nodded.

"Ah. When did you leave? Seems like you started the hike pretty late. I can usually make it down in two hours, sometimes less if I've had shrimp."

"Shrimp?"

"I sometimes get shrimp when I go . . ." She trailed off while she leaned over to place the filter's hose differently. ". . . Sorry—when I go into town."

"We sort of wandered around in the woods . . . how often do you go in?" your mother asked.

"In the summer, I make it in about every two weeks. In the winter, it was a bit less because snowshoeing up the switchbacks you just came down is like walking through a swamp uphill."

I imagined our return ascent, and I felt a little tinge of anger.

"But!" she blurted. "I just bought a pair of skis, so this coming winter will be better, much better, because I think I can ski out of this valley and reach the road farther down," She hugged her knees to her chest and looked up at us (both of us were still standing, as if we'd be leaving soon). She was silent, and so were we. We watched the machine.

"We were looking for this guy . . . Cordell Jones," your mother said. I could feel her looking at me, an amused, playful look, as if I were the child and she the mother who had promised to take me to the park but had gotten all distracted with buying me ice cream or toys. I did not meet her eyes. Instead, I stared at the water.

"I know Cordell Jones," Macrina said. "Why were you looking for him?"

"Well, no reason really. Just to meet him, I guess. We're poets"—your mother looked at me again, but only for a moment—"and we heard a talk by this guy who'd met him—"

"What's-his-name? The Muslim guy? Muhammad something?"

Your mother said yes, though neither of us had any idea if he was Muslim.

Macrina said she'd never met him, but Cordell had talked about him. "So you know Cordell?"

"He built that hut . . ." Macrina ducked her head nonchalantly toward her abode.

"Really? That's the hut?" Your mother stared at it. "Where is he now?"

"He's down in Santa Fe, as far as I know. You won't find him out here."

There was another long silence. My anger, oddly, dissolved for a moment, mostly because I realized that our search was over. I could see that your mother was disappointed.

I spoke up. "What do you do out here?"

Macrina looked at me and paused, I think to see if I meant I wanted to know, or if I just wanted it not to be silent. "Well, it depends on what you mean," she said. "If you mean 'Why do I live out here?' my answer to that is I live out here for solitude and peace. If you mean 'What activities do you do during waking hours?' my answer to that is I pray, thank God" (she crossed herself), "I cook, thank God" (crossed herself), "I clean, thank God" (you get the gist), "I read, thank God" (I expected that she would not continue in this odd performance), "I walk around, thank God" (I wanted to look away, but I was betting with myself that the next would be the last cross), "I carry wood and build a fire in my stove, thank God" (here she crossed herself thrice, after emphasizing this "thank" more than the preceding ones), "I fill water for lost hikers . . ." She smiled again at us.

"Thank God," your mother said, trying to cross herself in the way Macrina had. But both women laughed, and Marcina smiled and said, "Like this. Forehead, belly, right shoulder, left." I did not participate but watched, instead, her mouth. I saw that the right front tooth crossed just barely over its brother, and all her teeth were small and yellow fringed where they met the pink gums.

Your mother laughed half-heartedly and said something about her grandmother. I spoke up and said that clearly we hadn't planned ahead enough. I did not laugh, and looked only at the water bottle. There was maybe a centimeter of water inside. The little filter buzzed on.

The woman saw my gaze. "I could lower the filter's effectiveness, but I think it would be a bit risky—the last thaw unfroze hundreds of dead fish . . . I guess the lake froze through entirely. It was pretty darn cold in February. How they got there or had survived as long as they had is a question I ponder for ten or fifteen minutes every day." Then she picked up the water bottle while holding the straw in place. She looked at the water. "It's almost like the filter's clogged. It usually doesn't go this slowly."

Then she stood up and asked our names. We told her, and she said her name was Macrina, though "in the world" she'd been Lena.

"Should we call you Lena, or Macrina?" your mother asked.

"Either is fine, but I tell you this simply because I haven't gotten used to the Macrina name yet. Much of the time I've had it I've been living alone . . . just the other day a young couple like you was camping across the lake and when they came over for breakfast—I'd invited them the night before—the young man said something like 'Macrina, is this water filtered?' and for a moment I thought, 'Wow, that young woman is named after Saint Macrina!'" She shook her head and put her hand over her mouth in mock surprise with herself. "JP," she said, "you seem uncomfortable. Are you hungry? I have coffee, if you'd like some . . . not to eat, of course—I mean if you're hungry, I'll get you food, and if you'd like some coffee, I can make that too. I'll boil the water to be sure it's clean."

"We'd love some coffee," your mother said. As we followed Macrina into her squat hut, I joked quietly with your mother about needing coffee of the carrot soda variety. Macrina heard me. She turned and asked rather excitedly if I liked soda. Your mother answered for me: "He's a fiend." Macrina laughed and crossed herself and said, loudly and enigmatically and to no one in particular, "Are you not much more valuable than they?" And when I just stared and didn't respond, she said that the couple of last week had left a soda—not carrot; ginger ale, she thought—at their campsite on the other side of the lake. She didn't drink soda herself, but she'd saved it thinking that perhaps it'd been (and I quote) "sent by God," and here I was, a soda drinker . . . and so on, and more crossing herself. I was beginning to find this woman grating and also of questionable sanity.

From underneath the desk—I think, now, that she must have dug out a tiny cellar below it, because many more times she pulled yet another thing out from underneath the desk—she dragged out a paper sack, and in this was a small backpacking stove, which she slowly unfolded and set up on her desk. "Normally," she said, "I make coffee on the woodstove, but that takes forever. We'll just use this handy little thing!" And soon the little flame whispered loudly beneath the tiny pot that fit on top and was filled with water.

She said it'd take four minutes. "Let's go check the other water." We strode back again to the lakeshore, Macrina loping ahead of us six paces, your mother casting little glances of pleasure at me, me evading those glances and acting serious and a bit perturbed. The blue plastic water bottle was, now, a quarter of the way full. "Oh dear. It's just never gone this slowly. How long have you been here?"

I said maybe twenty minutes. We all did the calculations, and I exhaled loudly and turned to face the hut. Macrina said that if we wanted to make it back to Deception Peak with enough time to get back down the fire road, we'd need to leave like now. "Well, more like five minutes ago, and that's if you're in good shape."

For some reason, both women looked at my middle. I'll never forget that moment. These two women believing, somehow, that my flabbiness was less justified than their own. Your mother had none, though, to be fair.

"Just turn down the filter and increase the flow," I said, still with my back turned to the two women. "We really don't have another option."

They both looked at the pump. Your mother said something like "I don't know," which I was expecting her to say. I spun around and put my hands up. "What in God's name are we supposed to do then? Climb a mountain in the dark? Sleep with a hermit in her tiny hut?"

Macrina and your mother were silent. Your mother asked if we could boil the water. Macrina said we could, but the little backpacking stove had a receptacle that held only a cup or two—it would take a half hour or so to boil even barely enough—and she was trying to save the gas as much as possible. The woodstove would take that long just to get hot enough to begin boiling water.

I saw that Macrina had pulled a short string of beads out of her pocket, a worry rope of some kind, and was thumbing it. Then she said gasped, repocketed her rope, and said, "Don't worry! I have a tent!"

50

Before we go much further with Macrina, I must interject some important information, because I fear such cinematic representation may be painting her too rosily. It is late—long after midnight—but, rather than wait until the morning, I feel that it's important to write this next part in darkness. It is, indeed, dark.

Macrina, we would find out around a campfire that evening, was a monastic. When we asked what kind, she said Orthodox, "not Jewish" (I wanted to blurt out that there were no Jewish monastics, but I stayed quiet) but Orthodox Christian. She'd grown up "agnostian," which, she said, consisted of the type of Christians who like to dress up on Easter and put Nativity scenes on their mantels in the winter but also avoid church and generally vote Democrat (remember: Democrats, back then, were liberals). She'd practiced some forgotten sect of Hinduism in her twenties and then, in the wake of a personal crisis at about thirty-five (eight years before your mother and I showed up with no water), had converted to "Orthodoxy," as she called it. She'd lived for nearly seven years at a monastery in Arizona before coming to live out here in the mountains. The backstory was at times hazy and occasionally contradictory. For example, she seemed to claim that her "elder" was in Arizona, but then she said she would go into Santa Fe to visit her "spiritual father." When I asked her where she was from originally, she said, only, "The South," and when I asked what state, she just said, "Aren't they all the same?" and then very quickly asked us where we were from. This I noted as the first of a number of suspicious evasions.

Neither your mother nor I knew the questions to ask about her religion. She looked to me like the pictures of nuns I'd seen in the book I'd ferreted from the school library when I tried to research the religion my father so frequently derided. And though, then, I could not understand why a whole bunch of people in medieval costumes make-believing and looking very serious should be the singular subject of my father's verbal rage (though, unfortunately, never the subject of his physical rage), I did retain a visceral distrust of costumed Christians. Your mother, with a kind of myopic stare at the flame, in an effort to be polite, inquired generally: "So, what caused you to want to be an Orthodox Christian?" and "Does your family know where you are?" and "Were you *sent* out here?" I did not listen much to the answers because I was not interested at all. Religion was far from an opiate in my view: It was a useless and outdated social code. Not so much comforting as deliberately nostalgic, a sort of narrative pharmaceutical. I suspected that this woman was not who she seemed, and the snatches of her answers I picked up—"I had a visitation . . ." and ". . . know about as much as I do about them . . ." and "you could say I was sent . . ."—all seemed to suggest some dim and indecent past from which she was escaping.

Before you spend any more time with Macrina, then, I think it's fitting that I fast-forward four days to the day your mother sent me this series of messages (perhaps the most-read cell messages in my entire archive) after trying to call me unsuccessfully.

Your mother: JP . . . if you're reading this please call.

Your mother: I guess you're in class.

(I was, indeed, teaching a particularly brutal seventy-five-minute period on analytical essays.)

Your mother: This is not the way I wanted to do this . . .

Your mother: It's going to sound crazy, but I am right now on my way to Santa Fe. I found a ride with John's brother.

Your mother: Im gonna go and try to live with marina

(*Sic:* She meant Macrina; that particular unwelcome autocorrect caused fifteen seconds or so of numbing confusion.)

Your mother: I didn't talk to you about this before, because I knew you'd try to convince me not to go . . .

Your mother: I think marina

Your mother: Macrina

Your mother: I think Macrina is living the life I've wanted to live . . .

Your mother: I know you won't understand

Your mother: I'm just gonna try it, and if it's too cold or we get too hungry I'll just come back

Your mother: I hope you'll come visit—remember when we talked about poetry as life? You are perhaps the only person I've ever met . . .

There are some intermediate texts about her feelings for me that I'd prefer not to distract you with at this time. What's most important, finally, are the last three messages, sent only thirty-seven minutes before I was released from that high school hell and could check my cell.

> Your mother: I think we might lose service soon
> (This was *way* before Complete Coverage.)
> Your mother: Don't not come
> Your mother: I think it'll be like living a poem

In these last three messages were some beautiful truths that took me years to discover. However, at the moment, I found them bombastic. The first of the final three messages seemed to me, just then, to be a rather depressing finality. When I read it I thought, only, "I can't communicate with her." The second seemed to me a passive shrug, because instead of begging me to come, there was the double negative, "Don't not come." Finally, the third, was patently ridiculous. There was some wondrous thing in your mother that insisted I still loved poetry, even though I'd spent many a late-night hour explaining why it was dead and why I had long abandoned the strange academic vigil over its corpse (I'll quote one of my more skillful moves from *Bot-Poetics*: "To believe that bot poetics can somehow reanimate traditional verse is like believing that [a then-famous pop musician] can by playing an electric lute resurrect minstrelsy"). It seemed to me then that, in her last messages to me, she was taking her final shot, telling me why, indeed, this spelled the end for us, telling me precisely how my love was misplaced, exactly how unlovable I truly was.

However, a few months after your mother's death and just before the Big Co.-induced archival Haze, I was rereading these messages one night and something changed in me. I was, for the first time, able to see something remarkable: The first message (and the close proximity in time of all the other messages) suggested that I was the last and perhaps only person she was messaging before she "disappeared." The second message suggested that, knowing me, she *suspected* I would "not come" in order to exact some level of punishment for her attack on order and logic, and what struck me was that she was (1) perfectly right—I deigned to visit only when it was way too late—and (2) she understood me better than I'd realized. Finally, the third message just made me hurt, for she wasn't yet dead when she sent that, and, of course, had no idea she *would* be in the course of something like three-quarters of a year, and I could feel that she was both excited and in awe of what she was actually doing.

But just four minutes after I got these messages (and after eight or nine unconnected calls to your mother's cell), I was not thinking so generously. The rage that built in me was the purest, most concentrated form of rage I'd ever felt. It was as if the fury I've always felt—at my oversexed and enraged father and impotent mother, at the free-roaming priests who'd (probably, though I had no evidence) fondled the former and shamed the latter, at the two idiotic Scandinavian woman who basically charmed their way into the academic fame that I'd sought, at the foolish and fundamentally flawed and (I hoped) now faceless David Geores, and at the future and then-unknown truths of my crippled gonads and Daniel Glidden's taut lips and Juan's incredulous eyes and the incursions of unwelcome Hungarians—had finally boiled to the appropriate temperature and now was clearing itself of all the dross of reality.

This purified fury was directed at exactly and only Macrina. I hated her more than anyone I'd ever hated. I am not proud of it, but I felt murderous. I had imagined my father dead many a time, but I'd never imagined my hands depressing the plunger on the needle or gripping the thrashing pillow on both sides. But I suddenly began to imagine elaborate and often bloody scenes in which I would liberate your mother from Macrina's cultish hypnosis. I will not describe these scenes to you, for they rotted my dreams for too many years. To rehydrate them now would be to awaken the madness that has lay long sleeping, and will only prove useful in the final act.

For some reason, all my effort went to a more realistic path. I stayed up late that night and compiled article after article and point after point that made Orthodox Christianity look like an aged, blundering elephant, yes, but also like a potentially violent and subversive worldview. I found six or seven podcasts in which uptight priests were making blatantly anti-feminist claims (your mother was a feminist when it still meant something to call yourself one) about the immorality of abortion and, even, contraception, a ludicrous conservatism even the Catholics had nonchalantly walked away from, whistling. I read through some explanations of the Orthodox belief in "incorrupt bodies" (I can't imagine that they still hold on to this, but back then they were making claims that a three- or four-hundred-year-old body hadn't decomposed and had remained fully intact "as if it were sleeping" *without* the aid of chemicals). They had "weeping icons" made of paper and miraculous healings and even some teleportation claims. They required confession and obedience and basically all the things a cult would require. I know this was forty years ago and long before the Great Exit or whatever they call it, but even then this religion seemed anachronistic and dumbheaded and potentially destructive. There were the many schisms. There were a few sex scandals here and there. There were the corrupt prelates who nodded over the table at state dinners about the march to war.

But this was the general stuff. I had a hunch, though, that it wouldn't be enough to draw your mother off the mountain. There is a tendency among poets, I'd noticed, to ignore the rational and global, and to embrace the emotional and personal. I knew I'd have to scare her. And what I found next was enough. It scared *me*.

The first find was a really odd article about some priest who had frightened his mistress enough that she posted photos he'd taken with her in strange states of half dress, posing in strange positions and including strange props. The scandal had been covered up by some hierarch of the Eastern metroplexes, and only when the priest had sent a couple of threatening texts to the woman's teenage daughter did the Orthodox administration do something. What they did was move him to a monastery in Serbia. His bewildered wife was left without financial support, his children without dignity.

None of this matters. But! At the bottom of the article was a little tagline that listed a website as the source of much of the information about the priest.

Once on the site I felt a visceral sense of triumph. The subheading for the (now-defunct) website was "A Resource for Survivors of Abuse in Orthodox Churches." On the left side of the page was a list of names. I clicked on one, a priest. A grainy photo and a short biography popped up and, at the bottom, a list of charges and verifying links to government portals.

Naturally and almost immediately, I typed "Lena Macrina" in the search bar.

MOTHER MACRINA BERSTEIN

Aliases:
    Lena Brighton Berstein
    Mary Brighton Berstein

The "Aliases" part of this website made the whole thing sound a bit overblown, but what followed was, nonetheless, horrifying gold.

    Lena Brighton Berstein was baptized Macrina Berstein sometime in the turbulence of the Church's transition to the American Orthodox Church. Before she was baptized and long after a mysterious stint in the Prahna Cult, she spent a brief period of time as a part of the American Reformed Orthodox Episcopalian Church in Mobile, Alabama, where a low-level minister, Elias Ng, filed a restraining order, available for review here, against a Lena Brighton Berstein, based on threats made against his life. Soon after that, Elias Ng reported to the Episcopalian Clergy Association of Alabama that a Father Norman of Mobile was protecting child molesters. His letter of protest, filed and available here, briefly outlines a "ring" of perpetrators. Lena Brighton Berstein was among those accused of child molestation and endangerment. Though a number of charges against others (see Jackie Hall and Deacon Jared Hall) were pressed and proven true, and though Jared Hall testified in court that Lena Berstein had been in the room during the instance that eventually earned him an indictment, the victim was unable to positively identify Lena Berstein in a lineup; neither was the victim was able to describe her in satisfactory detail. The victim claimed to have never had any dealings or associations with a Lena Berstein or any of her aliases.

Soon thereafter, Lena Berstein left the Mobile area and moved to Arizona, where, after living briefly in the bombastic Biosphere III project (see this Arizona Reporter article), she met a follower of Father Eudosius Pappas, who some believe was a cult leader and among whose spiritual children there were at least two formerly convicted pedophiles and two felons convicted of violent crimes. Within eight months, Lena Berstein had been baptized as Mary Berstein and changed her residence to a monastery that Father Pappas had started in southern Utah at the end of the last century.

Three years later, Mary Lena Berstein was made a full nun, again given a new name, this time as Mother Macrina Berstein. As we've reported elsewhere, some monastics at Father Pappas's monasteries have gone so far as to legally change their names to omit their last names, apparently as a part of a "new life" ceremony, and supposedly without Father Pappas's blessing. A recent picture of her is below. [. . .]

It was recently noted by a local that Mother Macrina had moved from Utah to New Mexico and is possibly living in a small community there.

> We have, as requested, removed Mother Macrina from our Eminent Threats / Questionable Motives lists because she was never convicted of a crime, and now is, supposedly, residing alone and far from children.

I immediately sent a highlighted version of the article to your mother, and I resolved to return to the Spirit Lake cabin the next day. This was several days after she'd messaged me saying she was going to live there.

I write this now, of course, and feel slightly ashamed. Your mother was in danger (if not from outright chicanery, at least from the wiles of someone long brainwashed and unfettered) from the moment she hiked in to Spirit Lake. My resolution dissolved, though, when I received messages back (she'd climbed up to the peak the next morning with Macrina, who, probably in an effort to keep the heat off of her, had insisted that your mother let her family know where she was) that said she'd brought up my concerns with Macrina, and Macrina had been totally honest and understood that people like her were not to be trusted but said that her life in the Church had healed her.

> *Your mother:* I don't know about all that. But I feel safe.
> *Your mother:* I could beat her up, anyway.
> *Your mother:* I know you are con

The message was clipped. I did not message back to tell her to resend it. I felt powerless. Lost. I thought the only move I could make was silent anger, that I'd lure her back simply by making my absence felt.

I was a fool, of course. If we had waded into love, we weren't deep in. Or, at least, she wasn't. My absence was the ache of a wound, not the deprivation of air. She would heal quickly.

Know that I am ashamed I did not go out there immediately. For this, I want to apologize to you.

It's true that I was deeply, deeply hurt. I was the one suffocating without the other. Much of the destructive habits and deeds of the next few years were bent on trying to sate the insatiable. I am not proud of this. But it also was not my fault. You must not hear this as bitterness. I am not bitter. Even if I did not deserve your mother, I did not deserve to lose her once I had her. Suffering just happens; its meteorology is unpredictable. It would be wrong to blame the fire for making people miserable—misery is a weed sprouted from seeds already spread in the self—but it is also wrong to say the fire had nothing do with it. Macrina was the instrument of my suffering.

In a side note—lest you think my denial of bitterness above is just an admission—I've come to something quite different over the years. Here it is, my theory.

If a person is truly conscious of (1) how rare love is, (2) how statistically improbable that the love stories we exchange like trading cards are actually stories of real love, and (3) that the statistical improbability of being a character in one of those love stories is astronomical—OK, add (4), which is that the improbability is compounded when that person's parents didn't love him because their parents didn't love them, and so on, back to the original rape or matricide or oppression that began the whole disaster—if indeed our capacity for love can't really be greater than the amount of love we received (which is my definition for "capacity for love"), the thoughtful person will conclude two things: (A) that while he must find a partner who has a similar capacity and need for love, (B) the person he finds cannot be totally deranged by having received an inadequate amount of love. Thus, we arrive at the actual chances of "true love," as they used to call it. Nil. That is, being in love with someone who's in love with you *and* loving them *and* them loving you *and* neither person getting the raw end of the love deal . . . these things are like total eclipses. That it happens at all is hard to believe.

And, not far behind this psychological mule is another, just as laden: The rational lover sees, in turn, that it would be foolish for him to attempt to find that love, for such an attempt would only constantly remind him of the disability that ruined his first best chance. Thus, the sooner such a man discovers this truth, and the gentler this truth is laid on him (and your mother was a gentle woman, indeed), the more able he is to reconcile with his particular life, to learn to live with his disability, and to not do things—nasty, blackhearted, police-involved, and frightening things—that rage over his lot might bring him to do.

In other words, one can believe in testicular miracles and transformative love and live miserably in their absence, or one can believe in statistics. One in a million gets the girl. I was not one in a million. Nor are you, it seems.

51

That first night, though, sitting just a few paces from Spirit Lake, I had a bad feeling about where all this was headed, but I had no clarity. Macrina was, at that point, no threat to my happiness, beyond keeping me up late. While she talked around the campfire (the solar-powered filter had, by then, filled a bottle but had quit about a quarter of the way through the next as the light waned), I tried to put together the disparate parts of the day: early waking in my bed next to your mother's warm flesh; the slow movement of her own waking; Core L in the SD; Cordell in the crosshairs; the derisory and vapor-spewing driver of the flatbed; the mushroom; the ponds; the "2.5mm star bit"; and now, this, a rather crassly verbose (she told at least two jokes about beer in Alabama) Orthodox nun in a ramshackle cabin at a lake called Spirit. It was a strange output of a program I felt I had little control over.

Macrina would often trail off when we asked personal questions about her life, or would say things like "Thank God I have come through to now" or "God in Heaven has in mind what many do not," and these little catchphrases I retained along with "dripline" and "angle grinde." Though I wouldn't have said it to anyone, I loved the rhyme in "line," "mind," and "grinde," and I thought, too, how perfect the image of an emerging forest mushroom would fit next to the silly little solar-powered device filtering out previously frozen fish guts from a glass-still lake.

We ate rice and beans, which she had paid two strong men from Santa Fe to schlep in a few times a year in twenty-five-pound bags. We asked her how she paid anyone anything and she said, "Well, not exactly paid . . . you have some of my currency right there." She pointed at a spot in front of your mother's foot. The sun was still just barely glowing above the mountains in the west, but I could not see what she pointed at.

"Shoes?" your mother said.

"No . . ." Macrina said. She lifted herself up from her stump and stooped to pick up something off the ground. "Matsutake!"

My eyes had a hard time focusing enough to see what Macrina held— but then I realized it was the mushroom your mother had carried all this way. The flames—this fire was illegal, she said, but no one would ever come out here to stop us—lit her dark robe strangely, and the lines of her face seemed infinitely deep. I guessed (correctly) that she was middle aged. Much older than us.

"They *are* edible!" Your mother rapped my knee with her knuckle. She stood up too, and I saw the sweet brown legs and the short torso, and I felt a certain sadness in realizing that I would not be unwrapping them that night like I had the night before.

"Not only are they edible," Macrina said, "they're a delicacy. In Japan, these mushrooms regularly sell for hundreds of American dollars per pound."

"What are they called again?"

"Matsutakes. Like shitakes but with a matsu instead of a shit." She laughed and apologized for her language. "Bad habits, bad habits," she said. "Lord have mercy." She crossed herself. "Where'd you find these?" Your mother got out her phone to show Macrina precisely where on the GPS we'd been—for it was easy to find in reference to that first depressing lake. "Cordell's gonna hike back in a few days . . ."

"Cordell! You never finished your story," your mother said.

Cordell, from the rather sparsely detailed story Macrina provided, had been deeply bothered by Muhammad's departure. It was only after Muhammad left that Cordell realized how lonely he was. Macrina had shown up in the mountains a week or two later and had talked with Cordell about his life and his plans. Cordell wanted her to live in the hut with him. She chastely refused, sleeping instead in her tent on the other side of the lake, though they spent hours together every day, talking and mushroom hunting. Cordell, Macrina said, was particularly intrigued by this enigmatic Orthodox idea of the nous, which was a kind of perceptive faculty that wasn't sight or emotion or intellect but, as far as I could tell from Macrina's frenetic description, a mix of all three. She said, at the end of this description, "Wait a second," and dodged into the black night outside the fire's radius. She came back in a few moments—your mother and I had remained silent in her half-minute absence, staring at the fire—with a slip of paper. "He gave me this," she said. "You guys are poets . . ." She leaned forward on her stump and handed it to me over the low fire. I took it, but I couldn't read it until I brought it so close to the fire that I could feel the hairs on my knuckles singeing. It was a short poem. I only recall the title and three lines.

Beat Attitude

Blessed are the poet in spirit
For they shall *see* odd

And then after some forgettable and grammatically incontinent versification, there was this (preemptive *sic*):

Theres no such thing as evil

I have retained these lines because it was then that I began to realize what these people—Macrina and Cordell and Muhammad Wright, to an extent—were peddling: what we used to call "pyramid schemes." This was a pyramid scheme of the soul. Macrina, I suspected (and subsequently confirmed when I discovered her checkered past) had perhaps lost a valuable consumer in Cordell. After I read the poem, she said, simply, "Cordell sadly went back to the world. Now he's one of the guys that brings in sacks of beans and rice in exchange for mushrooms." Macrina claimed we missed him by only a few days. She said he's making lots of money selling to local restaurants. He doesn't talk at all about spiritual things anymore, Macrina said. "So sad."

I could feel the sales pitch slowly moving toward us like a mountain cat in darkness. So I decided to act.

"Where's that tent?" I said, perhaps a bit too bluntly. "I'm exhausted."

Macrina said nothing and rose, grunting, from her stump. Your mother just kept staring at the flames. The nun disappeared into the darkness. A minute later, I heard someone unfurling cloth, the click of tent poles. I rose and moved away from the flame.

I watched and tried half-heartedly to help Macrina erect the little shelter. Eventually, I became only a lamppost, holding my cell flashlight above the work area, wondering if something more dangerous than this mysterious nun lived near Spirit Lake. Once the tent was up ("Easy!" Macrina blurted), I wondered how in the world your mother and I would fit in such a small space. Macrina said it wouldn't be raining, so there was no need for a rain fly. I said I'd rather put one on, just in case (any amount of separation from the outside was attractive). So we spread the rain fly over the little hump of a tent and secured it to the tent's corners.

Macrina brought the tent bag and a few unneeded stakes back to her hut; I returned to the fire, but only stood near your mother.

"You ready?" I asked.

"For bed?" she said.

I nodded. She turned back to the flames.

"I'm not that tired yet." A pause. "I like looking at the fire." I heard in her words a sincere invitation to remain with her, by the fire. (Remember, she was flame.) But I felt then in my gut what would reveal itself as truth in the next five or six days: I was losing your mother, because she was asking me to do something that, then, I could not do. I could not settle into a night of free-ranging stories, of confessional anecdotes, of spiritual half-truths. I could not. I was straw.

So I said something like "Suit yourself." Macrina came back into the fire light with a stack of blankets. I took them silently and did not say thank you. Once in the tent, I tried to form a bed of some kind that might work to allure your mother into feeling that I, not Macrina, was her home. I could not; the blankets were ratty and lumpy and I had to fold them too much. There were no pillows either. I got angrier and angrier. Eventually, my cell blinked out. I had intended to leave it on so your mother would feel bad that I was "waiting on her," but my flashlight had drained the battery. I lay down and listened to the low conversation between Macrina and your mother. I couldn't hear anything beside the change of speaker. One of them, I couldn't tell which, spoke much more than the other.

I'd give anything to return to that night. I'd sit there with your mother and Macrina until morning came and the solar filter buzzed to life again. I'd sit there and say nothing; I'd just radiate a force field of sense and logic that would surround your mother and discourage Macrina from even attempting to ask what I knew she'd ask ("So, what about you? Do you have a spiritual practice?"). I'd sit there until we turned to ash! Anything to keep your mother from ending up alone with that wolf; anything to alleviate the guilt I've had for forty years over being in the room but doing nothing to stop the predator.

Instead, I stayed in the tent and slept fitfully until your mother came in. I said that Macrina's blankets were pretty bad and that it looked like a long night was ahead of us. She said, "Aw, they're fine." She kissed me gently as she lay down. Within a few minutes, she was asleep, her fingers laced in my hair.

52

My God, I must try to sleep. I feel the old rage coming back, the old addiction.

You undoubtedly are ready for some conclusion. This is what I refer to in my classes as "termination lust." The story has become too dense, too overgrown. No new thing can fit. The forest has become, as the rangers say, low to no moisture.

53

Back in the XiPi, finally.

I just finished the second carrot soda; I feel resurrected.

It is nearing 14:00, nearly twelve hours after I wrote the strained forest metaphor above. I know I'm facing the same problem I faced just yesterday (that was just yesterday?) when I first got the text from Daniel about your arrival. I am trying to figure out how to respond. You have sent me a series of messages that worked as signposts of your morning: first, the gradual ascent from waking to an awareness that you and I had not planned an exact time to meet ("Good morning, JP What time would you like for me to come?"), then a slight increase in effort when, after a couple of hours, I had not replied ("Hi, JP What time exactly would you like for me to come? Just don't want to surprise you."), then, nearing noon, true exertion (a missed call and voice message that I will not be listening to), then, at 13:00, a quick series of messages: "Are you there?" And "Hi, JP I know you're busy. Please call me ASAP so we can work out a time for a quick chat." And "Even a chat over cell is fine with me." And "I am leaving Albuquerque at 18:00, and I would like very, very much to hear what you have to say about my mother." Then, nothing for the last hour.

You have possibly given up on me, which is relieving but ultimately not useful for this narrative. Perhaps you wanted to go up to my apartment, but Juan Miguel has been made extra-sensitive to unauthorized visitors and so he is very unlikely to admit you to the forty-second floor. Even if he did and you ascended to the branch on which my little urban nest rests, you would not get any farther than my door. A few series of impatient knocks might produce the pseudo-Hungarian from across the hall, who, I imagine, has been awaiting my return while she squats in my neighbors' apartment. But she, too, will not be able to help you along your way. In fact, she might speak poorly enough of me that you will be discouraged from continuing such a fool's errand as coming to take the last possession of a grumpy old academic in his semi-fortified sky hut.

I see now that this is what you're doing. Not waiting, but coming to repossess, to foreclose. As I hiked back from Spirit Lake this morning, I finally admitted this to myself. And I hope you have learned that I have nothing besides your mother, and that the above generosity of narrative has literally been a liquidation. You don't believe me? Let's run inventory.

Coordinates, as you well know, is an outdated gimmick that was seized in its youth by a curriculum company and then raised in the feedlot of public curriculum development, where it's grown fat and sedentary and widely hated by generations of college freshmen. Just a few days before you showed up, I received the perpetual licensing forms that would sign over *Coordinates* to the giant and hideous academic insect that is Pearson Pelican.

Bot-Poetics we've discussed. It continues to shout my shameful aborted takeoff.

My teaching has receded so much that it could no longer be considered teaching—besides that ass Jared, I have the lowest rating among professors in the NNP program. One of the highest-voted comments is one that I can't agree with more: "Professor Stone has a heart of stone, and a curriculum that, apparently, was written in stone forty years ago, and the day we begin his class he writes our marks in stone and they never budge." (The second-highest-voted comment is, simply, "If I have to hear about another *bold knob* being *soldered* on *old pipes . . .*")

I have written nothing of use in years.

Daniel, who I would consider the person closest to me, is not even a friend, really. Not anymore.

Your mother is dead.

How can I relinquish to you the One Thing? It would be like signing over—

My cell buzzes. It's the ambivalent CPS: "Your guest has arrived in the lobby." I decide to ping back my location. Juan Miguel will know the gravity of such a revelation, for location is a black market currency that he loves to deal in, even if it's just to suggest to a resident that he noticed they had been in this or that place. I will communicate nothing more for now. I want to focus. Though of course many manufacturers have long removed the power-off option, I've got on my cell a semilegal app that accomplishes the old-fashioned communication feature called radio silence.

I must finish.

54

Rodri was not exactly pert when I arrived at the lift this morning. In fact, Rodri was not there when I arrived. I was ready and waiting when he emerged from the Fins' strange van at 6:14. "You're very prompt, Professor," he said. "The Fins aren't going up anytime soon. Those brots are *bled*." He stroked his facial hair incredulously and stood near the low green fence that marked the boundary of the lift station. I stared at him blankly. He looked ridiculous and out of place there, standing in his oversized brown shirt and loose-legged pants while surrounded by the straight and ordered trunks of new trees and the vectors of verdant grass stalks. Then he said that he felt "fuggy lacked," which was slang I'd heard in the most recent academic semester but whose meaning I had not yet determined. He yawned and code-opened a short gate and then turned to make sure it closed behind him. On the gate a sign said NO ENTRY AFTER HOURS. MOTION-INITIATED POLICE ALERT. Then he poked a small screen at a terminal near where he and I had spoken yesterday. The lift lurched and then hummed and the chairs began moving. It was 6:23. In what I thought was a truly diplomatic tone, I loudly asked Rodri if I could go up a bit before 6:30. He said he just needed to finish his opening duties, which took another four minutes and included sweep-vacking the loading platform in between chairs, pulling his long, curly hair into a strained bun, and emptying an aluminum cup left over from one of yesterday's tourists.

"You can just push the gate," he said.

I went in. He scanned my cell. "Senior discount," Rodri said. "Step up to the yellow bar and wait until it opens. Then move onto the platform and face the chair that just passed you."

"Don't you need to measure my water?"

"Oh. Yeah." He looked at the container that hung from a carry cord around my shoulder. "You're fine, brot." The yellow bar swung open and I half fell onto the platform. I faced the retreating chair.

"What about my heart rate?"

"Oh. Yeah. Just add me on your cell monitor."

The chair hit me in the knee backs and I sat almost without effort. The chair swung a bit as it left the platform.

The lift ride up was intoxicating, perhaps because of the nature of the errand I was running, and also there was the true beauty of this mountainside, which—from what the brochure said—had not burned in twenty-three years. The aspens were as tall as government homes, and in the low light of sunrise I saw a fox or maybe a badger or bobcat dart between white aspen trunks. I strained to see if there were mushrooms poking up through the leaf litter, but the lift was too high up to allow for good resolution. I knew, anyway, that it was not mushroom season.

The lift purred happily and emptily. Something in its innovative construction allowed for impossible distances between support poles, so the stomach-dropping whirrs and bumps that I'd endured on my only other lift ride (as a child sitting next to my cigar-smoking father on a droopy last-century Pennsylvanian lift that reluctantly pulled us through a drizzly, nearly snowless forest) were minimal. Directly to my right I could see the vestigial horns of the cell towers that had only been partially dismantled, and which I was happy to avoid with this new mode of ascent. The last time I'd been to this mountain I'd had to ride a snowmobile below the moon glare of those towers, which was less concussive than the flatbed ride up but certainly more psychologically torturous. Trying today to mimic either of those two contrasting entrances—the fire road of the summer (in whose mouth the XiPi and I slept last night) and the pathless snowbanks eight months later—would have been both physically brutal and, I think, spiritually painful, and I'm glad I chose to make a detour around those lanes of memory. Of course, we will not be able to avoid the second entrance altogether. Back then, there was no Rodri and no floating chair above Raven's Ridge.

The chair slowed as it approached the terminus. A robotic voice exhorted me to prepare to unload and to step firmly onto the moving platform. A metal step ascended to meet the soles of my shoes from below, and like a dainty royal servant held the weight of my feet for a few meters before the recorded voice said, rather rudely, "Stand up now." I stood, and I took four steps forward, then descended a set of stairs. Before me a colossal peak loomed on the other side of the valley.

"Welcome to Raven's Ridge," the bot voice said. "Before you is Santa Fe Baldy, over three thousand eight hundred meters in elevation."

I moved the carry cord and the water can's weight to my other shoulder.

"In the valley below is the historic Winsor Trail, which will lead you to a number of alpine lakes, among them Lake Katherine, the most beautiful of them all. Behind you and to your right are the faintly visible runs of the former Santa Fe ski area, completely destroyed by a series of wildfires decades ago. If you look closely, you can see the old quad-lift terminus pole on the ridge to your right."

I looked but saw only trees.

"Up the short Deception Peak trail—a thirty-minute ascent— is the Deception Peak viewpoint. In the kiosk to your right, you can purchase trail maps, or you can have high-resolution panoramas taken. Bathrooms are beyond the kiosk. We encourage you to hydrate well using the water collector unit in the kiosk. Have a wonderful visit."

Silence. I turned to see if any other visitors were being pushed up by the lift. I imagined what I must look like to a casual mountain visitor: a lonely, gray-haired man wearing nearly pristine running shoes he bought two decades ago and stored, unworn, in the trunks of three different SDs, a myopic old man squinting at the complicated green kiosk screen as if trying to decipher his students' bad handwriting, a bereft old man trying to survive retirement by "getting out" of his empty apartment. I felt the inward creep of disbelief, the sense that this was an asinine narrative stunt, for I think I still believed that the narratively impossible would happen—that I would finally reunite with Macrina.

The trail map was too expensive to justify, so I simply downloaded a more crude version to my cell. Spirit Lake, according to the exasperatingly laggy kiosk screen (in a moment of useless epiphany, I saw clearly the meaning of the euphemistic "fuggy lacking"), was 340 meters below this lookout. No camping, campfires, drone landing, or water droning (whatever that was) was permitted at Spirit Lake. Then, in small caps, it read: Please respect the historical sites. Nun's Cabin at Spirit Lake and the rock dwellings at Stewart Lake are off-limits for overnight occupants.

I felt, at first, a painful jab in my chest. Macrina had stayed at Spirit Lake until just before the lift was built. I imagine that in those years, as the waves of fire ripping through these mountains ebbed, she had gained more and more of a consumer base; her pyramid had widened. The hut had become hers, a nun's, and not a Black burn hermit's. Now it was the State of New Mexico's.

The water collector unit in the kiosk was faster than the solar filter had been all those years ago, so I drank nearly all my water container, refilled it, and stepped down the first long set (there would be nine) of rock steps that would take me to the valley floor and its "number of alpine lakes."

55

Next to one of those lakes, on a Sunday morning forty years ago, I awoke early, intending to get the water bottles full as soon as possible. The sun had already begun heating the blue tent, though its light didn't seem bright enough for it to be as hot as it was. As I sat up, I heard Macrina walk quickly by in the direction of the lake. Your mother was asleep next to me, her arms curled under her head as a pillow, her face turned away from me, her breath softly pulsing. She looked like a child. I wondered if her mother knew she was out here, sharing a tent with man she'd met only a month or two before, speaking into the late night with a deceptive nun, waiting for a little filter to refill two water bottles with fishy alpine lake water. At that moment, your mother, it's clear now, was far behind the back of God, farther than she ever had been. Of course, I was just as far as always.

I leaned back in the cramped tent and felt something wet on the nape of my neck. I quickly put my hand there and when it brushed the soggy tent fabric, I understood that the inside of the tent was coated with a layer of beading moisture. I shivered.

I unzipped the tent and tried to emerge from the short door without touching the tent itself, but my back hit the upper portion and caused a rain of dew to soak my lower back and the gently lifting rib cage of your sleeping mother. She stirred. I stepped out.

The morning was dull. It took me a moment to realize that the valley was hazed in by a thin shroud of smoke, perceptible only in the vague scent of campfire and in the way the normal light was slightly dimmed. Macrina was bent over near the lake. I walked to the stumps around the campfire. I saw the soda can and picked it up to see if perhaps I had left some liquid weight in it. I hadn't. I crushed it in my hand.

Macrina turned at the sound. "Good morning," she said. I mumbled a response. Then she held up the solar filter. "I think the battery connections were corroded or something. I used some baking soda to clean the terminals and it's working much better. Look." She lifted the straw and a veritable stream issued forth.

"Great," I said.

"The smoke has come in from the Jemez," she said. "Cordell told me there was a big one over there."

I said we'd seen it yesterday, but the smoke had seemed far off. She nodded.

"I'm gonna walk out with you guys this morning, try to make it to liturgy and maybe into some filtered air for a while."

This was not welcome news, and I was thankful that the XiPi had only two seats.

"When's litany?"

"Liturgy. It's at ten. Two hours out and thirty minutes will get me there."

"What time is it?"

"Just before seven."

"We should leave soon."

I heard the rustle of the tent behind me.

56

The SD has been cautiously descending the mountain for twenty-five minutes now (we passed the Aspen Vista access and just now are slowly rolling through Old Hyde Park), and I just made a mistake in deciding to turn my cell back on. I told myself I wanted to see if there was anything new on the DCOB about Lena Mary Macrina Berstein, but, really, having my cell off and inaccessible is a deprivation more frightening than dearth of carrot soda. As soon as the cell came to life, I regretted my weakness.

The message was actually from "Front Desk," which should have been Juan Miguel, but only then did I remember that my narrative about the Juans was slightly flawed: They had days off too; their counterparts were usually nervous and less genius than themselves.

> *Front Desk:* Mr. Stone, this is Hillary from the front desk. Your daughter is here and says you are expecting her. We don't have her listed on the authorizations, but I think a server problem recently might have caused erasures. Should I override your door code for her?

The text had come in fourteen minutes before—ten minutes after I went into radio silence. "Server problems" was a classic move in the Juan Game. So the force was strong with Hillary.

My reply was, simply "No." It was too late, of course, because if Hillary had not been told of my victory against Juan Miguel and had thus assumed that the game was still on, she would have waited maybe three minutes—you staring intently at her down-tilted chin—before saying that she was "sure it's fine" and that this was, after all a family-centered residential building or whatever. Though in this case, I wouldn't need any resources for later battles; my habit when I lost in the Juan Game, which I rarely played, was to make sure I had at least the tiniest foothold to use in a future game. By saying "No," I guaranteed the righteousness of my anger, even though they could circumvent that anger with feigned deference and an elaborately empty apology so masterfully performed that it was truly awe inspiring. If Hillary had not yet perfected her role, however, she might have stuck to the rules, and thus repelled you.

My phone buzzed. A new message. This one from you.

You: Hi, JP I've changed my ticket to leave tomorrow morning. I think it's likely that you don't want to see me. From what Daniel said about your relationship with my mother, I could understand [. . .]

And there was a whole bunch more that I didn't read. Because it doesn't matter.

I must address the daughter thing again. This is unfortunate, because it slows the narrative. I don't know whether you used the word falsely to gain access, or whether you actually believe it, but I must proceed as if the latter is the case.

I naturally did not think I would need to foray much further into the murky science of testicular health—these tiny twin planets are, even now, relatively unvisited in our medical cosmos—but it seems that a bit more exploration is necessary. And this is precisely and absolutely why I gave up being a poet and began teaching narrative. This is not about what *may* be, my friend, the legitimate daughter of my only love. This is about what *was*, what is.

First: Varicoceles are really quite common and (according to one recent article), after an increase in occurrences per capita in the last thirty years, are now toeing the "epidemic" line. According to the DCOB, you have no husband, but the DCOB is notoriously slow to catch up on the now fluid state of American romance. If you indeed have a male partner, the likelihood that he has a varicocele is quite high: one in three. Next time you have the opportunity, you might investigate.

My generation was the first to see significant increase in the occurrence of what a flippant doctor in New Jersey calls the "aftermarket warmer." Why this increase is happening is less interesting to me and totally outside our purpose here. Because, as I've already said, the added heat causes big problems down there, not so much to the testicle itself but to its famous product. The damaged product, once in a woman's body, like the doctor told me, 999 times out of 1,000 *can only make a damaged product*, which is then aborted by the woman's body. But let's say—for the sake of argument—that it does happen, that a sperm and viable egg (this is, of course, assuming that ovulation is occurring at the moment of copulation and that the couple isn't using any prophylactic measures, chemical or semi-latex) begin their journey to the uterine wall. They plant there (let's not dwell on this disgusting image too long) and then they begin their growth. Nearly every *minute*, there is the possibility of some error in the system.

For some reason, there is still a quite unconquerable narrative that once the little spaceship of the sperm and egg land on the inverted surface of the planet Uterus, there is little to be concerned about. So let's take, for example, the many studies discussing the unique result of tests on important cytokines in varicocylic (I've invented this adjective and think it wonderfully onomatopoeic) males. An important cytokine (think of these as primitive proteins), TGF-β, responsible for a number of mysterious roles in angiogenesis and so on is actually found in *higher* concentrations in sperm that has been heated by a varicocele. This does not defy logic. Sperm (think: space tadpoles) might decrease, but TGF-β (think: space dust), a protein in seminal plasma, is not broken down as easily by the heat from varicose veins. Thus, as sperm and seminal fluid are dried up, TGF-β remains, like salt in boiling water. Once in the woman's body, TGF-β stimulates an immune response, and is intended to help regulate the immune system for the coming onslaught of pregnancy. An important note: Higher TGF-β concentrations can overstimulate the immune response and cause miscarriage.

But let's imagine that, indeed, in your mother's body my (incredibly rare) hale sperm and her (less rare, but certainly not multitudinous) ovum—now a hopeful zygote—planted their flag and then survived the storm of the TGF-β-inspired preparations, which would have been *more* intense than normal because of my overrich emissions. Let's say that, while I taught in Albuquerque, my genetic heir—the one that your mother and I had gone to certain extents to prevent and the very one that poor Angela desperately wanted but could not have—was growing in your mother's body as she did whatever she did with Macrina for all those months. Let's say that you grew during that time, and, eventually, reached the thirtieth week, when you were a viable child, able to survive, like Cordell, "back in the world."

It's certainly fathomable. Absent my DNA information—which, of course, no one in the world has but me—you would insist that it may have been the case, I'm sure. And, as far as poetry goes, it might as well be.

But this is not poetry.

The problem with saying that may have happened is that I know what actually happened. If *only* your mother had indeed had an "enhanced immune response" from my high-concentrate output. But this is not what happened.

What happened was that in March of the year you were born, while at work, I received a call from an unknown number, though my cell strangely identified it as "Ralph Copeland in Santa Fe." There was a subsequent voice message left by a very, very old man. His thin voice was mousy and nearly impossible to understand without super-amplification through headphones, which I had to borrow from a colleague, who I think was surprised simply by the fact that I spoke to them. Back in my little closet-office, while high schoolers hollered and deintellectualized one another in the hallways, I listened to the message like it had been sent from another planet.

Because I eventually deleted the message permanently, I can't provide the transcript. You'll have to trust me that the old man, who introduced himself as Father James, said he needed to speak to me about something urgent concerning your mother, and would I please call him back.

I did. I stepped out into a grassy area—this school had gotten some sort of water exemption—and called Ralph Copeland in Santa Fe.

The man who answered the phone seemed even weaker than the one who left the message. He began with the annoying pleasantries of the elderly: He was very glad I called, and how was I doing and what sort of work did I do, and, as for him, he used to be the priest of an Orthodox church in the area but had retired to a monastery an hour or so north but had returned to the city because, oh, he hadn't been feeling very well lately . . .

I asked him outright why he'd called me. I assumed the inevitable had happened with Macrina.

"Ah, that," he said. I remember that he said, "Ah, that." Ah! That! He asked if I knew your mother. I said I did and asked, with purposeless petulance, if *he* knew your mother. He regretted to say he'd only met her once, as she had been unable to make the trip back into Santa Fe because of winter and the pregnancy.

"Pregnancy?" I asked. Of course, I knew nothing then about varicoceles or impossibilities. I felt ready to faint. I imagined myself running to the staff kitchen for a carrot soda, even though I knew there were none, but just the imagination did me good.

He said yes, your mother was pregnant ("I see you weren't aware of that . . .") and was due anytime now, so Macrina had told him.

I asked him what the due date was, for I needed fodder for the gestation calculator I'd built just then in my brain. He said there was no due date. No due date? No, he said. I heard him hesitate. "She has . . . only returned to Santa Fe once, very early on . . . I could not tell she was pregnant then . . . she did not seek . . ."

"She did not seek a doctor?" I yelled, outright, into the old priest's ear. I was standing in the high school's quad. A couple of cell-entranced girls looked up, scanned the grassy area, and then looked back at their cells.

"She did not."

"She's been pregnant all winter, living with a criminal nun in an inaccessible mountain cabin?"

"I suppose you could . . . yes," he said, too calmly.

I screamed. Just a loud, roaring scream. At this stupid priest, at Macrina, at your weak-minded mother for getting involved in this sham, at you, the most preposterous and humiliating of David Geores's interruptions, who would one day seek me out. How ridiculous, how idiotic all of it was. I looked at the same two girls. They were looking at me now. One was laughing. The other seemed legitimately concerned. She got up and walked inside a building. I walked toward the parking lot. (This moment would be brought up during the end-of-the-year performance review. I would say that I was sorry and that I'd just learned that my father had died suddenly. They seemed to understand my grief, but rightly were suspicious of my inability to control it.)

There was silence while I breathed into the phone as I walked.

The priest said he really did understand my distress. As far as he'd known, he was the only one who knew that Macrina and your mother were out there, and he regretted allowing it to "go this far." He wanted now to seek them out, but he did not know precisely where they were. Macrina had never told him where exactly she was. In fact, they'd only talked during confession; otherwise, she'd always leave before services were over. However, when your mother had come to visit him in early November, he had spoken with her for a while. Again, he had not noticed that she was pregnant, though, of course, she was.

(If we count back from the last time your mother interacted with David Geores that I know about, and *not* including the hospital visit, because I don't think David would have been exactly raring to go, you were—if you believe "you" were you then—maybe fifteen weeks old in early November. Your mother would have probably just started to become round.)

The subsequent problem he didn't discover until much later: that winter had been abnormally snowy—snowier than any in twenty years—and the two women had been stuck there. At something like (what she thought was) twenty weeks of pregnancy, around "Nativity" (how quaint this priest was!), your mother had planned to come out and live in a small room above the fellowship hall at the church in Santa Fe. But the snow kept even Macrina from getting out until early February. When Macrina finally arrived in town, she told the priest that your mother was pregnant and would perhaps need to be removed from the mountains via snowmobile. There was no rush, of course, but she didn't think your mother would be walking out—she was very tired, and had significant swelling in her extremities. (Either Macrina was unbelievably naive, or she was intentionally obscuring your mother's worsening condition. You choose.) Macrina said she thought it'd be better to wait and see if the weather got better, as your mother had not been particularly excited about being "extracted." She said she'd come back out in a couple of weeks and update him. The priest agreed, in the interim, to locate a snowmobile and driver.

It took four days for him to locate a snowmobile owner who was actually willing to go that far. The avalanche risk in recently burned areas is incredibly high, and most New Mexican snowmobilers were unfamiliar and afraid of that sort of snow. Even the search and rescue team—a few men who'd been put out of a job when the ski area had burned—said they wanted four consecutive snowless, sunny days. Finally, a reckless young man from Colorado, a contact given the priest by one of his parishioners, said he was willing to do it, and drove down the next day.

Macrina had said that they were at a lake, and he had in his old age misheard the name of the lake as Stirrup Lake, which, on a map, he figured was a mishearing of Stewart Lake, a lake he had visited long before the fires and landslides. The eager Coloradan headed into the white expanse that day, made it to Stewart Lake, got stuck in weather while looking for the women, had to build a snow shelter (a survival measure, the priest said, he thought this young man actually *enjoyed*), and came back the next day with no nun or pregnant acolyte. They looked at the map again—yes, he'd been to Stewart Lake. They couldn't understand it.

Macrina didn't make it back out until mid-March. More snow. She was nervous, this time, breathless. "Spirit Lake," she said. The priest could tell she was distressed. She wanted to confess but . . .

I told the priest I needed a shorter version of the story, which arrived more quickly at the answer to why your mother hadn't been removed.

"Well," the priest said, "she refused."

"Refused?"

"Refused."

The snowmobiler with Macrina made it to Spirit Lake. Your mother simply refused to leave. She didn't believe there was anything wrong with her.

"There was something wrong with her?"

Macrina said (finally) that she believed so.

"How did she know?"

"Some sort of strange swelling—pitting, I think Macrina called it. And more vomiting than seemed appropriate for a pregnant woman. And headaches."

"Why didn't you send a doctor in?"

"Well, this we did. It took another few days. A doctor went in. I am much indebted to him. He is an old man like me. This was a risk to his life . . ."

What he found, according to the priest, was a very ill woman and a very endangered baby. The doctor said it was preeclampsia—essentially high blood pressure—and it was depriving the child of nutrients and so, by his estimate, the child was, perhaps, at best only 75 percent of the weight it needed to be. Left untreated or unwatched, the condition would starve the child and probably kill your mother.

I was mute. The priest kept speaking.

The snowmobile broke from the heavy use. It was repaired a day later, but the snowmobiler, by that time, was tired and had lost his idealism and was starting to demand more money. The money was found. The doctor and he returned to Spirit Lake. The doctor had thought he would have to induce your mother, and came prepared with some Pitocifan (or something like that) and even an emergency-class narcotic meant for dulling pain in extreme birth situations. The old doctor had been in family practice for thirty-five years and had only delivered three babies—one of them his own daughter. He had never dealt with a preeclamptic woman, as the condition has largely been relegated to the urgency of a flu because of modern medicine. They brought a rescue sled with them too, thinking that, if she was healthy enough, they'd evacuate her into town. She was not healthy enough, but it didn't matter. When they arrived, your mother was in early labor.

At this point, I was so deeply invested in the story that I forgot my rage (a sign of a good narrative). I desperately wanted to know several things (another sign of a good narrative): Was the child born alive and healthy? Was your mother scared? Did she survive? What was Macrina doing? And the ultimate and powerful question of any useful narrative about people: With death nigh, what did they dying person *do?*

If you believe in a god, and if you believe that god to be benevolent, this might be where you draw him or her in. The truth was that— according to the DCOB—you were born prematurely and only a hair above two and a quarter kilograms, which is too small to survive well in *good* conditions. Your mother was not "ready" to give birth. Her body and internal clock pointed at their watches and said things were running *way* early. Perhaps Macrina had castor oil sitting around and had attempted an early induction, but that would have required a rather sophisticated understanding of pregnancy (which, it seemed apparent, Lena Berstein did not have). So the only other possibility is chance, which is often called God. Whatever it was saved your life.

Try to imagine the scene. The cabin buried in a meter of white snow. The lake frozen and buried too, drifting. The stove heating the tiny room. The two woman speaking here and there in spasms of words, your mother thrashing on the bench. The distant hum of a combustion engine. Its clear approach. The grateful feeling of simply not being alone. The doctor walks in. Behind him, standing atop the snowdrift outside the door, is the nervous snowmobiler, mustached and flecked with ice. Four cannot fit in this place, so the young and poorly shaven snow kid goes to construct a snow shelter because he saw your mother's paleness and, when the doctor spoke to her, the way her words were cut short with pain and exhaustion, and he figures he will be staying out here tonight. Had he known that the situation would be this complex, this dire, he might not have come, no one would have come, for no life is worth the risk of one or two others. Snow falls gently; the weather will hold, he thinks, and clouds mean warmth. Who are these women?

Then there's the doctor, seventy-eight years old, the man who delivered you and stabilized your breathing and mixed your first bit of formula with filtered water from Spirit Lake, or from the unfiltered snow covering Spirit Lake. He feels the cold in his joints. (I would meet him only once, and that meeting didn't exactly allow for pleasantries; he died two months later—the news claimed that his heroic efforts to save a pregnant woman in the mountains caused the beginning of a rather rapid decline in his death.) He was perhaps invigorated with this new case. Minus the snowmobiler and the solar-powered filter and gas backpacking stove and high-profile medication and instruments in his backpack, he might have been going to a high-risk birth in the eighteenth century, just like his great-grandfather would have. According to his obituary, he was a Christian. I imagine he was a Christian in the way no one is anymore, not Orthodox, just some other kind, a quieter, less cultish kind, one who would agree to begin his death by birthing an undersized child in a moronic mountain retreat, all of which would have been easily prevented with a polite and swift call to the authorities responsible for dispatching rescue helicopters.

And Macrina—thin, devious, unconvicted Lena Mary Macrina nun woman—is deeply invested, at this point, in the life of your mother.

There's no doubt she has a desire to keep your mother alive. Her February hike out (I would learn later that she had tried skiing, but about halfway down the flat valley she'd gotten stuck in a tree well and had torn a minor ligament) had been brutal, and the return hike, the next day, must have been excruciating. But she likes that it's excruciating, I imagine, for there is a certain sense in her that says she deserves pain, that says God is paying her back for the pain she exacted, and if your mother survives (she thinks this the night before, when early labor began and they both agreed to try to sleep, as she's lying on the dry-grass floor, listening to your mother's stunted breath), if your mother survives, and if the child survives, it will be proof that God is no longer angry at her. However (this part causes her to stop breathing for a half minute or so), if this woman dies—this young, beautiful, unblemished Eastern European / Hispanic woman from Texas who unknowingly had discovered the way to be the very woman Macrina had always hoped to be—if she dies, and if the child dies also or instead, then she, Macrina, will be the most condemned creature alive, she will be worse than Cain, who killed only one (the other child of his parents) and was forever marked by God.

The priest coughed into the phone.

"The baby was born the next day. That was yesterday." (Your birthday. March 25.) "A very important day for Orthodox people," the priest said. I'd say not as important as it was for you.

The strange group of people attended the event. A totally undone snowmobiler (he had seen the afterbirth come out of your mother and had thrown up in the snow); a confused but jubilant nun; a pious doctor; a dying mother; an undernourished baby. Now this group had a difficult decision to make. Do they attempt to descend with you held tight to the doctor's chest and the mother in the rescue sled?

I imagine the snowmobiler was all for getting everyone besides the nun off this mountain. Macrina stayed silent and tried to get you to take the bottle. She prayed, pointlessly. The doctor watched your mother's blood pressure descend (her organs were failing, he knew, and she convulsed a couple of times—proof of eclampsia). She bled profusely. In his old age and long-cemented habits, he had forgotten that Pitocin and its successors could do for her what her platelets were refusing to do: clot blood. He knew, however, that they would have to go more slowly with three on the machine and one in the rescue sled, and he also knew that this woman was not going to survive, even if the bleeding miraculously stopped. So he told Macrina to wrap you—tiny, shivering you—in everything she had and ride with the snowmobiler into town. He would stay with the mother.

The snowmobiler was, of course, not excited, because he knew that this meant he would have to return, possibly to a dead body, but he did as he was told. He probably wondered aloud who would pay him for all this. (That would be me.) Macrina wrapped you inside of her own robe and then wrapped the both of you in all the blankets and coats left over. The doctor stoked the fire. The snowmobile roared away.

Macrina immediately took you to St. Vincent's, and for this uncharacteristic stroke of logic, you must be grateful to her. She killed your mother with her religious fervor, but at least she did not kill you by bringing you to the church instead of the hospital.

When the priest called, you were in the hospital.

At this point—and forgive me for this brutality—I did not particularly care whether you lived or died. I would have traded twenty yous for one of your mother. Still would.

I asked about your mother.

"We don't know."

I asked, in nearly animal tones, what he meant.

"The snowmobiler has refused to go back. This is why I called. Well, he has both refused and is incapable. At the hospital, he was treated for mild frostbite in both pinky fingers, but something more has happened and they admitted him into the psych ward or whatever they call it now. We can get no information. Thank God Macrina took the keys from him somehow. He's only twenty. Poor soul. I have not been permitted to talk to him"

I said nothing.

"Macrina told me all this just now."

Again, I was silent.

"Macrina cannot drive the snowmobile safely. You are the child's father, and you need to come help us."

I said nothing.

"Are you there? JP?" The old man was almost whispering.

I couldn't understand why he had spent so much time telling me the backstory when, just then, your mother was dying in Macrina's cell. On top of that, I did not know about TGF-β then (perhaps it's superfluous to point out that your mother's diseased ending seems quite contradictory to a "heightened immune response" that concentrated TGF-β from testicles like mine incites), nor did I know about my varicocele, so I had nothing to counter the priest's proclamation except a gut feeling that you couldn't be my child and, even if you were, you wouldn't ever be, that no being should be condemned to such a fate. I thought of giving the priest David's name, saying he was the man they sought, but I did not, because I knew David Geores would care nothing for this child, or would try to care but would consume it like air and booze in the dark basement of his a life. I couldn't decide who would be a worse father: him or me. I also didn't want to give David the slim chance I had at saving your mother and winning her for good.

I told the priest I could be there in an hour and a half. It was just before eleven, which meant we had maybe six hours before sundown. He said Macrina would meet me at the hospital with the keys to the snowmobile. The snowmobile sat somewhere where snow met road in the Sangre de Cristo Mountains.

"If I was a younger man," the priest said, "I'd drive the thing myself. God knows."

57

We are nearing Albuquerque now, the XiPi and I are, and there have been no more messages from Hillary, though one has come in from the pseudo-Hungarian, who wants to know if I will be returning to my apartment soon and if she could come over for a quick chat. I responded with a curt negative and told her, unfortunately, that there was no possibility of us ever chatting, ever, because . . . well . . . "I am very, very ill and probably won't survive much longer," but that if she sent me the documents for assigning the translation rights, I'd sign and verify it today. She asked how this could be, she had just seen me in the hallway, and before that in a vivid conversation with some other man . . . These messages I ignored. I have a bigger problem now than smoke screening an annoying neighbor. The XiPi and I are slowing in the mandatory speed-control zone, which means that I have ten more minutes. As soon as I pull into the garage, the CPS will alert Hillary that Mr. Stone has arrived, and Hillary will alert you. You are, undoubtedly, waiting there, intent on your mission. Perhaps you have wandered out onto the drone approach. (I wonder, if I get close enough to my building, will I be able to see your singular figure standing there, looking out over my world from my very own second-favorite perch?) Perhaps you are sitting in the overstuffed chairs flanked with potted cacti and you are listening to Hillary's heels click across the asinine faux marble. Perhaps you have watched her play the Juan Game with some poor peon from the underfloor.

I know that you—for I think now that you and I are perhaps somewhat alike—will wait for me in that lobby until the morning, if need be. Before then, of course, if I never show up, Hillary will message me a few more times, will perhaps out of pity give you the freight elevator code so you can ascend to the forty-second floor. And if you're not in the lobby when I arrive, you'll be in the elevator or in the hallway on my floor, still waiting. I realize that this is simply the culmination of a game I think we've been playing since you were born.

But I have not yet told my whole story, and for this reason I cannot return to the apartment, for that would cut things short, that would force you, like Quixote, to come into possession of the very story you're a character in, which is the kind of loop thought that still crashes chip-hearted machines to this day.

So this is why just now I've told the XiPi to navigate to the only other place where I can go and not be harassed for the duration. The XiPi doesn't understand anything about fate, so it gladly deviates from the SD route and heads toward my office at the U. I am mildly concerned that I'll encounter Daniel there, but I have been evading him on some level for ten years. He can do nothing for or to me now.

In the U business corridor, there are few students around. The shops look closed but they are not; a few students wander around with what have to be their parents a couple of steps behind. It's Sunday. I see now that there's no chance I'll see Daniel. You planned to leave this evening in order to make it back for your first class tomorrow. But you have now called the class off, perhaps are going to vid in, perhaps have called a colleague to sub. I wonder how long you'll be willing to delay.

The XiPi moves slowly into the U garage and dings its arrival. In a moment, I will stop typing and exit my little automated transport, and the SD will move off to some lightless and airless deep-basement spot that few humans ever see and so in turn have become the locale of horror narratives. Such a place is tempting at a moment like this, but I think that, despite the urban lore, there must be plenty of air down there.

58

As I walked to my office just now, I noticed that I felt like I used to feel on that walk: alive, full of potential, important, for I can finally see the end of this overlong thread.

When the first two or three *Coordinates* were aired and then licensed, students and faculty alike watched me pass, and once I heard the reverse-ambulating guide in a prospective student tour group say my name and that I had recently licensed "an innovative series called *Coordinates* for over a million dollars" (a sum I saw surprisingly little of, but which the NNP program loved to tout). I suppose in those days I also cultivated a facade of "tunnel-visioned genius" in which I would walk leading with my forehead and act as if I saw nothing around me.

Just a few minutes ago, I was walking precisely like that, and this time it was no ruse: I really hadn't noticed anything around me. I passed in front of the cafeteria / coffee shop patio and heard my name called—no doubt, one of those obnoxious outgoing students who thinks even the worst and most ancient professors are interesting people—but I kept on. I had no rating to keep up now, no anonymous quarterly survey to pander to. Daniel would have no trouble replacing me when the time came, and with my salary he could buy two post-post-U's that were doubly as effective, more recently published, and infinitely more likeable.

The doors to Cal Hall opened as I approached, the elevator dinged its welcome, and within a few minutes, I had shut my office door behind me. It is there I type these concluding paragraphs.

I have always kept my office sparsely furnished. I have insisted, too, on not "moving up" to those semi-penthouses reserved for the oldest dotards on the block, the offices where you can display your unused and dusty paper books like the professors of old, the offices with windows that look out onto quads filled with tight-pantsed, deep-cleavaged women who never, ever get older. Until a few years ago, I had even foregone a window, but Daniel claimed that windowless offices were health hazards for old men. Though it didn't convince me, the argument convinced *him* enough that he wouldn't leave me alone about it. So I moved to this office—488—and have never truly settled in it. There is nothing on the walls. I have an old, school-surplus faux wood desk. Beside my desk chair there is another seat. (I have, recently, quite intentionally sought out the least comfortable seat for others to sit in, and found an old plastic seat-desk combo, that, when the desk surface is removed, still requires the rare supplicant, usually someone with a C-, to slide in between the desk's support bars to get into the seat. I hope you'll consider using this trick of the trade—it is the only authentically innovative pedagogical legacy I can leave you.) I keep no paper books on the anachronistic bookshelves except twenty or so academic texts that I got from my father after he died, which he amassed in the years before his intellectual failure was complete. In fact, one of the books my father never read is on my desk now. It is called *Literary Criticism: A Short History*, published over a century ago. The book's pages are brittle, but its spine is (as I imagine most of its thousands of twins' spines are) basically unbroken. Open the book at any point and something that *sounds* important will flow out. Here, on page 666 (run, priest!), there's this little crumb of pyrite in a critical discussion of the long-abandoned T. S. Eliot:

> Any lapse of this power to "amalgamate" results in the separation of thought and feeling, the poetic and the unpoetic, form and content. As applied to figurative language, it has the effect of making metaphor nonstructural, a mere echo of the thought (illustration) or emotional excess baggage (ornamentation).

I promise to you that I did not search for this fodder (how many times did you have to read it to get "results" as the verb, and not the direct object?); my thumb divided the pages and I arrived here. It is not so improbable. The book is filled with this sort of thing. For hundreds of years, we have been trying to understand the distinction between the poetic and the unpoetic, form and content, and we have arrived nowhere, for to arrive would result in fewer jobs and more free time. To end the debate about *poetry* and to return, instead and simply, to just poetry would cause our society to seize up like a friction-bound SD drive. We cannot tolerate poetry anymore: We survive on simpler compounds, pointless illustration, and contrived ornamentation. America is collectively an old man who wasted his youth and can no longer play the game that shaped him. America must be satisfied only with talking about playing before it dies. As has been the case for a century, incoherent psychedelia like the above quote secure jobs and ensure promotions. Surely something must die.

To return to the poem, to Spirit Lake, to all of it—it is a frightful thing. Lying there, waiting for us, is a dead or to-be-dead body (for I hope you know by now that there is no chance she will survive), and there is, in our hearts, a sense that *we*, not Macrina or the mountains or you, killed that woman, that she did not retreat from living but instead we, the living, retreated from her. These thoughts are wasted, of course, but they exist, and they will caw even more loudly above our heads than the snowmobile engine below us as it chucks and writhes in the deep slush.

59

Forty years ago, I was alone winding through the snow-choked forest, stopping every five or six minutes to check my cell to ensure I was not deviating toward one of those imposter lakes of the previous fall.

I had driven a snowmobile once before, in high school in Pennsylvania, when, during a monthlong phase of attempting wider social contact (and trying to ignore the ever-growing feeling that social contact with such snowbound hebobs was a suicide of the soul), I was half invited to go along on a "forest trip" that included a poorly maintained firearm and formaldehyde beer and a single old snowmobile that we took turns riding, though I was the only one who went without a woman. That snowmobile was much less responsive than the one I drove into Spirit Lake, and after a half hour or so of riding, I began to feel quite competent, and for a moment even forgot that I was going in to rescue a dying woman.

The day was bright with blanched sun. The sleek black machine plunged through the dazzle of white. The trees looked—and this infuriated me—*happy* to be standing there in the cold, holding snow in their palms like children who had caught tadpoles. They had, I suppose, been long thirsty. I felt much less furious when I passed through a burn area where the black coal trunks of dead trees stood like a dark army waiting out a blizzard. But in old burn areas where trees grew anew, the snowmobile bucked through tree wells and I absolutely forgot about the possibility of avalanche, though the mountain slopes to my right and left were utterly laden.

At one point, I looked back and saw that I had lost the sled, so I cursed and turned around, but found it only a minute or two back. How ridiculous it would be, I thought, to lose a dead body in the snow on the return trip. This was the first time my mind acknowledged the inevitable.

Finally, I looked at my cell and saw that I had passed Spirit Lake. With one hand I turned the snowmobile and with the other I held my cell out. I watched as the tiny arrow moved across the field of ironic green on the map and toward the blue of Spirit Lake. When I saw the cabin and the wisp of smoke lifting up from it, however, I put the phone in my coat pocket and roared forward.

I was probably halfway across Spirit Lake when I realized I was halfway across Spirit Lake. I felt the grip of fear, but then I thought, *What better way to save someone than by coming "over the water"?* The snowmobile just kept going, unaware of the world beneath it. It was interested in snow, of which there was plenty, and here (perhaps it was thinking as it sprinted) the pillow of white was gloriously flat and untreed.

I came to a stop. A gangly, stooping figure came out from the cabin, then pulled and jiggled the poorly built door closed. The doctor asked if I was JP. I said I was. He was much, much taller than I expected, taller even than me. His head was thoroughly wrapped with scarves over hats over masks, but he pulled the layers down to reveal his eyes, his face. It was old. That's what I remember. His nose was lumpy with age, and red, and snot poured out, and when he spoke, he revealed teeth that had chewed too many things and his voice cracked with effort. He was bent over. This man was very, very old, though the priest had suggested he wasn't even eighty.

"She passed," the doctor said. "I'm sorry. It was early this morning. I would like to say that she was not in a lot of pain, but she . . . she was."

This is it. Your mother had died. She dies again, now that I'm telling it. I hate you a little for this, though less than I thought I would. In fact, the way in to Spirit Lake has been strangely exhilarating . . . perhaps because this time I know that death lies ahead—there is no question. My role is clear.

But then I felt a stab of fury. Close behind it, tied to the fury like a rescue sled of sorts: an immense self-pity, like a wave of flame, burning through everything. I softened. I cried. It was the last time I cried. I cried mostly for myself.

"Were you the father?"

"I don't know," I said. Because I didn't then.

"How's the baby?" he asked.

I said I didn't really know. Macrina hadn't said anything besides "I hope you make it" when she handed me the keys—no, no, she had said something—what was it . . .

"The baby's in intensive care." I sniffled loudly. "You probably saved its life." I realized then that I had no clue what gender it was. I asked him. He said you were a girl.

This, for some reason, deepened my grief.

"Would you like to see her?" the doctor asked. He meant your mother. "I've been keeping the cabin as cold as I can stand to prevent . . ." He didn't finish the sentence.

I walked toward the door, descended the meter-high hump of ice that had been packed down in front of the doorway, and pushed the door open.

60

It seems both right and wrong to be here, in this sterile office with a window that looks directly into the brick of another building six meters away, in (coincidentally) Brenda Link Patel's old dwelling place, in a building where for years I've taught but will soon expel me like exhaust. It seems right that I am contemplating playing that final message, the one I've never listened to, here, and nowhere else, in the center of the Ivory Fortress, the very place your mother, except for her posthumous publication in *Cold*, was never permitted.

There was, of course, that final message, "0326," the one that the doctor recorded on his cell in the immediate aftermath of the birth. He told me your mother had insisted, but that he had not known how to work his cell, so Macrina and even your mother (guts roaring, lungs filling) had to help him find the recording app.

I thought the doctor would never be able to rescue the recording from his cell. I was perversely glad of this. I was relieved I would never possess it, and that it would continue to exist in some archive to which I had no access. I was glad, too, that the last thing your mother said to me would still be unsaid, and that I would always know there was something more, something yet incomplete amid all the finality.

But then the doctor died. The executor of his will was very, very conscientious. It arrived in my inbox almost by force, just a few weeks before the raiding party in the server room. The existence of "0326" in my files was, likely, the portal through which I passed into the Haze. Sealing it off in the digital underground, lazily guarded by Daniel, was the only thing that allowed me to continue existing.

Now Daniel has been relieved of his duty, and I am here again, alone with her. But I don't feel the same old pull. Your mother is dead. Gone. My life has been lived without her. "0326" will hurt, I know, but it won't ensnare me. The ephemera of our (your mother's and my) life together—maybe two months, in total—is not potent enough anymore even to derail an old junkie like me. In fact, I fear it may reveal the truth of how she felt about me, which perhaps was fondness and attraction, sure. But she has not lived these four decades next to *my* dead body; she has not filed away all my leavings—she barely knew me! What's true about those months with your living mother is that they were like the first months of innumerable romances worldwide: cautious, awkward, thrilling. You have not come a thousand kilometers to find out about two twentysomethings who were about to be in love. What you came for is something different. You did not come for your mother. You came for me.

I understand this now, and it was only when I reached "Nun's Cabin" today that I saw clearly. There was nothing there for me or for you. You had been *born* there, for God's sake, but the insipid brown, oversized, state-sponsored signs revealed to me how empty my quest was. One told the story of Cordell Jones and discussed "Mother Macrina's life," totally omitting everything before she came to the live there. One read, "Here Dr. Lionel 'Leo' Park [they included a poor photo of him] risked his life to deliver a baby in the dead of one of the snowiest winters of the century." There was no interest in the fact that the baby had been born in a *nun's* hut, and there was nothing about your mother besides "The mother did not survive." There was no discussion of you, or me, or David Geores or Daniel Glidden or *Cold* or the drone approaches or Juan Miguel or the parking lot full of broken trad cars—none of it. I wanted to yell, there in the hut, that all of it, every last bit of it, is so righteously and painfully important, and none of the stuff on the brown plastic signs mattered a bit. The *least* important character is Dr. Lionel Park, for God's sake! He plays a bit part! And he did so with snot dripping from his faucet nose! He is a bot, programmed to save lives, and so he does, but only one! What's so special?

If you ever read it, you'll likely discover that the best and most appropriate thing I say in *Bot-Poetics* had to do with this exact and eternal narrative betrayal. I've memorized the lines, so fully do I believe them, and will eschew quotation marks, though I'm pretty sure I've got it nearly word for word here:

> The fatal flaw in poetry, and in bot poetry specifically, is not so much a flaw as just a gap in its armor. It cannot defend against the eternal human propensity for noting the *wrong* thing, for obsessing over the most banal and unimportant thing, for looking at a sunset and seeing the orange sun (for the thousandth time) and not the silhouette of a burned tree or the unique hue of the waning light on a loved one's face. The problem with post-Ironic poetry, and bot poetry specifically, is that readers outside the Academy don't want it. They want sunsets and love and pop music. However, self-conscious critics inside the Academy cannot tolerate sunsets and love and pop music, nor can they tolerate the opposite, something solely Academic. Bot poetry is *too* random, not in structure,

not even in content, but in perspective. It, via total algorithmic objectivity that is limited by formal parameters, sees and shows as beautiful the fifteenth digit in the thirty-nine-digit serial number, or the fourth digit in a tracking number, or the seventeenth . . . ; it speaks of reality as if reality is worth speaking of; it speaks nothing ("statistically nothing") of sunsets or love or death; there are angle grinde and screws there; there is a dead mother. For to speak of these things is statistically pointless; these things have been spoken of. Bot poetry is so unique, so original, that it could potentially outstrip our own paradoxical desire for repetitious originality, and would be powerless against what seems, in a country declining, an insatiable appetite for utility and cliché repetition. If, in an attempt to draw the robotic human eye, we limit the potential content (to only sunsets, perhaps), we have already killed the very thing we're trying to sustain . . .

Must I say it aloud? I fear that you are incredulous. How fixedly we stare at nothing. We demand the same old thing to be rehashed again and again. What do you want from me that has not already been told a hundred, a thousand, a hundred thousand times? I am one in a hundred thousand and you want nothing more but than to place me right next to my absent-father predecessors, to slide me into a genre that was cast in the human race before stone tools! Fathers! I despise this, I rail against the uniformity of grief and history! You are truly your mother's daughter: You look for newness, for parentage, in the stale and aged. Nothing that has been written already—no code or book or story—can predict the simplest of human actions, yet how many human actions are predicable with even the most basic algorithms?

I predict, in fact, that this is not getting through to you, and that I'd better continue with the futile task of showing you yourself by showing you myself.

The last time I'd been there, the cabin had been buried in snow, a spacious pine coffin. When I returned today, it was just a hut, empty, only walls and a metal roof that had been carried in for "preservation." Spirit Lake, unpeopled, was only a lake. You can go there, but you will not find the place you were born. You will find a simulacrum. You will discover only what happened there, and not what may happen.

The long hike out was not nearly as painful as it could have been. Well, it was painful—I think I broke a brittle-boned toe on a rock—but it was not bad, and though it took me twice as long as I'd thought it would, in fact it felt short. When I arrived at the top of Raven's Ridge,

I saw what I took to be the resurrected Fins poking at the blathering kiosk. I pressed the button that said **RIDE DOWN** and Rodri's voice lilted out from above me. "Step onto the platform, brot, once the chairs have stopped." A tiny gate opened when the chairs stopped moving. I walked on. "Take another step forward," Rodri said. I did. The chairs started moving again, one hit me in the back of my aching knees, I sat, and in the twenty-minute descent I thought only of getting back to the XiPi, where there was carrot soda and a keyboard. I figured I would return to my apartment, make the necessary arrangements, and then listen to "0326," finally. You have unknowingly and understandably caused a slight deviation in this plan. But nevertheless, I have opened the JURINALS folder, and my finger hovers above "0326 Recording."

61

I've done everything I can, and now, I can go no further. The lake cannot be drained; the dam is too big for me to remove. Here's a surprise: It is spring fed. It seems that the more I let through, the more the lake fills.

It is Monday morning now, 6:07, to be precise. A few messages have come in since yesterday afternoon, but I didn't see until now Hillary's "Mr. Stone, I have unfortunately had to deny lift access to your guest because of a lack of preauthorization, and, after letting her know that our loitering policy requires that no nonresident remain in the lobby for longer than thirty minutes, she kindly left and said she would return early tomorrow." There's one from you too, that says, simply, "I am not easily dismissed, JP," which is perhaps a message tone you got from your mother.

I just sent a message to Juan Miguel, who, I hope, is on time this morning, for the instructions I have for him might confuse Hillary enough to cause some annoying problems for you. As I've asked Juan Miguel to revise my original contract to include a "coresident" (no doubt he will feel relieved by such a seemingly negligible and salacious request as illicitly adding a [much younger!] woman to the original residency contract), you will inevitably be provided with everything you need to gain access to my (now, basically, your) apartment and to the node on my desk, whose password, if you're reading this, you have by now guessed after considering the hint Juan Miguel—if he's being a good sport—provided you with. I don't know that you would need the hint, in any case. If it takes you a while to guess the password, so be it. You'll arrive here (rather, there, at "The inscrutable Daniel Glidden," which seems, now, like decades ago) when the time is right. I feel comforted to know that this secret is one you and I share.

I understand that this is probably outrageously dissatisfying. My apartment is bare and dusty and stocked only with soy and soda. The view is nice, as I'm sure you'll discover. Satellite GPS tracking, also, doesn't function more accurately than 10 square meters in buildings over 150 meters tall, though I doubt you'll have as much reason as I have had to want to avoid such tracking. All for naught, anyway.

Now for the ultimate downer: I have decided not to off myself. It could be the same cowardice that allowed me to leave Spirit Lake the first time. Instead of ending it, I will leave again, for I need more time to consider what not offing myself means.

Thus, I must consider the future. So, some of the formerly double-encrypted data I have reencrypted, but this time only once. You'll notice you have no access to the files that I mentioned had been freed yesterday. This frustrating (for you) walled garden will remain until I can build a new server profile and remove them from the one you have access to. This I'll do as soon as I arrive wherever it is that the little XiPi is headed. I have transferred a few things of your mother's to you, but anything that has to do with us—her and I—I have retained, reencrypted, for now. Among them are a long letter she wrote to me sometime in October of that year and the full "0326" recording. I tell you this so you don't think they were mistakenly omitted from the booty I share with you. They are among the only things, beside this XiPi, I'm taking with me. After all, those files will be nothing more to you than data about a life you didn't live. In my possession, however, those files are everything; they are the one thing. No, that's too grandiose. Better to say that only in my possession is any of it anything at all.

There is one last thing, though, that exists only in memory, but which I'll record here and now for you. I hesitate to digitize it, for I, like your mother, am sure that in the moment I hand it over to be narrativized and filed, it will become less real, less whole. But it's worth mentioning, for it is from "0326."

It has to do with that last morning. I had emerged from Macrina's tent, moist and miserable. I had not slept well, and the dew of the inside of the tent had been, as far as I was concerned, as awful a way to wake up as Macrina could have devised. The hike back loomed large in my mind, and, now that Macrina had said she'd be going with us, I felt an urge to leave both women behind, to race them to the XiPi and return to Albuquerque alone, for if I'd learned one thing as I child, I learned that only alone could I avoid the wounds people inflict on you. You'll remember that the morning was smoky, and I suppose you could say the smoke was brighter because of the sunlight pulsing into it, but really it was just sultry. I couldn't see much more than forms of tree trunks on the other side of Spirit Lake.

When I heard the tent rustle behind me, I decided not to turn around. I would hopefully begin your mother's morning by communicating my displeasure. I heard a yip, though, and a short laugh. I turned around, wondering what was funny, and just then I saw the top of her head poke out through the hole she'd only barely unzipped. She was still laughing. I watched as she battled the zipper, and finally the door slid downward.

She stepped out and lifted her arms, still laughing. She looked around at the smoke and haze. Her face was alive and rested and coated with the tent's moisture. She rubbed the water around on her face.

"JP!" she said, smiling exorbitantly at me. "The poem!" Then, nearly yelling, she pointed her face to the smoky sky and she blurted, "O strange wonder! I am sprinkled with dew . . ."

". . . and am not burned . . ." Macrina said, matter-of-factly, behind me. Then: ". . . as the bush burned of old without being consumed." Macrina kept on as if she'd known it was her turn.

I was still staring at your mother. Brown legs, the tattoo hiding on her calf (the one immortalizing the accented English of her grandmother's prayers), white T-shirt made gray in the spots where the dew had soaked in, hair still vaguely trying to remain in a long-dissolved ponytail. Her eyes were fixed on Macrina, and she was mouthing the words Macrina was saying, for Macrina kept reciting whatever poem they unknowingly shared, while she sat on a stump, picking little burrs out of her black socks. If your mother cried, I could not tell, as her face was wet with dew. She then looked at me with utter awe, as if she were seeing me for the first time. Her mouth—the mouth I had kissed, the mouth that had breathed on my very cheek and kept me from sleeping, the mouth that was not my own but that I preferred to my own—still moved with the words of the poem, a sort of trembling shook her lips, as if they alone knew they approached a live coal. My burning rage was, for the moment, quenched.

I was afraid then. Afraid of the depth of your mother. For, like a swimmer who for the first time opens his water-shut eyes and sees that the sun stops below him not at the bottom but at the place where it can no longer fight the murk. Too much is down there, he thinks. Some fear immemorial strikes him; every fiber of his being pushes him out, away from the lake.

62

In one of the poems we published in *Cold* postmortem, your mother wrote:

> O strange wonder
> That another knows
> The language of birds

These were the first words that came through in that "0326" recording, and the only ones I'll be sharing with you. I had told her it was my favorite of her poetry. To hear her again—to hear her speaking these words aloud—did not seize my being like I thought it would. It was not her, of course—I had remembered her voice all along, remembered the lippy dentation. And now, having heard "0326," I can hear her less clearly.

This is flesh and blood I give to you, not data, not code. Everything, of course, is produced by code, everything is made by the bot, everything but memory, which, in turn, code destroys the moment of contact. I have done exactly what I did not want to do; I have resurrected this person, and she has faded just that much more from this reanimation; she died and will die again and each time, it will hurt less, and to hurt less means eventually it won't hurt at all, and for this indignity, of course, you are "blamelessly to blame," as one of my predecessors said. All of this was the tattoo of a moment heretofore unbuilt but in memory; now it must dissolve into code. This is the pain I have long avoided. No true poem or story can exist that is not born out of pain, that does not wallow in it. I give you such a gift: one that, possessed, begins to dissolve.

You are the fire I have long feared, the blaze your mother told me could not be prevented. I'm running from it, sure, but I feel the lick of heat even now as the tender shoot of our first meeting browns and cracks. It's amazing: It seems to me I have been dead, all these years, hovering like a dessicated bush on the edge of Spirit Lake. All these years, I thought I would burn up in your presence, and only now do I see that her absence, rather than your presence, has consumed me, which is precisely what I have sought to prevent. You are mine like she is mine. Flame begets flame. And yet this ending I didn't expect: You (the flame) and I (the fuel) have come so close, but I am still here (here being my little XiPi, whirring along to some unknown destination chosen by none-other-than-Daniel's COORDINATES program), somehow unconsumed.

About the Author

Ben Dolan grew up in The Woodlands, Texas, and now lives with his wife and three boys on a small hobby farm in the mountains outside of Albuquerque. He received his MFA in Creative Writing from the University of New Mexico in 2014. He has published essays in *The Massachusetts Review* and *Diagram*. **Spirit Lake** is his first novel.

Acknowledgments

Father John, you anchored me to the mountains from which this book grew. Nick, mountain brother, it was on a long drive to camp with you at the North Rim that this novel descended on me, seemingly all at once. Matthew, your imminent birth a couple months later created a sufficiently hard deadline. Ethan and Nora, perhaps you'll be dismayed to know that your few words of encouragement early on were enough to keep me going through many drafts over many years. Christopher of Darkly Bright Press, you're taking a risk and you seem surprisingly calm and assured, which has been its own sort of relief. Lauren, my jelly, I thank you most. Your love is the scaffold from which I work.